EXILES

EXILES

ILYON CHRONICLES – BOOK FOUR

JAYE L. KNIGHT

Living Sword Publishing
www.livingswordpublishing.com

Exiles
Ilyon Chronicles – Book 4
Copyright © 2017 by Jaye L. Knight
www.ilyonchronicles.com

Published by Living Sword Publishing

Ilyon Map © 2014 by Jaye L. Knight

Cover Images
© Kjolak - Dreamstime.com
© kjpargeter - Depositphotos.com
© smaglov - Depositphotos.com
© piolka - Depositphotos.com

All Scriptures are taken from the New American Standard Bible, Copyright © 1960, 1962, 1963, 1968, 1971, 1972, 1973, 1975, 1977, 1995 by The Lockman Foundation. Used by permission. www.Lockman.org

ISBN 13: 978-0983774075
ISBN 10: 0983774072

JACE DRAGGED IN a deep breath to steady and compose himself, though his body fought to resist the effort. What would it say about him to look sick standing up in front of everyone in the meeting hall on this joyous occasion? He clenched his sweating fingers together to keep from fidgeting.

Why was he so jittery? This wasn't even his wedding.

For the hundredth time, his gaze strayed across the aisle. Kyrin stood opposite him with her mother and little Meredith as bridesmaids. This time she noticed and sent him a smile, her eyes a bit teary. She made a stunning image, standing there in her lovely yellow dress. His breath caught. So much for his composure. If he were to stand here as the groom one day, it would never be anyone but her at his side. That shouldn't make him so nervous.

Of course, she saw right through him. Her smile transformed from one of joy over the moment to one of comfort and encouragement just for him. His heart quieted.

Trask's voice registered again, and Jace snapped his wandering attention back to the proceedings. It was an honor for Warin to have asked him to stand up for him with Rayad and Jeremy, and he didn't take it lightly.

Jace focused on the man and his beautiful bride Lenae. Their announcement to marry had come as a surprise to him, though

Kyrin seemed to have seen it coming all along. Such things rarely escaped her notice.

Everyone had rallied around the couple with great enthusiasm. The glow on Lenae's face and Warin's perpetual grin proved how very much in love they were despite having kept it quiet all along. With Warin as Trask's right-hand man in leading the camp and Lenae acting as a mother figure to everyone, the union was fitting. To think, when Jace had first come to camp, it consisted of only a handful of single men living in tents. Now it was a small village of men, women, children, and blossoming relationships.

With Trask's pronouncement of man and wife, Warin drew Lenae into his arms and kissed her, sending a flurry of applause and cheers throughout the gathering. Arm in arm, the new couple led the way out of the meeting hall to close the ceremony. Meeting in the middle to follow, Kyrin tucked her hand into the crook of Jace's arm. Her touch and another reassuring smile soothed the last of his nerves.

Outside, an assortment of tables filled the center of camp, some laden with food and others set for dining. The young girls had done a fine job in decorating them with a festive array of wildflowers. Jace thanked Elôm for the bright sunshine overhead. It rained almost nonstop lately, and this celebration wouldn't be nearly so festive with wet weather. Warin and Lenae deserved a perfect day, and the clear sky was an answer to prayer.

The residents of camp eagerly approached the prepared feast and filled up their plates. At Warin and Lenae's table, Jace pulled out a chair for Kyrin to sit down and then sat beside her. Trask offered a prayer of thanks before the meal began amidst joyful chattering and laughter. Moments like these offered a glimpse of the peaceful life they all longed for and fought to attain.

However, halfway into the feast, Jace caught the sound of dragon wings above the trees. He looked over his shoulder. A crete dragon rider landed at the edge of camp—one of their messengers from Samara. Talk quieted around the tables. The crete approached King Balen, who sat a short way down the table with Trask. They spoke quietly, so as not to disturb the celebration, and the crete produced a packet of parchments. More messages from Baron Thomas and General Mason, no doubt.

Leaving food on his plate, Balen excused himself and stepped away to read the messages. Jace let his gaze follow the king and prayed the letters didn't bear bad news. Perhaps this time they may contain good news. With Daican's power growing like an ever-tightening noose, they could use a boost of hope. Ever since their defeat in Samara, it seemed as though they were always a step behind the emperor.

Warm, gentle fingers clasped Jace's hand, and he swung his gaze to Kyrin. Though she did not speak, her calming expression said enough. Fretting now wouldn't solve their situation. Best to enjoy this moment of celebration while it lasted. He gripped her hand more tightly and returned his attention to his food.

Once the meal concluded, everyone left the tables to mingle, full and satisfied after the feast. Kyrin spotted Elanor's happy, smiling face, and worked her way through the crowd. She gave the young woman a grin when she reached her side. She loved every occasion that brought Jace's sister out to camp. While Kyrin and Jace weren't actually married—yet—Elanor was already like a sister to her.

"Everything is so lovely," Elanor said. "You and your mother did a wonderful job helping Lenae put it all together."

Kyrin shrugged. "It's the least we could do after how kind she has been to us. Besides, I love seeing her and Warin together."

"They are adorable, aren't they? I'm almost jealous. I'm one of the only young women here unattached."

"Though not from lack of interest," Kyrin reminded her.

Elanor laughed. "No."

Not surprisingly, she had turned the heads of several of the young men with her mother's dark hair and deep blue eyes. However, between Jace and Elian—two formidable opponents— they kept a respectful distance. Kyrin found the broodingly protective looks Jace sent toward interested parties both amusing and endearing. It would take a very special sort of man to gain his favor when it came to his sister.

"Has anyone caught your eye?"

Elanor shook her head, and Kyrin gave her a probing look. It was easy to pretend not to have an interest in someone. She and Jace had gone months before sharing their feelings with each other. Thank Elôm those days were behind them now.

"Truly, there's no one," Elanor insisted. "Besides, I don't think falling in love with a fugitive is exactly what Mother had in mind for me here. Not that she would stop it, of course, but Father . . ."

She didn't need to finish. Goose bumps prickled Kyrin's arms at the memories of Elanor's father, Sir Rothas Cantan , and the time spent in his house. She still prayed every day for Jace's mother and what she had to endure as Rothas's wife.

"Poor Timothy." Elanor's comment broke Kyrin away from thoughts of the past.

Kyrin scanned the gathering to locate her close friend. Timothy stood with his brother and some of the other men, but his attention strayed away from them. She followed his gaze to Leetra at the opposite side of the crowd. The crete girl rarely wore dresses, but she did today—a traditional crete dress of pieced-together leather and a lavender blouse that matched her eyes and left her brown shoulders bare to reveal her family tattoos. No wonder Timothy kept staring. She was gorgeous in her exotic crete way.

"Now there's a man I wouldn't turn down," Elanor admitted.

Kyrin couldn't blame her. Timothy was one of the most kind-hearted, Elôm-seeking men she had ever known. He would make a wonderful husband one day.

"But I'll never have that chance," Elanor said with only a whispering of regret. "Do you think there's hope for him with Leetra?"

Kyrin considered what she had witnessed between them in the last year. Why Leetra always resisted Timothy was a mystery. Still, he was a patient man, and for being a race known for quick, decisive action, Leetra remained surprisingly neutral toward him.

"I wouldn't give up on them just yet. If Leetra wanted nothing to do with him, she would have put an end to it, and Timothy would respect that. I'd say there's a war going on between her head and her heart, and he knows it."

"Well, I hope one side wins soon, for his sake."

Kyrin agreed. They all loved Timothy.

"So . . ." Elanor leaned in a little closer, her eyes twinkling. "What about you and Jace? When will this be your day?"

Automatically, Kyrin sought Jace in the crowd, spotting him with Rayad and Elian. He was dressed in his best outfit—a black suede jerkin, pale blue shirt, and black pants. He'd pulled his hair back today, revealing his pointed ears. Though he didn't do it often, every day he grew a little more confident and accepting of his ryrik blood. His handsome form was enough to make her heart do a little dance, and she could certainly imagine him up at the front of the meeting hall instead of Warin.

She turned back to Elanor. "If it's meant to be, it will happen in time."

"Do you talk about it?"

Not outright.

"It's been implied in some of our conversations." Kyrin paused. "I'm waiting for him to bring it up. He's hesitant, and still

5

uncertain about things. I don't want to rush him or push him if he isn't ready."

A loving smile softened Elanor's expression. "I'm glad he has you and you're so understanding. I haven't known him for as long as you have, but I love my brother."

"So do I."

They shared a smile now.

Nodding in a different direction, Elanor said, "Well, however long it takes you, I'm sure it won't be as long as those two."

Kyrin looked to her right. Trask and Anne, of course. Trask leaned over Anne's shoulder, murmuring something in her ear. No doubt an attempt to coax her to accept one of his numerous marriage proposals. Were she to say yes, he would probably marry her on the spot. Anne just smiled coyly, looking anywhere but at him. Kyrin didn't doubt Anne's love for Trask, but she would marry him in her own good time. With a look of longsuffering, Trask seemed to concede this fact.

Kyrin released a light laugh. "Goodness, I hope not."

"Kyrin looks very lovely today, if I may say so."

Jace's attention shifted to Holden. He certainly wouldn't dispute that fact, since he had just been watching Kyrin and thinking the same thing. Before he could comment, Holden asked, "When will you ask her?"

Of course, that question was bound to come up. Jace let a slow sigh escape. He couldn't fault his friend's curiosity. He'd known all along that today would have everyone's minds set on weddings, and not just on Warin and Lenae's union. All week he had braced himself for the barrage of romantic speculations. He caught Elian and Rayad's pitiful attempt not to look interested in his answer.

"I don't know." Though he did contemplate it often enough. Holden shook his head. "I don't know how you can wait."

Once again, Jace sought Kyrin and watched her laugh and visit with his sister, lantern glow lighting up her face as the sun grew dim. How did he wait? She would almost certainly say yes. They could be husband and wife in a matter of weeks if they wanted, but he hesitated. Whether it was a sense of caution or doubt, he held back. She deserved only the best, and he wasn't completely convinced yet that he was it. Could he be the husband she needed and deserved? And what about beyond that? Could he be a father? He swallowed, his throat seizing.

Fear. He recognized the sensation. His future as a potential husband and father wasn't anything to take lightly.

Holden thumped him on the shoulder. "You all right?"

Jace worked to loosen his throat. He and Holden talked often, but this was different. Something too personal to speak of, even with him.

"It'll come," Holden said with a firm nod.

Though he surely didn't understand everything, his reassurance encouraged Jace. As an extra measure of comfort, he silently reached out to Elôm for guidance and to make His will clear.

Jace cleared his throat now. Time to turn the conversation away from himself. He looked at Rayad and couldn't hold back a smile. "So, when will you find a wife? Mrs. Hess has been very friendly."

The meddlesome widow had arrived early last fall and set her sights on Rayad immediately. She was never subtle in her hints of affection toward him, especially in the few days leading up to the wedding. And the more resistant Rayad was, the more determined she became.

He snorted. "No, we will not have this conversation."

Jace traded a glance with the others, and Holden let out a low chuckle. Rayad shot him a scathing look. While Jace might have liked to see Rayad settle down with a good woman, the Widow Hess wasn't the one. It would take someone of rare quality for that. After all, Rayad was very set in his ways having lived his life as a single man, and quite content with it. Jace wasn't sure anyone could change that.

Before long, the last of the sunlight faded, replaced by strings of lanterns in the trees. A lively tune of flutes and hand drums from a group of crete musicians quickly had everyone backing to the perimeter as couples stepped in to dance.

Jace sensed her near even before he looked down to find Kyrin at his side. Her tentatively hopeful smile tied his stomach in knots. He must have looked half-sick, because she grabbed his hand and smiled widely.

"Jace, you don't have to dance." Laughter tinged her voice. "It's perfectly all right. I only came to see if you felt any better about it."

The answer to that was a definite no. Dancing was not one of his strong suits. He was dreadful, actually. He could single-handedly take on five men and fight with perfect accuracy, but dancing made him clumsy. Even a couple of lessons with Kyrin leading up to the wedding hadn't produced any improvement.

"Really, it's fine," she insisted. "There are plenty of dance partners if you don't mind me dancing with someone else. After all, you men outnumber the women almost four to one."

She gazed up at him. Though she didn't appear saddened, it still must disappoint her, and that stung. She had been so enthusiastic about trying to teach him.

"I don't mind." The annoying itch inside him might not agree, but he wouldn't stop her from having fun tonight.

She squeezed his hand. "You try to enjoy yourself here, and I'll be back in a little while."

As she walked away in search of a dance partner, Jace let out a heavy breath. *Idiot.* He winced. He shouldn't be so hard on himself, but he still hadn't fully broken the habit. Just one of the many areas Elôm was working on.

Folding his arms, Jace watched Kyrin dance first with Aaron and then Mick. For the third dance, she found Timothy as a partner since Leetra did all in her power to avoid him. By this time, Jace shifted restlessly, the itch growing. He wasn't jealous, and certainly not resentful toward any of them. Kyrin's affections were devoted exclusively to him, of that he was certain, yet to stand here while she danced with everyone else ate at him. How could he let fear of something as trivial as dancing keep him from her?

Time to man up and do what he should have done all along. When the current dance ended, Jace wove through the couples toward Kyrin. Coming up behind her, he captured her hand and swept her around to face him. Her eyes rounded in surprise and delight. So what if he made a fool of himself?

Holding her as close as was proper, they joined in the new dance—a slower one, thankfully. At least he could try to do this right. His feet moved like lead at first, but after a minute or two, he let himself relax. How could he not while staring into her smile? Soon, even the music faded.

Somewhere in the middle of it, Kyrin murmured, "Jace, you've been holding out on me." Her voice was teasingly reprimanding. "You *can* dance."

Could he? He hadn't noticed, but now that he'd left behind his pride, it did come more easily. Well, good, because he didn't intend to share her any more than he had to.

Exhausted, Kyrin might have swayed on her feet if not for her hand tucked so securely in Jace's. She leaned into his shoulder with a smile. They had barely parted for the last couple of hours since he had stepped in to dance with her.

As the music wound down and the crowd thinned, the two of them walked toward Kyrin's mother, who sat on a bench at the edge of the gathering. Meredith curled up next to her, fast asleep. The little girl had done her share of dancing, but the late night had caught up with her.

"Looks like we need to get someone off to bed," Kyrin said.

Her mother nodded, smoothing Meredith's hair. "She fell sleep about a half an hour ago insisting she could keep dancing."

Kyrin laughed quietly.

"Would you like me to carry her inside?" Jace asked.

Kyrin's mother offered him a warm smile. "Thank you, Jace."

He released Kyrin's hand and bent down to lift Meredith into his arms. She gave a sleepy groan of protest but snuggled into his shoulder. Though Jace typically avoided children, he had formed a bond with Meredith due to the increased time he spent with Kyrin and her family. The sight of the two of them turned her insides to mush and rushed her thoughts far beyond the foreseeable future.

With her mother leading the way, Kyrin walked with Jace to the cabin. Jace carried Meredith up to the bed in the loft while Kyrin helped her mother light a couple of candles. When he stepped back down, he bid Kyrin's mother goodnight, and Kyrin followed him to the door, where they paused just outside. He turned to her, his aqua blue eyes so vivid and bright, even in the dark. The light inside them could bring fear to so many people, but Kyrin only saw the beauty.

"I had a lot of fun tonight," she told him.

"So did I."

His gaze dropped, and Kyrin's pulse quickened. Bending down, he placed a soft kiss on her lips. He didn't kiss her often, and not for more than a moment, but she cherished each kiss.

"Goodnight," he whispered.

She echoed him, meeting his eyes again. He gave her the smile that had become one of her greatest treasures—the smile of a man changed by Elôm and hopelessly in love.

"MICHAEL, PUT YOUR things here for now, out of the way. You can arrange them later. You too, Ronny."

Kyrin smiled from her place in the loft as her mother delegated below. Though they had always enjoyed sharing the cabin, now that Lenae had moved in with Warin, Kyrin's mother clearly liked running her own home again. And when she had suggested Kyrin's brothers all move in, they had jumped at the idea. They hadn't all lived under the same roof in years, and despite the cramped space compared to their large family home back in Mernin, they wanted to make it work. In a way, it would recapture some of their childhood cut too short.

While her brothers worked below, Kyrin arranged the loft to accommodate both herself and her mother.

Meredith sat on one of the small beds dressing her dolls. "When will I move into the new cabin with Mommy and Warin?"

"In a few days."

The little girl's brows gathered in a pout, and Kyrin straightened from placing her mother's clothing in the dresser. "What's wrong?"

Meredith looked up, her eyes wide and wistful. "I'm going to miss sleeping here with you."

"I know. I'll miss you too. But aren't you excited to have a loft to yourself? You'll have lots of room to play with your dolls."

"Will you come and play with me?"

"Of course." Kyrin sat down beside her and tickled her just enough to erase the frown and earn a giggle. "And I'm sure your mommy won't mind if you sleep over here sometimes."

This seemed to satisfy her.

"You'll always be my sister, won't you, Kyrin?"

"Always," Kyrin promised, giving her a hug. She may call Lenae Mommy now, but Kyrin had adopted her as a little sister ever since their days at Tarvin Hall.

She stood to get back to work. Downstairs, Liam walked in carrying one end of a cot. Jace followed him with the other. He glanced up and caught sight of her, breaking into a smile. Kyrin returned it, her mind quick to recall their time together yesterday. If only every day could be so carefree and wonderful.

"Do you think Warin will let me call him Daddy?"

Jace disappeared from sight, and Kyrin turned again to Meredith. "I think he would love that."

The little girl let out a long sigh. "I still miss my real mommy and daddy."

"I know. I miss my daddy too." Every time his face came to mind, Kyrin's heart constricted around the invisible wound there that never fully healed. He would have loved to see them all together in this cabin. Even more to see them all getting along and fighting for the same cause. They had lived too much of their lives in opposition to each other. Yet, if not for losing him, none of this would be reality. The loss had brought them together like they never were in the past.

When Kyrin finished arranging the loft, she joined her mother and brothers downstairs. By this time, Marcus had hung a couple of canvas curtains to partition off the back of the cabin where their five cots sat in a neat row. Michael and Ronny chattered and sorted their things, while Marcus and Liam moved a couple of chests and a dresser into place. The only one missing from the group was Kaden, who'd been absent since breakfast.

However, just before lunchtime, he appeared at the door with Talas. The two spent so much time together, the crete was almost like another brother to them.

"Ah, there he is." Marcus wore a teasing grin on his face. "Showing up after all the work is done."

Kaden smirked. "Clever, right?"

The rest of the family gathered around, and Marcus thumped Kaden on the shoulder.

"Let's have a look. I know you're itching to show us."

Kaden grinned and lifted his right arm, turning it over to reveal the underside of his wrist. Dark brown ink tattooed his skin in the shape of a dragon in flight. Beside him, Talas raised his right arm to display a matching tattoo.

"They look good," Marcus said. "Do all the riders have them?"

Kaden nodded, his eyes alight with satisfaction. "All thirty-four of us, including our two newest recruits."

Whatever happened from here on out, this tattoo bound the Landale dragon riders together for life. Kyrin thought it telling that Talas had joined himself to the group, being a crete.

Ronny stepped closer, admiring the tattoos. "I want to be a Landale rider someday."

Kaden nudged him. "I'll save a spot for you."

Ronny grinned, and Kyrin looked over at Michael. He didn't share their youngest brother's interest in the riders. At fourteen, he stood nearly as tall as Marcus and had his heart set on joining the militia under his brother's command just as soon as he turned sixteen. Despite the worry it would one day bring, Kyrin took pride in her younger brothers' passion. They knew the danger in it as well as anyone here, yet weren't deterred.

"Speaking of the new recruits," Kaden's attention shifted to her, "are the uniforms ready?"

"I just finished them this morning." She retrieved the two new, blue and gold uniforms from a nearby table.

Trask had come up with the idea for the uniforms after receiving an old Arcacian flag from General Mason in Samara. Kyrin and the other women had spent most of the winter outfitting Marcus's one-hundred-fifteen-man militia and Kaden's dragon riders in the original colors of Arcacia. Now, instead of a band of well-trained but mismatched woodsmen and farmers, they had a uniformed army that, though small, deserved respect.

She handed her twin the uniforms and admired for a moment how much he had matured in the last year. Stubble covered his chin and cheeks, partially hiding the scar left from his wound in Samara. He looked a lot like their father. His promotion to captain of the dragon riders last summer had burdened him with many uncertainties, but now he thrived on it. He certainly wasn't the hotheaded, rebellious young man he was at Tarvin Hall. Though that was still a part of him, deep down, being captain had taught him responsibility and self-control. Their father would be very proud if he could see him. Kyrin made a mental note to tell him that later when they had a little privacy.

Jace sat in the sun near the edge of the camp with his wolf, Tyra, sprawled out at his side. Two days of sunshine were a rare thing this summer. The warmth of it soaked into his skin, relaxing him, though not quite as much as the words he read. Elon's words. Kyrin and Timothy had made copies for him of everything they had heard Elon speak during their time in Samara. Everything he had missed out of fear. Thank Elôm for Kyrin's perfect memory. Jace longed to go back and listen to the words himself, but as he read, he could almost hear Elon's voice in his head. He couldn't get enough of it and always looked forward to his daily study with Kyrin and Timothy.

Dragon wings briefly caught his attention, but many came and went during the day, flying between here and the other two camps that Trask had set up deeper in the forest. The words drew him in fully again until the next interruption, this time with footsteps. He looked up. Holden approached with an apologetic expression.

"Sorry. Trask has called a meeting. A messenger just arrived from Valcré. He also wants to discuss Balen's latest messages."

Gathering up his parchments, Jace rose and dropped them off in the cabin he and Holden now shared with several of the other men—quite an improvement over the previous small hut that had sheltered them over the winter. At the meeting hall, he paused and let Holden go ahead of him. Kyrin was just on her way from the Altair cabin, and Jace waited at the door to open it for her. As she passed through, she gave him the soft smile that never failed to delight him.

Inside, they found seats at a large table with all the other members of Trask's council. The idea that Jace was even part of it still astounded him, yet he strove to offer whatever aid he could. He glanced around the table. Like all meetings lately, a heavy somberness hovered over the gathering.

With everyone present and seated, Trask began. "I called this meeting in part because I've received news from Valcré. Nothing significant, but it appears the Draicon Arena is scheduled for completion within a month. Daican intends to hold the first games there as part of his birthday celebration."

Jace shifted in his chair, the mention of arenas triggering the bloody memories of his gladiator days, and chilly, invisible fingers slithered down his back. He forced the images away to focus on Trask's voice.

"No doubt these so-called games will include mass executions of the believers that have been captured and imprisoned over the last couple of years."

They all took the news grim-faced, and Trev asked, "Is there anything we can do?"

"Unfortunately, I don't believe there is, but we must be prepared. Once Daican begins a public slaughter, we may have a sudden influx of refugees. Those who haven't yet sought safety may now feel compelled to."

Everyone agreed. With three camps now, they were better prepared to shelter a large number of people, but supplies would be their greatest concern. It would probably mean more hunting. Jace glanced at Kyrin. They hadn't gone out in a long time, and he missed it. Surely, one of her brothers wouldn't mind tagging along as a chaperone if he planned a hunting day with Kyrin.

He forced his mind back to the meeting. After all, he shouldn't be so eager about his plans when so many were in grave peril. He silently asked forgiveness for allowing his thoughts of Kyrin to distract him from the plight of others.

By now, attention had turned to Balen, who brought up the messages from Samara.

"Nothing has changed," he said, his expression drawn. "If anything, it has grown worse. People are slowly starving. Even some of the wealthy live like beggars under the emperor's heavy taxation." He sighed heavily. "I should be there with them. I'm doing them no good here."

"Knowing you're still alive gives the people hope," Josef, Balen's good friend and physician, told him. "That's important."

"Or they believe I've abandoned them to save myself. It's been a year and we've been able to do nothing."

Josef nodded slowly in acknowledgement. "Some may think that, but not those who are truly loyal to you and know your character and integrity as a leader."

"I only wish Elôm would show me how to help them."

"He will," Josef encouraged, "when the time is right."

Balen accepted this with a nod, and Trask said, "We'll know more once Sam returns from Arda. If he can convince the talcrins to join us, we'll be in a much better position to face Daican. And hopefully Captain Darq will gain the full support of the cretes. Until then, I'm afraid, we're powerless."

THREE DAYS OF sunshine were not to be wasted. Though a bit warm and humid, Anne and Elanor took the horses out right after breakfast with Elian to accompany them. The shade of the forest roads and paths offered the perfect relief from the heat. They talked and laughed, enjoying the time outdoors. Being cooped up day after day tended to make one gloomy, especially with all the bad news they received at camp. At least Anne had Elanor. Aside from the hardships of the past year, Anne greatly enjoyed her companionship.

"Well, I think you should just marry him and be done with it," Elanor announced.

Anne wasn't sure how the conversation had worked its way to Trask, but she laughed dryly. "I'm sure he'd be all for that."

"Why don't you marry him then?"

"Because I don't think it would work just yet. He can't come out of hiding, and if I were to run off with him, it could jeopardize the safety of my parents, not to mention you and Elian. Goler doesn't need another reason to come snooping around."

Elanor shrugged. "I still think you should do it."

But Anne was adamant. So far, Goler had not looked too closely into their loyalties, no doubt due to his infatuation with her. As much as she loved Trask, they had to take great care with every move they made these days.

When they rode up to Marlton Hall at the end of their ride, Anne groaned. Several soldiers and horses milled about in front of her house. One riderless bay belonged to Captain Goler. This was precisely why they had to be so careful. If she were an ordinary farm girl, she could run off to the woods with little notice. Yet, if she up and disappeared, Goler wouldn't just skulk back to the barracks to mope. He would do everything in his power to find her, and that search would start with her parents.

She grumbled under her breath. "Of course he would show up to spoil a lovely day."

They rode up to the stable and left the horses with the stableboy. Anne glanced over her shoulder as they approached the house to make sure Elian had followed. He was so quiet, but having another strong male presence around usually kept Goler on his best behavior. Elian had a way of staring down disreputable men that made them squirm. And Goler deserved to squirm, considering how insistent he was on having her as his wife, regardless of her or her father's objections.

When they reached the front door, Anne pulled her shoulders back as if preparing for battle. She stepped inside and scanned the large living and dining area. Goler sat in a chair near the cold fireplace, his legs stretched out in far too comfortable a manner. His dirty-blond hair hung in limp strands around his shoulders. He should cut it, or at least tie it back, but he apparently thought this made him more attractive. Anne barely held back an unladylike snort. It would take far more than a new hairstyle to make him attractive. A new heart would be at the top of the list.

Her father, Sir John, stood near the mantle, while her mother, Lady Catherine, hovered nearby. Anne caught her father's eyes before her focus settled on the second chair facing Goler, this one also occupied by a man in black and gold.

The men rose as they approached, and her father stepped forward.

"Captain Dagren, allow me to introduce my daughter, Anne, and Lady Elanor, daughter of Sir Rothas Cantan. She's been an extended guest in our home."

The unfamiliar man eyed her and Elanor calculatingly. Though he matched Goler's average height, he was only half as bulky. Gray streaked his jet-black hair around the temples and through his beard. While Anne always considered Goler an arrogant brute, this man possessed a far more sophisticated, yet dangerous air. He seemed the sort who would shake your hand while stabbing you in the belly before you saw it coming. Though only armed with a sword, Anne wouldn't be surprised to find a knife or two hidden in the folds of his uniform.

Dagren. His name echoed with familiarity in Anne's mind, but it took another moment for it to sink in. Goose bumps rippled across her arms. This man had once sought to kill Rayad and Warin. No doubt he still had revenge on his mind.

Keeping her features schooled, she spoke demurely, "A pleasure to meet you, Captain."

He merely nodded, his expression set like a grim sculpture.

"His Majesty sent Captain Dagren to aid in the search for the rebels," Goler announced. "A couple are of particular interest to him."

"Oh?" Anne replied, putting her best acting skills to use.

After all these years of fending off Goler, she had become an expert.

"Indeed," Dagren spoke at last, his voice refined, silky even, but icy enough to kill.

Another wave of prickles crawled along Anne's skin. He seemed far too cultured and cunning for a simple military captain— probably a younger son of a noble or other highborn family— and wouldn't be as easy to fool as Goler.

Anne's father cleared his throat softly. "Won't you all sit down? Tea will be prepared shortly."

Anne stepped toward the couch and caught eyes with her father again. His expression said he agreed with her assessment that they would all have to tread carefully.

Elanor sat beside her, and Goler resumed his chair. Dagren, however, remained standing and sized up Elian, who had stationed himself behind them.

"Who is this?"

"Lady Elanor's bodyguard," Anne's father answered.

Anne glanced up at Elian. He held Dagren's gaze without a twitch. At last, the captain sank into his chair, blinking slowly like a drowsy but watchful predator. However, when his gaze landed on Anne, it was anything but sleepy.

"You were in a relationship with the baron's son, who now leads the rebels."

It was more an accusation than a question. Anne smoothed her skirt and composed herself.

"We were fond of each other." Best give him as much truth as possible—it was more believable that way.

"Did you intend to marry?"

Anne glanced at Goler. Had he provided this man with such personal information about her and Trask? No doubt. She sent him a glare, eliciting no remorse, before returning her attention to Dagren.

"He asked. I declined."

Dagren's eyes bored into her. "Why?"

Anne straightened a little. "Because he was too impulsive and immature. I think you might agree, considering the present circumstances." A twinge of regret passed through her middle to speak of Trask in this way. Yet, knowing him, he would likely find it amusing. Besides, he would want her to do anything to avoid suspicion.

"If he had not been, would you have accepted?"

Anne paused for only a moment. Goler would love this. "Probably. He was the baron's son, after all. Why would I not have considered such an offer?"

She glanced at Goler again, entertained by his petulant expression.

Dagren's eyes narrowed slightly, probing. "And how do you feel about him now?"

Did he suspect her? He certainly wouldn't be blinded by any romantic feelings. Anne's palms turned clammy, but she resisted the urge to wipe them on her skirt.

"As you've said yourself, Captain, he is the leader of a group of outlaws. How do you think I feel about him?" Hopefully the ice in her voice would convince him.

He peered at her and gave another slow blink. Anne's insides squirmed, but then his gaze shifted to Elanor.

"And what is the purpose of your stay here, my lady?"

Anne looked over at her friend, who sat poised, but her dark eyes glittered hard.

"I became acquainted with Lady Anne last summer. I have no sisters so my mother thought I would enjoy her company."

"Does your father not have any prospects for you? You are of age."

Elanor went rigid, and Elian shifted behind them. Anne fought the temptation to smack the captain herself and let Elanor handled her own affairs.

Her voice prim, Elanor replied, "Captain, I don't believe my family's personal matters are any of your business, and I can't see how it has anything to do with your hunt for rebels. If it is really of so much a concern to you, I'll let my father know you inquired."

Anne caught the subtle threat of bringing Rothas into this and was quite sure Dagren did too. After all, Sir Rothas had

Daican's ear. He may not actually be on their side, but the threat was enough.

"No need," Dagren responded smoothly. His scrutiny returned to Anne. "You were out riding. Do you take the forest roads?"

Anne nodded slowly. "Yes."

"Do you ever see signs of the rebels?"

"Of course not. They are obviously very well hidden if you have not yet caught them." It was a strong jab, but she didn't regret it.

Goler grumbled, but Dagren just gave her the first hint of a cold smile. "That will change very soon."

Anne pasted on a smile of her own. "Then allow me to offer you early congratulations on your success." Inside, her stomach knotted like tangled embroidery thread.

Now her father stepped in, and Anne let her breath out quietly.

"Captain, are you through with questions for my daughter? I'm sure I can provide you with any information you require. Let's leave the women out of this business, if you please."

"Of course," Dagren replied, but his cool glance at Anne warned her that she hadn't heard the last from him.

"Annie, are you sure you should go?" her father asked, following her toward the stable. "Dagren and Goler could have men watching the roads."

"I won't take the roads." Anne glanced at the sun. Evening would soon descend. She'd waited all day to make sure none of Goler's men had hung around, but she couldn't set aside her unrest. "Trask needs to know about this."

"It's dangerous."

"I'll look after her."

Anne looked over her shoulder. She hadn't heard Elian

following. She nodded at him, and he continued toward the stable while Anne turned to face her father.

"If you ask me not to go, I won't, but I really feel the need to warn Trask. Goler and Dagren are up to something, and we must be prepared. A lot of lives depend on it."

Her father breathed out a slow breath. "All right, but be careful. And don't be gone long. You know how your mother will worry."

And you.

"I'll be careful." She stepped closer and kissed his cheek.

He clasped her shoulders. "You're far too brave for your own good."

Anne grinned at him. "You know where I get it from."

A few minutes later, Elian returned with Anne's white mare and his gray gelding. They mounted up, and Anne caught Elian trading a look with her father. A promise to protect her. He had become almost as much her bodyguard as Elanor's.

They rode away from the house, straight into the forest. As Anne had said, they avoided the roads and used extreme caution whenever they came near one. Almost an hour later, they arrived in camp. It appeared the men were just gathering for supper. She spotted Trask among them, and he broke from the group to meet her as she dismounted.

Normally, the sight of her would have lit his face up with a grin, but not tonight.

"What's wrong?" he asked. "As much as I'd enjoy it, you wouldn't be out here this late in the day unless something was up."

Anne scanned the men again. "Where are Rayad and Warin? They'll want to hear this too."

Trask turned to the gathering men and called to Jace to get Rayad and Warin. With a nod, Jace hurried toward one of the cabins.

Trask focused again on Anne as if he could gather information just by reading her face, but he didn't have Kyrin's skills. "What's this about?"

"Elanor and I returned from a ride this morning to find Goler had dropped by for a visit. He brought a friend. A particularly nasty friend."

Trask made a face, but Anne waited to give him the specifics until Rayad and Warin joined them.

"I met an old acquaintance of yours today," she told them. "Captain Dagren."

The two older men exchanged a look, their eyes growing. Though she wouldn't call it fear, apprehension settled in their expressions.

"Dagren," Jace said, lingering nearby. "The man responsible for Kalli and Aldor's murders?"

Rayad winced and gave him a short nod in confirmation. He looked at Anne. "He's here in Landale?"

"Yes, he arrived yesterday. The emperor sent him to help capture you. He knows you and Warin are here."

"How did he find that out?"

Trask shook his head. "Thanks to Falcor, I'm sure it wasn't difficult. No doubt the emperor had all our names circulated through Arcacia."

Anne gave them all a solemn look. "You must be careful. He is very confident in his plan to locate you. He's dangerous. Not that Goler isn't, but he's predictable and a fool most of the time. Dagren is cunning. I could just feel him weighing my every word."

Rayad scowled. "Yes, that sounds like Dagren."

"He had questions, but I think we managed to satisfy him for now." Anne paused, anticipating the future. "He'll surely return though."

"Is Elanor all right?" Jace asked.

"Yes. He started to question her, but she shut him down quickly. You'd be proud."

A flash of a smile appeared on Jace's face, but it didn't reach his eyes.

"I just wanted to let you know," she told Trask, "so you could be prepared and watchful. I'd better go now so I don't worry Mother and Father too long."

She turned for her horse, but Trask caught her hand.

"Walk with me. Just for a few minutes."

It was on her tongue to insist on hurrying back, but his eyes conveyed such earnestness that she couldn't say no. She let him pull her closer and followed him away from the horses. He remained unusually quiet until they were out of earshot. Then he turned, taking both of her hands in his.

"Marry me."

Anne's brows shot upward. It wasn't so shocking that he asked. Heaven knew it was probably the fiftieth time, and he had just tried two days ago, but this was different. The concern in his eyes sank right into her.

"Come live out here with me," he pressed on. "You'd never have to contend with Goler or Dagren again."

Ah, he was frightened for her safety. She recollected her earlier conversation with Elanor. "The moment I do that, they would know I'm part of the Resistance. What would happen to my parents? Or to Elanor and Elian?"

"They can come too. They're more than welcome."

"As of right now, they're free. How could I make them fugitives? And even if they were willing, what about all the servants? Most of them have family in the village. We can't just turn their lives upside down. They didn't ask for any of this."

Trask's forehead pinched, his jaw twitching, but then a mischievous little light kindled in his eyes and lifted the corners of his mouth. "I could kidnap you."

"What?"

"I could kidnap you and bring you out here to the forest. Goler would never have to know you came willingly."

Anne shook her head. What was it she had said about impulsive immaturity? "That would make you a fugitive *and* a kidnapper."

Trask shrugged and drew her a little closer. "So? Whatever it takes to protect and be with those I love."

A smile tugged at Anne's lips. Why did he have to make it sound so appealing?

"What are you thinking?" he asked.

"I'm trying to decide how romantic it is."

"Is that a yes, then?"

"No."

His face fell. "Why not?"

"Because I don't want you branded as a kidnapper. Not everyone will understand your motives."

"I don't care."

"But I do. Elôm willing, you will be Baron of Landale someday. Kidnapping wouldn't be a very flattering reputation."

Trask hung his head, and Anne couldn't hold back a soft laugh at his sulking expression. Such a little boy sometimes.

"There must be a way we can make this work," he said, almost pleading.

"Prayer."

He winced. "Ouch."

"Sorry, I wasn't scolding."

"No, you're right," he admitted. "I'm just impatient."

Anne loosed one of her hands and laid it on his cheek. "So am I, but I know it could lead to trouble if we don't think this through and act cautiously."

He perked up. "You do want to marry me then?"

She laughed again, smiling up into his eyes. "Yes, I do."

"So...does this mean you are actually accepting my proposal?"

"Yes, I am accepting."

He grinned widely. "Well, as long as I know that, I can wait forever."

"Hopefully not that long."

He drew her into his arms, and she tipped her chin up just enough for him to give her a kiss before she pulled away.

"I have to go home."

He took her hand again. "I'll ride with you and make sure you get there safely."

"No you won't. It's too risky. That's why Elian is here."

Trask blew out a hard sigh. "You just can't make this easy, can you?"

Anne bit back a grin.

He tugged her toward her horse. "Well, I can at least have one of our dragon riders fly over and make sure there's no one around."

And report to him when she was safe in Marlton, no doubt.

MOST OF AURÉA Palace rested in darkness as late evening overtook the city. Prince Daniel used the deep shadows to his advantage, creeping along carefully to avoid any echoing footsteps in the quiet halls. While most of the servants would be in bed or gathered in the Servants' Hall at this hour, he didn't wish to happen upon any guards making their rounds. And he certainly didn't want to stumble across his father coming from his office. *That* would be most unfortunate.

He reached a back door without detection and let himself out into the cool, damp air. Only ragged slivers of Aertus and Vilai shone through the thick cloud cover. A faint flicker of lightning lit up the sky to the west. He scanned the still courtyard. Though no guards were in sight, he slunk across the open ground cautiously. He had done this dozens of times, and could surely talk himself out of trouble; however, he'd just as soon his father not find out he had been sneaking around at night. Too much depended upon secrecy.

The palace temple loomed up as a dark, foreboding structure above him. He pressed himself up against the wall and waited, just to be sure. When no one followed, he snuck around the backside, where he had to work to squeeze between the temple and Auréa's surrounding wall. Here, hidden by many years' worth of tangled vines, stood one secret barred gate. Even his father didn't know about it. If he had, he would have had it filled in a long time ago. Besides Daniel, only one other person knew it existed—his old friend Alex Avery, son of the late Baron Arther. This little discovery as children had made them undisputed hide-and-seek champions back in the day. Now it was useful for more than simple games.

He pressed through the thick vines. The lock and top hinge of the gate had rusted away to leave it hanging at a precarious angle. Only the vines on the other side prevented it from falling.

And his father liked to think Auréa was impenetrable and inescapable since he'd blocked off the tunnel Kyrin Altair had used to escape.

On the other side of the wall, a rocky slope led away from the palace. He picked his way down, careful not to disturb the rocks. Raindrops pattered around him when he reached the road running along the palace toward the shore. He pulled up the hood of his cloak to shield his face more from curious eyes than from the drizzle, and headed deeper into the city.

Darkness cloaked the streets, which were mostly empty save for an occasional shady-looking figure. Though lanterns cast light at regular intervals, they were spaced too far apart to offer adequate illumination of every street. This wasn't Daniel's first foray into the city's nightlife, but he kept a cautious hand around the hilt of his sword in case of trouble.

Just ahead, a commotion of voices, raucous laughter, and out-of-tune singing drifted from a tavern. Someone entered, bathing the street in a momentary glow as the door swung open. It closed again, stifling both the light and the rowdiness inside.

Glancing at the door, he passed by. A couple of years ago, he would have eagerly stepped inside, especially since it held some interesting . . . well, *hazy* memories. He and Alex had snuck out the same as he just had and spent the night in the tavern.

How they even returned to the palace afterward, he would never know, since he didn't remember any of it.

He shook his head to himself. What he did recall vividly was the splitting headache the next morning and believing he would die of an exploded skull from his father yelling at them. He wasn't keen to repeat the experience ever again. Those wild days would stay in the past where they belonged.

After several blocks, Daniel arrived at a row of wealthy merchant homes. One of the largest was spacious enough to have its own walled courtyard and garden—rare luxuries in a crowded city like Valcré. At the gate, he paused to look up and down the street. Nothing stirred. Satisfied, he slipped into the courtyard and up to the front door. Dim light shone through the windows and in a thin strip under the door. With one more glance over his shoulder, he knocked—three quick taps, a pause, and then two more.

The rain fell more heavily as he waited, but in just a few moments, the door opened and spilled light into the courtyard. A well-dressed man with iron-gray hair stood on the other side.

"Daniel," he said with a welcoming smile as he opened the door wider and motioned him inside.

He stepped across the threshold into the warm house. It had taken almost a year to get the man to call him by his first name.

"I'm glad you made it." The man closed the door against the damp weather. "We missed you last week."

Daniel turned to him, shrugging off his soggy cloak and hanging it alongside a dozen others. Ben was one of the most successful merchants in the city, with his own large shop, warehouses, and several trading ships that transported goods all along the western coast of Arcacia. But more than that, he was one of the first people Daniel considered as a true friend.

"My father had a dinner he wanted me to attend," Daniel explained. "He wouldn't take no for an answer."

Ben nodded in full understanding and gestured toward a door across the room. "Almost everyone is here, and we even have three new members tonight."

His interest piqued, Daniel followed the man deeper into the expansive house and stepped into the drawing room. Though large, it only just contained the group of more than thirty people gathered there. His gaze touched on each face—men and women of varying ages, and even a few young children. Most were familiar to him, though three he had not met before.

"Daniel!" a warm and rich female voice came from across the room. A lovely woman Ben's age with olive skin and dark hair bustled toward him. Her large brown eyes exuded delight. "Thank the King you could join us tonight."

Daniel grinned as she put her arms around him and squeezed him tightly. "It's good to see you, Mira," he greeted Ben's wife. "Just keep praying that my father doesn't catch me sneaking away one of these nights."

"Every day."

Daniel had meant his words lightheartedly, but her face portrayed seriousness as she pulled away.

He squeezed her shoulders with a grateful smile and looked about the room again. The new members—a young couple and an older man—stared at him. He supposed he would do the same in their place. Everyone new reacted similarly. The last thing they expected was to see the prince of Arcacia in a secret and highly illegal meeting of Elôm believers.

Ben motioned to the newcomers. "Let me introduce you."

He led Daniel across the room and introduced him to the young couple and older gentleman. They greeted him with quiet reverence, bowing their heads and calling him by his title.

He smiled kindly at them. "Daniel, please. There's no need for titles here. We're all believers—not royalty or nobles."

They returned his smile, and then everyone found seats wherever there was room. Daniel took a chair near an elderly couple, who were some of the first people he had come to know since attending these meetings. Once the shuffling and murmuring stilled, everyone's attention focused on Ben at the front of the group.

"I am so pleased to see you all here tonight in spite of the danger, and we eagerly welcome our new members. Some would question our gathering, considering the risk and growing danger, but I believe it is Elôm's will for us to be here to learn and to praise Him together. I also believe He will protect us as we do so. Before we begin, let us bow our heads and pray for His blessing and protection tonight."

Daniel bowed his head and closed his eyes as those around him did the same. Ben's deep voice filled the room as he prayed for Elôm's guidance and protection for each person in the room and for other believers scattered throughout Arcacia and Samara, where the persecution was so heavy. Daniel let these words seep in and repeat in his heart. They held so much meaning compared to the worthless, empty handful of prayers he had ever offered to Aertus and Vilai.

After Ben concluded, they sang a couple of old hymns Daniel had never even heard of before last summer. Then Ben pulled out a crinkled piece of parchment. He read the words it contained— several verses from Elôm's Word. Daniel had heard them before but never tired of them. They were all thankful to have anything to read at all—these passages passed down through families and written reverently on scraps of closely guarded parchments— though they were but a handful of verses compared to the full collection of the King's Scrolls that Sam had smuggled out of Auréa almost two years ago. Thank Elôm that Daniel had let him go that night. He'd had no idea how much that would mean now.

For an hour, Ben expounded on the meaning of the verses. He was one of a few older men who routinely took turns teaching and sharing their knowledge of Elôm. Everyone received the teaching as if it were a meal after not eating in days—Daniel included. He hated when he had to miss these weekly gatherings.

After the session came a time of fellowship. Daniel mingled with the group, greeting everyone he had missed in the last two weeks. A large variety of people attended these meetings—from wealthy merchants like Ben to poor millworkers—but none of that mattered to them. They were friends.

No, more than friends. Family.

While he talked with a group of young men his age, the new attendees approached him tentatively, and the young woman offered a timid smile. "My lord . . ." She blushed. "Daniel?"

He offered her an understanding smile. For Arcacian citizens, showing proper respect to royalty would have been ingrained since childhood. He couldn't expect them to break such habits right away. "Yes?"

"Ben said you saw Elon after He rose and that is how you believed . . . could you tell us about it?"

Daniel's smile widened at her eagerness, and his mind drifted back, as it often did, to the day that changed his life forever. "Of course." A few others listened attentively as well. He had already told his story numerous times but never hesitated to share again how Elôm had changed him.

"I was there on the platform when . . ." He paused, the words 'when my father killed Him' sticking in his mouth. He hated the association, and he cleared his throat. "When He was killed."

Even now, the emotions flooded back, pressing down on his chest. "I knew it wasn't just another execution. I could feel that it was something much more profound than just one man dying for another. And then, just before He died, He looked at me—looked into my eyes. I knew in that moment He was everything He was said to be."

It was incredible, really. He was never so certain of anything as he had been in that moment. It had completely blown apart everything he'd thought he knew, yet had led to the discovery of all the answers he had searched for all his life.

"After He was gone, I felt lost and desperate to understand what had happened, but I didn't know where I could go or who I could trust. Three days later, I went out to the cliffs by myself and He appeared there, standing right before me. He told me that if I followed Him, He could use me to make a difference. Just before He disappeared again, He instructed me to come here and speak to Ben."

"And I'll never forget the moment I opened my door to find the crown prince of Arcacia standing on my doorstep." Ben's amused voice joined in from behind. Daniel smiled at him as the man continued, "I was afraid we'd been found out, but the first words out of his mouth were, 'Elon sent me here. I want to learn more about Elôm.'"

Daniel grinned, the eagerness of that moment still stirring within him. What a day that had been! He had spent the entire afternoon and evening talking with Ben and Mira. He would have stayed the whole night if no one at the palace would have missed him.

"I've never been as happy as I have been coming here over the last year," he said.

Ben put his hand on his shoulder. "And we're happy to have you. You're a testament to Elôm's power and how He works in the most unexpected and amazing ways."

Daniel agreed.

He remained at the house for another hour or so until most of the group had left. After trading goodbyes with Mira and those who remained, he followed Ben to the door, where they stopped and faced each other.

"I meant what I said," Ben told him. "You are a true blessing to us."

Daniel rubbed the side of his jaw. He hadn't been much of a blessing to anyone before last year. More like a royal pain in the neck if he were honest. "It's a blessing for me to be able to come here to learn and gain answers to my questions. I feel more at home and among family with you than I do at the palace." He smiled a little. "Every time I come, I wish I didn't have to leave."

"You are always welcome—any day, at any hour."

"Thank you."

The two of them clasped arms, and Ben said, "May the King protect you."

"You too."

Daniel put on his cloak and stepped out into the dark courtyard, where a gentle rain fell. He pulled up his hood and set out for the palace. He followed a different path this time just to be safe. Whenever he thought of Ben and Mira or the others getting caught, his heart nearly failed him. He would sooner give up his own life than see them executed.

On his return journey to the palace, he did not come across anyone on the streets in this wet weather, but Daniel didn't mind it. The quiet drum of the rain and the solitude did him good, and he took his time.

During the walk, memories of last summer returned to his mind. The moment Elon had looked at him just before death would never fade. He had witnessed such love in his Savior's eyes that it had convinced him beyond any doubt of Elôm's existence. Pressure built in his throat again, pushing up toward his eyes. He'd fallen straight to his knees on the cliffs where Elon appeared, unworthiness almost suffocating him. He still didn't know why or how Elôm would use him in this difficult situation when his own father led the assault against believers, but he prayed he would be ready when the time came.

At the palace, he picked his way up to the wall, careful to step only on the rocks so he wouldn't leave tracks in the mud. Though they would probably wash away by morning, he couldn't take any chances. Not unless he wanted to face the prospect of no longer attending Ben's meetings. He couldn't abide the thought. His faith constantly longed to be fed, and he needed the fellowship. Always being surrounded by those who blindly followed his father depressed him and left him in a mood unfitting for service to Elôm.

Pushing through the vines, he squeezed past the temple and eyed the courtyard. However, in such murky weather, he doubted anyone would notice him even if the guards were around. Still, he moved cautiously to the palace and let himself inside, where he brushed back his hood and breathed out a sigh. Tension uncoiled in his muscles. Such regular stress probably wasn't healthy.

He headed straight for his chambers to change into something dry and get to bed. Just when he reached one of the staircases, his father's voice echoed behind him.

"What are you doing?"

Daniel stiffened, and his heart choked for a beat. He turned slowly. His father's gaze swept his rain-soaked cloak. "I was out . . . for a walk."

His father lifted a brow. "At this hour in the rain?"

Daniel shrugged. "Why not?"

The two of them stared long and hard at each other. A wide chasm existed between them that Daniel wasn't sure could ever be bridged. Anger stirred inside of him, always lurking whenever he was near his father. He struggled to contain it. His own father had driven the killing dagger into Elon's chest. He prayed silently over the struggle and fought to calm his voice.

"I'm going to bed."

His father said nothing, and Daniel climbed the stairs. Once he reached the hall, out of sight, he breathed out heavily and hung his head, suddenly exhausted.

RAIN BEAT ON the roof as Jace bent over the table, his eyes trained on the words of the King's Scrolls. At the end of the page, he paused and glanced around. Timothy sat across from him, penning another message to share with the members of camp as he typically did a couple of times a week. Kyrin sat just to Jace's right with her elbow resting near his hand. Close enough to brush his fingers across it. But that wouldn't be appropriate since they were supposed to be studying. He did watch her for a moment. She was writing too, another copy of the Scrolls, this time all from memory. He didn't wish for her abilities, but what a gift to be able to recall any portion of Elôm's Word without struggle.

He bent his head again and refocused on the parchment in front of him, the rhythm of raindrops and the scratch of quills fading into the background. Several minutes later, the cabin door swung open. Aaron stepped inside, his dark cloak spattered with moisture. He pushed back his hood.

"Darq and Glynn just arrived. They're with Trask and Balen at the meeting hall."

Setting aside their study materials, the three of them rose and grabbed their cloaks.

"Did you hear any news?" Timothy asked his brother.

Aaron shook his head. "No, but Darq didn't look happy."

More bad news. Nothing seemed to work in their favor these days. Yet, Jace reminded himself that Elôm's plans didn't always make sense in their minds. After all, if Jace had not been captured and taken to Valcré last summer, he might still question Elôm's love for him. It was in the dark dungeon of Auréa Palace that Elon had declared once and for all that he did have a soul and was loved.

Outside, they rushed through the downpour to the meeting hall. What a miserable day for flying. Maybe that had something to do with Darq's mood. Others were on their way as they stepped inside. Trask and Balen gathered in the center of the large, open room with Darq and Glynn. The two waterlogged cretes stood with their long dark hair matted and dripping. Even so, Captain Darq made a proud, formidable figure despite standing almost a head shorter than Jace. He half scowled, his sapphire eyes as stormy as the weather.

". . . it's a stalemate." The crete captain paused and glanced at them in acknowledgement before continuing. "Half the clans want no part of it while the other half desire to fight. It's turned into a bunch of childish squabbling between the clan leaders."

"Can't those who wish to fight join us?" Trask asked.

"Individually, some will, but not as a whole. As much as they may desire to fight, they won't unless Lord Vallan is in favor of it, and he won't make that call unless the majority of the clans are in agreement."

"Which way does Lord Vallan lean?"

"Personally, he would fight. He's from the Hawk Clan, and we've always been fighters, but with the leaders split the way they are, he won't issue a call to war. If we had even one more clan on our side, things would be different."

Balen rubbed at the lines in his forehead. "None of them can be swayed?"

Darq snorted. "I tried. I spoke to every opposing clan leader multiple times. You'd think after Falcor's betrayal and the slaughter of the cretes at Amberin that they'd be more willing, but no. Stubborn fools. Even Falcor's clan, the Wolf Clan, won't sway, except for the Tarn family. They are with us wholeheartedly. When I left, Falcor's father said he would continue to speak to the other elders on our behalf."

The room fell silent under the weight of this disappointing news. They had placed so much hope on forming a military alliance with the cretes, especially after everything they had gone through to help locate Timothy and the Scrolls. It didn't seem right for them to refuse to offer aid. Couldn't they see that Daican's tyranny would eventually affect them too?

Slowly, Trask asked, "So what can we do now?" He glanced at Balen. "We can't take back Samara or stop Daican without help from the cretes. His firedrake force has grown too large for us to handle on our own."

"I've made them well aware of that." Darq, too, looked at Balen. "I believe we have only one action remaining. Lord Balen should accompany me back to Dorland. Lord Vallan and the clan leaders have only heard from me, not directly from Samara. It's not a bad idea to send at least one person to represent Arcacia as well. Perhaps it will be more difficult for them to tell you no."

Balen nodded. "I'm willing. How soon?"

"As soon as you are ready, my lord."

"I'd leave tomorrow if it would help Samara."

"We'll let the dragons have a day to rest, and we can discuss the details." Darq faced Trask. "What about you? Will you join us?"

Trask shook his head. "As much as I would like to, there are developments here in Landale I need to monitor. There are others, however, who can take my place." He gestured specifically

45

at Rayad. "And I'm sure you will agree that a strong security force is needed for the king."

"Of course."

Trask looked around the room, his gaze picking out certain people in particular. Jace glanced at Kyrin. If his inkling was correct, they were about to set off on another mission, this time halfway across the continent.

Jace sat on his cot and rummaged through his pack and weapons once more in preparation for their dawn departure. Even traveling by dragon, it would take over a week to reach the forests of northern Dorland—far too long a trip to risk forgetting something. What should he expect from the northern country? Despite what he had heard from Talas and the other cretes, it still failed to create a clear picture in his mind.

Though Holden and Timothy worked in silence nearby, Aaron, Mick, and Trev talked about the mission. When their discussion turned to the cretes' tree-dwelling lifestyle, a chill seeped down into Jace's chest and through his limbs. From the moment he had agreed to this mission, he'd fought to keep from thinking about how the cretes lived. He shared a glance with Holden.

Trev must have noticed his discomfort. "Sorry, Jace."

He shook his head. "Don't be." If he weren't so afraid of heights, he too would be curious about how the elusive cretes lived. He didn't want to spoil their interest. "I was just leaving. It's getting close to suppertime."

He closed his pack and strode out of the cabin to let his friends continue their discussion. On his way to the Altair's home, he passed Warin and Lenae's cabin and found Meredith sitting on a bench outside with the little white kitten Warin had given her. Her bottom lip stuck out in a pout, and he paused. She looked up at him, her wide eyes sad.

"What's wrong?" he asked.

Meredith sighed and dropped her gaze back to the kitten. "I don't want everyone to go. You were gone so long last time."

Her voice drew him to sit down beside her, where she looked at him again.

"Will you be gone long this time?"

"I'm afraid so," Jace said. "It's a long way to Dorland."

Meredith's pout returned full force. "It's not as fun without Kyrin here to play with me."

Jace couldn't help but smile. "Well, you do have Violet to play with now." He nodded to the kitten, who padded from Meredith's lap onto his. Stroking the kitten's downy coat, he leaned a little closer to Meredith. "And I'd be very happy if you played with Tyra sometimes. She gets lonely when we're gone too."

Meredith perked up a little. "I can play with her."

Drawn by her name, Tyra stepped closer to Jace and sniffed Violet curiously. The kitten scooted away, her ears laid flat, and hissed. Tyra took a step back and looked up as if to ask what she'd done wrong. Jace patted her head and handed the disgruntled kitten back to Meredith.

"Will your trip be dangerous?" the girl asked.

"I don't think so," Jace told her—unless one counted falling out of giant trees. He shoved the thought away.

"You will always take care of Kyrin, won't you?"

She fixed him with a serious gaze, and he matched it. "Always."

"Good, 'cause she's my only sister, and I don't want anything to happen to her."

"Neither do I, Meredith."

"Because you love her?"

Jace chuckled softly. "Yes." He half expected her to ask if they would get married. That seemed to be everyone's question these days.

However, Meredith's attention had shifted, and Jace looked up. Kyrin walked toward them, a particularly warm smile on her face

"Supper's ready," she announced. She focused on Meredith. "Your mommy said you get to have supper with us tonight."

"Can Violet come?"

"Of course."

Kyrin held out her hand, and Meredith took it, sliding off the bench. Jace rose, and the three of them headed toward the Altair cabin. He glanced at Meredith walking between them, and then at Kyrin. A thought struck him—what might it be like if Meredith was their child instead? He swallowed hard. If only that didn't terrify him.

Jace let them precede him through the door and then stepped in himself. All five of Kyrin's brothers had already found their seats. Jace, Kyrin, and Meredith squeezed into their empty places. Though a tight fit for them all, no one complained about bumping elbows, and Jace certainly didn't mind sitting so close to Kyrin. However, he focused on Marcus's voice as they bowed their heads in prayer. The moment he finished, Michael jumped back into a conversation they appeared to have been in the middle of earlier.

"Can't you just ask Trask if I can go along? You're just going to talk to the cretes. It's not like it's a dangerous mission, and I can handle myself anyway."

Marcus glanced at their mother at the opposite end of the table but didn't respond to his younger brother's request.

Michael slumped in his chair. "At this rate, everything will be over by the time anyone will let me help."

"As much as I wish that were so, this conflict won't end that soon," Marcus told him. "It'll take a lot of time and preparation to drive Daican out of Samara, and who knows beyond that. You'll get your chance. But . . ."

Michael's eager eyes locked with his brother at the promising word.

Marcus glanced at their mother once more and said, "I suppose I could ask him and see what he says."

Michael sat up straight, his face beaming. "Really?"

Marcus nodded.

Out of the corner of his eye, Jace caught Kyrin's smile.

"What about me? Can I come?" Ronny piped up.

"I think there are already enough people going," Lydia said gently.

Her youngest son let out an exaggerated sigh.

Liam nudged him. "You need to stick around and keep me company."

This drew a reluctant smile from the boy.

The meal passed pleasantly. Before it grew too late in the evening, Kyrin turned to Jace and suggested a walk. Hand in hand, they left the cabin and slowly circled camp. They talked about the mission and what they would see in Dorland. However, Jace could tell that Kyrin took care not to say much concerning the cretes and their treehouses. She was always so sensitive to his struggles.

When dusk had fallen, they returned to the cabin but did not go inside. Kyrin sat down on a bench in the light of one of the lanterns her brothers had lit, and Jace joined her. They sat for a couple of minutes in silence, looking out into camp until Jace sensed Kyrin's gaze. He turned to her. Her eyes were soft, yet piercing, as if she could read every thought.

"Are you still worried about Dagren?"

Ever since Anne had brought the news of the man responsible for Kalli and Aldor's deaths, Jace had struggled with fear of what chaos the man might wreak here and with underlying urges for revenge. If only his past didn't always try to creep in and torment him.

He nodded slowly. "Yes . . . but that's not what I was thinking about."

"What is it?"

He swallowed the uncomfortable knot in his throat. There would never be a time when he could hide any anxieties from her. But was now the appropriate time to discuss his uncertainties and fears? Was he even ready?

"Us."

She shifted to face him more fully. Jace hesitated, searching for words his tongue wouldn't rebel at. He had to tell her the truth, but every part of him fought coming right out with it.

"I'm . . . afraid." He winced. So much of his life had been characterized by the fears he fought to hide. To admit them still took great effort. "Afraid I can't be everything you deserve."

He searched her eyes, and her lips lifted in a little smile.

"I'm not looking for perfect. If I was, I'd be searching forever."

No one may be perfect, but he still failed her with his hesitance in considering a future as her husband. She deserved someone who was as ready as he sensed she was. Someone who would have moved forward by now.

She gripped his hand in both of hers. "Just think of everything we've been through. We've seen each other through just about the worst situations we could imagine, and I wouldn't choose anyone else to face the future with."

Jace breathed out slowly, a peaceful warmth growing inside him. If she would stick with him through this, then maybe, with time, he would figure things out. He looked her in the eyes. "I love you."

The smile she gave him only further quieted his anxious thoughts. "I love you too."

"Sometimes it just takes me a while to work through things."

"I know, and that's all right. I don't mind."

Across camp, Jace spotted Holden and Aaron heading for their cabin. "We should probably get some sleep before tomorrow."

Kyrin nodded, and Jace stood, drawing her up with him.

"Good night," he told her.

She echoed him, squeezing his hand before letting go.

He watched her until she was inside the cabin and the door had shut. Then he let out his breath in a long gust. If he would just marry her, then he would never have to leave her like this.

"WILL THIS RAIN ever stop?" Anne stared out the window at the streams of rainwater pouring from the roof. She envied those who had left for Dorland and the prospect of fairer weather. At least they had escaped being cooped up inside day after day.

"I pray so," her father responded. "If not, the whole region could lose this season's crops. It would mean a shortage this winter."

Just one more thing they had to worry about.

Anne turned back to the table, where her father worked on letters to various family members and friends and Elian sharpened one of his daggers. Her mother and Elanor sat sewing. She resumed her seat and took up working on a collection of dolls to give to Meredith and the other little girls in camp. They would need entertainment while shut up in their cabins. She would try to find something for the boys as well. Perhaps her father or Elian had an idea.

A knock rapped the front door. Everyone stilled. They didn't receive many visitors lately except for Goler, and now the threat of Dagren. Anne fought to steady her heartbeat, though it raced anyway when her father rose to answer the door. Elian watched him, a readiness hardening his expression.

Anne whispered a quick prayer as her father opened the door. She turned in her chair and leaned over to see around him. But no black and gold appeared, and she recognized one of Baron Grey's men. She gripped her chair. Had something happened in Landale?

"An invitation from the baron for you and your household, sir," the man announced.

Anne let out her breath, sagging a little. It would take a moment for her heart rate to return to normal.

"Thank you," her father said. "Would you like to come inside and dry off before you return to Landale?"

"Thank you, sir, but I have more stops to make and should be on my way."

Anne's father nodded and bid him good day. Closing the door, he returned to the table and scanned the parchment parcel in his hand. He broke the seal and read over it, his brows dipping.

"What does it say?" Anne's mother asked.

"The three of us and Elanor are invited to a celebration dinner at Landale Castle in three days to honor Captain Dagren and welcome him to Landale."

Anne exchanged a frown with her mother before she rose and looked at the invitation in her father's hands. "It is Baron Grey's handwriting, but why would he hold a celebration for Dagren?"

"He wouldn't, unless he was pressured to." Her father sighed and refolded the invitation.

"Will we attend?" Anne's stomach bubbled nauseously. It would be bad enough to face Dagren again but, at a party, she would have no way to distance herself from Goler. She shuddered. He would use every advantage this party offered him.

"I don't think we have much choice. This is no doubt a test to gauge the loyalty of the locals. We'll not only have to attend, but enjoy it, or at least make a concerted effort to appear to."

Anne groaned. A whole evening with Goler and Dagren would require great fortitude. Already her cheeks hurt with the dread of having to wear a fake smile.

The usual gray clouds blanketed the sky the next day but didn't drop rain all morning. When it still held after lunch, Anne announced, "I think I'll ride to Landale and see the baron."

"I'm not sure that's wise," her father cautioned.

"It's just a visit. He must get lonely since he never sees Trask anymore. Besides, I want to know more about this celebration. Trask will want details."

Slowly, her father nodded. "All right. I'll go with you."

"It might look more innocent if it's only me."

"Very well, but be careful."

"I'll go with you," Elanor offered. "I don't think two young women would raise suspicion."

No doubt she was as anxious to get out of the house as Anne was.

"I'll have the carriage hitched for you."

Anne's father rose from his seat at the table, but she stopped him.

"We can ride."

Her father shook his head. "Knowing how the weather has been, it's likely to start pouring the moment you set off."

Anne had to agree. As much as she would have enjoyed the ride, there was no sense in getting soaked and covered in mud.

Her father crossed the room, and Anne turned to look back at him. "Tell Elian to ride inside with us. I won't have him riding in the rain just because he's the bodyguard."

"I'll see if he'll listen," her father said with a chuckle as he stepped outside.

Twenty minutes later, Anne tied on a light cloak to ward off the dampness and stepped out to the porch with Elanor. The carriage waited for them. Elian stood at the open door to help them in. She did not see his horse, so he must have agreed to ride with them. Though he might as well be part of the family now, he kept many strict social rules. However, Anne cared less and less about societal expectations these days. Bodyguard or not, he was a friend, and there was no reason he should ride separately.

They stepped lightly across the soggy yard. Elian helped Anne into the carriage first, and then Elanor, before ducking in himself. He closed the door, and they settled into their seats. Anne peeked out the window as they pulled away from Marlton and onto the road. Even inside, she felt the wheels sinking into the mud.

"I hope we don't get stuck." She glanced at Elanor. "Then we'll wish we had ridden."

Such a prospect would mortify most noblewomen, but Elanor offered a little grin.

"We'd return to Marlton looking like the time James and his beastly friends threw mud at me when we were little."

"Trask did that once . . . I threw it right back."

They shared a laugh.

Anne looked across at Elian. "Did you ever throw mud at girls?"

"He would never," Elanor said, but her eyes were teasing.

Elian smiled. "I gave my sisters their share of grief."

Anne couldn't quite imagine it, but even quiet little boys had their moments.

Despite some rough patches, they made it to Landale without incident. They pulled into the courtyard of Landale Castle and stopped near the door. Elian exited first, turning back to help the women out. Anne stepped down and looked around. Regret needled her. She had not visited in some time. Trask had lived in hiding as an outlaw for two years now. Though he had his loyal servants, Baron Grey must be so lonely without his son. Not many people came visiting anymore since Trask's so-called treason.

At the door, the butler let them inside and showed them into the parlor. Anne and Elanor took seats on the couch, and Elian stood behind them while they waited. In just a couple of minutes, Baron Grey appeared, and Anne stood to meet him. That needle in her heart punctured deeper.

The once strong baron seemed to have aged ten years in the last two. Of course, the stressful situation took its toll on all of them. Even her father had deeper lines in his face and more gray hair but poor Baron Grey. He looked so frail, almost sickly now, and much thinner than in all the years she'd known him. However, his sad, tired eyes sparkled with a smile for her.

"Anne, Lady Elanor, what a pleasant surprise."

She smiled in return and gave him a hug. "It's been far too long since I visited."

"It's hardly easy with this weather," the baron said, but it was still no excuse for her absence. He gestured to the couch. "Please, sit. I've called for tea. You too, Elian. Join us."

Elian did not protest, claiming one of the chairs that faced the couch while Baron Grey lowered himself into the other. He coughed as he did so, and Anne's breath grew shallow.

"Are you ill, my lord?"

He waved off her concern. "It's all this damp weather. It's not good for my lungs. It'll clear up as soon as we get some sunshine."

Anne relaxed a little, yet couldn't completely shake her concern. Perhaps he was not ill now, but he could easily become sick and didn't appear to be in any condition to fight it.

"We all pray it comes soon, and for more than just a day or two at a time," she said.

Grey agreed. Then his smile returned. "It's so good to have young blood here again. Tell me, have you seen Trask lately? What's happening out at camp?"

Anne filled him in on all the recent events and developments—of Warin and Lenae's wedding and the mission to Dorland. Grey listened eagerly, asking many questions about Trask. If only the two of them could visit safely.

They spoke for a while over tea before Anne could bring herself to mention more serious matters.

"We received your invitation."

Baron Grey sobered.

"It was Goler's idea, wasn't it?"

"Goler insisted on it, but I believe the idea belonged to Captain Dagren."

"We met him," Anne said. "He stopped by with Goler last week. I wish he would go back to wherever it is he came from."

"Unfortunately, he doesn't plan on leaving any time soon. At least not until he gets what he's after . . ."

"Trask and everyone at camp," Anne finished.

The baron nodded gravely.

"Does he come here often?"

"Yes, and always with questions." Grey breathed out heavily. "Many of the same. I think he believes he'll wear me down and I'll finally tell him what he wants to hear."

Hot coals burned in Anne's chest. "He shouldn't question you like this. They have no proof that you have anything to do with the Resistance."

Grey gave her a weary shrug. "Perhaps not, but they have their suspicions, and that, it would seem, supersedes my rank. If I wanted to stop him, I'd have to go to the emperor. Since he sent Dagren, I don't see that it would be to my advantage."

Anne fought the outcry to make things right. However, just like the rest of them, Baron Grey was trapped by his circumstances. They all had to live with them until things changed, Elôm willing, for the better.

They talked for a time of less troublesome things until Anne decided to go before they wore the baron out. He looked so tired already, but their visit certainly added liveliness to his eyes.

On the way to the door, Anne said, "We will see you in a couple of days."

"I look forward to seeing your parents."

They traded goodbyes, and Grey said, "When you see Trask . . ." He paused, a wistful longing taking over his face. "Tell him I miss him and how good it is to know that he is well."

Anne rested her hand gently on his arm. "I will."

Back in the carriage, she set her hands in her lap but clenched them hard. They rolled away from the castle in silence, though her mind remained on Baron Grey and how she might help him. Certainly, she would visit more often.

Commotion outside jerked her thoughts and the carriage to a halt. She gripped her seat and exchanged a glance with Elanor before looking across at Elian. He leaned toward the window, his hand on his sword.

A moment of silence passed, and then the splash of hooves brought a dark horse in front of the window. Anne looked out, meeting Dagren's gaze. Her insides went cold, and she dug her fingers into the leather-covered seat cushion. Good thing he was outside the carriage so she couldn't slap him for being such a beast of a man.

"Lady Anne," he said, his voice more chilly than the damp air. His hard gaze drifted past her. "Lady Elanor." He didn't even acknowledge Elian.

"Captain," Anne responded in her sweetest voice, though it was a wonder it made it past her lips.

"A bit damp to be out and about, is it not?"

"We are eager to take advantage of any day it is not actively raining."

Dagren barely nodded, his gaze shifting to the road behind them. "I see you visited the baron." His eyes settled back on her. "Why?"

Anne stiffened and dropped a little of the sweetness. "The baron is a close friend of my family and, in case you hadn't noticed, he's lived alone ever since his son ran off. I like to visit and make sure he is well. He has no other family around to do it."

Dagren peered suspiciously at her. "Kind of you."

Anne forced a smile.

"Will you attend the celebration?" Dagren asked.

"Of course. Why wouldn't we be?"

A smile ghosted across Dagren's lips. "No reason."

"Is there anything else you need, Captain?" Anne asked, trying not to sound too impatient. "I'd like to get home before it decides to rain."

"No." His gaze touched Elian briefly but locked once more with Anne. "Good day, my ladies."

He moved his horse away from the carriage, and they rolled on.

Anne let out a breath and sank back into her seat, letting her rigid muscles unwind. It took a little longer for Elian to relax. A tense silence reigned until Elanor spoke.

"Would it be terribly uncharitable of me to hope his horse trips and throws him in the mud?"

A giggle rose to Anne's lips, and Elian smiled. However, Anne had to ask Elôm's forgiveness for hoping far worse things happened to the captain.

Despite the release of tension, the ride home passed in silence as each was absorbed in their own thoughts. It would be difficult for Anne to tell her father about Baron Grey's condition. They had always been such good friends.

Outside, the carriage splashed into a large puddle and slowed before jolting to a halt. The driver's voice urged the horses forward. The carriage lunged a couple of times but stuck in place. Following another splash, their driver appeared at the window, standing in almost knee-deep water.

"I'm sorry, my lady. I tried to keep her on the same path as before, but she sank deep this time. I don't think I can get her out on my own."

"How far are we from Marlton?"

"About a mile and a half, my lady. I can run and get help and horses for you."

Anne bit back a sigh. In this mood, she would hate to wait in the carriage for him to return. Straightening her back, she made up her mind.

"Elanor, Elian—you can remain here if you'd like. I'm walking." She would ruin her dress, but she didn't particularly care for the color anyway, and she'd worn boots underneath for just this situation.

"I'm coming with you," Elanor announced.

"Are you sure?"

Elanor's dark eyes twinkled. "You think a little mud will bother me?"

It was more than a little, but that was what Anne loved about Elanor. She looked at Elian, who shook his head.

"You're just like your mother," he said.

Elanor laughed at him. "Sorry you didn't get stuck looking after some prim princess who would never dream of setting foot in the dirt."

He chuckled and rose to open the carriage door. Anne and Elanor shared a smile as he stepped out.

Turning back to them, he said, "At least I can carry you out of this puddle."

Anne stepped to the door. The "puddle" was almost as wide as the pond near the house when it wasn't flooded, and came close to overflowing Elian's boots. She put her hand on his shoulder and prepared for him to lift her up, but a voice called out from other side of the road.

"What's this? Stuck are we?"

Her head shot up, her eyes meeting Trask's grin. He and a couple of his men, including Warin, sat on their horses at the edge of the water. She straightened as much as she could.

"Aren't you astute?" She waited a moment, and then said, "There are two women in this carriage who could use a ride to safety, unless you're going to make Elian tote us out himself."

Trask nudged his horse forward, looking entirely too pleased by their predicament. Warin followed. When Trask reached the carriage, he offered Anne his arm, and Elian helped her onto the horse. She wrapped her arms around Trask's waist. He directed his horse away from the carriage so Warin could reach Elanor and rode slowly so as not to splash her dress. She looked over his shoulder and could still see his grin.

"Don't look so pleased with yourself."

"Oh, come on," he replied. "It's not every day I get to rescue a certain damsel in distress."

"That's because this damsel is usually pretty good at taking care of herself."

"Which is why I have to take advantage of every opportunity."

Anne stifled a laugh.

At the side of the road, where the ground was more solid, Trask dismounted. He turned to lift Anne off his horse, his hands lingering around her waist for an extra moment until Warin and Elanor joined them.

She cast him a suspicious look. "It seems awfully coincidental for you to show up right when we needed help."

"One of my men saw you leave Marlton, and I thought I'd try to catch you on the way back."

"You have men watching my house, do you?"

"Not watching, exactly, but passing by every so often to make sure things are as they should be. And it's a good thing too, or you would be very wet and muddy by now."

Anne smirked at him.

"So what were you doing in Landale?"

"We visited your father. We received an invitation from him to a celebration dinner honoring Dagren."

Trask's forehead scrunched. "What?"

"It wasn't his idea, obviously, but he couldn't decline Goler's 'suggestion'."

He crossed his arms. "Are you going?"

"We'll have to."

He looked up the road leading to Landale, his expression growing darker. "A celebration means dancing . . . and drinking. Goler is already too possessive of you. I don't like it."

"Well, I'm certainly open to suggestions. I can't happen to be sick. Not even Goler would fall for that."

Trask chewed his lip, clearly attempting to come up with something on the spot. Anne touched his arm.

"It's probably best we just go to appease Dagren. It's surely a test of our loyalty."

Trask blew out a sigh and looked toward the carriage, where the men were about to push it out of the puddle. He moved to join them, but Anne held him back. There were plenty of men to do the job, and this was important.

"Your father misses you."

His gaze dropped to her. "How is he?"

Anne winced. This would be even harder than telling her father. "Your absence and the pressure he's under are taking their toll." She hesitated but had to tell him the truth. "He doesn't look well."

Trask's face grew serious. "I have to go see him."

"You can't. Goler and Dagren always have men watching. Dagren stopped the carriage right after we left the castle to ask why we visited."

"What did you tell him?"

"That your father is alone and has no family to look in on him and make sure he's doing well."

Trask hung his head, and Anne touched his cheek. "That's not a criticism against you. Your father understands why you can't come, and he doesn't want you to risk it. It's too dangerous. To see you die now would kill him."

"Still, somehow, I have to get in and see him."

Though Anne's heart stuttered in fear, she nodded. She would do anything to get to her own father in this situation, and Baron Grey needed to see his son.

"Just be careful," she murmured.

"Of course I will." He smiled and brushed a stray hair out of her face. "Did you tell him about us?"

"No, it didn't seem right. Not without you. But if you see him, you should tell him."

In another couple of minutes, the men had the carriage out of the puddle and waiting to move on. Elian lifted Elanor up and carried her over the worst of the mud to the carriage door. Following his example, Trask swept Anne up into his arms. She wrapped her own arms around his neck, relishing the moment, and smiled at him. The sparkle had returned to his eyes.

"You know," he said, "it would've been amusing to come along and find you traipsing through the mud. You're quite adorable when you're that determined."

"Oh, really? And what would you have done then? Thrown mud at me again?"

"Might've been tempting." Trask glanced at the carriage and smirked devilishly. "Now that I have you, I could just carry you off into the forest."

Anne shook her head, trying not to wish he would. "And if I scream?"

He lowered his voice. "It's just me and my men around. We made sure."

Anne let her head fall back with a laugh. "You're dangerous, you know that?"

He just grinned and eyed her lips. She fought to give him a stern look, but it failed miserably.

"My carriage," she reminded.

Trask screwed up his face. "You're no fun."

She laughed again, and he carried her to the carriage, setting her lightly on the step. She rested her hands on his shoulders as he looked up at her, his eyes more serious.

"Thank you for visiting my father."

"You're welcome."

He gave her a sweet smile, and she turned into the carriage. After taking her seat, she watched Trask return to his horse with his men until the carriage rolled away. Then she leaned back, a smile still on her lips and her heart lighter than when they'd left Landale.

"I can't believe you won't just marry him."

Anne glanced at Elanor and shook her head. "Don't start or you may just change my mind."

ANNE HELD UP a stunning emerald gown and scrutinized it in the mirror. The green satin shimmered even on a gloomy day like this one. It would certainly look dazzling in candlelight.

Elanor stepped up behind her and looked over her shoulder. "That one really brings out your eyes."

Anne scrunched up her face. "It's one of my favorites, but I don't want to stand out tonight. I'd wear a servant's dress if I thought it would make me less appealing to Goler." She shook her head. "I need something with an even higher neckline. The less I give him to stare at, the better."

Her cheeks warmed, but it was more the burn of ire than embarrassment. She would have to be careful to hold her temper this evening.

Behind her, Elanor shuffled through the wardrobe. "What about this one?"

Anne turned as Elanor held up a gown of moss green silk, a little on the dull side, with a neckline that would reach her collarbone.

"I guess that will do."

Not that it would deter Goler, but at least she wouldn't feel too conscientious. She returned the emerald gown to the wardrobe. A pity. It had been so long since she'd worn it.

The murmur of voices downstairs captured their attention.

"Sounds like company." Anne's stomach pinched. Company never boded well lately.

She led the way out of her room. Halfway down the stairs, she recognized a very distinct male voice.

Elanor gasped lightly and rushed past her. "Uncle Charles!"

Just below them, the handsome Viscount Ilvaran looked up with a warm smile, his stubbled jaw and travel-wrinkled clothes doing nothing to detract from his dignified air.

"Elanor." He caught her in a big hug. "It's so good to see you."

They parted with wide smiles.

At the bottom of the stairs, Anne joined her parents and Elian.

Charles's deep eyes shifted to her and sparkled, crinkling at the corners. "Lady Anne, it is a pleasure to see you again as well."

Anne smiled at him. She counted him not only a friend but also a powerful ally. After all, his plan had saved Jace from Rothas's intentions to hang him. "And you, my lord."

"What are you doing here?" Elanor asked.

Charles's gaze returned to his niece. "It's high time I came to visit you. I wanted to come sooner. I thought I would wait out the rain, but it doesn't appear that it will dry up any time soon. So here I am."

Elanor glanced around as if checking for others. "Mother couldn't come?" Disappointment tinged her voice.

"If she had, your father would have too, and no doubt would have taken you back. He doesn't even know I'm here."

"Is he still angry I left?"

Charles shrugged. "More frustrated that you're not there to marry off to one of the suitors he has lined up."

Elanor's face soured. It was the threat of suitors back home that had kept her here at Marlton for so long. Anne didn't blame her in the least and was happy to offer sanctuary.

Now that they had greeted one another, Anne's father offered to show Charles to a room. A short time later, once he'd had a chance to clean up, they all gathered around the table for lunch. Anne's father offered a quick prayer and conversation resumed.

Anne set her attention on Charles across the table, temporarily ignoring her meal. "How long can you stay with us?"

"A few days. I don't have anything pressing that demands my attention except to return before Rothas realizes I'm gone."

"Are you sure Mother will be all right without you to check in on her?" Elanor asked in concern.

"Your grandmother will stop by," Charles answered, a twinkle in his eyes. "And I'm confident that I left her in capable hands."

Elanor frowned. "Whose?"

The twinkle grew to a smile. "James."

Elanor's eyes rounded, surely matching Anne's own as they exchanged a glance. James was the very last person they would have trusted to take care of his mother. Elanor repeated his name incredulously.

Charles confirmed it. "Has your mother written to you about him?"

"Well, she did allude to some changes, but she was very vague about it."

"She probably wanted to be cautious should her letters fall into the wrong hands—namely your father's."

"So what *is* going on?"

Anne listened closely as well. She only knew James as the shameless, womanizing scoundrel who had flirted with her incessantly and tried to attack Kyrin. She couldn't imagine him any other way.

69

"You remember what he was like just before you left?" Charles asked.

Elanor nodded. "He was all sullen. He and Jace had it out the night Jace left. Jace never told me exactly what he said, but it did seem to bother James."

"That was only the beginning. After you left, it got worse. He was angry and withdrawn, and wouldn't speak to anyone. He wouldn't even have anything to do with your father."

Anne lifted her brows. Though she hadn't spent more than a few days with Elanor's family, James had appeared to be the mirror image of his father. It was hard to picture a falling out between them.

"He started drinking heavily," Charles went on. "And I mean drowning himself in liquor. Your mother didn't know what to do, and your father's only solution to everything is control, but James wouldn't have any of it. A few months ago, I rode out there to have a talk with him while your father was away. Perhaps it was not the most tactful approach, but I threw him out in the snow and kept him there until he would talk to me."

Anne nearly laughed to think of calm, dignified Charles doing such a thing, but desperate times . . .

"Why was he so upset?" Elanor asked.

"A guilty conscience."

Both Elanor and Anne looked at him in surprise. Did James even have a conscience? It certainly hadn't been in use when Anne met him.

"It's true. He felt guilty for the things he's done and had almost done." Charles's attention shifted to Anne, proving that he knew what had happened with Kyrin. "Whatever Jace said to him must have stuck like a hot coal, burning until it completely consumed him."

Elanor leaned forward eagerly. "So what happened?"

"We talked for a good long time, and I visited regularly. He still drank for a while, but gradually, things have changed. Now I can say with comfortable certainty that he has placed his faith in Elôm."

Elanor gasped, about ready to jump out of her seat. Even Anne experienced a thrill at the news. James was a perfect example of how anyone could change. It pricked her own conscience that she'd never had even the slightest hope that such a transformation could take place in Goler's life.

"Truly?" A smile beamed on Elanor's face.

"Yes. He's left his old ways behind him and is very attentive to your mother now." Charles chuckled. "I don't think your father knows what to make of it."

Elanor laughed lightly. "Just wait until Jace hears about this."

"How is Jace?" Charles asked, his eyes conveying his eagerness for news about his nephew.

Elanor immediately launched into telling him all about camp, with Anne supplying extra details along the way. Charles listened with great interest. After all, he and Rachel received very little information in Elanor's letters for the same reason her mother didn't write about James.

When an eventual lull came in the conversation some time later, Charles turned to Anne's father. "I haven't fully thanked you yet for your hospitality on such short notice. I hope I have not arrived at an inopportune time."

"Not at all," Anne's father replied. "We do have a celebration dinner to attend this evening. Elanor was invited, but I don't see any reason she can't remain here to keep you company. I'm sure she'd find that preferable."

"Oh? What sort of celebration dinner is it?"

"The kind where your attendance proves whether or not you're loyal to the emperor's cause."

Charles nodded slowly. "And I imagine, with Landale being the center of the Resistance, that everyone is seen as suspect."

"Yes, especially with this new captain, Dagren. The dinner is to welcome him, or so they say."

Before they could go on, Anne slid back her chair. "Speaking of the dinner, I had best get ready. It won't be long before we have to leave."

She excused herself, as did her mother. She hated to leave the table, but she needed a bit of time to prepare for her evening with Goler. The mere thought of him turned her stomach.

In her room, her maid Sara helped her change into the mossy green gown and fixed her hair in a pretty but understated style. On any other occasion, she may have done something more elaborate but not tonight.

When she finished, she dismissed Sara and sat in front of the mirror to contemplate what necklace and earrings to wear. In her head, however, she spoke to Elôm, praying for strength and wisdom.

A short time later, she left her room again and returned downstairs. When she reached the living room, she found her parents dressed for the evening, but they weren't the only ones. Elanor wore the deep blue gown she'd picked out earlier, and Charles had changed into more formal attire as well.

"What's this?" Anne asked.

Charles stepped forward. "Elanor and Elian told me about this Captain Goler. I thought, perhaps, you might like an escort for the evening."

Anne smiled widely. How could she not? Suddenly the evening didn't seem nearly so dreadful.

"I would be beyond delighted." She joined the group. "And were Trask here, he would offer his greatest thanks."

Charles grinned. "Ah, so he's the lucky man."

"Yes."

"Well, it will be an honor to see that you have a tolerable evening, for both your sake and his."

Rides through the countryside south of Valcré were vital for Daniel's sanity. Being stuck inside the walls of Auréa Palace would drive him mad otherwise. If only he didn't have eight members of Auréa's security following him everywhere. They were a necessity he'd learned to ignore, but he could hardly wait to free himself of them when he attended the meeting at Ben's house tonight.

He spent hours roaming the forested roads and small villages in the area. It was easy to forget out here that he was the crown prince of it all—easy to imagine a simpler life. However, his guards were quick to remind him of reality when they urged him to return home before it grew too late and started to rain. Reluctantly, Daniel complied.

Following a well-trodden road, they entered the city and clattered up the streets toward the palace. People waved greetings to him along the way, and he responded with smiles, genuinely enjoying the interaction. He liked people—well, most people. Often he disguised himself to mingle among them. He'd become convinced over the years that there were better men among the common people than in his father's circles.

When they trotted into the palace courtyard, Daniel pulled his gray steed to a halt and patted the gelding's neck. The horse tossed his head. He'd enjoyed a good run as much as Daniel had. The weather lately hadn't allowed them to get out nearly as much as Daniel would have liked. His mood had definitely taken a hit in recent weeks, but today had refreshed him.

Jumping down, he handed the horse off to the waiting groom and turned toward the palace entrance. Tension tightened his muscles. His parents were walking together across the courtyard. So much for his good mood. He rolled his shoulders to loosen them, and set off for the stairs. He met his parents there.

"Did you have a good ride?" his mother asked as she eyed him meaningfully. If any sort of bridge existed between him and his father, she was it.

"Yes, a very good ride." He gave her a genuine smile. The friction always bothered her, and he made a determined effort to shield her from it. He then glanced at his father, fighting to maintain his good humor. "I need to go change."

Though the rain held during the ride, the wet countryside had left him spattered in mud. He turned and took two steps toward the door before his father's voice halted him.

"We're having dinner with the Earl of Danthan and Baron Stant. I don't want you disappearing tonight."

The tension rushed back, only tripled. Daniel balled his fists. He wouldn't miss another meeting. He turned to his father, who speared him with a warning look.

"I doubt I could add anything to the evening."

"You will be there," his father said evenly.

"Why?"

"Because one day you'll be emperor, and I need to make sure you're capable of undertaking the responsibility and handling the sorts of people you will deal with."

Daniel gritted his teeth. If he were king one day—and it would be *king*, no more of this ridiculous emperor business— then many things would change, including the sorts of people he had in his advisor circle. Yet, he bit back a retort. He tried hard these days to avoid disrespecting his father, as difficult as that was.

"I think I'll manage." He turned again to leave, praying to avoid an all-out argument.

"I expect you at the table on time."

Daniel paused and dragged in a hard breath as he battled every impulse he would have readily given in to a year ago. He wavered a moment on the right course of action, desperate for the fellowship at Ben's, but convicted to obey his father in this instance. Over his shoulder, he ground out, "Fine."

He took another step.

"Are you ill?"

He turned back once more. His father stood at the base of the steps, his fists planted on his hips.

Daniel frowned at him. "What?"

"I asked if you were ill, because you've made it your purpose in life to defy me since your youth, and now that defiance has been glaringly absent. As much as I'd like to believe you've matured and are acting like an adult, these abrupt changes raise suspicion."

Daniel narrowed his eyes, that defiance closer to the surface than his father probably realized.

"Yes, well, whatever my reasons, you're certainly not making it easy for me."

He spun around, and this time did not stop. His father had already stretched his restraint thin enough. If he didn't leave now, he would snap and then have to deal with a guilty conscience later.

He strode inside and up to his chambers, slamming the door behind him. In the middle of his sitting room, he paused and released a long sigh.

"Why, Lord? Why tonight? The one night I get to spend with other believers? If this is a test of my patience, then it's certainly working."

He entered his bedroom, yanked off his muddy riding clothes, and changed into a clean pair of pants and linen shirt. He didn't bother with anything else. He'd have to change into something fancier for the evening in a short time anyway. Blasted formal dinners.

Back in his sitting room, he sank down into one of the chairs and rubbed his eyes with his fingertips, willing his ire to cool. The disappointment, however, lingered. He counted down the days to the meetings every week. To go another whole week without encouragement from Ben and the others would not help his thinning patience toward his father.

A knock tapped the door. Biting back a grumble, he pushed up from his chair. If his father had sent one of the servants with further orders for him . . .

He opened the door and drew his brows together. "Mother?"

"I think we should talk."

Daniel's frown deepened, but he motioned her inside. She stepped into the room, her eyes sweeping the area as if searching for something. Daniel remained standing by the door and watched her.

Finally, she turned to him. "Are you going to tell me what's going on?"

"What do you mean?"

"Your father is right. You've changed."

A grumble rose in Daniel's chest again. Couldn't they simply be happy with the change? He then closed the door and faced his mother, crossing his arms. "Is that such a bad thing?"

"No. In fact, under normal circumstances, I would be very proud, but . . ." she eyed him critically, "I too question your motives. You haven't been the same since . . ."

An expectant silence hung between them, and Daniel almost read the unspoken words on her face. He tipped his head. "Since when?"

His mother hesitated, her eyes flashing as if she suddenly regretted pressing him. "Nothing. Never mind." She stepped toward the door.

But boldness grew from Daniel's frustration. "Since he murdered Elon?"

His mother froze, her back stiffening. "It was an execution, not murder."

"He killed an innocent man. I don't see how that's not murder." He gritted his teeth. "He's killed many innocent people."

His mother held up her hand. "Stop it. Just stop. You're starting to sound like . . . like one of *them*."

Daniel stared at her, and some prompting overcame him that he believed was beyond himself. He never expected to do this here and now, but the words poured from his mouth. "I am one of them." His mother's face went slack and paled, and he affirmed, "I am a believer in Elôm."

She took a step back, shaking her head. "No." Her eyes flew to the door, but then she stepped toward him, her voice a sharp whisper. "You cannot do this. Not after everything your father is working to achieve for you."

Daniel barely restrained a hard laugh. "This isn't for me, this is for him, and he's going about it all wrong. Mother, he is slaughtering innocent people simply because we worship a different God. It's wrong."

"No, stop. You must stop this now. It's treason. You could be executed."

"That's a chance I'm more than willing to take. And do you really believe I'm guilty?"

His mother turned her face away and would not speak.

"Mother, do you believe I'm guilty?"

If she answered no, it would prove what he had said—that his father was killing innocent people.

Her gaze slid back to him, this time with a sheen of tears. Daniel didn't recall ever seeing her cry. She was always such a strong woman, and despite their disagreements over the years, she had always been there for him when his father wasn't.

He softened his voice. "I'm sorry, Mother, but the things I've seen and experienced have shown me that Elôm is real and that Elon is His Son. That will never change, and I've chosen to live my life serving Him."

His mother blinked hard and drew herself up. The tears disappeared, and her voice lowered. "I don't know if I can keep this from your father."

"I'm not asking you to."

This apparently wasn't the answer she wanted. A stormy mix of both fear and anger brewed in her eyes. "Do you have any idea of the danger you're putting yourself in? If this is some rebellious stunt against your father—"

"Mother," he cut in firmly. "This has nothing to do with rebelling. Quite the opposite. This is what compels me to do everything in my power to respect Father. And, of course, I understand the danger. I've witnessed execution after execution of the people who share my faith. I know exactly what this choice entails."

His mother breathed deeply in and out, sorrow morphing her face. "I will keep quiet for now, but please, do not continue down this path."

"I'm sorry, but this is my life now, whatever happens."

Slowly, she nodded and walked to the door, her head bowed as if in defeat. Just before she opened it, she looked back at him. "This will not end well, Daniel."

THE CARRIAGE ROCKED and splashed down the road toward
Landale, but their driver took particular care to avoid getting
stuck this time. Anne sat between her mother and Elanor, while
her father and Charles occupied the seat across from them.

Anne traded a quick smile with Charles. She really shouldn't
be so eager to see the look on Goler's face when she arrived with
such a prominent escort. Charles was sure to be the highest-
ranking noble at the party, which would mostly consist of
wealthy merchants, knights, and perhaps the neighboring baron
and his family. Anyone else of notable standing lived too far away
for a simple one-night dinner party. Being a viscount, and a
popular one at that, Charles would command the attention of
everyone present tonight.

"Anything more I should know about our *gracious* hosts?"
he asked.

Since he was looking at her, Anne answered. "Well, Goler
wants to be baron. If he wasn't doing such a poor job of
destroying the Resistance, I'm sure he would have found a way
to eliminate Baron Grey by now and take the position for
himself. He's also extremely jealous. I'm sure he'll be livid when
he sees that I haven't come alone."

She glanced out the window at the sodden countryside. "Dagren is the dangerous one. I've only met him twice, but he's very suspicious. We'll have to be especially careful with what we say and how we act around him."

Charles nodded but appeared up for the challenge.

They arrived at Landale Castle behind a line of carriages bearing the other guests. When their turn came, Anne's father and Charles climbed out first and turned to assist the women. Approaching the castle entrance, Charles offered Anne his arm.

"Thank you for doing this for me," she said as she accepted it.

"My pleasure." His tone changed from lighthearted to more serious. "One thing I can't abide is to see women taken advantage of in any sort of situation."

And that's what Anne appreciated so much about him. If only she had a brother like him, the way Kyrin had Kaden and her other brothers.

They entered the castle, where servants took their cloaks and ushered them into the sitting room. Around thirty people had arrived so far.

Anne scanned the spacious room and squeezed Charles's arm. "There's Goler."

He stood with a good view of the door, no doubt watching for her arrival. She rarely saw him in anything but his uniform, yet tonight he wore a burgundy shirt under a surprisingly well-tailored black doublet. It did nothing, however, to distract from that greasy hair of his and the ugly scar slashed across his nose. His eyes flickered to Charles, narrowing, but then locked on Anne. His expression like stone, he strode toward them. Anne drew in a breath, but Charles stood as a strong and steady protector at her side.

"Lady Anne," Goler said in smooth voice, yet his eyes glinted demandingly as he looked between her and Charles.

Anne put on her sweetest smile. "Captain Goler, allow me to introduce Lord Ilvaran, the Viscount of Dunrick. He's here to visit his niece and requested that he be my escort tonight." She said it with all innocence, as if she weren't fervently thanking Elôm that he had.

Goler stared at Charles for a lengthy moment with a sickening half-smile that suggested he was fighting the urge to curse. Finally, he must have controlled himself. "Lord Ilvaran, welcome to Landale."

"Thank you, Captain. It appears to be quite a charming place. I hope to see more of it, if the weather permits. I hear you have your hands full keeping the peace, what with traitorous outlaws running loose."

"Indeed," Goler spoke through his teeth. "In fact, I'm surprised your niece is allowed to remain in such a volatile area."

Of course, if she weren't, then Charles wouldn't be here to ruin Goler's evening. Anne fought an upwelling of smugness.

Charles gave a charming smile with not even a hint of subtle sarcasm. "Well, we trust the local officials to keep the innocent safe."

Anne bit down hard to keep from grinning. Goler couldn't argue against that.

"We do our best." Goler forced his smarmy smile wider, but it didn't hide the ice in his eyes. "I do hope you enjoy the evening and your visit."

His gaze slid once more to Anne, seething just as she'd expected, but next to Charles, she felt secure.

"Thank you," Charles said again. "I'm sure I will." He then led Anne off to mingle with the rest of the guests.

Once they were out of earshot, Anne released a quiet laugh and glanced up at Charles. "We need to keep you around. You handled him better than anyone I know."

Charles smiled handsomely. "I've had a lot of practice with such men."

They worked their way through the guests—all of whom were delighted to meet Charles—before they finally reached Baron Grey and Anne's parents. Charles and the baron greeted one another, but Anne grew distracted by Grey's appearance. She had hoped he would be in better health tonight, but he appeared fatigued, his skin sallow and sagging. It robbed her good humor, and she traded a look with her father. Though she had warned him, it must be difficult for him to see the deterioration of Grey's well-being firsthand.

They spoke briefly before parting as Baron Grey invited everyone to the dining room for the meal. Anne thanked Elôm that she didn't have to sit next to Goler. He did, however, claim the chair directly across from her. His burning gaze destroyed her appetite, though she put great effort into ignoring him. The woman to her left, the young wife of a knight, inadvertently aided her by being a talkative sort and monopolizing Anne's attention. She fairly gushed over Charles, far more than Anne thought proper for a married woman, but at least she was pleasant. And she wasn't the only one interested in Charles. As Anne had anticipated, he commanded the table. Questions came from nearly everyone, even those seated at the far end.

Everyone but Dagren and Goler.

Captain Dagren appeared less perturbed than Anne would have expected—more like a bird of prey waiting to spot his next meal. Goler, however, stabbed at his food, wearing a scowl. It darkened every time Charles drew laughter from the guests, which he managed with ease. Goler cast a withering stare at Anne, and she offered her most innocent, doe-eyed look while biting back a smile. Just as Trask had feared, there was plenty of wine and ale, and Goler guzzled down multiple mugs before the meal finished.

When they did conclude, the table emptied, and everyone filtered into the ballroom. A group of local musicians set up and began a merry tune. Remaining at Charles's side, Anne watched from the perimeter for a couple of minutes before he turned to her.

"I suppose we shouldn't just stand here or someone will get the idea to come claim you."

He offered his hand and guided her to join the dance. Anne was happy to participate. She didn't get to dance much anymore. She missed the summertime celebrations when things were normal before the Resistance. She and Trask had danced until they could hardly stand sometimes. Such a time seemed lost now, possibly for good.

Anne and Charles shared a couple of dances, all very enjoyable until Anne spotted Dagren and Goler talking together alone in the corner near the refreshments table.

"I wonder what those two are scheming about," she muttered under her breath as the current dance ended.

Charles looked over his shoulder. "Stay here. I'll be right back."

Daniel swirled the wine in his goblet but hadn't sipped any for a while. His father and their guests had already refilled theirs a time or two. Dessert sat before him, but he ignored the icing-drenched pastry. His father's guests and their conversations ruined his appetite. And "guests" was a kind term for the two men. Daniel could think of a few other, more fitting, words. He gripped his goblet harder when Baron Stant, an overweight glutton with a trail of crumbs down his beard and velvet doublet, brought up the topic of Elôm believers.

"My men caught five of them meeting in this old barn outside the village," he said around a mouthful of food. "I had them all hanged the next day. That should deter others. I don't know where they all come from. They're like rodents."

Daniel eyed his fork, unable to keep himself from imagining how it might be used as a weapon. Good thing the baron was across the table and out of reach.

"I've only had two turn up in the last couple of years," the Earl of Danthan responded.

"That's because your area is actually civilized," Daniel's sister Davira said. "Baron Stant is surrounded by a bunch of illiterate farmers who would believe anything."

The baron, earl, and Daniel's father all laughed openly. Davira sent Daniel a cruel grin. She knew how much he hated when she disparaged the common people. He stared coolly at her.

"Isn't that the truth? Have you heard the ridiculous rumors they are spreading?" Stant wiped his beard after a long swig of wine. "They claim that charlatan you executed last year rose from the dead of all things. The delusions of these people are astounding."

Daniel stilled and sat up a little straighter, shifting his gaze to his father, who said, "I can assure you that he was quite dead and stayed that way."

The satisfaction on his face pierced deeply into Daniel's chest, winding the tension inside him to the breaking point. He ground his teeth together, willing himself to keep his mouth shut, but words came out anyway.

"How do you know for sure? What if they're not just rumors?"

His father's gaze locked with his. A moment of silence surrounded them as everyone turned to stare at Daniel.

"Of course they're rumors," his father responded in a flat tone.

Daniel shrugged, yet he was anything but nonchalant. "Well, no one has ever risen from the dead before. Where would such a story even come from if there were no truth in it?"

"These rebels will do anything to further their cause and sway those foolish and weak-minded enough to believe their claims. Men don't rise from the dead."

His father spoke evenly, but suspicion clouded his eyes. Daniel was sorely tempted to ask, "What if He wasn't just a man?" but this time held his tongue. They glared at each other for another long moment before Daniel's father shifted his attention back to Stant and Lord Danthan. Daniel looked across the table, catching his mother's gaze. Her lips pinched, and she gave him the slightest shake of her head.

Charles poured himself a glass of punch and worked his way casually down to the end of the table where Dagren and Goler still spoke. He faced away from them and sipped his punch, straining to catch their conversation over the sound of the music.

". . . already tried questioning them," Goler grumbled.

"You think they'll simply give up the information without pressure?" Dagren hissed. "It's time to apply it. Surround the village with men. Anyone transporting supplies outside of it is to be detained and brought to me for questioning. That includes anyone in this room. And I want regular patrols on the forest roads. We only need to catch one traitor for the chance of further information."

The conversation ended, and one set of footsteps departed. The other, however, remained. Charles emptied his cup of punch and set it aside. When he turned, he found Dagren staring at him, eyes narrowed.

Charles stepped forward boldly and extended his hand. "Captain Dagren, isn't it?"

"Yes, my lord," Dagren replied as he grasped his arm and took stock of him.

"I hear you were sent to help deal with the rebellion. It's been going on for what, two years?"

Dagren's lip curled in the beginnings of a scowl. "Two years too long. It should've been eradicated before it even had a chance to begin."

"If I may, I'd guess you are far more capable of handling this than, well . . ." Charles glanced around for Goler. He drew his brows together to find the man working his way toward Anne. ". . . the current captain."

This drew a thin smile from Dagren. "You are correct, which is why His Majesty sent me."

Charles forced a smile of his own. "Good. My brother-in-law will be pleased to hear it. We would hate for my niece to have to leave due to the danger these rebels present. You've restored my faith in the handling of this situation."

Dagren's eyes sparked with a cold light. "I will not disappoint you. The rebels will be caught and dealt with. I guarantee it."

Anne spotted Goler moving through the guests like a predator on a scent and swallowed down her distaste. The only way she could have avoided him all night was to remain attached to Charles's arm, but that was unrealistic. She drew a fortifying breath just before he reached her.

"Dance with me." His voice was low and more of a command than an invitation.

Handling this as wisely as she could manage, Anne offered Goler a smile. "Of course."

Claiming her hand in a tight grip, he led her onto the dance floor, where he put his arm around her and pulled her closer than she was comfortable with. She tried to put more space between them, but his hold only tightened. Thank Elôm she had worn the dress she had, considering the way he stared down at her. Though not drunk, his eyes gave away the effects of alcohol consumption, and it wafted from his breath. It made him entirely too bold. Anne's breath trembled in and out as she fought to maintain her poise.

"You and Lord Ilvaran seem well-acquainted," Goler said as he leaned closer to her.

She turned her head away. "We got to know each other at Ashwood last summer."

"Has he expressed interest?" The question was a hard, slightly slurred hiss.

Now Anne looked him in the eyes, pausing for only a heartbeat. "Yes."

It wasn't a complete lie. Charles had said that, if he'd been younger, he might have sought her father's approval to court her.

Goler drew her yet closer so there was hardly any space between them. Anne gritted her teeth. Any nearer and she would stomp on his foot. She was, after all, a betrothed woman.

"And do you welcome his interest?"

"I would be a fool not to. He is the future Earl of Dunrick."

Let him think she and Charles had something between them. Perhaps it would keep him at bay until things finally came together for her and Trask.

Goler's jaw clenched, the taut muscles twitching. He could never compete with someone of Charles's standing.

Anne barely held in a sigh of relief when the dance finally ended. Sweat tickled her back and her hands had turned clammy in Goler's warm grasp. The moment he loosened his grip, she took a quick step away and prayed he wouldn't ask for another dance. He opened his mouth, surely to do just that, when Charles appeared.

"Lady Anne, here is your punch." He handed her a small glass of pink liquid.

"Thank you," she replied, truly grateful for something to soothe her prickly throat.

She took a sip, and Charles gave Goler a bright smile. "Thank you for keeping her company while I stepped away."

He extended his arm to Anne, and she latched onto it, little caring right now how it would infuriate Goler. She just wanted to put as much space between herself and the captain as she could. Her skin crawled with the lingering sensation of his hands on her.

With another seemingly innocent smile, Charles led her away. Yet, when they turned their backs to Goler, Charles's expression hardened. "Are you all right?"

Anne let out her breath slowly. Her heart still beat irregularly. "I will be as long as he keeps his hands off me for the rest of the night."

Knowing Charles, he wouldn't leave her side again. He guided her toward her parents and Baron Grey. Her father's grim expression said he wouldn't leave her alone either.

"Annie," he murmured when they neared.

"I'm all right." That's when she remembered the reason Charles had left her in the first place. She looked up at him. "Did you hear anything Goler and Dagren were discussing?"

Charles nodded and quietly filled them in on what he had overheard.

Baron Grey shook his head. "They are taking over the village. I have no control anymore."

"We have to warn Trask," Anne whispered. "Some of his men still come to the village for supplies."

"It won't be easy to get to him now," her father said. "Not with the patrols."

Anne resisted the urge to place her hand over her stomach as it sank toward her feet. What if she wouldn't get to see Trask anymore? However, she couldn't let her distress show here under such scrutiny. She cleared her face of emotion, prayed to Elôm, and did her best to fortify herself against her rising concerns. Worrying wouldn't solve things here.

Charles looked down at her again. "As long as you're with your father, I'll check on Elanor. I want to make sure Goler isn't anywhere near her now that I suspect I've just made him my mortal enemy."

For the rest of the evening, Anne remained close to her parents or Charles and Elanor. Any bit of enjoyment had vanished, and she counted down the minutes until they could leave.

At last, sometime close to midnight, the guests departed. The moment Anne stepped outside with Charles, she breathed deeply of the cool air and her whole body freed up. How much worse would it have been if Charles had not been there? *Thank You, Elôm, for Your gracious provision.*

While they waited for the carriage, Anne looked up at Charles's shadowed silhouette.

"I hope this won't embarrass or offend you." It did embarrass her some now, though in the desperation of the moment it had seemed like the right thing. "I let Goler believe that you have expressed your interest in me."

Even in the dim torchlight, Charles's smile was evident. "Well, considering that would be true under different circumstances and my affections are not yet spoken for, I see no harm in it if it can be of benefit to you."

"You're very kind, and I am incredibly grateful for how helpful you've been to me tonight. It's not an easy situation."

"I'm happy to help, just so long as your Lord Trask knows the rumors that are bound to circulate after tonight are just that."

Anne smiled. "I'll make sure he knows."

That is, if she even got a chance to see Trask again any time soon. Her smile faded.

The low hoot of an owl echoed overhead just after the last carriage rolled away into the night. Trask took this signal and let himself into the castle's back courtyard. He slipped through the deep shadows to the castle's rear door and glanced over his shoulder. Everything lay still and dark under the heavily clouded sky. He couldn't spot either of the two cretes on top of the wall, but they would warn him if anyone lurked nearby. He then unlocked the door and stepped inside.

Darkness engulfed him, but he knew every inch of this castle from roaming all the nooks and crannies as a child. He paused to breathe in the familiar scents, and pressure built in his chest, aching in his throat. He hadn't been home in months.

Trask made his way cautiously through the unlit halls to his father's office. Morris, the secretary, wasn't present, likely helping downstairs with the celebration. Trask lit a couple of candles and took a seat at the desk in his father's chair. Releasing a long sigh, he soaked in the sight of all his father's books. The same padded chair where he'd sat and learned to read as a young boy still rested against the wall. Hard to believe so much time had passed. His childhood imaginings of adulthood were nothing like reality.

A few minutes later, the door opened, and Trask pushed himself up as his father stepped inside.

"Trask!" he gasped, his eyes going huge.

Trask met him in the middle of the room, and they embraced tightly.

"Father," he whispered, his throat aching again. It had been such a long time, but he remembered his father being so much stronger. He was so thin!

Trask pulled away slowly to look into his father's face. Though Anne had warned him, it had not prepared him for how sickly his father appeared. It was perhaps the first time it truly sank in how old his father was becoming.

"Are you all right?"

His father smiled widely despite his worn expression and weary red eyes. "I am now."

"You don't look well."

His father shook his head. "I'm just tired."

"Sit down." Trask guided him to his chair and took a seat on the edge of the desk. He'd never seen his father so frail. "Are you sure?"

His father waved the question away. "There's just a lot going on here with Dagren and Goler."

Trask stared at him for a long moment. "I should take you out to camp. You shouldn't have to be here doing this alone."

"We both know that now is when I'm needed here the most. We can't let the people fall under Goler or Dagren's rule. There's not much I can do anymore to resist them, but it still encourages the people to have me as their leader."

Trask let a heavy breath seep past his lips. He'd always insisted that the people came before his own life and comfort, but it was more difficult to make the same sacrifices with his father's life.

A brief silence hung between them until his father said, "It does me much good just to see you." His eyes clouded. "But you took a great risk in coming here. Dagren seems to have men everywhere."

"Don't worry. I was careful. I brought two cretes with me. They're keeping a lookout on the wall."

"Just so long as you don't take the risk again. Dagren plans to increase his watch around the village and the forest."

His father filled him in on the captain's plans. With the dragons, they could get supplies from other villages, and they could scare off the forest patrols. However, his father was right that visiting Landale Village again would be a great risk.

Determined to lighten the mood while he was here for his father's sake, Trask let a smile grow. "I do have good news for you. Anne and I are betrothed. Officially."

His father's smile returned in full force. "Ah, that is good news. Do you know yet when you'll marry?"

"No idea, but at least there's no question of *if* anymore, only *when*."

"I'm so glad."

They went on to talk of camp, and his father mentioned the visiting viscount. Trask asked about the party and though his father mentioned Goler's treatment of Anne only briefly, Trask wanted to drag the man behind his horse.

An hour passed before Trask knew it, but he noticed his father growing weary. Reluctantly, he stood.

"I should get back to camp." He glanced at the door. "But, before I go, may I take a look at some of Mother's things?"

JACE CRANED HIS head back to stare up at the colossal Dorland trees until his neck ached. When he dropped his gaze back to the solid ground, he closed his eyes to ward off an assault of dizziness. At his first glimpse of the giant forest, he'd assumed it was a mountain range. Then came the real mountains in the distance. Mountains so tall and majestic, he half wondered if they'd all shrunk somewhere along the journey. Those soaring peaks surely rose twice the height of the Sinnai Mountains near Valcré. Was everything in Dorland this gigantic?

He opened his eyes again at a nudge from Gem. Patting the dragon's scaly cheek, he looked around the small clearing where they had stopped to have lunch. It was the only break they would take today before reaching the crete capital of Arvael in a few hours. Kaden and Talas stood nearby, good-naturedly teasing Michael about the crack in his voice, while the rest of their group finished packing their supplies. Jace secured his own pack and joined the others as they gathered around Captain Darq and Lieutenant Glynn.

"Once we reach Arvael, I'll introduce you to the Tarns. You will stay with them. Though Lord Vallan would welcome you, I want to stay where I know everyone. Too many people come and go from the citadel," Darq said. "I'd invite you to stay with my family, but they live farther north, and I think it would be best to keep you within the city."

He paused. "However, I'd understand if you have reservations. The Silvars live a bit closer, so you could potentially stay with them." He nodded to Timothy and Aaron. "Or the Folkans, though that would be a tight fit considering the size of Talas's family."

Everyone looked to Balen for his reaction to this arrangement. Jace hesitated at the thought staying with the Tarns. One Tarn had already turned traitor, and this time it was the king's life on the line. However, he remained silent.

"You fully trust the Tarns?" Balen asked Darq.

"I've known Falcor's father since I was a boy. He's always been a close friend of the Darq family. What's more, I'm the one who delivered the news of Falcor's betrayal and saw the pain it caused his family. I have no doubt Novan Tarn would defend you with his life."

Balen nodded. "Then we will give them a chance to repair what damage has been done to their name."

"They will be honored."

With these plans, they took to the air again. In Landale, they would have cleared the trees in a moment, but here, they had to climb much higher and longer to break free of the forest canopy. When they did, they continued east, toward the mountains.

After a couple of hours, Gem released a trill. Apparently, she recognized this as home. Ivoris echoed her, and Jace looked over to trade a quick smile with Kyrin. If only he could draw from his dragon's excitement, but his stomach had been like a rock ever since discovering the true size of Dorland trees. No words had prepared him for their enormity or for what he would have to overcome while staying here.

When the sun blazed red-orange behind them, a bare rocky point appeared ahead, jutting up out of the forest below. Darq and Glynn angled their dragons toward it. This must be Dragon Rest, their destination, just as the captain described it.

It didn't look like much until they drew closer. What had appeared to be only a bleak, solitary peak cut off from the main mountain range was actually an expansive formation riddled with caves and precarious-looking natural structures. The very stones seemed alive with dragons. Hundreds of them roamed about or soaked in the last of the sun's rays on the ledges. Darq's dragon gave an exuberant greeting as he swooped in to land. The rest of the group followed.

In a flurry of wings, they all alighted on a flat boulder protruding from one side of the peak. Jace wasn't quite sure he trusted it to stay in place. All it had to do was crack away from its foundation and crash to the forest floor, taking all of them with it. Shoving such thoughts away, he focused on the rest of their surroundings. Not only dragons populated the area, but cretes as well. They watched, their large, vibrant eyes evaluating them with some curiosity, but mostly wariness. Good thing Darq and Glynn were there to make introductions. Jace reached into his collar and tugged out the braided hawk pendant Darq had given each member of the group so it hung in plain sight in front of his chest—a sign of friendship with the cretes.

Following Darq's lead, they dismounted, but didn't get much farther than that before three imposing cretes blocked their path. The lead man stood at average crete height—several inches shorter than Jace—but was more heavily built than most cretes. His thick bare arms sported an array of brown tattoos, including one of a dragon, and he was armed as if to fight a war on this very rock.

"Captain Darq," the crete's stern voice rang out.

"Captain Lan," Darq responded, nodding respectfully.

"You bring visitors." His tone held accusation, as if he would sooner use the word 'intruders,' and his cool gaze touched each one of them with a measuring glance.

"I have." Darq's voice never lost its confidence. "Lord Balen, King of Samara, has come to speak with Lord Vallan."

Lan gave the group another examination. "And the others?"

"The king's security force, as well as men to speak on behalf of Arcacia."

Lan's gaze returned to Darq, losing a little of its suspicion. "Well, let's hope they present a compelling argument."

"And that the council is willing to listen," Darq added. He turned to the group. "Gather your things, and I'll take you into the city."

Jace turned to Gem to retrieve his pack and his bow and quiver. Once everyone had unloaded their belongings, they gathered around Darq and their other crete friends, who led them to a ledge winding downward around the edge of the peak. Thankfully, it wasn't too narrow, though Jace kept well clear of the edge. They followed this path around the peak until they stood almost directly below where they'd left the dragons some fifty feet above. Here, they reached another plateau surrounded by thick forest canopy. From the sheer edge, three rope and plank bridges stretched out into the trees. Darq stopped at the center one and turned to them.

"This bridge is the main highway into the heart of Arvael." A smile brought a sparkle to his eyes.

Jace gazed out across the bridge hanging suspended over the open space to its anchor point some sixty feet away. A thick band wrapped around his throat, his legs turning wobbly. He struggled to halt the rapid acceleration of his heart, but it defied him. All the same sickening sensations he'd experienced the first day he'd flown with Gem rushed back.

He found some small measure of comfort that he wasn't the only one who appeared to have reservations. Some of the others glanced nervously at each other, and Marcus took a cautious glimpse over the edge. Jace didn't have to join him to imagine the fall they would face if the bridge collapsed. This close to the treetops, they were at least two hundred fifty feet from the ground. He failed to swallow past his dried-out throat.

"I assure you, it is secure," Darq said, though Jace wasn't sure if it was only for his benefit or the whole group. "We maintain and inspect our bridges regularly. Safety is taken very seriously."

He and Glynn started across first, followed by Talas, Leetra, Timothy, and Aaron. One by one, the others stepped out onto the bridge, which swayed gently with their footsteps. Jace's knees weakened just watching them. He clenched his fists. He should have conquered this by now. Would he ever have victory over some of these recurring battles?

Rayad was one of the last to go and mumbled under his breath, "I'm getting too old for these sorts of adventures."

Jace almost smiled, but it died immediately. Now only he and Kyrin remained on the plateau. She stepped to the bridge and paused to turn back to him.

"We'll go together."

She gave him a heartening smile, but his feet fused to the rock. As much as he wanted to follow her, his blood had turned to immovable ice. His mind accused him of being weak and cowardly in front of her. However, her smile only grew, and she held out her hand.

"Come on, nothing will happen to us."

At her soft prompting, he took her hand, and the warmth melted the ice. He had led her to face her fears in the caves of Samara—now she would lead him. They stepped out onto the bridge. Jace gripped her hand tightly and used his other to hold onto the hand ropes, but he kept his eyes glued on her. His legs shook as the bridge shifted beneath them, but he didn't look down. He glanced at the others, who were still quite a distance ahead, and then focused again on Kyrin.

"How do you feel about staying with Falcor's family?" A conversation would help distract him from the crossing. Though Kyrin hadn't said anything when they'd discussed their lodgings earlier, her expression had seemed pensive to him.

She looked over her shoulder. "I'm not sure yet. I trust Darq . . . I just keep thinking about Falcor and how I should have trusted my instincts. I'm afraid that will cloud how I feel about his family. I just don't want to make the same mistake again."

"You won't."

Another faint smile grew on her lips. "I do agree with Balen about letting them repair their name. I know what it's like to live with the shame of having a traitor in the family. It—"

She stopped, peering out into the trees. Jace followed her gaze, and his eyes widened. Previously hidden by the thick foliage, an incredible view had opened up to them—a city unlike anything he could have imagined. Circular buildings of all sizes filled the giant trees—some built around the enormous trunks, and others built on the boughs that could have been trees themselves. Bridges crisscrossed between them, almost like a spider web. The place was alive with activity. Nearby, two crete children raced across a bridge as easily as one would run down a solid woodland path.

The sight drew Jace and Kyrin the remaining distance to a large platform where their friends waited.

"Welcome to Arvael," Darq said with a tone of pride.

"It's beautiful," Kyrin breathed.

And it was. The cretes didn't build with straight lines as most of civilization did. Their rounded structures flowed with the natural curves of the trees. Yet, the beauty of it dimmed for Jace with the knowledge that he would not just have to face his fear today, but every minute of their stay here.

Darq turned to face Balen. "I will take you all to the Tarns and then get word to Lord Vallan of your arrival. He may not be free tonight, but I expect he will want to meet with you as soon as possible."

They set off across another long bridge, Kyrin never letting go of Jace's hand. Though he kept his focus trained on her, he did take in quick glimpses of his surroundings. Many of the cretes they passed gawked at them. He could well imagine how he, Kaden, and King Balen stood out as the tallest men in the group. Most of these people had probably never seen outsiders within their city.

Two more bridges led them to what could only be described as a wide front porch to one of the crete houses. Darq stepped to the door and knocked as the rest of the group filed off the bridge behind him. When the door opened, Jace caught sight of an older crete woman.

"Verus. We didn't expect you back so soon."

"I've brought visitors." Darq glanced over his shoulder. "King Balen and others from Landale."

The woman's eyes rounded. "Please, come in," she invited, her voice quiet.

Darq led the way into the house. Jace had to duck to pass through the door, but the way the ceiling inside slanted upward left plenty of headroom. He stopped just inside and looked around. It was almost like stepping into the tree itself. Wood dominated the space—rich golden brown and polished to bring out its honey hues. Leather was another chief commodity and so were linens of deep earthly colors. It reminded Jace, in a way, of the cabin back at the farm, and he found it comforting despite being a couple hundred feet in the air.

"I'll get Novan," the crete woman said.

"Thank you," Darq replied.

She sent the group a glance that still held surprise and hurried to a half-log staircase that wrapped around the central tree trunk, disappearing on the other side.

Darq turned to the group. "That is Sonah, Novan's wife . . . and Falcor's mother."

Now that Jace thought about it, he could see the resemblance in the woman's face—in her serious expression and high cheekbones.

They waited in silence for a moment or two before Sonah returned with her husband. When Novan stepped into view, Jace's breath snagged in his chest. It was like seeing Falcor walk down those stairs, but twenty years older.

KYRIN'S HEART STUTTERED for a beat or two as Novan Tarn
approached them. He was so much like Falcor that her limbs grew
weak. Her father had died over a year ago, but seeing the Tarn
family resemblance brought the emotions rushing back with more
force than she anticipated. She drew a shallow, trembling breath.
Maybe she wasn't ready for this. If all she could think about
was the loss of her father, how could she respond appropriately?
What if she missed something that put them all in danger? They
relied on her to pick up clues and signals of potential threats.

At the gentle, reassuring pressure of a hand against her back,
she glanced up at Jace and received a comforting and protective
look. She steadied herself and let the emotions subside. She had
to remember why they were here. None of this was about her or
the past.

Darq introduced Balen first, working his way through everyone until he came to Kyrin and her brothers. Novan stood
before them, matching Kyrin in height. He glanced at each of
them, but his focus rested on Kyrin. She sucked in her breath.
However, though his eyes were identical to Falcor's in their
ocean-blue color, they were not Falcor's at all. They were softer,
deeper . . . sadder. Their gazes held, and he seemed to share her
hesitancy.

He spoke then, his voice low and heavy with regret she had to believe was genuine. "Welcome. It is an honor to meet and have you here in my home. I hope I can be of some service."

Though he was clearly a dignified man, Kyrin recognized the weight of family shame. After all, she had grown up under just such a weight. Her throat swelled and sent needles to her eyes, but this time the emotion didn't grow up out of fear as much as regret over how so many lives could be affected by the actions of just one person.

"Thank you," she murmured, and her brothers echoed her.

Novan nodded, deep remorse in his eyes, before he focused once more on Darq. "What can I do for you?"

"Lodging. I want to keep everyone here in Arvael, close to the citadel. I have no doubt Lord Vallan would happily extend them his hospitality, but I would prefer closer, more private quarters, considering the importance of the king's safety."

Novan's stance straightened as he shifted his gaze to Balen. "We would be honored, my lord, to offer you our hospitality. Whatever you need . . . any of you." His attention strayed back to Kyrin and her brothers. "And no harm will come to you within this house as long as I live and breathe."

The conviction with which he spoke boosted Kyrin's confidence in their safety with him. While men had fooled her in the past, she could detect no hint that he lied or wished them harm. Quite the contrary. She could almost feel his need to be of service to them, to atone for his son's betrayal.

"Thank you," Balen said. "I know we are a rather large group to accommodate."

Novan shook his head. "It's no trouble."

Darq stepped into the conversation again. "I will go see Lord Vallan and let him know of the king's arrival. The sooner they speak, the better."

Novan nodded, and Darq left the group to the care of their hosts.

When the door closed, Novan motioned to them. "Please, let me show you to your rooms so you may unburden yourselves."

He led them up the winding staircase around the massive tree trunk. Crete homes were certainly different from regular homes where rooms occupied the same floors. Here, the rooms branched off at different levels and directions—wherever a strong tree limb jutted from the tree. Kyrin glanced back at Jace. He'd seemed less nervous since they entered the house. At least everything was sturdy and enclosed. One would never know how far they were from the ground unless he looked outside.

They split up into three rooms—Kyrin and Leetra sharing a small guest bedroom just off the main stairs. Two canvas hammocks hung from the ceiling rafters. Novan offered to gather cushions for a bed on the floor, but Kyrin declined. She'd never slept in a hammock before, yet she was willing to try it.

She set her heavy pack down and looked around. There wasn't much in the way of traditional shelving and cabinets since the walls all curved. A small chest sat near each hammock with a couple of linen pillows propped against them and animal hides on the floor.

She stepped to the small arched window and peeked out. Lanterns twinkled to life around the city—those in the distance resembling fireflies. Laughter rang out nearby. Kyrin glanced down, but branches and thick leaves hid the forest floor far below. Bustling as it might be, Arvael didn't have the feel of a city. It was more of a community, a lot like camp, though on a much grander scale.

She turned to Leetra. "It's beautiful here."

The crete girl glanced out her window and nodded, the barest hint of a smile on her lips.

"You must miss it," Kyrin said.

"Yes. I always look forward to coming back." Her softening demeanor changed in an instant, her lavender eyes going hard once more. "But if we can't convince the clan leaders to stand up and stop Daican now, someday there may not be anything left to come home to."

Her face set as if ready for battle, she marched out of the room. Kyrin stood for a moment, and then followed her downstairs. In the main room, Sonah met them. She was a beautiful woman, but her eyes had such a sad, mournful look to them. Kyrin had noticed it the moment they'd walked into the house. The woman glanced between the two of them, her gaze lingering on Kyrin as she wrung a dishtowel.

"Please," she said a bit hesitantly, as if sorely out of practice in entertaining guests. "Sit and rest. I'll have supper ready shortly." She motioned to the living area, her expression painfully earnest.

Kyrin smiled, hoping to put her at ease. "Thank you."

Childhood memories floated in her head of her mother crying over how no one came to visit because of their reputation. No doubt the Tarns had suffered the same situation, not to mention the time they must have spent in mourning. According to crete customs, Falcor was as good as dead to them—perhaps even worse.

Sonah turned and disappeared under the stairs, where a hall must lead to the kitchen. Without a backward glance, Leetra followed her, leaving Kyrin alone. She looked around the quiet room, undecided, and then followed slowly. Maybe she could help in some way. They had shown up very unexpectedly right before mealtime. It would certainly take work to feed them all. Yet, when she rounded the stairs finding a door to the kitchen, she paused. Leetra and Sonah were talking.

"How are you?" Sonah asked.

A very long pause followed before Leetra answered tightly, "I'm still angry."

Kyrin backed away. Not long ago, Novan and Sonah were to be Leetra's in-laws. Kyrin would not interrupt them, especially when they spoke of Falcor. She returned to the living room and sank into one of the chairs, smoothing her hands across her skirt. Her gaze wandered over the large space. Like the bedroom, it didn't have much in the way of traditional furniture. Plenty of seating and low tables occupied the room, but no bookshelves, paintings, or tapestries. However, she took particular notice of a variety of different woodcarvings, mostly of animals. It was all very practical and straightforward, just like the cretes.

Soft steps drew her attention to the stairs. She couldn't stop the uncomfortable flip her stomach did when she saw Novan. He slowed, but then came nearer with a tentative smile.

"I hope you'll be comfortable in your room. If you find that a hammock doesn't suit you, let us know."

"I think it will be fine."

She glanced toward the stairs, praying for the others to hurry. Suddenly all her confidence disappeared at facing Novan alone.

"I'm sure they'll be down momentarily."

Her attention jumped back to Novan, and she scolded herself for making her discomfort so rudely obvious.

"They're probably making themselves comfortable." She tried to speak in a lighter tone. "It's a long journey from Landale."

Novan offered a brief nod. "Verus is very dedicated to travel it so continuously."

Kyrin agreed, and silence fell. She let her gaze stray back to the carvings and resisted the urge to clear her prickling throat. If only Jace were with her. She drew a measured breath and prayed for peace.

"I'm sorry I make you nervous."

Kyrin met Novan's gaze. She shouldn't act this way. She had no true cause to. "It's my fault," she said, shaking her head.

"No. It's my son's."

"Still, I should know better than most not to judge a family by the actions of one member. My grandfather is considered a traitor in Arcacia." She shrugged. "I guess we all are now."

"You have every right to be wary." He took a step closer, his expression earnest. "I know words mean nothing, but I meant it when I said you would be safe here."

Kyrin's breath seeped out with a final release of fear. "Thank you."

Still, emotion had begun rising up inside of her. She fought it, but it was bound to happen, considering the circumstances.

"I wanted to say . . ." She swallowed and cleared her tight throat. Her eyes burned, and she blinked hard, determined not to cry. "I don't hold your family responsible for anything that happened."

Her gaze faltered, but when she looked at him again, his eyes glistened.

"You're very kind," Novan murmured, though she knew he would still carry a burden. One couldn't just cast off such things in a moment or with simple words.

Before either of them spoke again, footsteps signaled the return of the men. Kyrin looked up and locked eyes with Jace. Concern filled his, but she gave him a brief smile of assurance.

The men gathered at the bottom of the stairs, and Novan invited them to make themselves comfortable. Talas and Glynn struck up a conversation with Novan right away, not allowing for any awkward silence. The other men soon joined in, and the atmosphere became much more comfortable. Enjoyable even. Kyrin did notice that Jace watched her often, likely looking for clues that something was amiss. She smiled at him again. Aside from the intense emotions from before, she found nothing to lead her to believe they weren't safe here. She trusted what Novan had told her.

Just before it grew dark outside, the door opened and a male crete walked in. The young man was around Talas's age, though a bit older, and clearly resembled Novan and Falcor. His expression lifted at the sight of the group filling the living room, but his gaze focused on one member in particular.

"Tal, when did you get here?"

Talas grinned. "About an hour ago." He met the man with a quick hug and slap on the back. "Good to see you. It's been a while."

"Darq says you've been busy."

"Oh, yes. Things are really growing in Landale."

"I've been thinking about joining you there."

Talas's grin resurfaced. "Well, now's the perfect opportunity to discuss it."

He turned back to the group, and Novan motioned the young man into their midst. With a hand on his shoulder, he said, "Everyone, this is my oldest son, Naeth."

He introduced him to each member of the group. Naeth was very stoic and quiet as Falcor had been, yet Kyrin detected none of Falcor's disgust in his eyes, and sadness lurked behind his subdued manner. Kyrin understood how difficult it was to have a brother on the opposing side of the fight.

"You're here to speak to Lord Vallan and the clan leaders?" Naeth asked Balen.

"I am."

"I hope you can reason with them." Naeth glanced at his father. "They don't seem to want to listen to us."

Before they could discuss it further, Sonah appeared to announce that supper would be ready shortly. Novan and his son set as many extra chairs around the table as they could fit. He then directed the group to take seats. Talas, Glynn, Aaron, and

Timothy offered to sit on the benches at the edges of the dining room.

Sonah and Leetra brought out the food a few moments later—a platter of thick meat steaks drizzled in a red sauce, a mountainous bowl of salad, and two pans of cooked vegetables that appeared to be carrots and a pink-tinted potato-like vegetable.

"I hope there's enough," she said.

Balen gave her a gracious look. "I apologize for showing up on such short notice."

"Oh no, don't. It's all right." She broke into her first soft smile. "Leetra was very helpful. I just wish I had more to offer."

"Trust me, this looks delicious."

Her smile strengthened.

They had all settled into their spots when Darq arrived and took the open seat saved for him. With everyone present, Novan offered a sincere prayer of thanks that further comforted Kyrin. His close relationship with Elôm was evident in his words and the ease with which he spoke them. Once he concluded, they passed the food around and attention turned to Darq.

"Did you see Lord Vallan?" Novan asked.

"Yes, he will meet with us and send for the clan leaders in the morning."

Though this was exactly what they wanted, Darq frowned as he spoke.

"Does he not wish to meet with Lord Balen?" Novan questioned.

"He does, but he's not optimistic that it will change anything." Darq set his gaze on Balen. "And, regardless of your presence, he will not change his stance without the majority of the clans in support of it. He made that quite clear when I left."

"How can half the crete people not see Daican as a threat we must all fight together?" Kaden asked.

Kyrin glanced at her twin. She would never have the guts to speak so boldly or directly. He'd clearly spent a lot of time with Talas and the other cretes in Landale, but then, he always had been that way.

Novan appeared amused by it. "As you can see, we have lived very secluded from Arcacia for years. Many of us have never even had contact with anyone outside of the Dorlanders. I'm afraid our isolated lifestyle has led to a deceptive sense of security."

"But why won't they listen to anyone like Darq and Glynn who saw in Samara what Daican is capable of?"

"Because we cretes can be very stubborn and set in our ways." Novan smirked. "You may have noticed."

Kyrin almost laughed. Kaden knew a thing or two about stubbornness himself.

"Let's hope we can redirect that stubbornness to stand up to Daican," Darq said, and everyone agreed.

WHEN JACE FINISHED dressing the next morning, he left the guest room while the others were still getting ready. He had slept surprisingly well last night, considering. At times, he almost forgot how high they were from the ground. Following the winding staircase, he passed the closed door to the room Kyrin shared with Leetra. He had no idea if she was up yet, but he didn't want to leave her alone like last evening. Though they had all settled in comfortably, staying with Falcor's family couldn't help but stir up many emotions. Jace had his own unpleasant memories of Falcor.

Down in the living room, he found only Talas talking with Naeth—clearly old friends. He hesitated to join them, but Talas bid him good morning, and the other crete acknowledged him with a nod. Jace responded, and his attention caught on the animal carvings he had noticed last night. He approached them to have a closer look. Expertly crafted, they reminded him of the pieces Aldor had made. There was quite a variety of animals, including impressive dragon carvings, but most were of wolves. When he came to one that reminded him of Tyra, he glanced at Naeth.

"May I?"

The crete nodded.

Jace picked up the wolf to inspect. "Who makes them?"

"My father and I, when we have time." Naeth's voice lowered. "Falcor used to, once in a while." He rose from his chair and stepped up onto another to reach for a wolf carving high up on a branch near the ceiling. "My grandfather made this one. He was a real master at it."

He handed it to Jace. It was indeed a fine and impressive piece of art. The details were incredibly precise. He couldn't imagine how much work had gone into it.

Talas joined them and told Naeth, "Jace is pretty good at carving too."

Naeth looked at him with interest, but Jace shook his head. "Not this good." He handed the carving back. "I don't get around to doing it much."

"You'll have to show them the new staff you made for Kyrin," Talas said. "She brought it with her, didn't she?"

"Yes."

"I'd like to see it," Naeth told him.

"I'll ask her to bring it down later."

They talked for a while longer about carving and the pieces in the Tarn's collection until the rest of the group joined them. A short time later, Sonah served a filling breakfast of eggs and flat cakes with chunky apple syrup that Kyrin's brothers practically inhaled.

When their plates were empty, Darq called for everyone's attention. "I'd better get you all to the citadel. The clan leaders will gather soon, if they haven't already."

He and Balen led the way. Novan and his son joined them. At the door, Jace paused to take a deep breath. Time to face the bridges once again. A bright world of greenery met him when he stepped outside. In full daylight, it was even more stunning and teeming with life, though not only cretes. An abundance of blue and gray jays and other birds flitted among the branches in perfect harmony with their crete neighbors. It was a captivating place to live if one could get used to the heights.

The group set off across one of the bridges. Jace's legs and chest stiffened up, but he followed before he could think on it too much, which earned him a smile from Kyrin. He focused on her and on keeping each breath even, but curiosity did tug his gaze to the scenery. The deeper they went into the city, the more closely grouped the dwellings became. He saw shops now, instead of just homes, with wares strung out on the branches. Many tanning racks sat outside where women worked on hides while children shrieked, played, and climbed nearby.

"There's the citadel," Darq announced.

Jace looked up. A hundred yards ahead rose the most magnificent tree he had ever seen—almost twice as wide as those in the surrounding area. Its massive boughs split off in all directions and cradled an impressive wooden structure resembling a castle, palace, and giant cabin all in one.

The bridge they traveled converged with a wider one that led directly to the entrance of the citadel. Two heavily armed cretes stood guard at the wide, arched doorway.

"I bring King Balen of Samara to see Lord Vallan," Darq told them.

The guards let them pass, and Darq guided them inside. Jace shifted his gaze upward, but he could not see any ceiling high above them—only an abundance of balconies and staircases winding amongst towering support beams. Branches from the main boughs flourished inside, covered with dark green leaves. It was as if a small forest grew right within the citadel. For being a smaller people, the cretes had certainly built a grand center for their government and defense.

Darq led them down what appeared to be the main bridge-like hall to the center of the citadel. More than fifty yards in, they entered a massive room. The wide plank floor was stained and polished to a golden brown. Large branches stood at regular intervals along the length of each side of the hall, rising up and entwining in the middle to form an arched ceiling.

At the far end of the hall sat an empty chair with twisted vines for armrests—a throne, yet lacking the splendor of one such as Emperor Daican's. In a semi-circle around the throne sat twelve less decorative chairs—six on each side. Behind them, at the perimeter of the room, were rows of benches where other council members must sit.

As impressive as the sight was, Jace's attention focused on the small group of cretes standing in front of the throne. One in particular stood out amongst the others. A dark blue cape was pinned at his right shoulder, and Jace guessed him to be about the same age as Captain Darq. The man stood tall and straight as he watched them approach, exuding the legendary pride of the cretes, however in a more dignified manner than many.

"Captain," he said as he stepped away from his group.

"My lord." Darq brought them to a halt before the crete lord and turned to motion to Balen. "Let me introduce you to Lord Balen, exiled yet rightful king of Samara."

Balen bowed respectfully, and Lord Vallan dipped his head.

"King Balen, welcome to Arvael. I do not know the last time my people entertained the royalty of one of our neighboring countries."

"Thank you for agreeing to speak with me."

"I'm not sure it will bring any change or settlement, but I am willing to talk." Vallan spoke without malice, simply with the factual bluntness of the cretes.

"I pray that it is Elôm's will that we can reach some sort of agreement." Balen matched his honesty.

Vallan eyed him a moment as if sizing him up. Though the crete fell far short of Balen's height, his presence was just as commanding. The slightest upturn of his lips seemed to indicate he liked Balen's reply. "So do I."

His gaze fell on the rest of the group, and Darq introduced them each in turn. The crete lord nodded his acknowledgement and offered another kind welcome.

Just as he finished, voices echoed from the other end of the hall, where a group of cretes entered.

"The clan leaders," Vallan told Balen. He motioned to the benches at the edge of the room. "The rest of your group may sit if they wish."

Darq led everyone but Balen to the benches as the clan leaders approached. Glancing at them, Darq lowered his voice.

"Crete or not, anyone invited into this hall is permitted to speak. So, if you have anything to add, feel free to step in and say it."

Kyrin studied each of the clan leaders as they approached the throne and found their seats among the twelve empty chairs. Most were Novan's age or older, and each wore an amulet in the shape of the animal representing their clan. She could tell immediately which half were opposed to their cause. While the others looked on them with interest and, perhaps, a hint of hope, these particular six peered with all the suspicion and stubbornness of the crete race. Kyrin did not envy Balen's task.

Captain Darq, Glynn, and Novan stood near one of the columns, their arms crossed over their chests. Darq traded nods with a couple of the sympathetic leaders, and then set his intense eyes on Vallan as the crete lord introduced Balen. Six of the leaders voiced their welcomes while the others regarded him silently.

With a gesture from Lord Vallan, Balen stepped forward to state their case, and Kyrin whispered a prayer for him.

"I have come to speak on behalf of my people held captive in Samara, as well as those under threat in Arcacia who have sheltered me during my exile."

He paused, and the leader of the Owl Clan cut in before he could continue. "I think we are all well aware of the situation in Samara and Arcacia. Captain Darq speaks of little else when he is here."

Darq shot the sharp-featured man a glare and refrained from replying, though it must have taken effort.

Balen faced the man, unruffled. "Then, no doubt, you are aware of my purpose here." He held the man's gaze for a moment before turning to address the rest. "I humbly request your aid, as allies, in driving Daican out of Samara and ceasing his conquest."

A heavy silence fell before the leader of the Hawk Clan rose to his feet. Kyrin looked between him and Darq. Surely, they must be related, judging by their similarities.

"I know I speak for half of us"—he cast a rather disgusted glance at the leaders on the opposite side of the throne—"in saying that we desire to offer you the aid you seek. The emperor must be stopped."

Directly across from him, another clan leader stood, this time from the Wolf Clan, and Kyrin caught Novan grimacing.

"And I speak for the other half in saying we should remain out of this. What's between Arcacia and Samara is none of our concern. We've already risked inciting the emperor's wrath by allowing some of our force to go to Samara last summer. I think we've suffered enough casualties already."

With these words, Darq received yet another scathing glance, and this time he joined in. From here, the back and forth arguing went into full swing. Balen stood his ground and presented his case as best he could when not interrupted. The opposing clan leaders seemed bent on distancing themselves from the struggle and blaming Captain Darq for trying to draw them into it.

After a while, Lord Vallan sat down on his throne and listened to the heated debate in silence. If only he would just choose a side. Around Kyrin, the others murmured to each other, their whispers growing sharper and more aggravated. Even Talas's good humor wore thin, and Leetra's scowl grew darker with every spoken opposition, especially against Darq. It was surely just a matter of time before she inserted herself into the argument. Did any of these debates ever turn violent? Kyrin slid a little closer to Jace. Beside her, Kaden shook his head and ran a hand through his hair. He probably wasn't far behind Leetra.

In the end, Marcus took the initiative and rose to join the dispute. Silence fell as he stood next to Balen. Though Kyrin could read the subtle hints of the same frustration they all shared, he spoke with his usual calmness.

"I am Captain Marcus Altair of the Landale Militia and formerly of Arcacia's army. There's one thing that seems to be forgotten in all this." He set his gaze on the opposing leaders. "You seem to believe Daican is no threat to you as long as you don't provoke him. If that's true, why has he created an army of firedrakes? If all he planned was to take Samara, his army was more than capable of accomplishing that without the trouble of breeding and training the drakes and their riders. You may have felt safe all these years because your people were the only ones with an airborne force, but that is no longer true. It won't be long before he possesses a force to match yours, and it will be every bit as strong as Arcacia's ground forces."

Kyrin was proud of her brother for standing up, but the Wolf Clan leader shook his head, apparently in dismissal.

"Perhaps he will match our numbers, but Arcacians will never match our skills or our dragons. We're faster and better trained."

"Perhaps," Marcus acknowledged, "but does your pride and superiority justify the damage that is inevitable? Firedrakes are destroyers. Against your dragons, they may ultimately fail, but you can be sure the damage they leave behind will be catastrophic. Do you want to see your women and children dead and this city in flames? Because that's what Daican is capable of accomplishing. Why wait until all your potential allies have fallen and you're next in the emperor's conquest? Why not stop him while he still has weaknesses and you still have allies to fight with you?"

The clan leaders all looked at each other, and Balen gave Marcus an affirming nod. The first to respond was the leader of the Deer Clan—an opposing clan, though one more reasonable than the others.

"You speak as though an attack on Arvael is imminent while there is no proof of such an event. Traitor or not, Falcor has said the emperor will not attack us."

"And you believe him and Daican?" Darq asked. "We can't trust either of them. Why would Daican stop at Samara if he could easily take the rest of Ilyon while her inhabitants are too foolish to stop him?"

The leader of the Owl Clan shot to his feet. "We are not fools, Captain."

Darq stared him down. "History may prove otherwise. I just hope there will still be free cretes left to learn from it." For a moment, it looked like the two of them might turn to blows, but Darq spoke again, more quietly than he had all morning. "The emperor will not simply ignore us and leave us to our own rule. To believe so will be the death of us all."

His gaze shifted past the other cretes and landed on Kyrin. She couldn't quite read his expression, but a light grew in his eyes that seemed to signal an idea. He looked at the leaders again.

"If you want to know the real Emperor Daican and not simply rely on these fantasies you've created to believe he wants peace with us, just ask Miss Altair. She's spent more time in his presence than any of us. She can tell you exactly what kind of man he is."

Kyrin's heart jumped into her throat as all eyes swung in her direction. She never imagined they would drag her into this. Her gaze swept each of the opposing leaders, and she brushed her hands across her skirt. Why would any of them listen to her? However, something strengthened inside her, and she stood. After all, she had stood up to Emperor Daican and denied his gods. This should be easy. With a quick glance at Jace, who gave her a nod of reassurance, she stepped forward to stand beside Marcus. Her pulse pounded, and she licked her lips.

"Captain Darq is right." She momentarily locked her gaze with the leader of the Owl Clan but didn't hold it. "I served at Auréa Palace before I was found to be a believer in Elôm and nearly executed. I've seen how driven and cunning Daican is. I have no doubt he is on a mission to expand Arcacia's power as far as it will reach. He wants to create a legacy and empire to honor his father's memory. I think you, of all people, know how family loyalty can drive a person. Anyone who stands in his way is seen as an enemy that must be eliminated without mercy, even his own people."

She drew a long breath, but no one tried to stop her. "My father, Captain William Altair, was a good soldier. He served Arcacia and he served Daican well. He held no animosity or hatred toward the emperor, and yet . . ."

Kyrin's voice faltered. She meant to speak of her father with pride and indignation against the injustice of his death, with passion and strength, but she couldn't stop the tears that overflowed and left warm tracks down her cheeks. She rubbed them away and cleared her throat, but her voice trembled.

"None of that mattered to Daican when he executed him simply for remaining true to his faith in Elôm. If Daican is willing to do that to Arcacian citizens, why would he treat you any differently?"

Silence fell for longer than it had all morning. Kyrin breathed hard in and out, fighting the threat of more tears. Marcus put his hand on her shoulder, and Kyrin closed her eyes to let the moment of loss pass. Finally, Lord Vallan's voice broke the silence, and she opened her eyes again.

"I believe Miss Altair makes a valid point that we would do well to consider. I suggest we break for lunch and resume this discussion this afternoon." He offered Kyrin a nod of support.

The leaders agreed and all rose. Amidst the commotion, Kyrin made her way back to the others. Kaden and Michael both shared her emotion. When she reached them, Kaden put his arm around her, and she rested her head against his shoulder while the rest of the pain slowly faded.

"Good job," he murmured. "Father would be proud."

FOR THE FIRST time in a week, the clouds over Landale broke up and gave them a longed-for look at the sun. Sadly, Charles had to leave that morning, but he left with the hope to return before summer's end to see Jace. The day passed quietly after the excitement of his visit.

Early that afternoon, Anne and Elanor took their latest sewing projects out to the porch to sit in the sunshine. Anne was determined to soak up as much of it as possible. She missed her usual summer glow. The wet, gloomy weather was making them all dreadfully pale.

"I hope you won't regret not returning to Ashwood with your uncle," Anne told Elanor as they settled in. Her friend had turned down the chance to return home, but with the growing danger here, Anne wasn't sure she should have. As much as she would miss her, she wanted her to be safe.

Elanor shook her head. "Anything I face here is far better than having to marry a man of my father's choosing."

Anne really couldn't argue with that. She would do almost anything to avoid a forced marriage to Goler. Her skin crawled at the mere thought of it. Not for the first time did she thank Elôm that her father cared more about her well-being than about securing a profitable marriage arrangement for her.

121

They sat in silence for a while, enjoying the sounds of summertime. The baby birds in their nests at the edge of the forest were especially exuberant today.

"Now there's a lovely sight."

Anne started, nearly puncturing her finger with her needle. Trask stood grinning at the end of the porch, his arms crossed as he leaned casually against the house.

"How long have you been standing there?"

"Long enough to enjoy the view of my bride-to-be."

A smile lifted Anne's lips, and she looked down at her sewing to hide the warmth creeping into her cheeks. Nothing had really changed by making their betrothal official, and yet giddiness fluttered through her nerves along with a pull to marry this man as soon as possible. Especially when they hadn't seen each other in days.

Beside her, Elanor rose with her sewing and spoke with a grin in her voice. "I'll just take this inside."

The moment she was gone, Trask crossed the porch and slid the now-vacant chair closer to Anne's before taking a seat. Stretching his legs out, he crossed his ankles and settled in as if he intended to be there a while.

"You're getting quite comfortable."

"I don't have anywhere to be."

"Well, you shouldn't be here. It's dangerous."

He shrugged, appearing unconcerned, and then looked over to study her face, his smile full of warmth.

"I'm serious. You're taking a huge risk."

"Don't worry. I thoroughly searched the area before I came."

He held out his hand. Anne couldn't bring herself to scold him again and entwined her fingers with his. If only this could be their daily life. She wanted it more than she'd ever wanted anything.

"I was afraid I wouldn't see you for a while. Dagren has set regular patrols on the forest road. It had me worried."

He grinned playfully. "You think a few patrols would stop me from seeing my betrothed?"

Anne laughed. He would not let her forget she had finally accepted his proposal any time soon. Truthfully, she enjoyed hearing it.

"Don't worry," he told her again. "My father warned me about them. Some of the cretes and their dragons *persuaded* them not to hang around the forest. I don't think they'll be back."

"I'm glad. It sounds like Dagren is confident that, if he can get to one of you, he'll be able to gain more information." She didn't want to imagine the terrible lengths he would go to just to get it.

"We won't let that happen." Trask looked around the puddle-spotted yard before his focus returned to her. "So, I was hoping to meet the visiting viscount," he said, though the way his attention strayed to her lips told her that he wasn't really thinking about Charles.

"I'm afraid you're a little too late. He left this morning. We wanted to bring him out to camp but didn't think it safe with the patrols."

"That's a shame." His eyes rose back to hers. "I hear he kept you out of Goler's clutches at the party. I wanted to thank him."

"He did indeed. The night would have been dreadful without him." She chose to leave out just how beastly Goler had been. No sense in raising Trask's ire on a lovely day like this. "However, you should know there could be rumors floating around since that night."

"Oh? What rumors?"

"About Charles and me."

Trask lifted his brows, but amusement played in his eyes. "Should I be jealous?"

"Not a bit. Charles is a good man and a good friend. Good enough to go along with allowing Goler to believe he has expressed interest in me and that I don't intend to turn him down. I hate feeling as though I'm taking advantage of his chivalry, but at least Goler doesn't believe I'm available now, which I'm not."

Trask's lips quirked. "Sneaky. I like it."

She laughed again. "Yes, well, it certainly upset Goler. Hopefully, he knows better than to tread on what he believes is Charles's territory." She prayed so. His boldness at the party unnerved her.

Trask stared at the road, almost grinning. "I'd love to see how he must be brooding down at the barracks." He let out a low chuckle.

"You shouldn't be so pleased," she scolded lightly.

"I can't help it." His smile remained undimmed.

They sat quietly for a couple of minutes, and Anne imagined their life once they were finally married. Trask's impatience was starting rub off on her. She looked over at him.

"When did you see your father?"

"The night of the party. I snuck in after everyone left." All traces of his smile faded. "He's not well."

Anne squeezed his hand.

"I wanted to take him out to camp. I offered, but he won't do it because it would leave the people to Goler and Dagren. He's right, but . . ." He shook his head. "I'm worried how he'll survive this if things don't change."

Though sharing such worries, Anne tried to encourage him. "I'll do what I can to visit him more often. Perhaps that will cheer him and he'll regain his health, especially now that he's seen you."

A slow, sad smile worked its way to Trask's face. He brought her hand to his lips and gave it a soft kiss. "I love you."

"And I love you," Anne replied. "So did you tell him about us?"

His smile grew. "I did. He was very pleased."

Anne grinned. That would certainly brighten the baron's mood.

"Speaking of which." Trask released her hand and reached into his pocket. He pulled out a small cloth bundle. "I wanted to give you something as a token of our betrothal. A ring would be too obvious and draw suspicion, but I hope this will do."

He carefully unwrapped the bundle to reveal a dainty, silver wirework pendant in the shape of a lily with a perfect white gem in the center. Anne's breath caught as he laid it in her hand.

"Do you like it?"

"It's beautiful," she breathed. "Where did you get it?"

"It was my mother's."

Again, Anne couldn't draw a full breath.

"Actually," Trask said, "my father gave me most of her things the other night. Whatever I could carry, anyway, just to make sure they were safe. As soon as we're married, they'll be yours. Consider it my father's wedding gift."

Tears wet Anne's eyes. Trask had loved his mother dearly, so to receive her things meant a great deal. "This is the most precious thing anyone has ever given me."

Trask stood to fasten the pendant around her neck before reclaiming his seat and her hand.

"You know," she said, "if Goler sees this, he'll think it's from Charles."

"Let him. I just want you to wear it."

Anne squeezed his hand again. "I will."

Kyrin and the others had their lunch with Lord Vallan in the spacious dining room of the citadel. The six supportive clan leaders joined them, so they did not have to worry about arguing at the table, thankfully. After listening to it all morning, pressure squeezed the back of Kyrin's skull and threatened to grow into a full-blown headache if she wasn't careful. The crete leaders were actually quite friendly. Their shared desires erased the typical crete suspicion toward outsiders.

Following the meal, Lord Vallan led them back to the great hall, but Darq stopped them just inside.

"I don't know what will happen this afternoon. Probably more arguing and just as tiresome. I have enough allies here to be confident of Lord Balen's safety, so not all of you have to stay. Perhaps Talas can show you around."

He glanced at the crete, who nodded eagerly.

"That is, if you're comfortable with it," Darq checked with Balen.

"Of course," Balen said. "Please, go. I'll not hold you here."

In the end, Rayad, Marcus, Glynn, and Novan chose to remain with Balen and Darq to argue their case. Just before they parted, Marcus turned to his siblings.

"Just keep an eye on Michael," he said, looking specifically at Kaden.

"Hey," Michael protested. "I'm not a kid. I don't need babysitters."

"Still, I promised Mother I'd bring you home in one piece."

And they all knew how seriously Marcus took his duties.

"Don't worry, we'll look after him." Kaden reached out to tousle Michael's hair.

With a grunt, Michael shoved his older brother away and glared at him, matting his hair back into place.

Marcus just smiled, and they all parted with the plan to meet back at the Tarn's house for supper. Talas led the way out of the citadel. At the main bridge, the group split again as Leetra, Timothy, and Aaron left to visit with their own families.

Talas turned to those who remained. "I'd love to take you to my family. My sister and my grandfather would be especially pleased to meet you."

Everyone responded with enthusiasm. Kyrin couldn't wait to meet his family. From the moment they'd met him, Talas had always been very friendly and easy-going. Not at all like a typical crete, something he said he had inherited from his grandfather.

They traveled for a while through the city to the outer edges. Kyrin felt bad for Jace at the number of bridges they had to cross, but he handled it well. The others probably didn't even notice the slight sheen of sweat on his face. She gave him a quick smile to keep him encouraged.

The group finally slowed when they approached a dwelling that appeared the same as any other crete house, yet more rooms and floors spread out around the tree than the Tarn's home. With a light spring to his step, Talas reached the door and knocked. He flashed a grin back at everyone just before it opened.

"Talas!"

A slender woman a little older than Sonah looked out at him with wide eyes.

"Mother!" He immediately swept her into his arms and kissed her cheek.

"When did you get here?"

"Last night." Talas turned and motioned to the group behind him. "I brought a few friends with me."

His mother eyed them in bewilderment. Kyrin smiled when the woman's spring green eyes met hers, hoping to ease her hesitation. After all, not everyone in Talas's family shared his enthusiasm toward strangers and outsiders.

"Oh, well, please come in," she said, finding her voice. She motioned them in but raised her brows at her son.

Talas's grin lacked any contrition.

One by one, they entered the Folkan house, and Talas's mother closed the door behind them. They turned to face her, and Talas said, "Everyone, I'd like you to meet my mother, Tress Folkan."

They all smiled as he introduced each of them. Then an eager female voice exclaimed his name, drawing everyone's attention. A crete girl rushed into the room, straight into Talas's arms. She was barely five feet tall and about fifteen years old—nearly an adult by crete standards, but to Kyrin she still looked young. Behind her came three more successively older women—all with long dark hair and green eyes, which seemed to be the dominant trait in the Folkan family. Talas greeted them fondly and introduced them as his sisters. Apparently, he had two older brothers as well, though they were married and in their own homes. The youngest of his sisters, Trenna, exuded delight upon meeting them, while the older sisters were more reserved like their mother. Trenna's sparkling grin matched Talas's, lighting up her eyes and radiating interest. Kyrin caught Michael fixing his hair again and smoothing his jerkin. She bit her lip to hold back a smile.

After the greetings, Talas asked his mother, "Where are Father and Grandfather?"

Tress motioned deeper into the house. "They're building on to the back porch . . . and having one of their debates, I believe."

Talas's lips quirked wryly, and he motioned for everyone to follow. Up a short flight of steps and around the other side of the tree, they entered a spacious living area with a wide door leading out to an equally large porch. Just outside stood two crete men. The first was middle-aged with a profile like Talas's. The second was older, his dark hair heavily streaked with gray. They faced each other, the first crete pinching the bridge of his nose, and Kyrin just caught his exasperated words.

"It's more than sufficient already. There's no need to go wider."

The older crete shrugged. "I don't think another couple of feet would hurt."

He said it nonchalantly, but Kyrin detected a subtle humor in his expression, almost like a teasing child. Talas did refer to his grandfather as a bit of a rascal.

Talas cleared his throat, and the two men turned. He stepped out to the porch and embraced his father, and then his grandfather, who gave him a couple of hearty slaps on the back.

"I was just wondering when you'd show up for another visit." The older crete grinned and then his attention shifted past Talas to Kyrin and the others. "You've brought friends, I see."

Talas motioned them all out. Kyrin lingered near Jace, who remained well away from the edge of the porch where the railing was not yet completed. Another round of introductions followed, and they all greeted Talas's father, Thel, and his grandfather, Varn.

"How long will you be here?" his grandfather asked.

"Until King Balen can convince at least one of the clan leaders to change their position," Talas answered. "At least that's the plan."

"Well, he's got a difficult task. I shall aid him with my prayers."

"He'll surely appreciate that. We all will."

Talas stepped to the edge of the newly built section of the porch, as if one stumble didn't mean a fatal drop of a couple hundred feet. Though Kyrin didn't fear heights like Jace did, she had a healthy respect for them and would never get so close.

"So, you're building on?"

His grandfather joined him. "Yes. Your father thinks we should stop here, but I say add another couple of feet. What do you think?"

"Well, if you're going to do that, you might as well extend it to that branch out there." Talas gestured to a limb some ten feet away.

His grandfather laughed and clapped him on the back again. "Now you're talking."

Talas winked slyly at his father, who shook his head, but looked more amused now than perturbed. Such exchanges were no doubt a regular occurrence in the Folkan family.

"But enough about the porch. I want to know more about your friends," Varn said. "Let's go inside."

They all turned for the door again and gathered in the living room. Thel joined them, as did Trenna, who appeared as eager as her grandfather. The other women hovered nearby, listening but not fully participating. They discussed all the happenings in and around Landale. Kaden was particularly popular and fit right in. Toward midafternoon, Tress brought them a tray of soft, nutty cookies. By this time, she seemed to have warmed to their presence.

Perched on a small stool at the edge of the group, Trenna said excitedly, "We should give everyone a proper welcome and have a celebration at Flat Point."

"Good idea," her grandfather agreed. "A proper welcome for the king. It will give the people a chance to get to know him, and perhaps raise their sympathies toward the struggle in Arcacia and Samara." His gaze swept the group. "Do you think he would like that?"

"I think he would do anything that might help gain support for Samara," Talas said.

"Good. I will talk to the Darqs. They'll help set it up. The Silvars and Almeres too, I would expect."

"Lord Vallan, I'm sure, would make a contribution to the preparation."

His grandfather nodded, and plans seemed set for an up-coming celebration.

Her eyes full of excitement, Trenna turned to her brother, the small beaded braids in her hair swishing across her shoulders. "Oh, Talas, we must take them to see Glimmer Falls!"

Talas grinned as he eyed the group. "Anyone willing to get up before the sun tomorrow morning?"

JACE STEPPED OUT of the darkened room with the others and left most of their companions still asleep. He wasn't so sure about this pre-dawn excursion of theirs since waterfalls meant heights, but Kyrin had seemed eager to go. Only he, Kaden, Michael, and Marcus had gotten up when Talas came to wake them. He couldn't blame the others for wanting to sleep this morning, especially those who had spent the previous day at the citadel debating. Though there may have been a slight shift in Balen's favor, none of the clan leaders had changed their position yet.

Just down the stairs, Talas knocked on the room Kyrin and Leetra shared. "Hey, Lee, are you two up yet?"

The door opened, and Leetra stepped out. "We're up."

Kyrin came out from behind, her eyes bright and eager.

"Where is everyone?" she asked.

"We couldn't get them out of bed," Kaden answered, "but we did manage to drag Marcus along."

"This had better be good," Marcus said, his voice still hoarse from sleep. "I could use more rest after yesterday."

"Who knows if we'll get another chance to visit Dorland again? We'd better see everything there is to see."

They continued downstairs to the living room, where Captain Darq, Glynn, Novan, and Naeth all sat as if they had been up all night. Naeth rose to join them, and they trooped outside. Night-time darkness still rested over the forest, however, the city already buzzed with activity. Jace doubted that cretes even knew what sleeping in meant since they only needed a couple hours of sleep a night.

Talas took the lead, and they followed the same bridges they had traveled when they'd first entered the city. When they reached Dragon Rest and circled around to the top, they found Trenna waiting for them with a sleek female dragon.

Talas led them all into one of the many caves where the cretes had stashed their saddles. When Gem spotted Jace, she trilled and met him with a hot breath to the face. He chuckled and patted her on the neck. "Missed you too."

After all, he was much more comfortable at this altitude when he was with her.

Once everyone finished saddling their dragons, they gathered and mounted up.

"Just follow us," Talas said.

In a flurry, they all took to the air, following Talas and Trenna eastward toward the nearby mountains. The sky stretched out above them in a deep, purplish blue where the stars had begun to fade. Ahead, the horizon glowed with the first hint of orange sunlight. Leaving all signs of the crete city swallowed up by the vast forest below, it was as if they were the only souls for miles around. A shiver raced through Jace from both the chill of the morning and the wonder of just how big this land and its terrain were.

Twenty minutes later, a rumbling noise grew over the sound of dragon wings, promising of something magnificent. They soared over the top of a ridgeline, and just to their left, a river at least a hundred yards wide gushed over the edge of a cliff and plummeted hundreds, perhaps a thousand feet straight down into a deep ravine.

Still at the head of the group, Talas and Storm dove downward with the waterfall. Jace let Gem follow with the others, but his stomach did a flip on the way down. He would never get used to these sharp dives. Halfway to the bottom, a rocky point jutted from the mountainside not far from the falls. They all landed there and dismounted, gathering in a close group to hear each other.

"Just give it about ten minutes and you'll see what we came to show you," Talas shouted over the roar of the water.

He walked toward the farthest end of the point. Everyone followed, but Jace stopped before he came too close to the edge. Kyrin stayed at his side. Michael tried to follow Kaden and Talas closer, but Marcus snagged the back of his jerkin to stop him. His face turned deep red as he cast a glance at Trenna.

A fine mist from the waterfall landed cool and soft on Jace's skin, but the powerful rushing of water vibrated in his chest. He could only imagine its crushing force when it hit the riverbed below. His mouth turned cottony with the unwelcome thought of the ledge they stood on giving way.

They waited, engulfed in the thundering of the water. The sky brightened overhead until the first rays of sunlight spilled over the opposite ridge. Light struck the mist, turning it into a shimmering, undulating gold cloud. A rainbow appeared above them, and everyone gazed at the sight, mesmerized. Perhaps Jace should have tried to get Rayad and Holden to join them. They would be sorry they missed it. It was worth the early hour and even his discomfort of standing over such a deep ravine.

The sight lasted about twenty minutes before those first golden rays of morning faded as the sun climbed higher. Though still a spectacular view, the light show ended. Moving slowly, still casting looks back at the falls, they returned to their dragons and followed Talas up to a plateau above the ravine where they dismounted again. The rumble of the falls still rose around them, though much quieter up here, and they could actually hear each other without shouting.

"That was incredible," Kyrin breathed, her hair and face damp.

Talas grinned, and they all gazed down at the falls shrouded in white mist. The rainbow was still visible, even up here. Then Talas led them to the other side of the plateau overlooking the thousands of miles of forest stretching out below them.

"This place is amazing," Kyrin said.

Trenna looked at her. "It's a popular spot for picnics and courting."

She and Kyrin shared a grin, and Jace felt Kyrin's hand slip into his. He squeezed it, enjoying the moment, despite the heights. It would make a romantic area for a picnic, especially at sunset.

"It's hard to believe you have a whole city down there," Marcus said. "No one would ever know unless they'd been there."

Trenna and Talas agreed, and Kyrin said, "It's easy to see why so many of your people don't want to get involved with the war against Daican. You do feel so isolated here, and it would be hard to imagine the emperor ever being able to reach you."

Jace could see it too and could understand how the cretes felt. After Kalli and Aldor died, all he'd wanted was to lose himself in the wilderness and pretend Daican and Arcacia's troubles didn't exist or concern him. He would have if Rayad hadn't convinced him to go to Landale.

"But they are wrong," Trenna said quietly. "We aren't untouchable. That kind of arrogance will get us all killed."

Silence settled over them. The cretes' stubborn pride was just as strong as Jace's lack of concern had been for what went on outside his own life. He'd had to learn to look beyond himself, but how long would it take for the cretes to learn the same lesson? *What* would it take?

"Well, we should get back for breakfast," Talas broke into the silence. "If we're still not needed at the citadel, I thought we could explore the city today before the celebration tonight."

Once they had made it back to the Tarn's, Sonah had another delicious breakfast prepared for them of eggs, bacon, and warm bread with jam. The eggs were different from usual chicken eggs. They were much deeper in color and had a richer taste. When Jace inquired about them, Novan explained that they were from a breed of large quail that were plentiful in the mountains.

After breakfast, everyone who did not accompany King Balen to the second round of meetings with the crete leaders remained at the Tarn's for a time. Talas, Trenna, and Naeth happily entertained them with stories from their childhoods. Many of these tales included rather harrowing mischief.

"How do any crete children survive childhood?" Jace had to ask at one point.

Talas laughed and said, "By learning very early on to be mindful of our surroundings. When not inside, young children who are too young to understand usually wear a harness and are tied to something secure. I can tell you many a crete child has learned from experience not to wander near the edge."

Jace shook his head. He was willing to bet Talas was one of those children. How did their parents survive raising them?

Midmorning, when everyone headed out on a tour of the city, Timothy excused himself. He had something he needed to take care of now that he was back in Arvael. There was no telling when he might visit again after this.

On his own, he walked to the opposite side of the city, greeting and nodding to everyone he recognized. He didn't quite fit in with his shorter hair and brown eyes, but he'd spent enough time in the city two winters ago for most to know who he was. Cretes had excellent memories when it came to remembering their friends and neighbors.

In a quieter area south of the city, he arrived at a particular house and paused at the door. Closing his eyes, he breathed a quick prayer. Even after the many times he'd thought about this, he still didn't feel entirely prepared. Still, he pulled his shoulders back and knocked on the door.

A minute later, it opened, and a middle-aged male crete looked out at him. "Timothy."

"Mister Almere."

The strong-faced man invited him inside.

"You're here alone?" Raias Almere closed the door and looked at him curiously, his vibrant blue eyes holding a hint of stormy purple like Leetra's.

"Yes. If you're not busy, I would like to speak with you."

Raias peered at him as if sizing him up and then nodded. "Come with me."

They walked deeper into the house and met Raias's wife along the way. She had Leetra's youngest sister balanced on her hip while the other five children were scattered around playing. She said his name in surprise, and he greeted her kindly.

Raias led Timothy back outside to a private covered porch where the sound of children inside was only a low hum. Though chairs sat around the perimeter, neither of them took a seat. They both stopped, and Raias faced Timothy.

"My instincts and the circumstances tell me this is about Leetra. That, and the veiled exasperation in her letters."

Timothy hesitated, though he should have assumed Leetra would have mentioned his interest in the letters she always sent home with Darq or one of the other cretes who came and went from Landale. He cleared his throat. Though half crete, he didn't think he could ever comfortably say whatever was on his mind. However, for this conversation, he believed it best to speak his thoughts outright.

"Yes, sir, it is about Leetra. I don't know when I'll be here again, and I wanted to make my intentions clear, either to gain your approval or to accept your rejection."

Raias watched him—neither reassuring nor disapproving. "Go on."

Timothy drew a breath and attempted to recall everything he'd rehearsed in his head on the way here. "I have a keen interest in your daughter. I desire to court her with the intention of it leading to marriage one day . . . if she'll have me." He paused. If only Raias would give him some sort of signal, whether or not he would approve. "However, she hasn't been entirely open to my interest. I would like to continue to pursue her with complete respect for her feelings, and perhaps change her mind, but not without first gaining your permission."

He couldn't explain his feelings for Leetra, at least not in any coherent way. Even Aaron suggested he was wasting his time on her. Yet, under Leetra's tough façade, Timothy had caught glimpses of a softer, more vulnerable side—a side he believed to be the real Leetra and a side he had quite inexplicably found himself falling in love with. He just wanted a chance to draw that side out.

Raias crossed his arms and considered him for a long moment without speaking. Slowly, he nodded as if to his own thoughts rather than to Timothy.

"Normally, I would tell you no—that if she has spurned your interest, to leave her alone—but I'm not so sure that's what has happened, judging by her letters and her reaction when I mentioned it yesterday."

"I will accept whatever you decide," Timothy assured him. "I know I am only half crete and don't have much to offer except for my love and faithfulness, should she be open to them."

"I do not know you as well as I would like, but I do know your reputation and your devotion to your faith. I have no doubt you would devote yourself to my daughter as well."

"Yes, sir."

A hint of a smile claimed Raias's face. "I do admire your courage in coming to me. Crete fathers are notoriously difficult to approach, especially if you're not a crete." His smile faded as quickly as it appeared. "You're not what her mother and I envisioned for her . . . but then, what we believed was a perfect arrangement turned out to be a terrible mistake."

"You couldn't have known," Timothy said quietly. It wasn't as if Leetra had been unhappy with her attachment to Falcor before his betrayal.

"Still, it was my job to protect my daughter and see her with a man who would protect and care for her." Raias subjected him to an intense scrutiny before finally nodding. "All right, you have my permission. You may pursue Leetra, providing you continue to respect her wishes, and if she turns you down completely, you will accept it and move on."

Hope filled Timothy, but he remained serious. "You have my word. I will not push her."

Raias nodded again. "You will understand if I discuss this with Talas and Verus Darq and ask them to monitor the situation in my stead. I expect you to respect them as you would me."

"Of course."

"Good." Raias's protective tone softened a little with love. "Leetra is very stubborn and has had both her pride and her heart deeply wounded. It will take great care to heal them. Honestly, I'm not sure a crete man could do it, but I think you may just have a chance if you can manage it without her pulling away. I want my daughter to be loved and happy. She's her own worst enemy. I hope you can change that."

"Thank you, sir, for allowing me the chance."

They talked for a while longer, and Timothy could tell that Raias made an effort to learn more about him. After a time, they went inside to visit with the rest of the family. Timothy loved getting to know Leetra's younger siblings. They were a rambunctious group but took to him well.

With the approach of midday, Timothy took his leave to meet back up with the others. He bid the Almeres goodbye, and Raias showed him to the door. When he stepped outside, Leetra was just coming off the bridge to the house. She stopped and stared at him, her brows scrunching together as suspicion narrowed her eyes.

"What are you doing here?"

Timothy motioned to the house. "I came to talk to your father."

Her frown grew even deeper, her purple eyes igniting with what might have been panic, but he smiled pleasantly and asked, "Are the others at the market?"

The question didn't seem to register at first as she continued to stare at him.

"Yes," she said finally, her voice cool.

He nodded. "I'll see you later then." And he went on his way.

Leetra stared after Timothy, her heart thumping her ribs as her mind spun with the implication of his words. She then whirled around to where her father stood in the doorway. Crossing the porch, she stalked inside and slammed the door.

"What was he doing here?" she demanded in a sharp whisper. Of all things, she hadn't expected to see *him* walking out of *her* house. It was far too uncomfortable to consider his reasons.

"He wanted to talk to me . . . about you."

Leetra's blood pressure rose. "Why?"

"To ask my permission to pursue a courtship with you."

Leetra's mouth fell open. It was just what she feared. "And?"

"I gave it to him."

"Father!"

"What?"

Was that amusement in his eyes? Because this was anything but funny. "How could you?"

"You don't wish to consider being courted by him?"

Leetra sputtered. "It's not like I've encouraged it."

"But have you turned him down?"

She floundered for the right words before crossing her arms with a huff. She couldn't believe he had done this to her. It didn't matter if she'd outright turned Timothy down or not. "How could you just give him your permission? He isn't even a crete! He isn't . . . isn't . . ."

"Isn't Falcor?"

Leetra went cold and felt the blood leave her face. Something pained in her chest, but she forced it away.

"No, he isn't," her father said more gently, soberly. "Thank Elôm for that."

Leetra swallowed hard. She couldn't do this. Not right now. Her voice came out rough. "He isn't like us."

"No . . . but maybe that isn't such a bad thing." He stepped closer, resting his hands on her shoulders. "I know how Falcor hurt you, but someday, you'll have to move past it or you will miss out on a life of love and companionship you could have. Timothy is a good man and desires to give you that."

Leetra ground her teeth together and a couple of tears forced themselves from her eyes despite how she fought to hold them back. She pulled away from her father and swiped them away. "I don't want to talk about it."

KYRIN LOVED EXPLORING Arvael's marketplace. Large platforms built around the trees held a multitude of small shops and stalls containing unfamiliar and interesting food and other wares. Talas, Trenna, and Naeth bought them lunch from the various items available—fresh rolls and honey from a small bakery, plump red berries that tasted a bit like blueberries, and smoked pheasant. They spent the majority of the afternoon exploring the area and learning about the city.

Late that afternoon, once they'd seen almost everything there was to see in the market, Talas turned to the group. "We should probably get ready for the celebration. It'll begin at sunset."

Trenna whirled around to face Kyrin. "Will you let me get you ready for the celebration? I think you would look amazing in a crete dress."

Kyrin smiled. "That sounds like fun." She'd always liked Leetra's dresses. She didn't want to miss an opportunity to wear one, and she hadn't packed anything suitable for a party anyway.

"The problem is, we need someone whose clothes would fit you." Trenna looked down at her own. "I'm too short."

"What about Katia?" Naeth suggested.

Trenna's face lit up. "Perfect." She looked back at Kyrin. "Katia is one of the tallest women in the city. Almost as tall as

143

you. Come on. I'll take you to see her. I'm sure she would be happy to let you borrow something for tonight."

Kyrin glanced at Jace and her brothers. While she felt perfectly safe with Trenna, she wasn't sure they would be entirely comfortable with her going alone.

Jace stepped forward. "I'll go with you."

He sounded like it was a casual decision, but Kyrin knew better. It might be overly cautious on their part, but after everything they had been through, it was hard to trust just anyone. There could be enemies here just as easily as there were in other places.

"We'll meet you back at the Tarn's," Trenna told the others.

When they turned to go, Naeth also joined them, and they left the market. As they crossed one of the first bridges, Trenna looked back. "Luckily, Katia has blue eyes like yours."

"Do cretes always wear clothing that matches their eye color?" Kyrin asked. She had never seen any of the cretes at camp do otherwise.

"Typically, yes, though once in a while we try something different." She shrugged and flashed a smile at Kyrin. "Always wearing the same color can get boring."

Kyrin laughed. Cretes were anything but boring. "For ten years, I wore only black and gold every day. I don't think I ever want to wear those colors again."

Not far from the market, they stopped at a crete house. A few moments after Trenna knocked, a young crete woman opened the door. She was only an inch or two shorter than Kyrin and had a similar shade of blue eyes, though much more vivid. She looked at Kyrin and Jace in surprise before turning a questioning look to Trenna.

"Katia, these are my friends Kyrin Altair and Jace Ilvaran." Trenna drew Kyrin forward. "I want to dress Kyrin up in crete style for the celebration tonight, but I'm too short to have anything that would fit her. Would you mind letting her borrow something?"

Katia eyed Kyrin again, but said, "Sure." She opened the door wider to let them inside. As they passed through, Kyrin caught Katia and Naeth sharing a smile—the sort of smile she and Jace shared. Now she understood why Naeth had joined them.

"Everyone else is out," Katia said. She gestured into the living room and told Jace and Naeth, "You can make yourselves comfortable."

They nodded, and Katia led Kyrin and Trenna to one of the winding staircases across the room. On the way up, she glanced at Kyrin. "So, you're from Landale?"

"Yes."

"Naeth talks about joining the Resistance."

Kyrin caught a slight hesitancy to her voice. She couldn't blame her. She didn't know what she would do if Jace left to join some faraway struggle.

When they entered a bedroom, Katia opened a knee-high chest.

"Will you be at the celebration tonight?" Trenna asked her.

Katia nodded. "Father wants us all to be there to show our support for King Balen."

Trenna leaned closer to Kyrin. "Katia's father is the leader of the Eagle Clan."

Kyrin thought back to yesterday. The man had been one of their staunchest supporters. "I know I speak for everyone when I say that we really appreciate your family's support."

Katia looked over her shoulder, and at first Kyrin wasn't sure she felt the same as her father, but then she said, "It's men like Daican who have caused us to isolate ourselves here in Dorland. We're not about to let him take away the freedom we do have. Fighting together benefits us all." She turned back to the chest and pulled out a blouse a moment later. "This should work."

She handed Kyrin the light blue linen-like garment. Kyrin unlaced her overdress, while Katia searched through a second chest, and changed into the blouse. The long sleeves were split down the side starting at the shoulder. A couple of small stitches held it together near the elbow, but otherwise it was open for the full length of the arm. An embroidered vine pattern decorated the edges and the neckline.

Next Katia handed her a soft leather skirt tanned a grayish brown. The bottom hem had raw, uneven edges. It wrapped around her waist over her leggings and fell almost to her ankles. Over the blouse, she wore a matching leather bodice constructed of several pieces stitched together decoratively and laced at the sides.

"Perfect," Trenna said with a grin. "Now we just need to do your hair and paint."

"Paint?"

"Whenever we have celebrations, we accent our tattoos with colored paint. You don't have any tattoos, but we could do some pretty designs."

It seemed a little odd to Kyrin to paint designs on her skin, but she was willing to experience the crete culture to the fullest while she was here. "All right."

She sat down on a cushion, and Trenna and Katia both went to work on her hair. They brushed it out and then added varying shades of blue beads. On the right side, Trenna attached a couple of long, narrow feathers with black at the tips that gradually lightened to a blue hue streaked with white.

Then came the paint. Trenna took a place at Kyrin's right shoulder, while Katia worked at her left. Each held a fine tipped brush. Before they started, Trenna asked, "What is your favorite animal or flower?"

Kyrin thought about it for a moment. Then a memory from her childhood came to her mind.

"Trilliums," she said quietly and cleared the sudden tightness from her throat. "I like trilliums."

Trenna nodded but said nothing about her slightly hoarse voice. Using a light blue base color, she and Katia painted flowing designs and dots on Kyrin's arms, starting at her shoulders and working down her upper arms to where the sleeves came together. Kyrin sat very still and watched, marveling at their steady hands. They must have had a lot of practice to do it so well. Once finished with the light blue, they accented the designs with dark blue and black paint.

After letting it dry for a couple of minutes, Trenna pronounced it finished. Kyrin lifted her arm to see her right shoulder better. In the middle of her upper arm, Trenna had painted a small trillium. The designs around it were just as lovely.

"It's beautiful," she said, smiling at the two cretes. If only she had a full-length mirror like the one she'd had in Auréa Palace.

"Good." Trenna gave Kyrin a wide grin. "Let's go down and show Jace."

Downstairs in the living room, Jace and Naeth waited for the women to finish. Though Naeth tended to be on the quiet side, Jace found himself surprisingly at ease with him. They talked a little of the city and Naeth's family before discussing the division between the clan leaders.

"My father was nominated for leader of the Wolf Clan, but he declined." Naeth shook his head. "He regrets it now. If he were clan leader, things would probably be far different. No doubt it would be seven to five in our favor."

"Why did he decline?"

"My father isn't one to seek such elevation, and it was around the same time Falcor started acting more distant. My father thought it would be better to focus on our family. Unfortunately, we had no idea why or just how much Falcor had changed."

He spoke blandly, as if simply stating facts, but his eyes revealed more emotion.

"Do you know now why he changed?"

Naeth shrugged. "He always held this bitterness and a warped view that humans have forced us into a lesser life than we had before. It's not an uncommon view, but most don't act on it. He had this group of friends, and I guess they chose to do something about it. We don't know how they contacted Emperor Daican, or whose idea it was to provide him with the means to breed firedrakes—theirs or Daican's. They must have made a deal they think will gain them power. They're certainly not doing it because they want Daican to succeed."

He paused. "We just never expected such betrayal, so we didn't look into things the way we should have. I should have seen it. I thought he was just being difficult."

Jace offered him a sympathetic look. Now that he had siblings of his own, he understood the feeling of responsibility as the oldest to look out for them.

A moment later, the women came down the stairs. Jace pushed up from his chair and turned just as Kyrin reached the bottom of the steps. He paused and didn't immediately draw another breath as he took in her appearance. Their eyes met, and she approached him slowly and a bit shyly.

"Do you like it?" She smoothed her hands down the front of the skirt.

He gave the new style another long look. He hadn't really expected to see her in something so completely crete. He met her gaze again. "It's different."

She bit her lip, but he quickly smiled.

"You look good in it . . ." he lowered his voice so only she could hear, "beautiful." And she was. The colors and even the ruggedness of it suited her because it was both feminine and strong like she was.

She returned his smile and pink dusted her cheeks. "Thank you. It was fun to let them dress me up like this."

Jace glanced at the designs on her arms, particularly her right one. "A trillium?"

Kyrin nodded, tipping her head to look at it too. "Trenna asked what my favorite flower was. My father always used to bring in bunches of them for my mother in the spring. They remind me of him."

Jace tucked that bit of information away in the back of his mind.

With evening fast approaching, they all turned to the door. Kyrin thanked Katia on the way out, and they set off for the Tarn house. By this time, the sun had sunk lower in the sky and shadows engulfed the forest city. When they arrived, Trenna split from the group to head home to prepare herself for the party. Jace, Kyrin, and Naeth stepped inside where all the men spoke in the living room.

Kaden was the first to notice them. He looked his sister up and down and nodded. "Nice."

"Better than my makeover at Auréa?" she asked with a laugh.

"Much."

Kyrin glanced at the others and asked, "So, how did today go at the citadel?"

Kaden shook his head. "Doesn't sound any better than yesterday. The opposing clan leaders are still being stubborn."

She sighed and kept her voice low. "This isn't going to work, is it?"

"Well, maybe Varn is right and Balen can gain some support tonight," Kaden said hopefully. "So far, he has only spoken with the clan leaders. Maybe the rest of the people will be more open to talking. The leaders can't remain stubborn if the majority of those in their clan want to fight."

Jace wasn't quite so optimistic, but they had to hold onto some hope for this trip.

"FLAT POINT IS just ahead," Talas announced.

Jace and the others had followed him though the city, crisscrossing one bridge after another for over twenty minutes now. Most of the city seemed to be heading in the same direction. Where could there be a place large enough to accommodate so many, especially at this altitude? Jace assumed from the name that it was another rocky point like Dragon Rest, though he saw no sign of it through the thick trees.

However, in another moment or two, he caught sight of flames flickering up ahead. Crossing a final bridge, the trees opened up to reveal a massive, flat-topped peak just a little lower than the treetops. In the center, a bonfire crackled and popped. Lanterns and torches burned along the entire perimeter. And all around, cretes stood talking. Jace had never seen so many all at once. Hesitation crept in. Though this celebration was in their honor, would the people receive them well? Cretes as a whole weren't known as the most welcoming or gracious of hosts. He would have been more than content for them all to spend the evening at the Tarn's house instead, but if this could help their cause, they had to be here.

When they stepped off the bridge and onto the solid rock of the point, Lord Vallan and a couple of the clan leaders met them.

"My lord." Vallan inclined his head in greeting to Balen and acknowledged the others with a nod. "I hope you will enjoy the festivities tonight."

"I'm sure we will," Balen said. "I'll be sure to thank the Folkans for setting it up."

Vallan motioned to the gathering. "Come, I will properly introduce you to everyone."

They followed the crete lord closer to the center of the area, and Vallan called for everyone's attention. The conversations and laughter grew quiet as everyone turned in their direction—the cretes' many colored eyes like bright gems. Jace was glad to be in the midst of a group and not singled out for attention. So far, no one seemed to notice the signs of his mixed blood, or at least weren't alarmed by it. Hopefully tonight wouldn't change that.

"Thank you all for coming. As you know, tonight is to honor and welcome Lord Balen, King of Samara." He gestured to Balen.

Applause and hearty cheers rose up, though not from everyone. More than a handful of cretes stood silent and looked on in suspicion. Apparently, they'd come to enjoy the celebration and nothing more.

"No royalty from another country has visited our city in generations. I expect you to show him and his companions respect and make us all proud."

Again came the applause and nods of agreement. Following this introduction, several cretes stepped forward to meet Balen and the others personally, including the Folkans. Jace smiled at how enthusiastic Varn was to meet the king. He was so much like Talas. They also met Darq's two brothers, who were just as imposing as the captain. Others may have found them intimidating, but they had spent so much time with Darq their intensity felt familiar.

In the midst of the greetings and conversations, Timothy cut in.

"Kyrin, Jace."

The two of them turned, and he beckoned them over to an elderly crete man with long gray hair. Something about him seemed vaguely familiar.

With a smile, Timothy said, "I'd like you to meet my grandfather, Tolan Silvar."

Josan's father. That's where the familiarity came from. Jace and Kyrin greeted him, and he smiled kindly, especially when his eyes rested on Kyrin.

"Ah, the girl with the perfect memory," he said. "A remarkable gift."

Kyrin smiled and nodded. "It has drawbacks, and some things I would rather forget, but I've learned to cherish it for everything I can remember . . . for the memories I carry of loved ones."

They traded a knowing look, their expressions wistful. After all, they'd both lost someone to Falcor's hand, whether directly or indirectly.

His gaze switched to Jace and lifted to his face. Jace almost felt as though he should bend down so the man wouldn't have to look up at him.

"And you are the one Elon saved from Daican."

"Yes," Jace affirmed.

Tolan nodded slowly as if imagining what had taken place. "An incredible moment that must have been."

"Life changing," Jace replied, his throat constricting a bit as it always did when he spoke of that time and the sacrifice Elon had willingly made for him.

"I can see it in your face."

Jace smiled.

"I thank you for all you did for both my son and my grandsons," Tolan told him and Kyrin.

"We were happy to do it," Kyrin said. "Timothy and Aaron have both been a great blessing to us at camp."

Tolan looked with pride on his grandson, and Timothy humbly stared at the ground.

They spoke with the crete a while longer before turning their attention to others. Despite the less enthusiastic attendees, there were quite a number of people eager to meet them. In between the conversations, Jace's attention wandered around the party area. At least a couple hundred cretes had shown up. Several tables sat off to one side holding refreshments for the night.

Before long, the distinct sound of crete flutes, hand drums, and tambourines rose above the hum of voices. Immediately, crete couples paired up to dance to the lively tune. They certainly did enjoy their music and dances. Everyone from Landale stayed clustered together for a while as Balen and Lord Vallan spoke to each other and others who came and went.

After a couple of songs, Trenna appeared and joined their group. The crete girl had more beads in her hair than earlier and green paint highlighting her tattoos. She grinned at Kyrin. "Aren't you going to dance?" She cast a prompting glance at Jace.

"Oh, I don't know," Kyrin replied.

Was her hesitation for Jace's benefit, or did the size of the crowd make her reluctant? It was one thing dancing in front of friends back at camp but something else entirely to join in on a crete dance in front of half a city.

"I've danced to some crete music but not much," she continued.

"Don't worry about it," Trenna said. "A lot of us aren't even good. We just like to dance."

"We'll see."

"All right, but I hope you change your mind. It's really fun." Trenna's infectious grin turned to Kyrin's left—to her brothers, specifically Michael. He gave a shy smile in return before looking down bashfully.

"Do you want to dance?"

His head shot back up at Trenna's question. He glanced around before meeting her eyes. "Me?"

She nodded.

"Um, sure." He smiled again, his eyes alight with both nerves and excitement.

Trenna grabbed his hand, and they headed off toward the other couples.

"Someone's going to be good and disappointed when we have to return to Landale," Kaden said. He and Marcus shared a laughed, and Kaden glanced at Talas. "Looks like we might end up really being family."

Talas grinned good-naturedly. Apparently, he had no qualms about his sister's potential interest in a non-crete. "Might as well make it official."

Kyrin shook her head at them. "Come on, Michael is still just a boy and already you're playing matchmaker."

Marcus shrugged. "Father was nineteen when he married Mother. Michael's less than five years shy of that."

"Well, he's always going to be my little brother." Kyrin looked between them. "Besides, you two aren't even married yet."

Talas slapped Kaden on the back. "We'll have to go about fixing that, now won't we?"

Kaden shook his head. "Don't get any ideas. I'm perfectly capable of deciding who and when I want to marry. And I don't see you out there dancing with a special girl."

Talas shrugged. "True."

Jace chuckled at their banter. Thank Elôm that he had Kyrin and wasn't the object of any matchmaking schemes.

Conversation continued as they watched Michael and Trenna and the other couples. Kyrin seemed to enjoy watching the lively dances. Whenever Jace looked at her, she wore a contented smile on her face. It was good to see her so relaxed after the stress of arriving at the Tarn's house. In the midst of these thoughts, he caught sight of a couple of young crete men nearby. The way they looked at Kyrin spoke of obvious interest, clearly not put off by the fact that she was human. And she did make an attractive sight standing there—Jace didn't dispute that—but they would have to look elsewhere for the attention of a girl. He moved closer to Kyrin, enough to gain their attention, and gave them a cool look. Not necessarily threatening but enough to let them know Kyrin was taken. They seemed to get the message.

Jace scanned the area for any others who might have the same interest. It would probably be a good idea to make his claim clear, and there was only one sure way to do that. He looked down at Kyrin. "Let's dance."

Her eyes widened as she looked at him. "You really want to?" She glanced around. "It's a large audience."

Jace nodded without giving it too much thought. He'd done all right in Landale—in fact, he'd even ended up enjoying it—so he could manage here. "I don't mind if you don't."

Her smile blossomed. "I don't mind."

He offered his hand and, feeling surprisingly confident, led her closer to the bonfire where another lively crete dance was underway.

Leetra crossed her arms and surveyed the gathering. She used to enjoy these parties . . . years ago. As a child, she'd raced around with Talas and their other family and friends getting into all sorts of mischief. Something about the nighttime air, bonfire, and music always put them in a rowdy mood. A smile tugged at her lips when she spotted a couple of her siblings dashing past just as she had once done. One of her little sisters let out a squeal, and she laughed.

But it caught in her throat when she spotted Timothy nearby.

She narrowed her eyes. Two young crete women stood talking to him. One, a girl even more petite than Leetra, with the largest and most brilliant green eyes she had ever seen, giggled and gazed at Timothy adoringly. He smiled kindly at them but didn't appear entirely comfortable. Leetra rolled her eyes with a huff and determined to ignore them, setting her attention on the nearby dancers. Five seconds later, her gaze shifted back to the trio.

She wasn't jealous. No. Those girls just didn't know half the man Timothy was. But who cared? She didn't . . . she really didn't. She stiffened, her blood zinging through her veins. What if he was doing this purposely to make her jealous? Yet, the thought died instantly, along with her ire. Timothy wouldn't do that. Falcor might have, but Timothy? Never.

The musicians started a new song. One of her favorites, actually, before memories of Falcor had tainted it. She scowled. She'd sworn never to dance to it again . . . but . . .

She grumbled to herself. *Fine.* She would save Timothy from an uncomfortable situation and that was it. It wouldn't mean anything. After this, he was on his own. If he didn't avoid the girls, that was his problem.

She marched across the gap between them, her beaded braids slapping her back. Though the music and conversation covered the sound of her footsteps, Timothy noticed her coming, and his sudden diversion of attention alerted the other girls. All three stared at her. She set her focus on Timothy.

"Do you want to dance?" She only realized after the words left her mouth how perturbed she sounded, but she wasn't doing this for fun.

Timothy glanced at the two girls. Leetra speared them with a stern look as well. They exchanged glances and shifted back a little. Satisfied, she fixed her gaze on Timothy expectantly. If he was so sweet on her then he'd be a fool to turn her down.

Finally, he smiled. "I would like that."

He gave the other girls a parting nod, and Leetra spun around, heading toward the dance. Drawing near to the other couples, she turned again to let Timothy catch up. When they stood facing each other, neither acted for a moment. Only now did it sink in that she'd saved Timothy from an uncomfortable situation just to land herself in one. She'd forgotten they actually had to dance *together*.

With a hard breath, she put her hands up. Looking much more comfortable than she was, Timothy stepped closer and put his arm lightly around her waist, taking her hand in his free one. This was probably the closest Leetra had ever been to him. She swallowed, her throat suddenly prickling and dried out.

Timothy easily took the lead and guided her into the midst of the other dancing couples. As soon as they settled into the rhythm, he spoke.

"That was rather abrupt."

Leetra looked him straight in the eyes, daring him to imply she'd been rude. "They don't deserve you."

Amusement played on his face. "Do you even know them?"

Leetra huffed. "Yes."

Well, maybe she didn't *know* them, but she knew who they were.

He stared down at her with a slight smile, and her heart sputtered. He was the perfect height, she couldn't help but notice—tall by crete standards, but not too tall. She gave herself a firm mental shake. It didn't matter how tall he was.

"So who does deserve me?" he asked in a teasing tone.

But Leetra wasn't joking. "I don't think anyone could truly deserve you."

All hint of teasing and amusement faded from Timothy's face. His eyes deepened. "I can think of someone."

Leetra couldn't tear her gaze away at first. Brown eyes were so strange for someone with crete blood, yet they were so . . .

She jerked her head down and focused on one of the buckles of his jerkin, stubbornly refusing to meet his gaze again. "Well, I can't."

A long silence fell between them. When Leetra couldn't stand it anymore, she chanced a peek up at Timothy. He was watching her, a soft, almost sad expression on his face. She did a double take. Falcor had never looked at her with such tenderness. Not once.

"You look beautiful tonight."

She barely heard his quiet voice over the music but felt every word. When was the last time someone other than her family had called her beautiful? She couldn't even recall a specific time Falcor had—not that she wanted to. And she hadn't even dressed up for tonight like all the other girls. She was just the same as she always was.

She struggled to swallow again. Her heartbeat echoed in her ears as she fought to stop the walls inside her from crumbling. It would be easy to let them fall away—far too easy. But there were reasons she had built them in the first place. She straightened her shoulders and the walls with them. Disappointment crossed Timothy's face, but she would not be swayed.

They finished the dance and came to a stop near the bonfire. Having accomplished her mission, Leetra turned away from Timothy, but her hand remained captured in his. She tugged against him, but he wouldn't let go. She looked back to send him a glare, but his expression was too kind to follow through.

"Are you sure you don't want to keep on? When was the last time you spent a night at home dancing?"

He had a point, and she could enjoy it if she let herself. It wasn't as if she had anyone else she preferred to dance with.

"All right," she conceded, but this time she would keep her walls strong and intact.

Kyrin's delightful laugh mingled with the music as she and Jace both missed a step, putting them completely out of rhythm. But Jace didn't care. He loved to hear her laugh and see her having such fun. It didn't matter who was watching. They tried to get back into the rhythm of the music but failed miserably.

"I think we'd better give it up," Kyrin said with laughter still in her voice. "This one's far too complicated for either of us."

They stepped away from the dance toward one of the refreshments tables. After so much dancing, Jace could use a drink to wet his throat. At the table, they found at least five different types of punch filling the air with a tangy, fruity scent.

Kyrin looked at him. "Which one do you think?"

He shrugged. "Your guess is as good as mine."

"Well, why don't you try one and I'll try another?"

He nodded, pouring himself a glass from a large bowl of cherry red liquid while Kyrin served herself from a bowl of darker purple juice. They each took a sip, and Kyrin made a face.

"This one's a bit tart."

"Try this instead." Jace gave her his glass of much smoother and sweeter punch.

She smiled her thanks and sipped it, nodding. "Much better."

Jace tried hers. Though tart, he didn't mind. They both turned to watch the dancers, all silhouetted by the large flames of the fire. After a moment, Jace looked over at Kyrin, and his gaze settled on a pale ridge along her left shoulder not quite hidden by the blue paint.

"How did you get that scar?" he asked.

"I was eight," she replied with barely a pause to think about it. "One of the bullies at Tarvin Hall pushed me, and I fell into the edge of one of the stone benches in the courtyard. It really wasn't much more than a scratch, but it did hurt at the time."

Jace pulled his brows together in a frown as he thought of a young Kyrin in such a hostile environment. She deserved to have had a happier childhood.

However, she smirked. "Kaden gave him a bloody nose."

A smile crept to Jace's lips. At least she hadn't had to face it alone.

"That was the first of many fights he got into, mostly on my behalf."

"It's good to know he took care of you."

They shared a smile, and Jace had to fight the pull to draw her close and kiss her. They were in public, after all.

The music stopped abruptly. Jace turned toward the dance where the couples looked around in confusion. Then he spotted a group of mostly younger crete men making their way through the gathering . . . straight toward King Balen and the others from Landale. Stiffening, Jace set his cup aside and took Kyrin's hand securely in his as they moved to join the others before the group of cretes reached them.

JACE AND KYRIN reached the others at the same time as Michael and Trenna—just before the group of cretes did.

"This doesn't look good," Kaden muttered.

Jace glanced around. Everyone was on alert as the cretes approached Balen. None of them had brought weapons—this was a party, after all—but Jace didn't have a good feeling about that decision now. The head crete, a man about Talas's age, stopped just a few feet short of the king. Captain Darq stood a little ahead of Balen, his stern gaze set on the young man and no doubt would have intercepted had he come any closer. The crete, however, didn't give him more than a passing glance before focusing on Balen.

"We hear you've come to drag our people into your war," he ground out the accusation.

Balen gave the entire group a sweeping glance, but said calmly, "I've come to ask your people for aid. We are allies."

The animosity brewing in the crete's eyes told Jace the man wouldn't have any of it. He'd come here to fight—whether with words or more, Jace couldn't say just yet. He carefully watched the crete's every move. If this turned violent, there would be little warning.

The man scowled. "I don't remember hearing of Samara putting up a protest when the cretes had to leave Arcacia."

Darq snorted, but Talas was the one to step forward and approach the crete, a cajoling smile on his face.

"Come on, Cray, let's not ruin a good party." He put his hand on the crete's shoulder as if to guide him away from the group, but Cray shoved his arm away.

"You stay out of this. You've been with them so long you're hardly even a crete anymore. You never were much of one."

Talas stiffened, and his smile vanished. Considering the pride cretes had in their race, this was a serious insult. To Jace's left, Kaden shifted as if preparing to join his friend in a fight if need be.

His expression and voice now unusually cold, Talas replied, "Oh, so you have to be ignorant and narrow-minded to be a crete?"

Cray stepped closer, and they faced each other down. The other crete lifted his arm to hit Talas, but Novan jumped in, forcing them apart.

"Now is not the time or place for this." He glared at Cray. "No one forced us out of Arcacia. We left by our own choice. It's the innocent people of Samara and Arcacia who are oppressed, and don't think for a moment that Daican won't bring that oppression to us. If you really want more power for the cretes, then you should be all for standing with our allies and putting a stop to Daican's conquest."

Cray scoffed. "Why? Let the humans fight themselves. What's that to us? Once they're weak, maybe then we'll regain our power."

A murmur rippled through the other cretes, and not only those in Cray's group. Several outside of it also nodded their heads. By now, Captain Darq and the rest of their crete friends stood in a line in front of everyone from Landale as if to create a barrier Cray and the others would have to cross to get to them. A barrier against their own people. Jace glanced over his shoulder just to be sure no one came at them from behind.

Darq spoke icily. "Don't you understand what's happening? Samara was conquered. She can't fight back without our help, and while we bicker over whether or not to grant it, Daican only grows stronger, not weaker."

Cray didn't buy any of it. "And maybe, like Talas, you've just spent so much time away from your own people that you've let their plight blind you and cause you to forget what it is to be a crete."

"I don't remember when it became the crete thing to do to throw aside honor and turn our backs on friends in need of aid."

"I see *your* friends, but when was the last time Arcacia or Samara were actually friends of the cretes?"

Darq's fists clenched, but Lord Vallan stepped forward.

"Enough." He sent Cray a glare. "This is not a debate. We gathered tonight to honor King Balen, not to argue."

Despite the crete lord stepping in to Balen's defense, Cray's scowl deepened. "So, because of a bunch of humans, we are no longer able to speak our minds?" He turned to the crowd. "Sounds suspiciously like what drove us out of Arcacia in the first place, does it not?"

The grumbling grew louder.

Lord Vallan shook his head. "You know that is not what this is."

"No?" Cray again addressed the crowd. "Haven't you noticed how things have been changing ever since Captain Darq saw fit to involve us in the struggle in Samara? And how many crete lives were lost because of it? Now they're asking for more. How many will it take before they're satisfied? Was it not better when we didn't have this contact with the humans?"

Agitated murmurs spread through the gathering, both in agreement and disagreement with Cray's words. Jace shook his head. So much for a celebration. The people were as split as their leaders.

Kyrin tugged his hand, and he looked down to see her gaze darting between Cray and the surrounding crowd of cretes. He didn't like the tense look on her face when she turned to him and spoke in a low, urgent voice, "We need to leave. It's not safe here."

Panic flashed in her eyes and tremored in her voice. Jace needed no further prompting. He grasped her hand more tightly and stepped closer to Balen.

"My lord," he said when they reached the king's side. "We should go."

Balen turned to them, looking first at Jace before his gaze lowered to Kyrin, whose face was almost pleading with him, thinly veiled fear peeking through.

Before he could utter a word, she told him, "I think we're in danger."

Jace waited for his response. Would he think Kyrin was over-reacting to the situation? Jace wasn't used to seeing her so shaken, but if she said they were in danger, he believed her.

Balen nodded and turned to the others. "We're going."

Kyrin breathed a sigh but cast a wary glance toward Cray and his friends. Jace squeezed her hand again. These cretes would have to come through him to harm her or any of them.

Word passed through the group and everyone gathered closer to Balen, including Darq's brothers, who looked thoroughly disgusted with their brethren. Balen gained Lord Vallan's attention and said, "I think it would be in everyone's best interest if we took our leave."

Lord Vallan gave a short nod, his face grim. "I apologize for this. I don't know what has gotten into everyone. My men and I will make sure no one follows you out."

They all turned toward the bridge back into the city. Darq, Rayad, and Talas led the way while Darq's brothers and the Tarns brought up the rear, keeping Balen well protected in the center of the group. They crossed into the city, and the sound of upraised voices slowly faded behind them. Jace kept Kyrin at his side and scanned every bridge for danger. The city was quiet with so many at Flat Point, and they encountered only a few cretes along the way.

Jace breathed much more easily once they reached the Tarn's house. They all filed inside, filling up the living room. While no one spoke immediately, Captain Darq looked angry enough to hit someone. Had they stayed, he probably would have. Even easygoing Talas appeared to be in a fighting mood. That alone told Jace they had made the right choice in following Kyrin's warning. Bloodshed between the cretes certainly wouldn't have helped anyone.

After a moment to compose himself, Darq faced Balen. "I sincerely apologize, my lord. I expected more from my people."

Novan, Glynn, and Darq's brothers expressed their own regrets.

"I would hope I speak for the majority of the cretes in saying it was a shameful lack of courtesy and honor," Darq continued. "I don't doubt Lord Vallan will have a thing or two to say to Cray and his friends."

"I am only glad we left before things grew too far out of hand, thanks to Kyrin's warning," Balen said.

Darq turned his attention to her. "Did you see something that presented a danger?"

"I believed us all to be in danger, yes," she said. "Do you remember last summer in Samara when you met with my grandfather and Falcor at the river? Marcus said that Falcor told you to let the humans fight amongst themselves. That's what Cray said. It could be coincidence, but what if it's not?"

Darq narrowed his eyes. "You think Cray could be a traitor too?"

Kyrin lifted one shoulder in a shrug. "I don't know. He probably isn't, but he and the others gave me a bad feeling. The last time I ignored such feelings, disaster happened. Maybe he's not with Falcor, but he's certainly not with us. Everything about his behavior threatened ill will. And you saw how many were listening and responding to what he was saying. That's why I thought we should leave." She turned contritely to Balen. "I'm sorry if I overreacted."

Balen shook his head. "No, don't be. You were right to warn us. It was best we left when we did. It wasn't worth the risk to stay."

"So, what is our plan now?" Rayad asked. "If Cray and his friends are traitors, what's to stop them from coming for us here?"

"Naeth and I will set a watch outside," Novan said, "to guard the house."

"We'll join you." Darq nodded at his brothers and Glynn. "That should deter anyone from snooping around or attempting any surprise attacks."

"It will only be for tonight," Balen told them. "I think it's time we left Arvael. Arguing with the clan leaders isn't getting us anywhere. Even if Cray and his friends aren't traitors, tempers are high and everyone is on edge. We should leave now before the whole thing gets out of hand."

Darq sighed. "As much as I hate it, I agree."

"So, we're going back to Landale?" Talas asked.

"No," Balen answered, surprising everyone. "First, we're going to Bel-gard. I want to speak with King Orlan. Perhaps if the giants will help us, the cretes will change their minds."

"Do you really think the giants would agree to go to war?" Rayad asked.

"There's only one way to find out."

Kyrin glanced warily at the window near her hammock. They had closed and bolted the shutters, but what if someone prowled around out there in the darkness? At least Darq, Novan, and the others would stand guard. Surely no one could get past them unnoticed. She tried to rest easy as she prepared for bed knowing that even if someone did manage to get to one of the two bedroom windows, Leetra wouldn't sleep for hours, if at all.

Changing out of her borrowed clothing, Kyrin put on a pair of linen pants and a short-sleeved shirt. With the uncertainty of tonight, it felt better to remain fully dressed than in a nightgown. At the washstand near the door, she wet a cloth and pushed up her sleeves to wash away the paint Trenna had applied. She scrubbed her left arm clean first before turning to her right one.

When she came to the trillium, she hesitated and stared at it for a long moment. Trenna had created such a lovely design. She turned to Leetra. "Do you have any tattoo supplies?"

Leetra looked up from fiddling with a feather from her hair. "Not with me, but I'm sure Sonah does. Why?"

"Can you duplicate this trillium?"

Leetra's brows lifted, but something resembling respect lit her eyes. After all, tattoos were a significant and meaningful part of crete culture that most outsiders probably had no interest in. She nodded. "Sure."

She slipped from her hammock and out the door.

While she was gone, Kyrin finished cleaning all but the trillium from her arm. A couple of minutes later, Leetra returned with a small wooden box containing three jars of brown ink and a collection of brushes. She nodded to the floor. "You can sit down."

Kyrin knelt on the floor, and Leetra sat cross-legged beside her. She had never considered Leetra a close friend but, right now, they shared a certain camaraderie.

"Just hold very still," Leetra instructed. "Once this goes on and sits for a few minutes, it's permanent."

Kyrin nodded, stiffening her body and breathing carefully. She watched Leetra open the lightest bottle of ink and dip in a very thin brush. Then she went to work tracing an outline around the painted on flower. Once it was dry, she wiped off the rest of the paint and filled in the outline.

"So what's the significance of a trillium?" Leetra asked, her voice unusually soft.

"It reminds me of my father." It would be a way to carry the memory of him with her, much like the stone necklace she almost never took off. She touched the stone with her left hand and breathed deeply to stop the emotion from taking hold of her.

"I'm sorry."

Kyrin looked over at Leetra again and met her eyes. In the dim room, they were a deep royal purple and filled with a solemn seriousness Kyrin hadn't seen before.

"I'm sorry about your father," she went on, her voice still soft and earnest.

Though Kyrin had seen how what took place in Valcré had affected her, Leetra had never spoken of it like this.

She shook her head and dropped her gaze. "I really should've seen Falcor for who he truly was. I don't know how I was so blind."

Kyrin just stared at her for a moment. She spoke without anger or detachment. Her walls were down, allowing a rare sincerity to shine through.

"Thank you," Kyrin murmured. She tipped her head a little to get a better look at Leetra's face. "But it wasn't anyone's fault. Elôm allowed my father to die for a purpose. I may never fully heal from it, but at least I know his death wasn't meaningless. In the end, it brought my family together in a way it never was before—not even when I was young, before Tarvin Hall."

Leetra nodded slowly and met Kyrin's gaze for a moment. "He also left behind a legacy in his children that would bring great pride to any father."

Kyrin's lungs tightened up and pressure welled in her eyes. She had never heard Leetra pay anyone such a meaningful compliment, considering how seriously cretes took their family legacies. A smile grew on Kyrin's face, and to her surprise, Leetra offered a genuine and open smile in return. It was as if Kyrin were catching a glimpse of the real Leetra for the first time.

Quiet settled around them again as Leetra worked on the tattoo, but it was a comfortable silence. Sometime later, Leetra announced she was done and now they just needed to let it dry. Several minutes passed before she took a rag and washed off the excess ink to reveal the finished tattoo. Kyrin twisted her arm around to inspect it. Though only in brown and not the vibrant blue paint, the new tattoo was even more beautiful than the temporary one. Leetra had done a masterful job in blending the different shades of brown to create a very lifelike depiction of a trillium.

"It's perfect." She smiled again at Leetra. "Thank you."

Leetra nodded as she gathered up the supplies to return to Sonah. "It was an honor to do it for you."

JACE RUBBED HIS fingers against his tired eyes. His life seemed characterized by sleepless nights. Though he had tried to rest and trust that Darq and the others had the house secure, every little sound had him wide-awake. But dawn arrived without incident. He thanked Elôm for this and asked forgiveness for his lack of trust. As much as he had learned and changed in the last year, he still found it difficult not to expect the worst of both situations and people. He comforted himself with the fact that he hadn't been the only one. Rayad had tossed and turned all night long, as had others.

Yet, despite the lack of adequate sleep, a sense of determination and new purpose surrounded them this morning. As intriguing as parts of it were, Jace couldn't say he'd be disappointed to leave Arvael behind. It would be good to set foot on solid ground again.

After folding and stacking the bedding they'd used, they all left the bedroom, their packs in tow. Female voices drifted from the dining room as they descended the stairs. Kyrin and Leetra were setting the table and talking almost like old friends. Odd. In the two years she'd been in camp, Jace hadn't known Leetra to be very talkative unless angered. They quieted, and Leetra darted a glance at Timothy. Kyrin had pointed them out dancing last night, which was a huge step forward, considering how pointedly Leetra had ignored Timothy at Warin and Lenae's wedding.

But Jace's attention didn't linger on them, instead focusing on Kyrin. When she reached to set a cup on the table, a brown trillium tattoo peeked out just below her sleeve. He wasn't surprised. When she looked up, she met his eyes and offered a smile, though the weariness in it said she probably hadn't slept any more than he had. It would be good for her to get out of Arvael as well. It seemed to dredge up too many painful memories.

Just as the women finished getting breakfast on the table, Captain Darq and the other crete men joined them from outside.

"Did you see anyone last night?" Rayad asked.

Darq shook his head. "No. Everything was quiet."

Before breakfast began, Talas, Leetra, Timothy, and Aaron excused themselves to say goodbye to their families. Once they had left, everyone bowed their heads while Novan offered thanks for the food and prayed for the safety and success of Balen and their group. They then passed around the food.

From the head of the table, Novan looked at Balen. "Naeth would like to accompany you—not just to Bel-gard, but back to Landale. We all feel there should be Tarns actively fighting on the right side of this struggle."

Balen nodded. "We appreciate the help. Your people have been instrumental in our fight."

"Speaking of which, Glynn is going to remain here and work with Novan to find out just how many cretes will fight with us if we were to try to take back Samara," Darq said. He shrugged. "Perhaps it will be enough."

Shortly after they finished their meal, Talas and the others returned with Trenna so she could say goodbye. Everyone gathered up their belongings, said farewell to Sonah, and thanked her for her hospitality. With Darq and Novan in the lead, they left the house and headed for Dragon Rest.

Along the way, Jace fought to overcome his fear of heights and take in the scenery one last time before leaving it behind. After all, he probably wouldn't visit again, at least not very willingly. Despite the heights, he liked the cretes' rugged lifestyle. Even their city life didn't feel as confining and oppressive as cities back in Arcacia. He could happily live in the forest like this had the city been built on the ground instead.

Arriving at Dragon Rest, they gathered their dragons to saddle them and load their supplies. Just before they finished, Jace spotted Lord Vallan and his men along with a couple of the supportive clan leaders.

"We wanted to see you off," Lord Vallan told Balen. "It pains me that you're leaving on last night's terms, though I understand your decision."

"It's no reflection on you," Balen assured him. "Regardless of last night, we've received great hospitality here. We just don't want to cause any further discord among your people."

"Perhaps someday, Elôm willing, you can visit under better circumstances and receive a more fitting welcome."

"I'd like that."

Lord Vallan glanced around at the group. "I wish you all well and pray that things go as you hope in Bel-gard." He lowered his voice a little. "I cannot guarantee it, but, should you convince the Dorlanders to join you in your fight, it may go a long way in convincing the other clan leaders to change their minds. Whatever the clans feel about Arcacia and Samara, I don't believe any of them would turn against the giants. They're our closest allies."

"Then we too will pray that they will be inclined to offer us aid."

The two lords shook hands, and Vallan bid the rest of them farewell.

Ready to depart, everyone traded final goodbyes. Novan shared a hug with his son, and though both of them maintained a strong face, Jace understood how hard it was to part from family. Especially under uncertain circumstances. This was especially evident when Trenna gave Talas a tight hug. The girl wasn't as good at hiding her emotions. Tears wet her eyes, but she kept up a bright smile.

After saying goodbye to Kyrin and Kaden, she turned to Michael. Jace worked to hide a smile as they traded a rather awkward, but sweet farewell.

At last, they all turned to their dragons and mounted. Calling goodbye, they each took to the sky, and Dragon Rest shrank behind them, soon disappearing amidst the trees. Putting the sun on their left, they turned south toward Dorland's capital of Bel-gard.

Anne welcomed another two days of sun with only one day of rain in between. It provided the perfect opportunity to take the horses out for a good ride. Not to mention an opportunity to make good on her promise to Trask to visit his father more often. She hadn't seen him since the party a week ago.

After changing into their riding clothes after lunch, Anne and Elanor met Elian outside, where their three horses were saddled and waiting. Anne took up her horse's reins and pulled herself up into the saddle. The white mare danced in place a little, eager to set out. Anne didn't blame her. It would be nice to go for a good run if the roads weren't still so muddy. They would have to take it easy until things dried up a bit . . . if they dried up. Anne was beginning to wonder.

They set off at a brisk walk. Anne angled toward the forest road first, unable to keep from hoping Trask might just happen to meet them somewhere along the way. It depended on just how closely his men watched Marlton. As good as the sun felt, the shade was nice. All the moisture in the air created very humid weather. Even so, getting out was freeing from the heavy weight of uncertainties that hounded them lately. Anne even found herself enjoying a couple of good laughs with Elanor over purely silly things.

An hour and a half after they left Marlton, they made their way to the edge of Landale. A little of Anne's joy faded when they spotted Dagren's guards ahead, but she was determined to keep up a cheerful attitude for Baron Grey. So, she pasted on a smile when they neared the guards, who called them to a halt.

"What's your business in the village?" one of the men questioned.

"I am Lady Anne of Marlton and this is Lady Elanor. We've come to visit the baron." Anne spoke sweetly despite her irritation with the situation. The more innocent they appeared the better.

The man gave her a long look before shifting it to Elanor and Elian as if searching for something amiss. Anne resisted the urge to make sure the dagger she had in a sheath under her skirt remained well-hidden. Of course, it wouldn't be very effective against armed soldiers, but she felt better lightly armed than not at all these days.

"Is there a problem?" she asked after a moment. She put on her best innocent damsel act. "Surely you can't suspect two young women of causing any trouble."

The guard met her eyes again before waving them through. "Carry on."

Anne nudged her horse forward again, and they rode into the village. She glanced at the surrounding fields along the way. They could hardly be called such—just large patches of standing water and mud. Only scattered clumps of sickly, waterlogged crops had broken through the brown sludge. Her father was right. If things didn't change soon, it would be a hard winter for many people.

They rode into the courtyard of Landale, and a smile broke across Anne's face. Baron Grey stood out in the sun and appeared much healthier today. Though still too thin, his eyes were not so tired and held a twinkle, and color had returned to his face. Trask's visit must have done a world of good. He offered a wide, welcoming smile as they halted the horses and dismounted.

After handing her horse off to one of the waiting stable hands, Anne met Grey with a hug. "You're looking well, my lord."

He nodded as they parted again. "Yes, this sunshine certainly helps."

Anne agreed. "The roads are still a bit sloppy for riding," she said as she glanced down at her mud-spattered riding skirt, "but it's so good to be out."

"I was thinking of taking a ride myself later. I want to see just how bad the crops are."

"We noticed the fields on the way in. It doesn't look good."

"That's what I've been told." Grey grimaced, and then shook his head, recovering his smile. "But let's not talk of that while you're here." He greeted Elanor and Elian and motioned for them all to follow. "Why don't we talk in the garden? No sense in being inside on a day like this."

They walked around the castle and into the garden. Many of the decorative flowers had failed to bloom in the wet earth, but enough greenery managed to survive to brighten up the place. When they reached a grouping of benches near the central fountain, they all took seats.

Baron Grey set his gaze on Anne. He spoke quietly, but with enthusiasm. "Trask told me the news. Congratulations. I can't tell you how happy I am for you."

Anne grinned. "I'm sure he'd agree with me in saying it was time. Now, we just have to go through with it."

And, hopefully, it wouldn't take as long to get married as it had just to become betrothed.

"I pray it will all come together for you. I think it would do you both a lot of good."

Anne nodded in agreement. She was more than ready now.

"I see you are wearing one of Katrina's necklaces."

Anne glanced down at the pendant. "Trask gave it to me the other day. He thought it would be less suspicious than a ring."

Grey smiled warmly. "It looks lovely on you, just like it did on his mother. It was one of her favorites. Do you remember her?"

"Yes, I do. She was a very lovely woman." Though she'd had darker hair than Trask, she'd had the same green eyes. Trask looked a lot like her. He also had her driving compassion for others.

"She used to watch you and Trask and say, 'those two will marry one day.'"

"Did she?" Anne laughed, considering how Trask had teased and tormented her more than anything as a child. "I suppose she never expected it would take so long."

Grey shrugged. "Well, Elôm has a way of working things out when they're supposed to."

Anne nodded, praying that the wait all these years had been the right choice and that it would soon be over. It was difficult not to know when she and Trask could actually marry.

"Whenever it finally happens, I'm sure we can find a way to make you a part of it."

"I would like that," Grey said, his eyes crinkling with another smile.

THE RINGING ECHO of blades bounced off the circular walls of the training court inside Auréa. Daniel blocked a high strike and pressed against his opponent's blade. The young man backpedaled, leaving Daniel with an opening to attack. He swung low and then across the man's middle. Both attempts were blocked, but with another thrust, Daniel had his sword point pressed against his sparring partner's chest. He breathed out hard and shook his head as he lowered his blade. The young man hadn't even made an effort to block that last attack.

"How am I supposed to know if I am a halfway decent swordsman if you always let me win? You're not going to hurt me with a blunt blade, and even if you did, it's not like I'd have you arrested." He tried to temper his frustration and soften his tone. He hadn't minded so much when he was young and it was all fun and games, but he took it more seriously these days.

"Now, come on. Fight me. For real this time." He raised the sword for a second match, but the young man sent a questioning glance at the other instructors. Daniel sighed and let the sword drop. Shaking his head again, he turned to look around the room. He put his arms out in exasperation. Surely, someone had the guts to actually try to beat him. "Is there anyone who will give me a proper fight?"

"I will."

Daniel's gaze shifted to where Aric stood in the doorway. How long had he been there? Daniel had watched him spar before. The man was one of the most skilled swordsmen at Auréa. He had to be to have secured the position as head of security.

Daniel nodded eagerly. "Thank you."

Aric strode in and unbuckled his jerkin and sword belt. "Like you said, you won't know what kind of swordsman you are if you're never challenged." He handed his jerkin and sword to one of the attendants and took the blunt practice sword from Daniel's previous sparring partner, who backed quickly to the perimeter of the room.

Giving the sword a few test swings to get the feel of it, Aric faced him. Daniel took his own sword in both hands. He had the distinct feeling he was about to get exactly what he wanted, and he honestly couldn't say how he would fare against it. Both excitement and hesitance rose up inside him. He could look like a complete fool in the next few minutes. He fought to keep his ego in check these days, but it would sting nonetheless.

Aric nodded his go ahead, and Daniel attacked, tentatively at first. They traded a few blows in relatively slow succession before the tempo increased. Within the first couple of minutes, Daniel could tell he faced a far more skilled and determined opponent than he had previously. He liked it. It allowed him to fight with the same determination. It also required far greater concentration.

The minutes stretched out. Moisture built on Daniel's skin and plastered his shirt to his back. When was the last time he'd built up such a sweat in practice? Even his arms started to burn. As far as he could tell, the match was pretty even—both of them attacking and defending equally. However, there were several moments when Aric's sword nearly found his flesh. Though he reacted in time to block, his rapid defense was awkward and sloppy. If he'd had a moment, he would have sent his trainers a scowl. So much for their praise of his "flawless" technique. He wouldn't have had them punished for accidentally injuring him in a real training session, but he just might for lying and coddling him.

A long ten minutes into the match, Daniel barely blocked a stinging blow to the shoulder, but it threw him off balance. In the split second before he could recover, cold metal rested against the side of his neck, and just like that, the fight was over. He stood for a moment in surprise, his chest heaving as he stared down at Aric's sword. No one had bested him since his early days of training. A grin split his face and a breathless laugh escaped. Finally, someone who treated him like a man and not just royalty. Though he'd always held Aric in high regard, his respect grew a hundredfold.

Aric removed the sword from his neck and met his gaze.

"Thank you," Daniel said, working to catch his breath. "That's the best workout I've had . . . ever."

Aric nodded, also breathing heavily. "You're good. You have a few areas to work on, but you'd be a match for anyone, save the most experienced swordsmen."

Daniel appreciated both his honesty and praise. Very few men besides Ben spoke to him so openly. "I'll be sure to work on those areas." He cast a hard look at his trainers, who ducked their heads. "Providing I can find someone to properly spar with."

"I'd be happy to," Aric offered.

Daniel smiled "I would certainly appreciate that."

"Tomorrow then?"

Daniel nodded. "Tomorrow."

Aric gathered his jerkin and sword and left the training court. Daniel turned and approached his trainers, who looked at him rather sheepishly.

"I'm not a fragile piece of glass that will shatter at the first misstep," he said. "I can take a hit."

"Yes, my lord," the oldest of them replied with a bow.

Daniel didn't believe for a moment that any of them would change their ways. But at least he had Aric to practice with now. He already looked forward to tomorrow. Maybe he would take a few hits. Not that he relished the pain, but he was sick of being treated like a woman when it came to his training. Sometimes pain was the best way to learn. It encouraged focus and discipline.

He handed off his practice sword and strode out of the court, heading in the direction of his chambers. When he reached the family wing of the palace, Davira's door opened ahead of him. His sister sidled out first, a saucy smile on her face. One of the security guards, Collin, followed on her heels.

Daniel hadn't failed to notice their little rendezvouses over the last year, though he'd just as soon be ignorant. Disgust boiled up in his stomach. It was bound to happen, of course. It always did when an attractive new face arrived at Auréa. He supposed he couldn't blame Collin entirely. His sister was a master at luring men in and trapping them for her own personal amusement before thoughtlessly casting them aside as soon as she was bored. By the time they realized their mistake, they were already too entangled in her web to free themselves from her control without risking ruin. Daniel had witnessed several staff dismissals and disappearances of a highly suspicious nature over the last few years.

They didn't notice him at first, but when Collin turned to leave, he caught Daniel's eyes. Surprise, and then shame, claimed his face as he dropped his gaze.

"My lord," he murmured, keeping his head down as they passed each other.

He definitely bore the look of a man who knew he'd been trapped and had no escape. Regret stung Daniel. He should have warned Collin about his sister's wiles when he'd first arrived. However, back then, Daniel was so bent on defying his father and having his own way that he hadn't much cared what went on with Davira and the staff.

But the men's shame wasn't even the worst of it. How many pregnancies had his sister aborted because of these trysts? Three, at least, that he was aware of, and only because his mother knew. No doubt Davira had kept even more secret. It hurt Daniel now more than it had a couple of years ago to think of the nieces or nephews he'd lost. Surely, he would meet them one day in eternity.

He slowed when he neared Davira and received her conceited smirk. She seemed to dare him to condemn her lifestyle. As much as she loved their father, it did surprise him that she lived so promiscuously. If there was one thing he could praise his father for, it was being a faithful husband to their mother all these years. It was the one and only thing Daniel sought to emulate, though he credited his mother more for this desire. She'd drilled her insistence that he save himself for his future wife into him from the moment he'd first noticed the female gender. Though he'd taken some of his past "relationships" further than he should have, her persistent voice always echoed at the back of his mind and prevented him from taking actions he knew he'd regret now, thank Elôm. He really needed to make sure he took the time to thank his mother properly as well.

The fact that he didn't imitate his sister's behavior seemed to infuriate Davira, and she never grew tired of badgering him over it. He set his gaze ahead, intent on distancing himself from her before she could make any of her lewd comments. Just as he passed, she said, "Father was looking for you."

He paused and glanced back. What could he want now?

Davira sashayed a step closer, but stopped short, wrinkling her nose. "I suggest you find out what he wants. But wash up first. You smell."

He snorted, half tempted to pull off his sweat-drenched shirt and toss it at her, as he would have when they were children, just to hear her shriek. Now that they were both adults, he wasn't sure that was wise. His sister had a very dangerous way about her. Best not provoke her since he honestly didn't know how she might respond.

"You're lucky I'm in a good mood," he muttered as he stalked on down the hall.

Nearing his room, he made a sudden direction change. Davira was right about one thing. He did need to clean up and one pitcher of water from the washstand would hardly be sufficient.

Back on ground level, he headed out the back of the palace to the covered pool overlooking the garden. The still water offered promise of refreshment after his intense workout. Maybe he could wash away thoughts of Davira along with the sweat. He tugged off his boots and stockings first and then peeled off his shirt. He paused when he caught sight of a young maid nearby, waiting with a towel for when he finished his swim. How did the servants always know exactly where to be even when he wished they wouldn't? He couldn't very well send her away without making her feel like she'd done something wrong, so he just sighed and decided against removing his pants. Even in undershorts, he wouldn't have been comfortable, and the poor girl was already halfway to blushing as it was, though she did avert her eyes.

Daniel waded into the pool up to his waist and then dove in to submerge himself completely. The cool water washed over him, soothing the fatigued muscles in his arms and back that would surely be sore come morning. He stayed under until his lungs craved oxygen and then pushed to the surface. The refreshment did indeed restore his good mood.

In no hurry, he swam the length of the pool a few times before climbing out. He stood at the edge, dripping, and the servant girl hurried forward with her towel. He took it from her before she got too close. Davira would just stand there and let the servants towel dry her, but he wasn't about to do anything of the sort. He was more than capable of drying and dressing himself. Thank Elôm he'd convinced his manservant of that a long time ago.

He scrubbed the towel against his wet hair and then swiped it across his arms. "Would you get a couple more towels please?"

The girl nodded and hurried to do his bidding. When she returned, she handed them over and stepped back.

"Thank you," he said.

She looked down shyly, not meeting his eyes. She was a pretty thing with a sweet and innocent face, though a bit young. Not that his father would ever allow him to entertain such thoughts as seriously pursuing one of the servants or any other woman of such a lowly position. It would have to be someone of noble birth if his father were to approve. Daniel hadn't met any noblewoman yet that he felt a real connection to. And he couldn't imagine having a wife who didn't share his faith in Elôm, though, at the rate his father was imprisoning and killing them all off, he was probably doomed to remain single for the rest of his life—a gloomy prospect. He offered a silent prayer to Elôm that this wouldn't be his lot.

With the extra towels, Daniel dried his pants as much as possible, so he wouldn't leave a trail of water through the palace, and went inside. He took a route to avoid running into Davira again and reached his door. He pushed it open, halting after his first step inside. His father sat in one of his chairs, waiting for him.

DANIEL STOOD IN the doorway and stared at his father. Tension wrung his previously relaxed muscles. He made a cursory scan of the room to make sure he'd hidden the verses he'd been studying earlier. His father almost never came to his chambers. He'd have to be far more careful about what he left lying around from now on. His father did have a thin stack of papers in his hand, but they did not look familiar.

Finally, he stepped fully into the room and closed the door. "Father," he said, unable to hide his suspicious tone.

His father must have picked up on it. "Since you do everything in your power to avoid communication, this seemed to be the only way to get you to talk."

Daniel locked his teeth together to keep from retorting and complaining over the invasion of his privacy. Apparently, he couldn't even count on finding solitude in his own rooms anymore. Working to cool the flame of ire, he strode past his father and into his bedroom to his wardrobe, where he changed into a pair of dry clothes.

"I heard you sparred with Aric." His father's voice came from the sitting room.

"Yes." Daniel shoved his arms and head into a linen shirt and tucked it hastily into the waistband of his pants. He grabbed his boots and walked into the sitting room to face his father. "It was the first real match I've ever had. Honestly, if you're the one who ordered the men to take it easy on me, you're doing me a great disservice. I didn't even know until today that I had areas in need of improvement."

Daniel dropped down in the chair across from his father and pulled on his boots. "So, what was so important it has you waiting for me in my room? I doubt it has anything to do with my sparring session."

His father lifted the papers in his hand. "It's high time you were more involved in the running of things here at Auréa."

Daniel barely bit back a sigh. Of course, what prince wasn't expected to work alongside his father in learning the ins and outs of running a kingdom? But that was just the problem. He hated to share the same space as his father, let alone work with him. Still, he swallowed his objections, bitter tasting as they were. If there was any chance of reconciliation between them, wouldn't Elôm desire him to seek it? After all, maybe a willing attitude might just soften his father, perhaps even to the point that Daniel could broach the subject of Elôm.

"What sort of involvement did you have in mind?" he asked, careful to hide his lingering reluctance.

In response, his father narrowed his eyes probingly.

For pity's sake, couldn't the man just be thankful he was attempting to curb his rebellion instead of greeting it with suspicion?

Not finding whatever answers he sought, his father replied, "My birthday celebration is little more than a week away, as well as the opening of the arena."

Daniel's innards recoiled. He'd stayed as far away from the arena as he could over the years. He hadn't liked the idea of such violence from the beginning, never mind now when he believed just like the people who would die there in droves. If there were any way he could put a stop to it, he wouldn't hesitate to do so.

His father continued. "Final preparations must be made. I want you to go down to the prison camp near Fort Rivor and choose some of the strongest prisoners to bring back for participation in the games."

Heated resistance flushed through Daniel's body. He would compromise and work with his father on some things but never something like this. He shook his head. "No."

Their eyes locked.

"Why not?"

"I won't choose people to die in the arena. I want no part of it."

His father's expression hardened. "They're criminals. What difference does it make if they die in the arena or at the execution block?"

"I won't do it."

Suspicion returned to his father's eyes, though much more pronounced. "They deserve to die for their treason."

Daniel swallowed hard and sat up straighter, leaning toward his father. "Well, I don't believe it's right."

Their gazes held for a charged moment, and then his father slapped his papers down on the short table between them. "Come with me."

He pushed up from his seat with a glare that dared Daniel not to follow. Daniel sat for a moment, all the old rebellion holding him in place, but finally he complied. His father stormed out of the room. Daniel followed, stormy emotions brewing inside of him.

"Where are we going?" he demanded, but his father wouldn't answer.

They strode through the palace, their angry footsteps echoing in the halls and sending the servants backing away quickly. Exiting the rear entrance of the palace, they headed in a direct line across the courtyard . . . straight toward the temple. Daniel stopped, and his father turned on him the moment his footsteps ceased.

Daniel threw out his hands. "What is this? Are you really going to drag me inside and test my loyalty? Your own son?"

His father stepped closer, and they squared off, just like they had so many times in the past.

"Your behavior has been questionable as of late, and I aim to get to the bottom of it."

"Oh, so I start acting more responsible and that makes me a traitor?"

"It's your apparent sympathy for traitors that has called your loyalty into question. Now get inside that temple and prove to me those sympathies haven't turned you into a rebel." His father's voice lowered dangerously. "Unless you refuse."

Daniel glared back at him before his gaze slid to the temple. This was it. Now the truth would come out. He stepped around his father and marched determinedly toward the temple. Cool shadows swallowed him as he passed through the doors and headed straight into the belly of the cavernous structure. The hazy red glow of candles drew him right to the golden figures upraised on their altar to tower over all who entered. He planted his fists on his hips and glared at them in defiance before turning to his father, who followed just behind him.

"Well, I'm here."

His father scorched him with that daring look again. "Now bow and prove your devotion."

Daniel couldn't contain a scoff. "They're idols. They can't even see or hear me."

"They are your gods." His father's voice thundered against the walls.

"No, they're not . . . I believe in Elôm."

There, it was done. No more hiding. No more pretending. He might die for it, but he wouldn't tiptoe around it anymore.

His father's eyes bulged, but Daniel wasn't finished.

"Furthermore, these rumors you're so quick to dismiss are true. Elon has risen from the dead. Three days after you put that dagger in His chest, I saw Him. I stood before Him and spoke to Him."

His father looked ready to explode. "You're lying!"

"You think I would bet my entire life on a lie?"

"I killed him. I—"

"Yes, you did," Daniel cut in. "It's something I will never forget. He did die that day, but then He rose from the dead as Savior of Ilyon, and He will forever have my allegiance."

He let a long sigh seep out as his anger faded to a quiet determination. "Father, please, just listen to me. I'm telling you the truth. Elon is alive, and I did speak with Him. I know you see believers in Elôm as traitors, but we are not your enemies. We're not a threat to you. The only reason there is fighting is because *you* are making enemies. You're taking away liberties, not only from your own people, but from those who should be our allies. Please, stop and think about this. You can continue to worship Aertus and Vilai just as you please—that is entirely your choice— but give us the freedom to choose to worship our God. People don't have to keep dying over this."

His father stared intensely at him with an expression Daniel couldn't interpret. For one incredible moment, hope grew that his father might actually consider what he'd said, until the next words out of his mouth.

"You've been brainwashed."

Daniel let his head slump forward with a groan. He wanted to pull his hair out.

"You've let their lies corrupt you! This is exactly why they must be eliminated."

Daniel shook his head, grinding his words through clenched teeth. "I'm thinking perfectly clearly. If anyone's been brainwashed, it's everyone who believes a few hundred pounds of gold or two balls of rock in the sky are capable of hearing or answering prayers and receiving worship."

His father's amber eyes sparked like molten metal, and he gestured sharply to the entrance of the temple. "Get out!"

Daniel didn't wait to be told twice. He strode through the short hall with the growing desire to burn the whole thing to the ground, starting with the idols, just for the satisfaction of watching them melt into a puddle.

Outside, he slowed, but his father barged out behind him and gripped his arm. "Inside." He shoved him toward the palace.

Daniel yanked his arm away. If his father wanted to throw him down in the dungeon or even take him straight to the execution block, he could walk there himself. They entered the palace the same way they'd left. Just inside, they happened across Aric.

His father snapped his name and motioned to Daniel. "Take him to my office and keep him there until I'm ready to speak to him." He shot Daniel a furious look. "Use force if necessary."

Daniel glared back at his father, tempted to resist just to spite him, but he thought better of it. Instead, he set off for the office without even pausing to see if Aric followed. When he reached it, he shoved the door with enough force that it banged against the wall when it swung open. He sat down hard in the chair near his father's desk and rubbed his fingers into his forehead. He needed to control his temper, but it was so blasted infuriating that his father wouldn't listen to an ounce of reason.

Aric entered the room and closed the door. Daniel breathed deeply in and out and let his anger cool. It took a while, and all that time he figured his father must be deciding his fate. Once calm, he looked up at Aric, who stood in silence.

"Don't worry. I won't try to escape." Whatever befell him because of this was in Elôm's hands, as much as his father would insist otherwise. Surely, his father wouldn't go so far as to execute him. After all, Elon had said He could use Daniel to make a difference. Then again, he supposed that difference could come from his death. But whatever fate Elôm allowed, he was ready to face it.

Aric tipped his head curiously. "What happened?"

"I guess you might as well know, since the whole palace will hear by suppertime." Daniel sat back in his chair. "I'm a believer in Elôm. A *traitor*."

To his surprise, Aric showed almost no reaction at first. When he did react, it came in a slow-growing smile.

Daniel frowned. "Why does that amuse you?"

Aric glanced at the door before taking a couple of steps closer and lowering his voice. "Because, my lord, I too am an Elôm-believing traitor."

DANIEL'S EYES ROUNDED. Aric was a believer? Since when?

Before he could voice these questions, heavy footsteps echoed outside the door, and Aric hastily returned to his guard position. Daniel still gaped at him a moment and struggled to refocus on his own plight rather than on the stunning revelation that one of his father's most trusted men had been living under the same pretense as he had. And doing a much better job of it, apparently.

The door swung open to admit his father, and his mother and Davira followed. Daniel pushed to his feet and shared a look with his mother, whose deep green eyes held a dire solemnity. His gaze then tangled with his sister. If looks could kill, his father wouldn't even need to execute him. He almost feared she might somehow spit venom at him.

Tearing his eyes away, Daniel focused on his father. Though he appeared to have calmed, anger still simmered in his taut expression.

"I hope you've had adequate time to consider the foolishness of your actions and are ready to dismiss them as some sort of joke."

Daniel crossed his arms. He would do his best not to let his temper take over this time. "It's no joke to me."

His father threw up his hands and turned to Daniel's mother. "You see?"

Her face pinched, and he spun around to face Daniel again. "Do you understand what this is? This is *treason*." His voice lowered. "I could have you executed. Anyone else would already be in the dungeon. I can still give the order."

Daniel drew a fortifying breath. "If you'd go so far as to execute your own son and heir, then it just proves you've taken this way too far."

His father's fist balled as he glared at him, but behind the anger, Daniel caught a glimpse of something else—a tortured indecision. Maybe his father really did care what happened to him.

His mother stepped in and rested her hand gently on his father's arm. She spoke quietly as if only for him to hear, but Daniel still caught her words.

"Just give him time to see the error of his ways."

Well, that would never happen, but, considering his life was on the line, Daniel wouldn't argue.

His father breathed hard, angry breaths as the indecision still warred on his face. Before he could respond, Davira cut in with words like poison.

"What will happen if word gets out that you spared him? All the other traitors just like him will feel that they've won a victory."

Daniel glared at his sister. Did she really want him dead so badly?

Their father glanced at her, but when his eyes refocused on Daniel, much of the tortured uncertainty had subsided. "You will be confined to the palace grounds until you get some sense back into your head." He turned to Aric. "Let all the guards know he is not allowed beyond the wall under any circumstances, by my order. And if anyone leaks any of this to the outside population, they are to be arrested and executed."

"Yes, my lord."

Aric shared an apologetic glance with Daniel.

However, Daniel's attention snapped back to his father, who said, "I don't care how long or what it takes, I will not allow you to continue down this path."

The almost desperate way in which he said it led Daniel to wonder if, in some twisted way, there was love behind it. Miss Altair had said she thought his father loved him. He hadn't believed it, but if it weren't true, why wasn't he on his way to the dungeon right now? Something deep down must be staying his father's hand.

But then the more familiar hardness returned to his father's face. "Now tell me who convinced you to believe such rubbish."

"I did tell you. Elon."

His father shook his head in a stubborn refusal to believe Elon had risen from the dead. "I know you must have talked with someone. Who was it?"

Daniel sighed and rubbed his forehead. This would give him a headache yet. "Even if I did talk to someone, there's no way in Ilyon that I would give them up, so you might as well quit trying."

"One way or another, I will find out," his father promised. "And until you come to your senses, you will not leave this palace."

"Then I guess I'll be a prisoner here for the rest of my life." With that, Daniel turned for the door. He hesitated just a little to see if his father would order him back into the office, but he didn't. Relieved, Daniel headed for his room. Just before he reached his door, his mother called to him. He slowed and waited for her to catch up.

"Daniel, I know you're angry right now, but you must let your father see your repentance over this. Let him see it as a temporary transgression."

Daniel shook his head. "I'm not repentant. This is what I believe, and I won't apologize for it."

His mother grabbed his arm to stop him. "Then pretend," she said with surprising force. "I'm doing *everything* I can to keep you alive."

Daniel released a heavy sigh and rested his hands on his mother's shoulders. "I'm sorry, Mother, but I can't do that. My faith is what it is, and if it gets me killed, then that's the will of Elôm. He can just as easily keep me alive and doesn't need me to cover up my faith to do it. I accept whatever He chooses for me. Besides, do you really believe Father would execute me? He has no other heir."

"I don't believe he has any intention to, but I'm not completely certain he can't be persuaded to change his mind."

"By Davira?"

"Her and others who might think that not even you should get away with treason. Just, whatever you do, don't provoke him. He may do something in a fit of rage that he wouldn't normally do otherwise."

Daniel remained in his room through suppertime and spent the evening hours praying and contemplating. He prayed he hadn't acted recklessly at any point and made his faith known too soon. The last thing he wanted was to jeopardize the plans Elôm had for him.

Evening bled into nighttime, and his candles burned low. He sensed a quietness about the palace that signaled most had gone to bed. Sometime around midnight, he pushed out of his chair and stepped to his door. He eased it open and peered up and down the hall. Nothing stirred. He grabbed his cloak and left his room, creeping past his parents' chambers, which set his heart to pounding even more than usual.

Downstairs, he followed his usual path to the rear door into the courtyard.

"Are you sure it's wise to sneak out tonight?"

Daniel just about jumped right out of his skin at the low voice in the shadows. He spun around as Aric appeared. Daniel breathed out a gusty breath and tried to slow the rib-shattering pounding of his heart. He shook his head, yet his voice came out a bit winded. "How do you know I was sneaking out?"

Aric looked at him keenly. "Because you've been doing it for the last several months."

Daniel raised his brows, and Aric said, "Don't worry, no one else knows."

Thank Elôm. No one but Aric could be trusted with this secret.

"There are people I must see. They need to know what has happened so they can pray for me."

Aric regarded him a moment, but then nodded. "Just be very careful."

"I will." Daniel turned for the door but paused to look back at Aric. "How long have you believed?"

"Quite a few years."

"How have you hidden it so long?"

Aric shook his head, a pained expression on his face. "By doing some things I wish I did not have to . . . or not doing things in hopes of bringing about the greater good."

Captain Altair came to Daniel's mind. Hadn't he and Aric been good friends? Aric had been right there the day Captain Altair was executed. Daniel grimaced. Would he have been able to stand and watch a friend die?

"I'm sorry," Daniel murmured. "I'm sure it's been difficult."

Aric nodded.

"Thanks for letting me know how you believe. At least I have an ally here now."

"Whatever you may need, my lord, I am here to help."

Daniel let a smile grow. "We'll start with that sparring session in the morning."

Aric smiled in return and gave a nod before Daniel let himself out of the palace. Though no rain had fallen all day, clouds blanketed the sky, for which he was thankful. Moonlight would only make him easier to spot. With extreme caution, he crossed the courtyard and slipped out through the hidden gate.

Once within the city, he paused a few times at dark street corners to watch and make sure no one had followed him. He waited extra-long when he reached the corner of Ben's street. Satisfied that no one had tailed him, he crept to the merchant's house and up to the door. No light shone through any of the windows. He hesitated to wake them, but Ben had said he was welcome any day, at any hour. Daniel was going to take his word for it.

He raised his fist and knocked firmly but not so loudly as to raise undue suspicion from any nosy neighbors. After waiting a minute or two, he tried again. In another moment, a dim filtering of light came from under the door and the bolt inside unlocked. The door opened a few inches, and a flickering candle lit up Ben's sleepy face. His eyes widened to full alertness.

"Daniel." He opened the door wider. "Come in."

Daniel slipped through the opening, and Ben closed the door behind him. Mira stood just inside, concern knitting her brow. Ben turned, his candle lighting up the little circle around them.

"Has something happened?" he asked.

"My father knows I believe in Elôm."

The couple's eyes went wide.

"Come, let us sit down." Ben ushered Daniel toward the living room. He lit a few extra candles before joining them at the couches. "The fact that you're here and not in the dungeon awaiting execution tells me that Elôm is at work in this."

With their full attention fixed on him, Daniel shared all that had taken place at the temple and in his father's office. It truly was a miracle he wasn't spending the night in one of the cold cells beneath Auréa, bound for torture and execution. Someone like Ben or Mira wouldn't have even been given the chance to plead their case. He almost felt guilty.

When he finished, he shook his head. "I don't know what to do." He paused, but his heart spilled its inward desire. "Honestly, when I left the palace, deep down I didn't plan to go back. I just want to get out and go to Landale or somewhere—anywhere but here. But how am I to know if that's Elôm's will or if it's to remain at the palace?"

"That is a difficult question," Ben agreed. "What do you believe Elôm is telling you?"

Daniel leaned forward and rubbed his eyes. He wasn't so sure he wanted to know what Elôm was telling him. Finally, he looked up to meet Ben's gaze.

"Running seems like the easy way out . . . the coward's way. The thought of having to deal with my father and sister is difficult to face, but I have more opportunity to do good here than hiding in Landale."

Ben nodded slowly. "Then I think you have your answer."

Though not the answer Daniel wanted, he would have to accept it. "Just pray for me. Davira wants me dead, and there may be others with her who will try to sway my father. I'm not sure if I'll be able to attend the meetings regularly, if at all. I can't stand the thought of losing the fellowship, but thank Elôm that I did discover another believer at the palace. At least I'll have someone to talk to. Pray for him as well. I can't imagine how difficult it has been to hide his faith for as long as he has."

"You can both count on our prayers."

"Thank you," Daniel breathed, weary yet ready to do his Lord's will.

For hours, the three of them sat in the living room and talked quietly about how Daniel might make a positive difference at the palace and how Elôm could use him. It strengthened his heart for the challenge, though he put off leaving until nearly four o'clock in the morning. He had to get back to the palace before daylight. However, the idea of returning was even harder than he thought it would be.

Ben and Mira walked him to the door, where he turned to face them. Though they had been up most of the night, they each had a strong and encouraging smile for him.

"I'm sorry to have wakened you and kept you from your rest," he said.

Ben shook his head. "You don't ever have to apologize for seeking our help. We all need to be there for each other if we are to face these dark days. If the middle of the night is the only time you can come, then you come. The time is not important."

This brought a smile to Daniel's face. "I don't know what I'd do without you two."

"It is our joy to be in this with you," Ben said. "Now, let us send you back to the palace properly with a word of prayer."

The three of them bowed their heads, and Mira took Daniel's hand in a comforting, motherly hold.

"Lord, as Daniel, Your child, returns to the work we believe You have called him to, we pray for Your wisdom, guidance, and protection to be upon him. The dangers are numerous, but we know nothing can touch him without Your permission. Continue to stay his father's hand, and show him what good he can do by facing this challenge and not running from it. Give him both the courage and the strength to stand strong and remain focused on the path You have set before him. We pray this in the name of Your Holy Son, Elon, who called him to this work. Amen."

"Amen," Daniel murmured, using his free hand to rub the sting of tears out of his eyes. What would he do without this incredible couple?

Just before he left, Mira pulled him into a loving hug. "We won't say why, but we will let the others know to pray earnestly for you."

"I appreciate it."

He turned to Ben. They clasped arms, and Ben drew him into his embrace as well, clapping him encouragingly on the back.

"I know the days ahead will be rough, but Elôm wouldn't bring you here and then abandon you. You can count on His presence to guide and strengthen you."

Daniel nodded and they traded their goodbyes, which seemed much more difficult than any other visit before. Finally, he left the house, carrying their love with him as he trudged back to the palace.

When he arrived, he stopped and looked up the slope toward the hidden gate. His heart thumped hard and heavily, and his legs resisted going farther. He glanced over his shoulder to the east, in the direction of Landale, and then down the road to the shore and all the moored ships. So many different escape routes beckoned to him.

"Lord, I don't want to go back in there. I don't want to have anything to do with my father." He paused. Ever since stepping into the temple yesterday, the thought of execution hadn't scared him. Yet, standing here alone, staring up at the palace walls, the fear crept in with all the gruesome images of the executions he'd witnessed. His throat constricted, strangling his voice to a hoarse whisper. "I don't want to die. If there is another way, I need You to make it clear to me."

He waited a long moment, listening to the stillness. Only quietness surrounded him highlighting the gentle nudging toward the palace that a lingering, selfish part of him fought to ignore. With a quiet sigh, he nodded. "Whatever You will."

And he climbed up to the gate and crept back into the palace.

A DAY AND a half after leaving Arvael, the thick forest below thinned and gave way to enormous rolling slopes of fertile meadowland. Kyrin followed the others as they landed in one of these meadows for lunch and found that the lush grass almost reached her waist. Daisies and large blue bellflowers swayed in the breeze gusting down from the mountain peaks that towered just to their left. Meredith would have had such fun exploring the meadow and collecting daisies to weave into crowns.

Pulling her lunch from her pack, Kyrin walked over to Jace, where Gem stared intently off into the distance. A hundred yards away, some sort of deer trotted off toward the mountains. Kyrin's eyes widened. The animal was as large as a horse. It seemed everything was bigger in Dorland, including the wildlife.

Gem let out a low grumble when the animal disappeared over a hill. Kyrin laughed, and Jace patted his dragon on the neck. "We'll see about getting you something to eat soon."

With deer that big roaming around, all their dragons would be able to eat enough to last them a week.

"We'll reach Bel-gard within an hour," Darq announced. "The Dorlanders are used to cretes coming and going from the city, so we'll be able to fly straight to the royal palace."

"Isn't that a bit careless of them?" Rayad asked.

Darq shrugged. "Hospitality is their way. They give everyone the benefit of trust."

Kaden snorted and nudged Talas. "So the exact opposite of the cretes then?"

Talas gave a dry laugh. "Basically."

"Don't get me wrong, though," Darq went on, "they won't tolerate any kind of hostility or cruelty. If there is one area Dorlanders move swiftly in, it's justice when someone has been wronged." He peered off to the south. "I'm hoping Prince Haedrin will be present today. King Orlan is a good man but doesn't have the fire in his blood that younger Dorlanders might. The prince could potentially help sway his father if he were inclined to offer us aid."

Kyrin silently prayed for Prince Haedrin's presence when they met the giants today. Though everyone put up an optimistic front, she could sense the frustration they carried over their failure to secure allies in Arvael.

As much as she would have loved to linger in the peaceful mountain meadow and explore it with Jace, they were in the air again within twenty minutes. They flew lower now, allowing a good view of the surrounding terrain. Kyrin spotted many more large deer along the way, as well as herds of shaggy, gray mountain sheep in the foothills.

Almost an hour later, the untouched meadows gave way to cultivated fields full of equally fertile crops. Now, instead of deer, the grassy meadows were alive with cattle—large reddish-brown beasts with shaggy hair and long horns. Though they grazed placidly, Kyrin didn't think she would want to come across an angry bull or a cow with her calf.

The farms were scattered and widespread, consisting of sturdy log houses and barns. Even from a great height, they appeared incredibly large. Kyrin couldn't imagine what it would be like to come face to face with the giants. She felt small enough around Sam and Tane.

At last, a city appeared in the distance, constructed of hewn rock and built on the slope of a towering mountain, whose snow-capped peak disappeared into the clouds. Everything looked half again the size of a normal city. Though built with simple architecture of clean lines and arches, it appeared as strong as the mountains themselves. From the top of a great wall that put even Samara's border wall to shame, scarlet banners rippled in the breeze and sported some sort of white symbol. It wasn't until they drew nearer that Kyrin was able to make out the shape of a hammer and pickaxe crossed at the center—simple and non-threatening.

Just ahead, on a plateau overlooking the city, rested an enormous castle built right into the mountainside. Again, it lacked the elegance of Auréa, but its magnificence far surpassed any other royal dwelling Kyrin had ever witnessed. At the base, behind a containing wall, lay an open stone courtyard. Here they angled downward and came to land near the gate. From the ground, they all stared up at the castle, rising at least eight stories above them in a magnificent display of precise construction.

The approach of solid footsteps dragged Kyrin's gaze down from the almost dizzying sight of the castle, and she gained her first look at the giants. Two strode toward them, both barrel-chested and at least eight and a half feet tall. Each wore a matching black shirt and long red tabard the color of their banners. Thick leather bracers that could have been leg armor for anyone else were cinched around their massive forearms, and broadswords that must have been nearly as tall as she was hung at their hips. Neither made a move to reach for or even touch the weapons as they curiously regarded the group of dragon riders that had just landed right outside their stronghold. Even so, their alert eyes scanned the entire group. Kyrin wouldn't want to be their enemy. Those swords could easily cut her right in half.

Darq slid off his dragon first to meet the two men, appearing as a mere child next to them.

"Captain Darq," the older of the two guards said in a deep, powerful voice.

Darq nodded politely. "Halsen."

The giant smiled through his thick chestnut beard, which had braids and metal beads woven into it. "You have an interesting group with you. Who have you brought to Bel-gard?"

"King Balen of Samara, as well as several from the Resistance in Landale. We seek audience with King Orlan."

"King Balen," Halsen said in surprise.

Now the rest of the group dismounted, and Balen joined Captain Darq. Even he looked small next to the giants. "Yes. My adoptive father, King Alton, knew your king well, but I have yet to personally make his acquaintance."

"Welcome to Bel-gard, my lord," Halsen said as he and the other giant offered a respectful bow. "Allow me to take you inside to King Orlan right away."

He turned to the other guard. "See that their dragons are fed and left undisturbed."

Kyrin shared a look with Jace. Considering the amount of meat required to feed all of their dragons, the giants were hospitable and generous indeed.

They followed Halsen across the courtyard to the wide steps of the castle entrance. The steps themselves were almost twice as tall as normal, and Jace offered Kyrin his hand to help her climb them. She glanced back at Leetra, who was the shortest of the group, just in time to see her grudgingly accept Timothy's hand. Kyrin shook her head. Thank Elôm that she and Jace hadn't needed to go through such a tedious process.

They passed through the arched gateway into the castle, which had not one, but two portcullises ready to drop into place, as well as an iron-enforced door that two hulking guards pushed open ahead of them. Inside was dim and a bit cold, but torches and tapestries of simple designs chased away much of the bleakness. Kyrin could barely make out where one huge building block ended and another began, they fit together so precisely. It was almost as if the entire castle were carved out of one single piece of stone from the mountain. The deeper they went, the more it appeared that way.

Down a long central hall, they reached another set of impressive doors. Just on the other side lay the grand throne room. Sturdy pillars along each side of the room supported the towering fifty-foot ceiling and led the way to the fur-draped throne at the far end. A man sat there, a little hunched, but with wide, powerful shoulders. His long hair and beard were nearly white, and his mustache was braided into two long braids with thick silver beads at each end. A simple silver crown rested on his head, and what looked like black bear fur trimmed the long scarlet cape draped around him.

Two more giant men stood before him, their backs turned to the group. Both bore long hair—one dark and the other a bit lighter. The lighter one had a two-edged axe strapped to his back, while the other had a longsword. Their rough leather and linen clothing wasn't as fine as the guards' apparel. More like farmers or woodsmen. Even so, they too sported braids and metal beads, which seemed to be typical of Dorland style.

As they drew nearer, the giant with the axe spoke, his voice taut with restrained aggravation. "We need men to help secure the ford and the surrounding area. Three men and a little girl have already died. It's time a detachment of soldiers was sent to drive them out for good."

King Orlan shook his head, his face regretful. "I cannot put soldiers near the border. Our relationship with Arcacia is tenuous. Any show of force could be seen as aggression."

"By defending our own land?" The other giant threw his hands out in disbelief. "And what if Emperor Daican is behind these raids in the first place?"

"You said they were ryriks," the king replied skeptically.

"Yes, but since when do groups of ryriks work in such an orderly fashion or together? Something is going on."

"I will see if there are any volunteers to form a militia to help you defend your farms," King Orlan told him in a pacifying voice. "Until then, I suggest you return home and take whatever precautionary measures you must."

The other giant shook his head, clearly agitated.

Kyrin glanced at Balen. This already didn't look promising for their group. If the king wouldn't even send soldiers to defend his own people, how would he ever agree to help the Resistance?

"And tell Jorvik what?" the giant demanded. "That we're on our own unless a militia decides to form and come to our aid? We all know the chances of that happening."

Before King Orlan could reply, his attention shifted to the approaching group. They all paused several yards from the throne, and Halsen said, "Wait here."

He walked up to the king and murmured something near his ear. The king's thick white brows rose as he peered at their group again. His attention then returned to the other two giants, who had glanced back over their shoulders to see what had caused the interruption. Both were about in their thirties.

"I am sorry," the king said, and the two giants turned to him once again, "but the ford has been a difficult area for centuries. Unless it presents a direct national threat, I cannot send soldiers there and risk a misunderstanding with the emperor."

"Won't, you mean," Kyrin caught the older of the two giants mutter under his breath. His voice rose. "Our family has guarded the ford for generations, but if it falls now to enemy hands, it won't be our fault."

He gave a curt bow and turned to leave. The younger, darker-haired giant followed. They cast a curious glance at the group as they passed but did not stop on their way out of the throne room. When they were gone, the king's attention settled solely on the group as they drew nearer to the throne. His light eyes held kindness and good intentions more befitting an old grandfather.

"King Balen," he said, inclining his head.

"Your Majesty," Balen replied, and everyone gave the giant king a bow.

"Welcome to Bel-gard. It has been some time since a king of Samara has visited these halls."

"Thank you. I've long desired to visit your land. King Alton spoke of both you and your people with great respect."

King Orlan smiled. "He was a good man and a good friend." His gaze shifted to Balen's left. "Captain Darq. It is good to see your face again. How is Lord Vallan?"

Kyrin exchanged a look with her brothers and Jace. The king was very gregarious but seemed oblivious to more urgent matters.

"He is well, though there is much debate going on in Arvael." Darq paused and seemed to be searching before he asked, "Is Prince Haedrin here? I know King Balen would be very pleased to meet him."

Orlan gave a regretful shake of his head. "Sadly, no. He is up north inspecting some of the mines. But he should return in a few days. You're welcome to stay and wait for him."

A grimace crossed Darq's face. King Orlan clearly didn't notice, because he turned another welcoming smile to Balen. "What is it that brings you all the way out to Dorland, my lord?"

Balen glanced at Darq before he spoke. "I'm sure you've heard that Samara has fallen into the hands of Emperor Daican, and I've been living in exile in Arcacia for the last year."

King Orlan's weathered face finally took on a grim expression. "Yes, a terrible situation. You have my deepest sympathies."

Kyrin held back a sigh. It wasn't his sympathies they needed.

Balen took a step forward. "It is my intention to reclaim Samara and free my people from Daican's oppression, but I can't do it alone. That is why I am here—to seek the aid of you and your people who have long been friends and allies to those in Samara."

Orlan's face changed from sympathy to a more evasive frown. "It is not the way of the Dorlanders to become involved in these disputes. We are not a fighting people, nor do we have a large fighting force. It is better to resolve things peaceably than with war. I cannot advocate action that would make Emperor Daican our enemy."

"What if he is already your enemy?" Balen questioned. "Has not Arcacia already claimed land beyond the river that rightfully belongs to Dorland?"

"That was before my time," Orlan said. "As of now, Dorland has no quarrel with Arcacia."

"Even if it's Daican's plan to seize control of Dorland?"

The king's eyes narrowed. "You know this for a fact?"

"It is his intention to create an empire. He won't content himself with simply ruling Arcacia and Samara. The resources that come out of Dorland alone are enough to draw his attention. Most of the gold and precious jewels in Ilyon come from your mines. That would tempt anyone with Daican's ambitions."

King Orlan regarded him with thoughtful eyes before shaking his head. "Without proof of your speculations, I cannot take action. I won't be the one to declare war."

Kyrin let her shoulders sag. That was it then. Just like that, it seemed their final hope for their mission to Dorland had failed.

"I truly am sorry for your plight," King Orlan said in a consoling tone. "Please, accept my hospitality and remain here as my personal guests for as long as you wish."

Kyrin watched Balen to see if he would press the issue, but they all seemed tired of arguing their case.

He gave a brief nod. "Thank you, my lord. I will discuss it with my companions and let you know when we make our plans. We will be out with our dragons."

The king nodded and motioned for Halsen to show them out.

As Balen turned, however, Kyrin caught a look of determination that said they weren't going out just to discuss whether to return to Landale. The king may have turned them down, but Kyrin didn't believe Balen would give up just yet.

THE MOMENT THEY stepped out of the castle, Kyrin heard Jace take a deep breath as the sunshine and fresh air hit them. She didn't really like the solid stone interior either. Despite its size, the cave-like solidness to it threatened to make her claustrophobic. One wouldn't even have the hope of getting out if trapped inside.

Jace took her hand again when they reached the stairs, though the descent was easier than the climb. At the bottom, Balen stopped and everyone gathered around him.

"I am sorry, my lord," Darq said in a tired voice. "I feared there would be no reasoning with him. That is why I had hoped Prince Haedrin would be present. He might be more inclined to listen."

Balen didn't seem to hear him as he stared toward the gate, where the two younger giants from the throne room stood with their horses.

"Do you know who they are?" he asked Darq.

The crete captain shook his head. "I've never met them. The ford they mentioned must be Andros Ford. The Trayse River is very swift and rough, and the ford is the only passable area this far north. You'd have to travel a good four-hundred miles downriver into ryrik territory to find another adequate crossing."

"So it's the only safe way into Dorland by land?"

"Pretty much . . . and presents a straight shot to Bel-gard, which is why it's guarded by the families in that area."

Balen nodded slowly, a calculating expression on his face. "And if Daican were to invade, that's exactly where he'd send his soldiers." He glanced at the group. "Let's find out more about these attacks. There must be a reason they mentioned Daican. If this is part of the emperor's scheme, the king needs to know before it's too late. If Dorland falls to his power, then our hope to stop him will surely fall with it."

They set off across the courtyard. As they drew near the gate, the giants' powerful horses captured Kyrin's attention. The heavily built animals' withers rose taller than she could even reach. Their brown and gray coats were a bit shaggy—not short and sleek like Maera's or Niton's were at this time of year—but she supposed thicker coats were important in the cooler temperatures close to the mountains.

The two giants noticed them coming and turned to face them.

"I'm sorry, but we couldn't help overhearing your conversation with the king," Balen said. "I understand you are having difficulty with ryriks?"

The older giant with the axe nodded. "Aye. We've dealt with multiple attacks in the last month."

"And you have reason to suspect it might somehow be related to Daican?"

The giant traded a glance with his younger, darker haired companion. "More a gut feeling than any sort of proof. Living so close to the forests of Wildmor, we're used to ryrik raids, but there's something different about these attacks. They seem more . . . organized. It just doesn't add up to the usual sporadic attacks we've had to deal with in the past. They seem more bent on destroying than looting, which is unusual."

Everything Kyrin had heard about ryriks growing up was that they were killers and thieves. They lived off what they looted from their victims. It wasn't unusual for them to destroy their targets but not at the expense of their loot.

"This is simply our speculation," the giant continued, "but it seems as though they are trying to destroy everyone around Andros Ford."

"How far is that from here?" Balen asked.

"About two days' ride by horse." The giant gestured to their dragons. "Half that if you were to fly."

"Are you returning there?"

The giant nodded. "Our older brother sent us for help and stayed behind to watch over our farm. We need to get back there to help him fend off any attacks."

"Would you mind if we joined you?"

The giant traded another surprised glance with his brother, and Balen said, "If this is some scheme of Daican's, we want to get to the bottom of it. If not, then at least the presence of us and our dragons may discourage further attacks."

"Well, we'd certainly appreciate the help." The giant shot an irritated look at the castle. "We didn't exactly find it here." He held out his hand. "I'm Halvar, and this is my brother Levi."

Balen shook his hand, which was humorously like watching a child shake the hand of a grown man. "I am Balen, from Samara."

Halvar peered at him. "Isn't Balen the name of Samara's king?"

Balen gave a slow nod. "Exiled king now."

"It's a pleasure to meet you, Your Majesty, and an honor that you would concern yourself with our situation."

"The last thing I want is for Dorland to fall to Daican as Samara has. I don't wish for your people to suffer under his rule, and I won't be able to free my own people if he continues to gain power. I will let the king know we are not staying. You ride on ahead. We'll follow you from the air and join you when you make camp this evening."

Halvar nodded, and he and Levi turned to their horses.

Guiding the rest of the group with him, Balen said, "Prepare to leave. If we can find evidence that Daican is behind these ryrik attacks, then King Orlan will have to take action. And if we don't, we can always return here in a few days and speak to Prince Haedrin. I'll let the king know we're leaving."

"Will you tell him what we're doing?" Darq asked. "He might not like the idea of dragons near the border."

Balen paused for a moment. "Why don't we see what we can find out first?"

A faint smile grew on Darq's face.

The first scattering of stars sprinkled the deep blue sky overhead as the pink glow on the western horizon ahead of them grew dimmer. At the front of the group, Balen and Darq's dragons angled toward the ground. Glancing down, Jace spotted where Halvar and Levi had stopped and dismounted in the meadow below them. He directed Gem to follow the lead dragons.

By the time they landed, Levi had a small but growing fire to light the area and cook their dinner. Following Balen, they all gathered around the giant brothers.

"I apologize if we pushed on later than you would have," Halvar said. "We just want to get back as soon as possible."

"If you're worried, I could take a couple of us on ahead to scout the area around the ford and make sure there aren't any ryriks around," Darq offered.

Halvar gave him a grateful look. "We'd be much obliged. Our older brother's watching the farm all on his own. He insisted Levi and I both go to Bel-gard in case we met up with trouble. I tried to stay with him, but he wouldn't hear of it. It's foolish if you ask me, but that's Jorvik—always putting our safety above his own."

"Give us a couple of hours to rest the dragons," Darq told him, "and then we'll head out."

They gathered their provisions from their packs and sat with Halvar and Levi around the fire. The two giants had many questions about Samara and the Resistance in Landale. None of it was pleasant to recall, especially when they spoke of the losses they had suffered. Kyrin grew quiet when they mentioned her father, and Jace reached over to take her hand. She'd had to relive the memories of his death too often lately.

Thankfully, Balen changed the subject. "So it's only the three of you on your farm?"

Halvar nodded. "Our pa was killed by a she-bear with cubs about three years ago while he and Jorvik were out hunting."

Jace winced. Considering how tall and powerful Halvar and his brother were, just how big were bears in Dorland? He decided right then and there that he didn't want to find out firsthand.

Halvar continued quietly. "Our ma didn't handle it well and there wasn't much fight in her when she got sick that winter and died."

"I'm sorry," Balen told him.

Halvar shrugged. "That's just part of living way out here. It can be a hard life, but we wouldn't trade it."

"We heard you say your family has been guarding the ford for generations."

"We're the closest to the ford—only about three miles—so we've always looked after it and paid attention to who came and went."

"Have you personally suffered from any of the ryrik attacks?"

"We were the first. They burned down our chicken coop, but we drove them off before they could get at the barn or cabin. I don't think they were prepared for such a fight. After that, they moved on to the other farms in the area, but they'll no doubt try again."

"And we pray to Elôm they haven't while we've been away," Levi joined in.

Halvar murmured in agreement.

"Well, whatever the ryriks are up to, we hope we can figure it out and help you put a stop to the raids."

With all this talk of ryriks and their trouble with the emperor, Jace was glad when, during a lull in the conversation, Halvar started singing what must have been a giant folk song. Levi joined in midway through. For being such a simple people, they were quite impressive singers. Everyone applauded when they finished. Just before starting a new song, Talas jumped up to get his flute from his pack. Between the brothers' deep voices and Talas's lively flute playing, the mood lightened considerably.

NOW SEEMED TO be as good a time as any for Anne to master the spinning wheel. Her mother had wanted to teach her for years, but after one very unsuccessful attempt, Anne had lost interest. However, with the continually foul weather, she was ready to try just about anything to stay occupied. She might start to lose her sanity otherwise. After most of the morning, she was finally getting the hang of it. The sound of Elanor reading from one of Anne's favorite books made the attempt more enjoyable. They'd begun taking turns reading chapters every day while working on their various projects.

They were just about to break for lunch when a sharp knock at the door cut through the gentle sound of the rain outside. They all froze. The knock came again with more force than it should have if someone had simply dropped by for a social call. A moment later, Anne's father came down from his study and went to the door. Anne held her breath.

The door swung open and the sight of gold and black filling the doorway sent a jolt into her chest. But it wasn't Goler or Dagren, which only raised her suspicions further.

"Good morning," her father greeted cautiously. "Can I help you?"

"Captain Goler and Captain Dagren have called a gathering of all the locals in and around Landale Village. Attendance is mandatory."

"Right now?"

The soldier nodded firmly. "They plan to make an announcement at noon. We are to escort you and your household to the village."

Anne pressed her hand to her stomach. Whatever announcement required an escort into Landale could not be good. Her blood flowed like ice water through her veins. Could they have been found out? She fought to calm herself. If Goler knew her family followed Elôm, he would have had them arrested . . . unless this was some scheme concocted by Dagren.

After a tense pause, her father nodded. "Very well. Let me see about having the carriage hitched."

He turned to the women, not quite masking the tension in his expression, though he spoke calmly. After all, what could they do but comply? "Get your cloaks. It will be wet out there."

He then stepped out, giving them privacy from the soldiers waiting on the porch. A heavy silence fell when the door closed behind him, filled only by the erratic beating of Anne's heart. Finally, her mother took the first action and pushed to her feet.

"We'd better get our cloaks," she said, her voice low.

Wordlessly, they tied them on and waited near the door. Anne tried to convince herself that this was more posturing by Goler and Dagren to intimidate the locals, but a cloud of doom pressed down on her. She drew a deep breath and prayed inwardly. *Lord, whatever this is, protect Your children.*

Her father returned several minutes later and escorted them out. The carriage waited near the porch, and just behind it, a wagon for the servants. Elian stood near the carriage with his horse, his face taut. The four guards had mounted and waited to leave. Anne's father helped the three women into the carriage before climbing in himself.

The soldiers' horses splashed around outside, and then the carriage lumbered forward. As they rolled away from Marlton, Anne's mother looked at her father, her hand clutching his arm.

"What do you think this is about?"

He shook his head and murmured, "I don't know."

Anne kept praying to keep her mind from all the worst-case scenarios. She peeked out the window a couple of times and could not help but hope to catch a glimpse of Trask or his men. It would ease her mind to know help was nearby.

Silence followed them the rest of the way to Landalc. When they reached the edge of the village, Anne spied more than one soldier out the window.

"That's a lot of security," she whispered.

Her father nodded solemnly. "They must know people won't like whatever announcement Goler and Dagren plan to make."

Dread rose up within Anne and turned into a gnawing urge to flee. But, as the carriage rolled to a stop, she sent up another prayer and stiffened her spine. They had faced and overcome more than one trial in the last couple of years. She had to believe they would overcome whatever this brought as well. Her father helped her down from the carriage. They stood at the edge of the village square, where it appeared most of the villagers had already gathered.

A cold mist coated her face, and she shivered. She pulled up her hood and walked beside Elanor as her parents led them into the gathering. Murmurs surrounded them. The confusion on the villagers' faces told Anne that they were no more sure of what was happening than she was. A terrible thought invaded her mind. What if this was a move to flush out believers, and they would all be required to bow before Aertus and Vilai?

But with a quick scan of the area, she could find no sign of any idols, and a little of the pressure squeezing her lungs let up.

A few restless minutes after they arrived, Captain Dagren stepped up onto a flat wagon that elevated him above the crowd, and the murmuring died. Several soldiers stationed themselves around it. A hush fell across the entire square as they all peered up at the captain.

"People of Landale," his voice rang out, "I have called this gathering to address a problem—a problem that affects every single one of us: the problem of rebellion."

He said the last word with a sneer. Anne peeked at those standing near them. Most of the people she knew maintained loyalty to Baron Grey and Trask as well as faith in Elôm, but their faces remained a bland mask.

"For over two years, Landale has found itself at the very center of rebellion and treason against His Majesty, Emperor Daican. Violent rebels hide within your forests. Criminals who would use dragons to make forest travel unsafe and increased security necessary."

Anne resisted a scoff. The people of Landale would have to be blind to buy any of this. Dagren and his men were the ones responsible for making the area unsafe. However, she checked her anger toward him.

"The emperor sent me to put an end to it once and for all. To eradicate such rebellion, one must destroy it at its heart. It didn't start with the lowlifes and outcasts—it started right here in the very center of your community, with your leaders."

He swept his arm to his right and all eyes followed it. The door opened on a nearby building, and a group of soldiers, including Goler, led Baron Grey out in chains. A gasp escaped Anne's mouth, but the other audible reactions all around her drowned it out.

The soldiers led him through the crowd and up to the wagon.

Anne covered her mouth with her hand as tears poured into her eyes. Bruises and bloodied gashes covered the baron's face, yet, when he looked out over the people, he appeared stronger than he had in a long while.

With a solid thud, soldiers set an execution block on the wagon. Anne's heart lurched inside her, and panic burst through her body.

"Father!" she gasped. She turned to him, and his eyes mirrored her desperation. "We have to do something."

The slight shake of his head told her there was nothing they could do. Even if they tried, unless the whole village joined them, they would never get past Dagren's men alive.

Her attention jerked back to the wagon, where Dagren spoke again.

"Baron Grey of Landale has been found guilty of treason against the emperor, denying the gods, and aiding the rebels. He is therefore sentenced to death. Treason will never be tolerated. Not by the lowest of Arcacia's citizens, nor the highest."

He motioned to Goler, who pushed Baron Grey forward and forced him to kneel at the block. Anne's entire being screamed for them to stop, but she choked back the words. This couldn't be happening. They couldn't kill him. Her gaze flew around the area, desperate to see Trask and his men somewhere in the crowd ready to intervene. Surely Elôm had put one of Trask's men near Marlton to see the soldiers escort them away. With news like that, Trask would have come to investigate. He had to be here. Elôm had to have a rescue ready!

Goler pushed Grey down against the block, and Dagren drew his sword, taking the place of executioner. Women around Anne broke into quiet sobs. Her own tears fell hot against her cold cheeks.

"No," she almost cried aloud.

Her father's arm wrapped around her, and Elanor clutched her hand.

Please, Elôm! This can't be! It just can't be!

Dagren raised his sword, and Anne squeezed her eyes shut. *No, no, no! Elôm, You can't allow this to happen!*

The sword fell. Cries erupted from the crowd. Anne went numb as a sob ripped from her chest. She clung to her father and Elanor just to stay upright, but all she wanted was to sink into the mud and scream. Tears leaked from her still-closed eyes. She couldn't make herself open them. *Elôm, why?* A small voice warned her to get a hold of herself and keep up appearances, but she couldn't contain the flood of sorrow and horror without it suffocating her.

Unable to bear it any longer, she pulled away from her family and fled through the crowd. Tears blinded her, causing her to bump into people and almost trip, but she pushed forward until she broke from the gathering. Then she ran—ran until she reached the outskirts of the village and her legs finally gave out. There, beside the road, she sank into the wet, mud-spattered grass and cried as she never had before.

Soggy footsteps approached sometime later.

"Annie."

Her father's husky voice rose above the rain as he knelt down and drew her into his arms. She clung to him, crying as her breaths came in shallow, choking gasps. She could see the baron's face from only two days ago when they'd spoken of her betrothal to Trask. Could see his smile at the thought of their wedding. Now he would never be there to see it happen.

"Trask," she cried weakly. "How will I tell him?"

Her father pulled away, cupping her face in his hands. Tears wet his bearded cheeks. "I'll help you."

He pulled her up with him and guided her toward the carriage waiting nearby. Anne followed, her body leaden and tears still streaming as if they would never stop again. She climbed inside where her mother and Elanor were both crying. Elian was there too and had a comforting arm around Elanor. Even he had tears in his eyes. Anne sank into the seat with her parents.

The trip back to Marlton was the longest and most painful Anne had ever experienced. Her sobs would not subside. When they did arrive home, everyone climbed out of the carriage and wagon with bleak, tear-streaked faces. No one spoke a word as the men led the horses away to unhitch. Anne paused before she reached the porch and looked toward the stable. Her father tried to usher her into the house, but she turned to him, her voice barely making it past her swollen throat.

"I need to go to camp. Word will reach there eventually, but it must come from me. Please."

Slowly, her father nodded, his eyes almost overflowing again. "First go inside and change. You're soaked through. I'll get the horses and go with you."

Anne stepped onto the porch and into the house, numbness taking hold again. She couldn't even say anything as she passed her mother and Elanor and climbed the stairs to her room. She pulled off her cloak and wet dress and let them drop in a heap. Her movements were reflex; her mind thinking ahead to what she had to do. Before she even really knew what she had done, she was dressed and on her way downstairs. She took a second cloak from the peg just as her father came in. He went to her mother first and held her for a moment.

"I'll be back as soon as I can."

She nodded against his chest. He then tried to give Elanor an encouraging look before joining Anne at the door. When they stepped outside, Anne looked at her horse, almost crippled by the question of how she would break the news to Trask.

She pulled herself up into the saddle, her arms shaking, and let her father take the lead. During the ride, Anne struggled not to think—struggled to keep the swirl of emotions at bay. She fought hard, but when they neared camp, the weight grew too heavy. Her tears turned the forest into an indistinguishable green blur. Finally, she had to pull her horse to a stop as sobs gripped her again. Her father drew up beside her and leaned over to put his arm around her.

They sat this way for a while, but Anne only felt worse with each passing minute. The dread of facing Trask mounted in her chest until all she wanted was to collapse near a tree and wait for the day to pass. She couldn't bear the thought of how it would devastate him. But she had to tell him and be there for him, so she straightened and wiped her sleeve across her cheeks. "Let's go."

Her father squeezed her shoulder, and they rode on.

All too soon, they reached the edge of camp. They rode up to Trask's cabin, and Anne was afraid she would be sick as they dismounted. The moment her feet touched the ground, the cabin door opened.

"Anne?"

Trask's voice shot a dart of pain through Anne's heart. She squeezed her eyes shut, the tears already swimming again. *Elôm, help me.* Slowly, she turned to face him. His brows sank as he eyed her face and stepped closer.

"What happened?"

Anne swallowed with great difficulty, unable to summon her voice. He stared at her, his expression growing more and more tense. Her tears spilled over before she could stop them, and her father's hand pressed against her back.

"What?" Trask asked, his voice rough. He dragged in a breath. "My father?"

Anne forced her tongue to work. "He's gone." She bit back the sob rising in her throat. "They executed him."

Only shock registered on Trask's face for the space of three heartbeats before a wave of other emotions filled his eyes—anger, disbelief—but the grief overwhelmed all the others. His face crumpled as the sorrow took hold, and tears overflowed. The already broken pieces of Anne's heart shattered even further. She stepped forward and wrapped her arms around him, and they cried together.

After a time, Anne's father and Warin guided them both inside the cabin, out of the rain. They sat at the table where Anne held tightly to Trask's hand just to let him know he wasn't alone in this. He used his other hand to wipe his face, but the tears in his eyes still threatened to fall. He tried to speak but had to clear his throat.

"When?" he finally managed.

"Just a couple of hours ago." Anne shook her head, choking. "Soldiers came to the house to escort us to Landale for Dagren and Goler to make an announcement. We didn't know. I would have gotten word to you, but it happened so fast. We had no warning."

Trask squeezed her hand, but his expression was still so broken. "I should have brought him out here when I had the chance. I should never have left him there."

Anne reached over and put her hand on his cheek. "No, don't put that on yourself. He stayed for the people of Landale. If he had wanted to leave, he would have asked you. This isn't your failing."

He closed his eyes, his tears coming freshly.

For a long while, they sat there at the table, sometimes murmuring to each other, but most of the time not saying anything at all. News spread through camp and people came and went to offer their condolences.

A miserable eternity later, Anne's father spoke. "It's getting late. We should go."

Anne shook her head and looked at him pleadingly. "I need to stay. Please." She couldn't leave Trask's side when the loss was so fresh.

Her father stared at her for a moment and then looked over at Warin, who sat nearby.

"I'll see she gets home safely when she's ready," Warin said.

Slowly, her father nodded and pushed up from his chair. "Don't be away too long," he said gently.

Anne understood his concern. She needed to be home in case Goler or Dagren dropped by. The thought of ever facing either of them again turned her stomach, but she nodded.

Morning dawned without much notice. After the long hours of the night, Anne couldn't find the energy to care. She stared into the fireplace where the small fire they'd built was only a couple of red embers. Blinking the grit from her eyes, she looked over at Trask. Neither of them had said a word since well before dawn. Pain seared through her chest at his tired, faraway look. She shifted, her body protesting the hours she'd sat in this hard chair. Only then did Trask snap from his daze.

He met her eyes, and Anne saw the exhaustion they both shared—the point where the sorrow still held its full strength, but the tears had drained and all the usual functions of grief shut down. He gave a weary shake of his head.

"After everything we've faced and all the death that has surrounded us, somehow you trick yourself into thinking you won't be the one it touches personally." He let out a long, heavy breath and hung his head. "I always prayed and wanted to believe that, somehow, this would be resolved and I could return home to him again . . . that things would one day return to normal."

Anne put her hand on his back and rubbed it. "I know."

"Now, even if I were to return to Landale, nothing would be the same." He looked over at her again. "Who has taken over control of the area?"

Anne shook her head. "I assume Goler or Dagren."

The spark of anger flared in Trask's eyes but died just as quickly. "As hard as we tried, it still fell into their hands."

"You did *everything* you could," Anne assured him. "Both you and your father. You have to leave it in Elôm's hands now."

He nodded. A moment later, the barest of smiles lifted the corners of his lips, and tears formed in his eyes.

"What?" Anne asked.

"I was just thinking about how my parents are together again now. They loved each other so much."

One by one, the tears dripped over. Anne laid her head on his shoulder and let her own tears fall silently. Once they subsided, she wiped her face dry and fought to scrape together her strength. She hated to do this, but it was time.

"I need to return home."

Trask just sat for a long moment, staring at the fireplace ashes as if he had not heard. Then he stood. "I'll take you."

They left the cabin with Warin and saddled the horses. After sending one of the cretes to fly ahead and make sure the forest and roads were clear of danger, they mounted and rode out. It was a quiet ride, and Anne didn't see much of it. She was just too tired for her senses to work properly. When they arrived at the edge of Marlton, they stopped in the trees.

"You shouldn't go any farther," she told Trask. At least if soldiers spotted her riding out of the woods, she could claim she'd been out for a morning ride.

They looked at each other. Trask's expression held the same longing Anne carried inside. A moment later, he put words to that longing.

"I don't want you to have to leave . . . ever. I want to marry you and have you with me every day so I know you're safe."

Anne breathed out a trembling breath, her eyes smarting. She didn't want to do this anymore either. If not for her family and their safety, she'd give it all up right here, ride back to camp with him and marry him that very day. But her family was here, and the danger to them was very real. She tried to swallow down the longing.

"We'll figure it out," she said, fighting with everything inside her to believe it. She reached out to Elôm for Him to make it so. "Somehow we'll figure it out."

He nodded, determination coming through his weary eyes. He moved his horse closer and leaned over. Anne met him in the middle, welcoming his kiss. It was different from the kisses they'd shared before—subdued by grief, but fueled by the longing for a better future.

AFTER A FULL day of flight over the rolling meadowlands and another night of camping, Kyrin spotted a line of trees far off in the distance. Nearer, however, lay a sprawling farm. Over a hundred head of the shaggy Dorland cattle grazed on one side, while thriving crops grew on the other. In the middle of it stood a huge log house and gigantic barn. Below them, Halvar and Levi trotted into the farmyard. The entire group landed around them.

Before any of them had a chance to dismount, another giant man came striding from the barn. He was a bit taller than Halvar and Levi and built like the bears Kyrin had heard about. He had long dark hair like Levi, and despite his simple farm clothes, the confident and commanding way he held himself pointed to him being more of a warrior than most of his kin. He analyzed each of them, but his focus settled on Halvar and Levi.

"Jorvik!" Halvar exclaimed. "It sure is good to see you're still here."

Jorvik offered a brief smile to his brothers before his attention returned to Kyrin and the others as they dismounted.

"When I sent you two for help, I was expecting something a little different."

Halvar laughed and motioned him closer to the group. Balen stepped forward to meet him, and the others gathered behind. Halvar introduced each of them, surprising his brother when he introduced Balen. Jorvik greeted the king with respect and welcomed them all as a group.

"They overheard us talking to King Orlan about the attacks and wanted to look into it with us," Halvar explained.

"We appreciate the help." Jorvik glanced eastward, the way they had come. "The king didn't send any men, did he?"

Halvar shook his head. "No. He doesn't want our soldiers seen at the border and cause Emperor Daican to misread our intentions."

Jorvik snorted but did not comment on the king's lack of assistance. "All the more reason to be thankful for the help we do have."

"We would like to see you get to the bottom of these attacks," Balen said, "especially if they have something to do with Daican as your brothers suggested."

"I thank you for coming." Jorvik gestured to his brothers. "Let us help you unload your dragons."

They turned to the animals to unsaddle them. With the help of Jorvik and his brothers, everyone carried the supplies up to the cabin and then inside. Just through the door, Kyrin stared in awe. The wide, open front room welcomed them with a great stone fireplace towering at the opposite wall. Massive timbers supported the ceiling, and the openness of the cabin gave the dwelling a feel of amazing spaciousness. Even after seeing the way giants lived in Bel-gard, she still had to get used to the size of everything. She and Jace could have easily shared the one-person chairs near the fireplace.

"I'm afraid we don't have much to offer in the way of spare rooms or beds," Jorvik said as he led them toward a half-log staircase. "But we'll do what we can to make you comfortable."

"We've spent more nights on the ground in the last weeks than indoors," Balen told him. "Anything is better than that."

Upstairs, along a balcony overlooking the living room below, Jorvik opened two doors. "These two rooms are free."

Balen turned to the group. "Kyrin, Leetra, you can share one. We'll take the other."

Kyrin offered a grateful smile that he and the other men would all cram into one room and let her and Leetra have their privacy in a room that was more than large enough for two. In fact, just the room alone appeared almost as big as one of the cabins back in Landale.

She and Leetra stepped inside to set their things down. A thick bearskin rug lay on the plank floor at the foot of the largest bed Kyrin had ever seen. The top of the quilt-covered mattress reached her chest and was wide enough for four people or more. She then scanned the rest of the plain, but homey room. When she turned, she found Leetra staring up at the ceiling with a calculating expression, her rolled up hammock in her arms. Kyrin had to bite back a laugh at the thought of how she might go about getting her hammock strung up. The ceiling beams were a good twelve feet above the floor. Leetra just might have to settle for sleeping in a normal bed tonight. She seemed to realize this and wrinkled her nose.

"At least a bed is better than the ground," Kyrin said.

Leetra arched her brow and did not reply. Her expression said she didn't agree. Kyrin just shook her head to herself over the cretes' strange aversion to traditional beds.

Once they'd arranged their belongings, they joined the men downstairs. Halvar and Levi carried a table and two long benches into the house from somewhere outside. When they set it down near the other table, Kyrin found that it was a more normal-sized one.

"We don't get company besides our neighbors very often, so this will need a bit of dusting," Halvar told them, "but at least you won't have to try to sit at our table."

Kyrin almost laughed at the thought of them all seated at the larger table.

"Levi, why don't you get a rag? I'll help Jorvik in the kitchen." Halvar gestured to his brother and then addressed the group again. "We're just throwing together some beef sandwiches. I hope that's all right."

"That sounds excellent," Balen replied. "I'm curious to see how your beef tastes compared to the cattle in Samara and Arcacia."

"It can be a bit tough if you don't know how to prepare it, but our ma was an expert, and Jorvik learned all her secrets."

After Levi had cleaned off the dusty table, he invited them to sit down. The benches were just long enough to accommodate them all comfortably.

A few minutes later, Jorvik and his brothers carried out the food. They set a large platter on the table, filled with sandwiches. Each one was cut in half but, as a whole, they were as large as a normal-sized dinner plate. Kyrin's mouth watered at the sight of the thick, crusty bread, tender slices of lightly pink meat, and rich yellow butter. Halvar carried a stack of plates to the table, which must have been desert plates due to their smaller size, and Levi brought a couple of jars of preserved apples and a plate containing a large cream-colored cheese wedge.

With the food set before them, Jorvik and his brothers brought their own plates to their table, and Jorvik offered a simple but sincere prayer. Then they passed around the food. Kyrin's first bite of her sandwich was every bit as delicious as it had looked. She tried a slice of the cheese wedge, which was a little bitter, but rich and smooth. Along with the honey-sweetened apple preserves, they were the perfect complement to the sandwich.

All around the table, the men voiced their appreciation for the food.

"Do you make everything yourselves?" Balen asked the brothers.

Jorvik nodded. "We stock up on necessary supplics a few times a year from one of the nearby settlements, but otherwise everything we eat comes from right here on the farm."

Kyrin smiled to herself. The thought of these three brothers baking and storing up preserves for themselves was endearing. Her brothers certainly couldn't do it. If she and her mother left, they'd all five starve no doubt.

Now that conversation had begun, Jorvik asked about Landale, and they spoke of the Resistance. When Balen explained what had brought them to Dorland and how their meeting with King Orlan had gone, Jorvik said, "If it were up to me, I would help you take back Samara. Whether Daican plans to conquer Ilyon or not, someone ought to show him that he can't just take whatever pleases him."

His vehemence surprised Kyrin. She wouldn't have expected this from a giant, especially considering how passive their king was. But then, Darq had mentioned the giants' aversion to injustice, and the takeover of Samara was exactly that. If only King Orlan felt as strongly as Jorvik and his brothers.

"We appreciate the support. At least we know we have some friends here," Balen said. "So what can you tell us about the ryrik attacks? How large is the raiding party?"

"It was a good dozen men, at least. Perhaps more that we have not seen. We've killed a couple, but that hasn't deterred them. We may have the size advantage, but the farming families around here aren't large in number. Even for us, it's difficult to take on so many ryriks at once." Jorvik's face grew solemn. "We lost two of our nearest neighbors. One of them had a little girl who was killed in the attack."

Everyone sat silent for a moment at the tragic loss.

"Your brothers told us how coordinated they are and their apparent disinterest in looting. Have you noticed any other strange behavior?" Balen asked.

At this, Jorvik rose from his seat and crossed the room to a small closet. When he returned, he laid a sword on their table, which drew an immediate reaction from Marcus.

"That's an Arcacian military sword."

"That's what we thought."

Marcus picked up the sword to inspect closer. "And not a standard issue foot soldier's sword either. This would be for officers or given as gifts to decorated men."

"Of course, it could have been stolen in a raid somewhere," Jorvik said, "but it's odd to see something like that way out here. There isn't an Arcacian barracks for more than a thousand miles. It doesn't prove anything, but it could be worth looking into."

Anne stared numbly into the fireplace, unable to let herself think for more than a couple of minutes without tears forming. She ached for Trask. Leaving him that morning still tore at her. Inside, the house was gloomy and quiet as everyone mourned in their own ways. Her mother and Elanor kept busy with their sewing, but whenever Anne glanced at them, their faces were downcast and their eyes moist. Anne felt cold and too heavy to move. Her father too just sat in silence, no doubt reflecting on the lifetime he'd known Baron Grey. She wiped the corners of her eyes and swallowed around a hard knot of grief.

A strong knock at the door shot a jolt through every frayed nerve in Anne's body. What would it be this time? Her heart beat sluggishly as her father stood up to answer it.

"Captain Goler," he said in a low, flat tone.

Anne's insides convulsed, and she clenched her fists.

"Sir John," Goler replied, sounding disturbingly pleased.

A long, heavy silence passed.

"May I come in?" Goler asked finally.

"I'm not sure now is the best time."

"I have news I wish to share with Anne," Goler responded, with just enough force to show he wouldn't take no for an answer.

Anne rose stiffly and approached the door, unsure if it was truly wise. It would take all her strength not to slap him. She came up behind her father, and Goler's hard face brightened.

"Anne."

What gave him the gall to skip her title? She sent him her coldest glare, and the pleased smile dropped from his face.

"Are you ill?"

Anne could hardly believe him. Was he truly so ignorant and self-absorbed? She ground out her words through her teeth. "What news did you wish to share, Captain?"

He hesitated as if taken aback. However, he recovered himself and stood up a little straighter, the remnants of his smile returning as his eyes beamed with pride. "I came to tell you that I've been named Baron of Landale."

Anne stared at him. The selfish, inconsiderate, arrogant boor! Good thing her father stood between them. Tears flowed, and she couldn't contain them.

"How dare you?" Her voice trembled but gained volume. "How dare you come out here to tell me that after yesterday!"

All the pride and satisfaction vanished in an instant, and he stammered, "I thought . . . you might be pleased for me."

Anne's fists clenched more tightly, and she shook. "How could I when Baron Grey had to die for you to gain this position?"

Goler's brows bent. "He was a traitor."

"He was my friend!" she choked through a sob. "You have no idea how to treat or understand a woman if you expect me to just get over it. I don't wish to speak with you right now."

She turned her face away from him though, out of the corner of her eye, she caught the way he blinked, and his mouth opened before snapping shut again. For just that moment, he appeared truly perplexed.

"Anne . . ."

"Go away!" she almost screamed at him before turning her back completely.

Her father stepped in then. "I suggest you leave and let my family have the time and space we need."

A moment of silence followed, but then, without a word, Goler's footsteps thumped across the porch. The door closed, and Anne turned back to her father. He reached out to her, and she collapsed against his chest, crying inconsolably.

Daniel pulled on a fresh shirt and winced at the throbbing pain in his ribs. Three days of sparring with Aric had left him with a collection of painful bruises and sore muscles, but the sessions were one of his favorite parts of the day. It offered him a distraction from the matters weighing on his mind and the already suffocating feeling of the palace. Not to mention a way to get his aggressions out. He hadn't thought house arrest would be so bad since he had his secret escape, but the inability to do something as simple as go out for a ride ate at him. If it was this difficult after just a couple of days, what would it do to his sanity after a month?

Well, he might not go riding for the rest of his life, but he could at least visit the stable and make sure his horses were properly exercised. Any excuse to get outdoors. He buckled on his jerkin and left his room. On his way downstairs, one of the footmen intercepted him.

"His Majesty requests your presence in the throne room, my lord."

Daniel didn't stifle a sigh. "Now?"

The footman nodded.

Altering his course, Daniel fought mightily to rein in his rebellious emotions. After several hours of deep prayer, he'd reached the conclusion that the best way to try to get through to his father was through submission and respect as long as it didn't go against his faith. After all, what better way to show Elôm's power in his life than to do well in presenting himself as the changed man he was?

With a deep breath and another plea for aid, Daniel entered the throne room. His father stood near the dais with Aric, but Daniel's attention latched onto the eight other men nearby. They were his security detail, and all eight of them stood in chains. Daniel frowned and faced his father. "What is this?"

"It has occurred to me," his father said in his deceptively conversational tone, "that anyone you met who might have swayed you to follow your misguided beliefs would have been witnessed by your men. They, however, insist they know nothing."

Daniel shook his head. "They don't."

"I don't see how that's possible if they were supposed to be with you every minute you spent outside this palace."

Daniel shifted his jaw. Not every minute. "Come on, Father, just let them go. This won't gain you anything."

"No? Well, I will not tolerate treason, nor any who aid traitors." His father motioned to the other security guards. "Have them taken to the arena. They can help provide the entertainment once it opens."

Daniel's jaw dropped. "Father, what are you doing? These men are innocent!"

"Unless you can prove that, I'm inclined to believe otherwise."

The guards led the men toward the door as some tried to protest and plead their case. His father ignored them, staring expectantly at Daniel. Clenching his fists, Daniel stepped forward to stop them. Other guards grabbed him by the arms and held him back. He fought against them, but they would not relinquish their hold.

"Father, you can't do this. They can't tell you anything because they don't know anything. They don't deserve this." But his father didn't budge. Daniel expelled a rough breath. There was only one way to stop this, but to do so would destroy the only escape he had left. He looked at his men. If they died in that arena, they would never have another chance to turn to Elôm. He couldn't let that happen. He jerked around to face his father. "I sneak out of the palace alone at night."

Everyone stopped. His father peered at him, eyes narrowed. "How?"

Daniel bit down until his teeth hurt, the trapped feeling already descending on him heavily, but he came out with it. "An old gate hidden in the vines behind the temple." He winced. Now he truly was a prisoner.

He held his father's gaze, ill feelings passing between them before his father turned to Aric. "Find the gate and have it filled in immediately. And check the wall for any more such gates." To the guards leading away Daniel's men, he commanded, "Take them out. They are relieved of their duty here at Auréa, and should they speak a word of what's happened, they are to be executed immediately."

Daniel hung his head in regret that he had cost them their jobs, but at least they would live. The guards released their hold on him, and his father stepped closer. His voice dropped to a low, dangerous tone.

"If I find out anyone in this palace has aided you in sneaking about, I will have them executed." The intensity of his eyes drove home his point. "And you will not leave this palace again until you are ready to kneel in the temple and commit to the life your gods have given you."

THE CALL OF early morning birds beckoned Jace outside. He'd slept well last night—better than in Arvael—but awoke earlier than everyone else, save the cretes. He stood on the porch for a moment and walked down to where Darq and the others stood with their dragons. He said good morning to them, and then to Gem, who bent her head for him to rub her chin. Smiling at her purr, he looked around the yard. He hadn't been on a farm in so long. All the sights, sounds, and smells reminded him how much he missed it and revealed a deep ache for the little valley near Kinnim.

When he saw Jorvik and his brothers working on chores, Jace left the dragons and approached them. He gazed up at the barn in awe. Aldor's had probably been a quarter of the size.

"Morning," Halvar greeted him cheerfully.

Jace responded, and then nodded to the wide, open barn door. "Mind if I have a look inside?"

"Not at all." Halvar motioned for him to follow and led the way.

Large stalls lined the long corridor down the center. One of the first held a tall sorrel mare whose sides bulged.

"She's about to drop a foal any day," Halvar said.

The mare dipped her giant head over the rope across the stall, and Jace rubbed the white star on her massive forehead. He still couldn't get over the size of Dorland horses. A horse like this would make quick work of plowing a field back in Arcacia. He looked at her swollen belly again.

"Today or tomorrow, I'd say," he told Halvar.

The giant agreed. "Are you familiar with farming?"

"I lived on a farm for a couple of years before joining the Resistance." A shallow sigh escaped him. "I miss it though."

"Maybe someday you'll get back to it."

Jace looked up at Halvar and shrugged. He couldn't really see that. As long as Daican ruled, he and the others would be fugitives. No doubt they'd spend the rest of their lives in hiding, if they survived the advancement of the emperor's power.

They moved on, and Halvar gave him a tour of the rest of the barn and let him have a closer look at the cattle that, despite their size, were rather docile. Jace was interested in learning more about them, as well as the crops the brothers had planted. He forgot all about the time until Jorvik's booming voice called everyone in for breakfast.

Jace and Halvar walked away from the pasture and back to the cabin. When Jace entered, Kyrin was already at the table, and he slipped into the spot she had saved for him. She gave him a soft smile and asked, "Where have you been?"

"Halvar was showing me around the barn and the cattle." He paused. "It brings back memories."

A hush fell for Jorvik to offer a prayer. When he concluded, Jace opened his eyes and looked around. A mountainous bowl of fluffy scrambled eggs sat in the center along with an equally large bowl of fried potatoes and onions. On one side sat a platter of enormous strips of bacon. Another plate sat to the opposite side with slices of buttered toast just waiting for a thick slathering of jam. Jace's stomach growled. The giants sure knew the value of a good, home-cooked meal. He'd take this over fancy fare any day. The others seemed to agree, especially with the way Kaden filled his plate until it nearly overflowed.

Kyrin leaned forward past Jace to see her brother. "You're really going to eat all that?"

"Sure. Why not?"

Kyrin shook her head. "You'd think Mother and I starve you."

Jace chuckled at them and eagerly filled his own plate, though not quite as full as Kaden's.

Though they enjoyed the meal, they did not linger over it. After helping Jorvik and his brothers clear the tables, they left the cabin to saddle their dragons and horses. Jorvik had offered to take them to the ford to see if they could spot anything he and his brothers hadn't. They all headed west, toward the trees in the distance. It wasn't long before Jace spotted a sparkling ribbon of water ahead. The closer they came, the more he distinguished its features. Though not wide, it flowed swiftly, riddled with rocks and steep banks. Not good for crossing, as Darq had said—all but in one area.

When they reached the ford, they landed near the pebbly shore. The opposite bank sloped up gradually about fifty feet across from them, and though the water still moved along at a quick pace, it appeared shallow. They dismounted as Jorvik and his brothers joined them.

"This is the ford," Jorvik said. "Individually, one might find crossing points at other places along the river, but as a group with supplies or horses, this is the only safe way to cross into Dorland on foot."

They approached the river to have a better look. Jace studied the ground for any signs of people, but it didn't appear anyone had passed this way in at least a week. However, dozens of deer tracks left deep impressions in the moist dirt. He looked upriver. A couple hundred yards off, the tree line started. Thick towering pines that would offer cover from detection—just what a ryrik raiding party would want.

"Naeth and I will take a look around on the other side," Darq said. "Talas, you and Leetra fly around the area and see if you spot anything unusual."

The cretes returned to the dragons and took off.

"Why don't we spread out?" Balen suggested. "Jace, you can make a search to the north, and I'll go south. We'll see if we can find anything."

Jace nodded and headed north with Kyrin and Holden while everyone else stayed close to Balen. They moved along slowly, and Jace scanned the ground for any imprints or disturbed soil. When they reached the trees, he searched for paths that led in and out of the forest. He also kept a close watch, just in case someone was hiding in the underbrush waiting for them.

"Find anything?" Kyrin asked.

He shook his head. "If anyone has passed this way, it hasn't been for a while. Either that, or they've covered their trail well." Which was very possible. They were ryriks, after all. No other race of people was more skilled in the woods.

They turned back to the ford. Just as they joined up with the others, Darq, Naeth, Talas, and Leetra landed nearby. The captain spoke urgently. "Talas and Leetra spotted a lot of smoke northeast of here."

Jorvik looked in that direction. "Go; we'll meet you there."

Everyone scrambled to their dragons and launched into the air. Jace loosened his sword once Gem had leveled out. With the dragons, chances were they wouldn't even need their weapons, but his blood still stirred in anticipation of a possible fight. It wasn't long before a thick, gray plume of smoke billowed on the horizon. His gut cramped. Something big was burning— something like a cabin or barn.

In less than five minutes, they reached the source of the smoke, confirming his suspicions. A barn similar to Jorvik's blazed with roaring flames shooting through the roof. He looked around for the culprits. Only four giants occupied the yard. No ryriks were in sight, but the forest stood only a hundred yards from the cabin, providing a quick and convenient escape for the attackers.

They landed near the cabin and dismounted. The four giants were a man and woman and two children—a boy and girl—who, though young, stood nearly as tall as Jace. Both cried and clung to their mother. Their father sat on the ground, clutching his arm to his chest. Blood wet his sleeve, and a sword lay at his side. All four of them looked at the dragon riders in awe and, perhaps, some fear.

Darq approached the family first. "We're here to help you. We saw the smoke and came as quickly as we could."

Leetra hurried up to them, her familiar leather medical bag in hand. "May I see your arm?"

The man blinked in surprise. Leetra was so tiny next to him, and Jace had a feeling they'd never seen cretes before today. Still, he let her inspect the long gash to his forearm. Everyone else gathered around but kept enough distance so as not to crowd them or make them uncomfortable.

"What happened here?" Balen asked.

"Ryriks. They came out of the forest." The giant jutted his bearded chin toward the trees. "We didn't even know they were here until the barn was already in flames. They tried to set the cabin afire too."

"Did you kill any of them?"

The man gestured with his good arm toward the cabin. "One, yes."

Jace glanced that way. A dark body lay near the corner of the porch. Marcus and Kaden left the group and walked over to it. Stooping, Marcus picked up the dead ryrik's sword and turned back to them.

"Take a look at this. Another Arcacian sword. One could easily be explained by a raid somewhere in Arcacia, but two . . ." He shook his head. "That's more suspicious."

Balen looked grimly at the others but then focused again on the giants to introduce himself and the group.

"I'm sure glad you showed up," the man, whose name was Sev, said. "As soon as the ryriks spotted you coming, they ran off. If you hadn't come when you did, we would've lost the cabin, and much more." He looked at his wife and children.

"Thank Elôm we were nearby," Balen replied.

"Aye," Sev agreed.

Behind them, a horse's loud shriek echoed from somewhere in the forest. A jolt shot through Jace, and he gripped his sword as everyone spun toward the trees.

Sev growled. "The beasts ran off with one of my best mares."

"We should try to find them," Balen said. "It might be the only way we find out what's going on."

The men all seemed to agree, and they pulled out their weapons. Jace had to swallow his reluctance. The last time he'd faced ryriks, he and Kyrin had been lucky to survive. They were a strong group this time, but were they strong enough?

Most of the group moved toward the trees, commanding their dragons to follow, but Jace hung back and turned to Kyrin. "Stay here." Whatever they found in that forest, he didn't want her anywhere near it.

She nodded, but her wide eyes filled with unease. "Please be careful."

"I will." Jace turned to catch up to the others and found that Marcus had also hung back and was gripping Michael's arm. The boy had a scowl on his face.

"I can help."

252

Marcus shook his head and spoke with the firm and unrelenting tone of a captain. "You're staying here with Kyrin."

Michael opened his mouth to argue, but Marcus was already hurrying after the rest of the group. Jace cast Michael a quick look as he passed before he focused on what lay ahead. He called to Gem and caught up to the group at the forest's edge. They paused a moment before Balen pointed out the large hoof prints leading into the trees. "This way."

They plunged into the shadows of the forest, and Jace could only pray they had a large enough group to outnumber the ryriks and that their dragons would be as useful on the ground as in the air.

Kyrin watched the men disappear into the trees and hugged her arms around herself, a chill passing through her even in the bright sunshine. She couldn't stop the clear images playing in her mind of the time she and Jace had met the band of ryriks in the forest near camp. It still made her shiver and brought occasional nightmares.

"Please, Elôm, protect them," she whispered.

With a deep breath to calm herself, she shifted her attention to Michael. Her brother stared off at the forest, his shoulders sagging in a deflated stance.

"Hey, Marcus is just keeping his promise to Mother."

He turned to her, his brows still bent low. "I'm getting old enough to decide for myself if I want to face danger or not."

Kyrin couldn't help but smile. "I don't think older brothers are ever all right with letting their younger siblings put themselves in harm's way."

Michael just huffed, and Kyrin motioned to him. Together, they turned their attention to Leetra, who had also remained behind to stitch Sev's arm. After cleaning away the remaining blood, she applied a salve, and then wrapped it in bandages.

"There," she said. "In a few days the stitches can come out. Just keep it clean."

"Thank you." Sev pushed to his feet, taking his wife's hand and patting his still weepy little girl on the head. "We're all right."

"But what are we going to do about the barn?" the girl whimpered.

They all turned toward it. Flames consumed the entire structure now.

"We'll just have to build a new one," Sev said optimistically. "The important thing is we're all safe."

Kyrin smiled at the little girl's pouty face. She reminded Kyrin of Meredith, though she had thick wavy hair the color of ripe wheat.

An uncomfortable prickle crawled along the back of Kyrin's neck, and she sensed more than heard the movement behind her. A strong arm hooked around her waist, yanking her back against a hard chest. She gasped out a cry as another arm encircled her in a hold of iron.

Leetra and Michael spun around, whipping out their swords. Leetra's lavender eyes flashed wide, and she took a step forward but stopped at the thick, gravelly voice that growled in Kyrin's ear.

"Hold it right there or I'll break her neck."

A hand rose menacingly to Kyrin's throat. Her stomach plummeted at the glimpse of distinctive black hair along the man's forearm. A ryrik. *Elôm!* A tremor raced through Kyrin's body, and she struggled against him, but his hold wouldn't budge. He dragged her backward, toward the trees

Ivoris let out a menacing growl and charged at them. The ryrik swept Kyrin around, using her as a shield against the dragon.

Ivy slowed, growling and hissing threats, the air shimmering around her mouth.

"You'd better get her to back off or you'll die right now."

Kyrin swallowed against her fear. She hesitated but complied when the ryrik's grip on her neck tightened.

"Ivy, *tolla.*"

The dragon hissed again but didn't come any closer. Leetra's dragon growled and paced behind her. They resembled angry dogs that couldn't come to their master's aid.

Kyrin's gaze shifted to Leetra and Michael again. Her brother could only stare at her, mortified and helpless, while Leetra's eyes sparked with the desire to take action. However, they both knew how any attempt at a rescue would end.

The trees drew closer and any hope of help sank further away. With it the fear mounted, filling Kyrin's chest and jolting through her frantic heart. She fought the panic to think clearly. Her dagger! The one Jace had given her that she'd hidden behind the panel of her overdress.

Carefully, she moved her hand toward the weapon. *Please, Elôm, please help me.* Her fingers wrapped around the hilt. Gritting her teeth, she yanked it out with the intent to drive it back into the ryrik's thigh. But he was too quick. He snatched her wrist in his large hand and twisted it hard. She cried at the sharp stab of pain that pushed tears to her eyes, and the dagger dropped out of her hand.

"You're a feisty one." His breath warmed her neck, and she tried desperately to squirm away, but he was far too strong.

When they reached the tree line, she couldn't contain her panic any longer and screamed Jace's name. The ryrik's hand immediately clamped over her mouth, cutting off any further cries for help.

EVERYTHING ABOUT THIS screamed of danger to Jace. He wasn't the only one who had faced ryriks before and understood how dangerous they were, but should he have protested when Balen chose to go after them? It's true they were here to figure out what was going on, or, at the very least, end these raids, but what if there were more ryriks than Jorvik and his brothers knew about? Maybe they should have waited for the giant brothers to arrive to help them. Of course, the ryriks could have completely disappeared by then, leaving them once again with no answers.

Jace carefully scanned the trees and undergrowth as increasing unease churned inside of him. They couldn't be far from where the horse had whinnied. Would the ryriks be there? Or would they circle around and surround the group? If only he had Tyra here to help sense for danger. In this thick forest, ryriks could hide anywhere. Though the pines weren't as tall as the trees the cretes built in, they towered taller than any pine Jace had come across back home, shadowing the forest floor.

After another few yards, a powerful thudding vibrated the ground. He paused to listen more closely. Hooves.

"I think the horse is just ahead," he murmured.

They moved with extreme caution. The pounding of hoof beats grew louder and distressed snorting joined it. Coming upon a small clearing, they found the horse. The massive animal pawed and churned up the mossy ground with her enormous hooves. Blood ran down the side of one of her haunches. Her lead appeared stuck in some brush, but when Jace got a closer look, dread socked him in the gut. The lead wasn't stuck—it was tied. She had been left here deliberately.

He spun around to face the others. "It's an ambush!"

The words had barely left his mouth before an arrow swished right past his ear and narrowly missed Holden before slamming into a tree. Everyone jumped into action to protect Balen, backing to the edge of the clearing where they had more trees for cover. More arrows pursued them but missed, thank Elôm. They ducked into the brush and attempted to catch a glimpse of their assailants as the dragons growled behind them.

Then a sound reached Jace's ears that turned his blood to ice—Kyrin's scream. It echoed faintly in the trees but rang in his head like an alarm bell. He gasped her name. Every instinct and impulse urged him to get to her. His body was all ready to obey, but duty crashed in and halted him. How could he just run off with Balen still in danger? They were here to protect him.

But Kyrin!

His mind nearly tore itself apart in that split second battle before Rayad grabbed his arm. "Go!"

Jace needed no further prompting. Not even concerned by any arrows from behind, he raced back the way they had come—toward Kyrin's scream.

Blood surged hotly through his veins. There had only been one scream. What did it mean and what would he find? The last time he had heard her scream his name, his own brother had nearly assaulted her. His heart matched his pace. Images of riding into the farm back at home and finding Kalli and Aldor lying lifeless in the yard flitted through his mind. He shook them away.

When he broke from the trees, he stumbled to a halt. Leetra and Michael stood a few yards away, their swords in their hands.

But no Kyrin.

Jace could barely breathe. "Where is she?"

"A ryrik grabbed her." Leetra shook her head. "I wanted to stop him, but he threatened to kill her."

Jace's heart pounded with the force of a sledgehammer as the news sank in, rendering him momentarily paralyzed. But the flames inside him came roaring back. "Where did he take her?"

"Into the trees." Leetra gestured to the forest about thirty yards from where they stood.

Jace almost bolted straight for it but restrained himself. "We were ambushed. Help Balen and the others, and then come find us."

He didn't wait for her response—he just ran. On the way to the trees, a shard of metal caught the light in the grass. Kyrin's dagger. He snatched up the blade and stuck it in his belt without slowing. His blood throbbed inside him with the frantic desperation to reach her before she was harmed. *Elôm, please protect her! Please guide me!* He couldn't let himself consider what would happen if he couldn't find her. He *would* find her.

Only when he entered the forest did he slow. He needed to find a sign. Something to show him the right direction. If he chose wrong now, it would give the ryrik captor time to get away. He searched the ground, which seemed void of clues. There had to be something. He drew a deep breath and forced himself to focus. Then he spotted the faint impressions of footprints in the leaves and moss. Following them a few yards, he found where Kyrin had struggled and dragged her feet.

"I'm coming," he gasped.

He scanned the forest for any bit of movement. He couldn't be far behind. Pressing on, he continued to find signs—sometimes faint, other times obvious. After another hundred yards, he stopped to listen, struggling to hear over the thundering of his heartbeat. The forest was eerily silent. He had to be close. The fact that he hadn't found her yet nearly sent him into a panic. He swallowed down the fear rising in his throat and called her name.

Out of the dead silence came a muffled cry.

Jace's heart lurched. He gripped his sword in both hands and moved cautiously toward the sound, battling the urge to charge in. When he stepped around a grouping of saplings, he froze in his tracks. Four ryriks stood waiting for him. His gaze went straight to Kyrin. They had already bound her, and her captor had his arm firmly around her, a large blade pressed up under her chin. One quick move and she could be dead, just like that.

Only when one of the ryriks took a step toward him did he tear his gaze away from her to size the man up. He was the only one who didn't have a weapon drawn. His calm expression said he was in control and knew it. He was tall and strong like the other ryriks, yet something about him didn't add up—something Jace couldn't quite pinpoint. But all that mattered was getting Kyrin away from these men before they could cause her serious harm.

"Came alone, did you?" The ryrik's lips curled in a satisfied smile.

Jace looked him straight in the eyes. "Let her go."

The ryrik snorted. Of course, they never would.

"How about you drop your sword and surrender or . . ." he motioned to the man holding Kyrin, "she'll get hurt."

Jace's attention jumped back to Kyrin, who drew in a sharp breath and tried to tip her chin up away from the dagger that pressed against her skin.

"I'd hate to have to cut such a pretty throat right away," her ryrik captor said. He nuzzled his bearded cheek against her neck with a cruel chuckle. Kyrin squirmed but couldn't distance herself from him.

Furious heat burst through Jace's chest and limbs. He barely restrained himself from fighting his way to her. Only his fear for her safety held him in place.

"Let her go," he ground out.

"Not going to happen. You've got ten seconds to drop your sword before I order him to kill her."

Jace dug his fingers into the hilt of his sword. To surrender would leave him with no power to protect her, but he couldn't stand there and watch her die either. Even if he stalled long enough for the others to find them, the ryriks would kill her the moment they showed up. His fingers loosened.

"No, Jace, please don't." Kyrin's voice trembled. "Please, just go."

She was so brave, but he would never just leave her with these monsters.

"Time's wasting," the head ryrik said.

Before Jace could respond, Kyrin kicked her foot back into her captor's leg. He growled and spat a curse. Kyrin released a soft cry as his dagger cut into the flesh at her jawline. Jace stepped toward her, but two of the other ryriks blocked his path. Kyrin's captor forced her to her knees and grabbed her hair to yank her head back and place his dagger at her throat again. For a moment, all Jace could see was the blood trailing down the side of her neck.

"Jace, just run," she cried with a desperate tone that Jace could hardly bear to hear. Two tears rolled down her cheeks.

That was enough. Jace couldn't take the risk. He threw down his sword, silently begging Elôm for help. He would not leave her. Not even if it meant having to die with her. At least she wouldn't be alone. He would have to trust the others to find them and mount a rescue before that happened.

The two ryriks rushed in and grabbed him by the arms. They shoved him up against a tree, knocking the breath from his lungs and bruising his ribs, and tied his hands behind his back.

He twisted his neck around to look at Kyrin. Her head hung, more tears cascading down her anguished face. Blood still trickled down her neck. Jace strained against the ryriks, longing to reach her.

Once they'd searched him for weapons, the ryriks yanked him away from the tree and forced him to stand in front of their leader. Jace held his piercing eyes firmly. The man smirked and turned to Kyrin's captor.

"Bring her to me."

"Yes, Geric," the man grumbled as he slipped his dagger back into his sheath. He hauled Kyrin up and shoved her forward.

Geric took her securely by the arm and motioned the other man over to Jace. "Ruis, you keep an eye on him." His attention turned to the ryriks on either side of Jace. "You two cover the trail. We need to get out of here before the others show up."

Dragging Kyrin along with him, Geric turned and strode deeper into the forest. Kyrin looked back at Jace. He tried to offer her a look of reassurance, as if, somehow, he would get her out of this. But could he?

"Move." Ruis prodded him forward.

Jace followed Kyrin, staying as close to her as he could. Though it went against his usual instinct, he tried to leave as many tracks to follow as he could without alerting Geric and Ruis to his intentions. The ryriks behind them would cover most but, Elôm willing, they wouldn't completely erase all signs. Right now, the only escape Jace could see was a rescue from their friends. He couldn't stomach what would happen once the ryriks felt they were out of danger . . . what would happen to Kyrin. He swallowed back the fear of it and begged Elôm not to let her suffer at the hands of these monsters. He'd do anything, just so long as she got away safely.

A mile into the forest, his hopes for a quick and easy rescue faded when they joined up with a group of seven other ryriks.

Their vulturous eyes simultaneously locked on Kyrin. Jace clenched his fists, testing the strength of the rope around his wrists.

"Did you kill any of them?" Geric asked.

One of the ryriks shook his head. "We couldn't get close enough with their dragons there."

Geric scowled. "Well, at least we've got the Altair girl." He dragged Kyrin deeper into their midst, and Jace's heart gave a hard thud. How could they possibly know who she was?

She looked back at him again, her face held taut. Her confusion was as plain as the fear in her eyes, but he could see her fighting it. He wanted to tell her it would be all right, but too many ryriks stood around them. How could he be certain? *Elôm, please give me a way to rescue her.* He ground his teeth together, his blood still coursing with heat. *And don't let them harm her.*

"We'll have to watch ourselves," Geric said. "Those dragons will be flying over any time now." He nodded to one of the nearby ryriks. "Gag them. I don't want them calling out for help."

The man pulled some old cloths from his pack and tore two long strips. He handed one to Ruis and used the other on Kyrin. Jace glared defiantly at Ruis, but it didn't stop the man from forcing a wad of fabric into his mouth and tying the gag tightly at the back of his head. Jace grimaced at the bitterness of the cloth against his tongue.

Now that their captives were muted, the entire group of ryriks set off, heading south. Jace took a quick glance over his shoulder, praying their friends were just behind them, but the forest was void of anything to offer hope.

Kaden was the first to break out of the forest with Marcus right on his heels. He'd heard Kyrin scream, and it had taken every ounce of willpower to fight his instinct to race to her aid. Instinct probably would have won out if Jace had not gone.

His gaze swept the farm as he prayed to Elôm that he would see his sister standing unharmed with Jace, who would have kept her safe no matter what. Jorvik and his brothers had arrived and stood with Sev and his family, but where were Kyrin and Jace? He took another desperate look around, just to be sure, but found no sign of them.

Kaden rushed up to Sev. "Have they come back?"

The giant shook his head, his eyes full of regret. "Not yet."

Kaden's heart punched his ribs like an iron-covered fist, urging him to race into the forest after them. But he reined the impulse to a halt. Rushing into an unknown situation wouldn't help anyone. He needed to think, not react recklessly.

He spun around to face Marcus, who seemed to be going through the same thought process. "We need to find them."

His brother nodded.

By this time, the others gathered around them, and Captain Darq took charge. "Talas, you take Leetra and see if you can spot them from the dragons. The rest of us should split up—half of us to remain here with Balen while the other half searches for them on foot."

Balen immediately protested. "You might need me to help track them."

"I'm sorry, my lord," Darq replied, "but I just can't agree to that. It's too risky."

Balen frowned toward the forest as if contemplating whether or not to go anyway. Before he could speak again, Halvar stepped forward. "I'll go. I'm a good tracker. I've done a lot of hunting in this part of the woods."

They looked at him and then at Jorvik, who said, "He's right. You should take him."

Darq nodded and quickly chose Kaden, Marcus, Rayad, Holden, Timothy, and Aaron to go with Halvar while the rest stayed behind to guard Balen. Once it was settled, Michael stepped in. "What about me?"

Marcus faced him. "I want you to stay here."

Michael's mouth fell open. "But I want to help. You can't just keep leaving me behind."

"Michael, just do as I say." He did not yell, but he spoke firmly enough to show Michael and Kaden both just how worried he was.

Michael grumbled but didn't argue, and now was not the time to worry about his feelings. Every moment they stood here debating, Kaden's gut twisted itself into tighter knots. They had to get going. Anything could be happening to Kyrin and Jace.

The search group headed toward the trees with Halvar in the lead. A deep, churning wave of dread rolled inside of Kaden at the thought of what they might find, and he prayed earnestly that Kyrin and Jace were all right.

DESPAIR DRAGGED AT Jace for every mile and hour they traveled, the gloom only growing heavier. The ryriks forced them on at an arduous pace past midday and through the afternoon. His legs burned from the strain, and his throat ached for all the moisture the gag sucked away. Kyrin must be miserable. Every time she stumbled, he wanted to reach out to her, but his bound hands were useless behind his back. If only he alone were the captive.

The sun sank low and nighttime overtook the forest. Just before full darkness set in, the ryriks stopped in a hollow rimmed with tall ferns that provided cover.

Looking around, Geric nodded. "We'll stop here but no fire."

He led Kyrin over to a tree and told her to sit. Jace sank down close beside her, his legs welcoming the rest. Geric untied Kyrin's gag, and she bent over coughing. He removed Jace's next. Jace sucked in a deep breath now without the obstruction but, like Kyrin, he almost choked on the dryness of his mouth and throat. He tried to swallow, but his mouth was too parched.

He rejoiced when Geric handed Kyrin a waterskin. She grasped it in her bound hands and guzzled the water. A little bit ran down her chin. When she finished, she turned to Jace and held the waterskin to his lips. Though it was warm and stale, he gulped the water before Geric snatched the waterskin away from them. Jace swallowed his last mouthful and turned his attention to Kyrin. The cut on the side of her jaw had quit bleeding a while ago. With a closer look, it appeared to be little more than a nick to her flesh. Then their eyes locked. They said nothing, but he could almost read the question in her gaze: *What are we going to do?* All he knew was that he would do whatever it took to keep her safe.

Around them, the ryriks dug into their packs for their provisions. Geric tossed a small linen sack between Kyrin and Jace. "Eat."

Kyrin reached for it. Inside were strips of dried venison. She pulled a piece from the sack. After biting off some for herself, she tore off another small piece as best she could and held it to his mouth.

"Thank you," he murmured between chewing the leathery provisions.

She nodded, her eyes looking a little too moist. His chest ached with the desire to protect her. All day he had prayed not to be stuck with these men overnight.

But here they were.

They ate in silence; however, the ryriks filled the hollow with their coarse talk and crude jokes. Such crassness had surrounded Jace during his days as a gladiator, but that was such a long time ago, and he hated for Kyrin to be exposed to it. If only he could shield her from words as well as physical actions.

After some time, he noticed Geric didn't join in the conversations as much. Though clearly the leader, he seemed like an outsider as well. Jace watched him, trying to pinpoint that difference he'd detected earlier. It wasn't until Geric brushed back his hair and Jace caught a glimpse of his ears that he realized—they weren't as sharply pointed as the other ryriks' ears.

"You're not a full-blood ryrik."

Geric's eyes trained on him. He almost looked amused by Jace's observation. "No. I'm half, like you." He smirked. "You thought you might be the only one, didn't you? My father had a human wife. It's rare, but there are a few of us around."

One of the other ryriks made a comment about Geric's mother and Jace squirmed. Geric shot the man a glare, his eyes flickering with that dangerous ryrik light.

"You want to say that to my face?"

The other man remained silent this time, but his hard expression retained a challenging stubbornness.

Conversation resumed between the men and only grew rowdier as they passed a flask of alcohol around. Jace kept a close watch on them, his every nerve taut with a growing sense of impending trouble. He prayed he was wrong, but after a couple of hours, Ruis stood. His gaze fell on Kyrin, and she stiffened next to Jace. Though, by now, it would have been too dark for her to make out many details, the eerie glow of Ruis's eyes would be easy even for her to see. What she probably couldn't see was the lecherous look on his face. Jace clenched his bound fists, his blood temperature rising rapidly.

The ryrik strode toward them.

"Ruis," Geric warned.

"I'm just going to have a look at her," Ruis snapped, but his eyes said otherwise.

Jace shoved to his feet and took a stand in front of Kyrin. He strained his wrists against his bindings. *Please, Elôm, break these ropes. I need my hands!*

Ruis stopped short and glared at him, yet his lips curled with cruel amusement. "You think you're going to stop me?"

Jace let his fighting blood flow through him. He didn't know what he could do without the use of his hands, but he had to do something. Ruis reached to shove him out of the way, but Jace lowered his shoulder and rammed it into Ruis's chest. Caught off guard, Ruis stumbled a few steps before recovering. He twisted away and used Jace's momentum against him. Without his arms to catch himself, Jace lost his balance and fell hard to the ground.

With a low chuckle, Ruis made his way to Kyrin once again. A small cry escaped her when he grabbed her and pressed her up against the tree.

"Not so feisty now, are you?" he sneered in her face.

Jace scrambled back to his feet, energized by Kyrin's struggles. Again, he used his shoulder to slam into Ruis. He had no other recourse. Ruis staggered away from Kyrin. Jace didn't stop until both he and Ruis crashed to the ground. Growling, the ryrik flailed around in the leaves, and Jace struggled to regain his feet first. However, as Ruis pushed himself up, he swung out his right arm. A glint of metal caught Jace's eyes. He scrambled away, but it caught him across the shoulder and left side of his chest. After a momentary sting, any pain disappeared amidst the heat of his blood.

Ruis lunged toward him, dagger still in hand. Jace attempted to recover his feet again, but the man grabbed his ankle, and he fell to his back. Kyrin gasped a split second before Ruis was on top of him. The very tip of the dagger pierced the skin of his stomach just below his ribs. He tensed, waiting for the rest of the blade to follow.

"Ruis!"

Geric's voice halted everything. Jace stared up at his would-be murderer. The pressure on the dagger increased, slicing a bit more flesh, and Jace held his breath. However, Geric spoke again.

"A dead prisoner is of no value to us."

Ruis let out another low growl in his throat and leaned down to sneer in Jace's face, "You're lucky, half-blood. I'd gut you right here."

He pushed to his feet and stepped away. Jace let out the breath trapped in his lungs. He then rolled to his side, maneuvering himself to his knees as he watched Ruis and Geric come face to face and stare each other down.

"From now on, you'll keep away from the girl," Geric commanded, his voice low.

Ruis scowled. "You just want to keep her for yourself."

"I'm keeping her for the emperor. If all you want is a girl, then go back to Arcacia and raid a village. I intend to collect that gold Daican promised, and you can bet she and whoever else we manage to bring him will be worth a small fortune. If that doesn't mean anything to you, then get out of here and don't come back."

Ruis only glared for a moment, but he returned to his place with the other ryriks, muttering dark threats under his breath. Geric cast a look at Jace, though he said nothing. A second later, Kyrin was at Jace's side. She said his name in a trembling voice, and he looked into her face. Her cheeks were wet and her skin almost white, but she was unharmed. She helped him to his feet and back over to the tree. Here, she looked down at her hands, and her expression tensed as her eyes flew back to him.

"You're bleeding."

Red coated both her palms, and only then did he register pain—a deep, stinging pain that spread across his shoulder and just below his collarbone. He looked down to assess the damage. His shirt and jerkin had a long slice through them.

"Sit back," Kyrin told him. "I'll try to stop it."

Jace leaned against the tree, and Kyrin placed her hands over the wound, applying pressure. He winced a little and could feel her hands shaking against him. If only he were free of his blasted bindings! He longed to wipe her tear-streaked face and hold her until the fear left her eyes.

"Are you all right?"

Her gaze met his briefly but faltered. She nodded, biting her lip as she stared down at her hands.

Jace tipped his head to try to see into her eyes. "I'm going to do whatever I can to protect you."

Her chin rose a little, and her gaze met his, holding this time. She blinked at the moisture gathering near her lashes. They both knew it was a futile promise. After all, Ruis had been only a breath away from killing him. Any further confrontations and he would probably succeed. Still, Kyrin seemed to draw strength from his words. She pulled in a ragged breath and nodded again. She then glanced over her shoulder and spoke softly to let the hum of conversation behind her mask her words.

"It's true. They are working for Daican. And they intend to hand us over to him."

Jace stared past her, determined to find a way to escape before that happened. If only the men weren't ryriks. They were entirely too good in the woods and anything like darkness would be of no advantage in an escape. His attention shifted back to Kyrin.

"It's a long way to Valcré. Anything could happen before then." Good or bad, though he prayed for good.

After a time, Kyrin removed her bloodied hands from his wound. "I think it's stopped. I wish I could see how bad it is."

"Try to pull the fabric apart so I can see it," Jace said.

Carefully, she spread the ripped edges of his shirt apart near his shoulder, giving him a glimpse of the wound. It was deep, as he suspected, but she was right that the bleeding had stopped.

"It'll be all right," he told her.

She stared at him as if not quite sure.

"It could use stitches, but for now, it's fine." And the least of their worries.

Her face still taut, Kyrin wiped her hands in the leaves and stepped around to his other side, where she sat down next to him, their shoulders resting together. She breathed out a long, tired breath.

"Try to rest, if you can," Jace said. "I'll keep watch."

Hesitancy overcame her expression, but after a moment, she leaned her head against his shoulder.

The hours passed slowly. Jace's eyes grew tired, but he would not close them. Not even for a moment. Especially not when it seemed Kyrin had actually fallen asleep. By now, most of the ryriks had settled down and slept as well, except for Geric. He sat fiddling with his dagger, casting a look at Jace and Kyrin every so often. Some may have tried to escape during the long periods he wasn't looking, but Jace knew better. They wouldn't get fifty yards.

Nighttime quiet stretched out around them, unbroken, until a low howl resonated in the distance. Jace had heard wolves all the time on the farm, but the tone of this one prickled the hair along his arms and neck. Kyrin jerked awake beside him, and Ruis and several of the other ryriks looked up from their bedrolls. Geric swore and sent Ruis a fiery glare.

"Now look what you've done. His blood will draw them right to us." He gestured at Jace.

Agitated murmurings came from the other ryriks.

Jace shared a tense look with Kyrin. If a large group of ryriks were disturbed by a wolf pack, then these were no ordinary wolves.

Geric pushed to his feet. "Everyone get up. We're moving. Maybe we can lose them. I won't have them tailing us back to camp. We've lost enough horses as it is."

The ryriks hurried to pack their belongings. As they finished, Jace caught Ruis giving him a stomach-turning look. The man then walked up to Geric.

"I know how to lose them."

Geric's eyes narrowed. "How?"

Ruis nodded at Jace. "We leave him behind as bait."

JACE'S HEART STALLED in his chest, and he heard Kyrin's breath catch.

Geric immediately dismissed the idea. "I intend to hand them both over to the emperor."

But Ruis pressed on, and Jace suspected this had more to do with their confrontation than drawing off the wolves.

"What's he worth? Not nearly as much as the girl. You have her and can use her to catch some of the others. Better to leave him here than to have a pack of wolves on our heels. He can't be worth that much. He's a troublemaker anyway."

Geric peered at Ruis for a long moment in consideration, and Jace held his breath. *Please don't separate me from Kyrin. She can't be left alone with them.*

However, Geric nodded, and Jace's heart dropped to the bottom of his stomach.

"Fine, we'll leave him."

Ruis grinned wickedly and motioned to a couple of his companions. They started for Jace and Kyrin. Heat pulsed through Jace as Kyrin held onto his arm. His breaths came hard and fast. He couldn't let them take her. Somehow, he had to stop them.

One of the ryriks grabbed Kyrin and ripped her away.

"No!" she cried.

Jace shoved to his feet and lunged toward them, but Ruis and another ryrik caught him by the arms. He struggled against them with all his might, but a third ryrik joined in to subdue him. Suddenly, the ropes released from around his wrists. A burst of raging energy swelled inside him, and he fought like he never had before to get to Kyrin. Yet he just couldn't match the ryriks or break their hold.

They slammed him back against the tree and wrenched his arms around it, once again binding his wrists. As an extra measure, they wound a rope around him and the tree twice, rendering him powerless.

Ruis stepped back to admire his handiwork. Jace glared at him, his blood flowing like fire in his veins. Every muscle squeezed taut for action as he strained against the ropes, but they held fast. Sneering, Ruis reached out and tore Jace's blood-streaked sleeve from his arm. He then pressed it roughly to Jace's wound, which had begun to bleed again during his struggles. Jace sucked in a breath through his teeth at the jolt of pain. Using his sword, Ruis hung the sleeve, now blotted with fresh blood, from a branch above Jace's head. It swayed in the breeze—a breeze that would carry the scent far into the surrounding forest.

"Enjoy the wolves," Ruis said.

He turned to join the others.

Jace's gaze locked with Kyrin's. He had seen her in many difficult situations, but he'd never witnessed the kind of terror that filled her eyes at that moment. Geric took her by the arm.

"No." Her voice rose in panic as she fought against him. "You can't just leave him here to die. Please!"

She pulled and strained, but Geric dragged her right along with him. "Jace!"

"Kyrin," he gasped her name.

Tears flowed from her eyes, and she screamed for him again just before they disappeared up over the lip of the hollow.

No! He yanked at the rope around his wrists and leaned hard against the bindings across his chest. *Please, Elôm!* He had to break free. He struggled with all his strength, driven by the carrying sound of Kyrin's pleading, but after a couple of minutes, all sounds of life died away.

A new wave of despair crashed over Jace. They'd taken her. Kyrin was gone—the captive of a group of ryriks—and he hadn't been able to stop it. He was stuck here, helpless, while they were free to do whatever they wanted with her. *Elôm, You can't let this happen.*

"Please," he gasped. Moisture filled his eyes.

But then the despair hardened to steel inside of him. He wouldn't give up—not now, not ever. He would fight for her until his last breath. Heat engulfed him again. He had to get out of this. He strained and twisted against the ropes at any angle he could manage.

Minutes later, he paused, panting. They hadn't budged. He dragged in a couple deep breaths, forcing himself to think. Then he rubbed the ropes around his wrists against the rough tree bark. Maybe he could fray and weaken them enough to snap them. It was his only hope now.

Jace's arms cramped and burned. He struggled to draw in a good breath against the ropes. Somewhere amidst his fight to get free, the sun had risen, but he didn't think about the time or even about the wolves he'd been left behind for—only getting free. He blocked out the pain from his mind by picturing Kyrin. He had to save her.

However, his attempts to free himself grew sluggish as his strength depleted, and he paused for the first time in what could have been hours. He gasped for breath, his lungs burning from exertion, and looked up toward the sky. Through the thick pine boughs, he could just make out the sun. It was nearly midday. Cold washed over him despite the sweat that covered his body. Even if he did break free, Kyrin and the ryriks would be miles ahead of him by now.

Despair crept in again. He hung his head, which had begun to pound. His vision blurred, but he blinked it back into focus, his gaze settling on the blood that dripped down his jerkin. All his struggling had caused the wound to bleed more heavily. It soaked the ropes near his shoulder and dotted the grass below him in crimson.

Still trying to catch his breath, Jace closed his eyes as the full weight of his helplessness descended on him.

"Elôm," he whispered past his dried-out lips, "please, help me. Please, break me free." He didn't even realize tears had leaked from his eyes until they dripped off his chin. "Please let me get to Kyrin before they can hurt her. Please protect her."

He swallowed hard, the weakness that had overtaken his body settling in. He didn't feel as if he had anything left in him with which to fight. "Elôm, I need Your strength."

Gritting his teeth, he lifted his head and looked to the last spot he had seen Kyrin before they had taken her away from him. The fire inside him that had long since cooled flared back to life.

"I won't stop, Kyrin," he gasped out. "I won't stop."

His blood flowing hot again, he went back to grinding the ropes against the tree. He would continue until they snapped or until the wolves showed up. Twenty minutes later, he paused to test the ropes again. They seemed to have slackened just a little. He tugged and twisted as hard as he could, straining to the point where his bones threatened to snap. But it didn't matter. He only needed to get free. With a hoarse cry, he gave a final yank and, at last, the ropes gave way and his hands broke free. He gasped. *Thank You!*

He reached up for the ropes bound around his chest and pulled them up over his head. When he took a step away from the tree, he dropped straight to his knees, his chest heaving. His entire body shook with the effort of the last hours.

Gathering his ragged remnants of strength, he forced himself up. After a couple of wobbly steps, his determination took over and drove him forward. Kyrin was out there, and he was going to reach her.

Kyrin had faced some dark days of fear and loss that she had prayed never to have to experience again, and today was one of those days. Jace was probably dead by now, and here she was alone with the monsters that had left him to the wolves. Every time she let herself think of it, tears rushed into her eyes. She'd struggled against despair until her body and heart were just too heavy to fight anymore.

Hours later, she stumbled along in a daze. Her prayers had become little more than desperate internal cries of, *Elôm, please help* and *Please don't let him be dead*. She had nothing else. If she thought too deeply about losing Jace or what lay ahead, she would fall apart completely.

They marched on and on through the thick forest without rest. Geric dragged her along at a grueling pace until she thought her legs would give out.

Her eyes blurred with weariness and tears, making it difficult to see where she was going, much less care, until her foot sank into a hole. Her ankle twisted, and she fell to her knees with a cry. The group halted. Kyrin bit her lip, struggling to hide her pain and the weakness ryriks preyed upon. Even so, the tears flowed out before she could stop them, and she cried with all the pain of her broken heart.

She'd lost Jace.

And all her captors did was sneer and taunt.

After a minute, Geric ordered, "Get up."

Kyrin didn't want to get up. Her ankle throbbed, and she had no strength. Yet, to give up would surrender total victory to these ryriks. She had nothing to fight them with except her courage and determination. Though she wasn't sure she had any left, she begged Elôm for His aid and forced herself to rise, terrified of the future, but unwilling to quit.

Pain shot through her ankle, and she almost collapsed again. Gritting her teeth, she took another couple of steps, but it forced a groan to her throat. She swiped the tears from her cheeks and looked at Geric, fighting to stop her voice from trembling. "I twisted my ankle. I don't think I can walk on it."

Geric gave a peevish sigh. He then bent down and hoisted her up over his shoulder before she could protest. Kyrin squirmed but then gave up. This was the only way they would get where they were going, and they all knew it. Struggling would only waste her energy.

Kyrin winced at the way Geric's shoulder pressed into her ribs and stomach, but settled in as comfortably as she could. Closing her eyes, she prayed desperately for deliverance and a miracle for Jace.

Jace pressed on as fast as he was able to pick up signs of which way Kyrin had gone. The ryriks didn't leave much behind, but it was enough to keep him going in the right direction. As long as he knew which way to go, he wouldn't stop until he caught up.

His breaths came in short puffs, and his throat ached for moisture. He had no food or water besides a few berries he'd found along the way, but he had no time to worry about that. Right now, he had to gain ground . . . before night set in and the ryriks stopped. Before Ruis had a chance to finish what he'd started last night. Jace didn't know what he'd do without weapons when he did catch up but, somehow, he would find a way with Elôm's help.

Mid-afternoon, he paused and knelt to study the leaf-littered ground for tracks. When he pushed to his feet, dizziness assaulted him. He closed his eyes and pressed his fingers to them, willing the sensation away. Opening them again, he blinked to refocus and spotted a couple drops of his own blood in the leaves below him. He focused on his wound. Though not bleeding heavily, it hadn't stopped.

He flinched as he moved his left arm to tear off his other sleeve. Wadding up the fabric, he stuck it under his jerkin with the hope that it would staunch the flow of blood. It was the best he could do without supplies or time.

He drew a head-clearing breath to continue his pursuit. Just before he moved, a stick snapped. He froze, his senses sharpening, and peered into the trees. Nothing stirred. Not even birds. Maybe he'd made up more ground than he thought. A chill tickled the back of his neck and spine. The forest might have appeared empty, but eyes watched him. He could feel it. He waited a moment to see if a ryrik arrow would puncture his chest and then scanned the area around him. A sturdy stick lay a few feet away. He bent to pick it up.

When he straightened, his heart lurched. Ten yards away stood a wolf unlike any he'd ever encountered. As big as a bear, it stared him down with cold yellow eyes. Its lips curled to reveal long fangs, and a deep growl rumbled in its throat. Jace gripped the stick in his hand more tightly. Movement flashed in his periphery. Three more wolves stalked toward him. Checking his other side and behind him, he realized the grim truth—the pack had him surrounded. While he'd focused on tracking his own prey, the pack had stalked him.

The first wolf took a couple tentative steps toward him, saliva dripping from its mouth as it sniffed the air. Jace pointed the stick at it, and it growled again. Slowly, the other wolves closed in on him. Jace racked his brain for a plan. He'd been in countless dire situations, but all his training and experience gave him no solutions for taking on a pack of wolves more than three times the size of Tyra without a real weapon.

The first wolf drew within striking distance. Jace raised the stick and brought it down with a crack on the wolf's snout. It jumped back with a yelp, and the other wolves retreated a few yards before immediately beginning their advance again. The moment one came close, he swung at it with a shout, praying they would decide he was not worth the trouble. However, after only a few minutes, the wolves grew bolder. Soon they would realize he wasn't a true threat and charge in.

He swung the stick around, but the deadly circle was closing. Then one of the wolves grabbed the stick before he could swing it. He yanked on it, but another wolf lunged toward him. All at once, they moved in. He bolted toward the only opening in their tight circle, but one of them snapped at his leg, its teeth only stopped by the leather of his boot, and he fell.

It was over. He would die.

He put his arms over his head and neck in a futile defense. In a flurry of snapping teeth and growls, the pack converged on him. Fear and a heartrending hopelessness coursed through him. The ryriks had succeeded, and he had failed.

Jaws clamped over his arm, but before the teeth could fully sink in, one of the wolves let out a loud yelp, and then another. A shout echoed above it—a man's shout. Others joined him, and the wolves scattered.

Jace slowly looked up, gulping for the air he truly hadn't believed he would still be breathing moments ago. Yet it died in his chest when his eyes rose to his rescuers.

Ryriks.

JACE HOBBLED TO his feet, shaking from the adrenaline and terror of near death, and stared at the men. They weren't the same ones who had taken Kyrin, but they were ryriks—each of them as strong and tall, if not taller, than he was. A couple had bows, but the others carried longswords. His gaze settled on the man who was just finishing off one of three dead wolves. Wiping his sword clean, the man slid it back into the scabbard and turned to face Jace. He had his raven black hair tied away from his bearded face and was dressed like a woodsman rather than in an odd combination of stolen clothing like most ryriks. All seven men in the group dressed similarly.

"I don't know how you got out here, but I've never seen anyone so narrowly escape death."

The man spoke in such a conversational, non-threatening manner it took Jace aback. Did they believe him to be a fellow ryrik? Was that why?

The man's gaze dropped to his bloodied clothing again. "Looks like wolves haven't been your only trouble. What are you doing out here? You're a long way from any settlements."

Jace hesitated and glanced warily at the others. Should he answer or try to get away without confrontation? His eyes slid back to connect with the other man's, which were bright with what appeared to be genuine curiosity.

"I was captured by ryriks." He paused to gauge their reaction.

The man's black brows drew together, and his eyes narrowed, a light growing in them. "The ones terrorizing the giants?"

"Yes," Jace answered slowly. "I was injured last night. When they heard the wolves early this morning, they tied me to a tree as bait. I managed to get free, but the wolves followed."

The man exchanged glances with his companions. "If we hadn't shown up when we did, there wouldn't be much left of you. You can thank the King we did."

Jace's eyes went wide. "The King?"

"Yes, King Elôm." The man stood taller as if prepared to fight for the truth of his words. "The God of Ilyon."

Jace could only stare as his thoughts spun in circles. *Elôm?* These ryriks were believers? Then the dizziness returned, and his knees gave out.

"Whoa, easy." The man knelt in front of him. He braced Jace's good shoulder and handed him a waterskin. "Drink this. Looks like you've lost a lot of blood and are dehydrated."

Jace brought the waterskin to his lips and gulped the water that was a lot fresher than Geric's had been, soothing his throat.

"We better get that wound looked at."

Jace swallowed another mouthful and shook his head. "No, I have to go. I wasn't the only captive. The ryriks also took a woman. I have to get to her and free her before . . ." He swallowed hard. "Before anything happens to her."

He moved to rise, but the ryrik held him down. Heat flared in Jace's chest, and he tensed to fight. However, he paused at the understanding in the man's expression.

"You won't be much help to anyone in this condition. At least drink more water and eat something. Then we'll help you go after them."

"You'll help me?"

The man nodded. "You can't very well take them on your own. You don't even have a weapon."

Jace let out a huge sigh, so overwhelmed he didn't even know how to thank them or Elôm.

A kind smile spread across the man's face. He offered his other hand to Jace. "I'm Saul, by the way."

"Jace." He gripped the man's hand firmly.

"All right, Jace, you just keep drinking that." Saul shrugged off his pack and pulled a leather pouch of dried berries out of it. "And eat some of these. First thing we need to do is get you out of those bloody clothes or the wolves will keep trailing us."

"Whatever you do, please hurry," Jace urged him. "The ryriks are at least a couple of hours ahead of me."

"Don't worry, we have horses a short way back." He turned to the other men and sent them to get the mounts.

After Jace put a handful of berries into his mouth, Saul helped him remove his jerkin and shirt, revealing the deep laceration from his shoulder almost to his throat.

"You're fortunate this isn't more serious. It needs stitches, but we'll worry about that later."

Saul wet a cloth from his pack and handed it to Jace to clean away the blood from his chest and arm, as well as from the bite wound that had barely broken skin. It wasn't until that moment he noticed how chafed and raw his wrists and the backs of his hands were. Blood had caked there too. He cleaned up quickly and let Saul cover his wounds with a roll of bandages. The man then offered him a clean shirt from his pack.

"Thank you," Jace said as he slipped it on.

After a few more mouthfuls of berries and water, he was ready to go again. Saul rose first and offered him a hand to pull him to his feet. Looking him in the eyes, the man said, "We will get your girl back."

Nightfall crept in like the approach of an unseen but deadly enemy. Kyrin had prayed for it not to come, yet couldn't stall the sinking sun. A shudder passed through her. Now that Jace was gone, would Ruis leave her alone? Would Geric stop him if he didn't? She grew cold at the memory of Ruis's hands on her last night and the powerlessness of her situation.

"Jace." His name passed her lips in a silent whisper, and her already sore eyes stung. She could hardly bear to face these men on her own, let alone deal with the sorrow that Jace might be dead.

No, she wouldn't let herself believe it. He was strong and resourceful. If anyone could get free, it was him. And he knew the forest better than anyone. He'd escape the wolves. *Oh, Elôm, please let it be so!*

She shifted to try to relieve the pressure on her ribs. They were starting to ache, and it was hard to take a decent breath. She wanted to get down, yet as long as they were still moving, she didn't have to fear Ruis. Once they stopped, that changed.

Fear slowly rose like a flood inside her, but she squeezed her eyes shut, battling it with prayer. *I might feel alone, Elôm, but I know I'm not. You are here, just like in the dungeon in Auréa. I am so afraid. Afraid that I've lost Jace for good and afraid of what will happen to me.* She swallowed hard, fighting to enforce her weak thread of courage. *I don't know if I can stay strong. Please strengthen me. Please rescue me.*

Her eyes popped open at the sound of rushing water. It grew in volume until they stopped.

"Now, no squirming unless you want to end up in the water," Geric said.

Kyrin twisted around just enough to see that they stood along the Trayse River, which ran swiftly several feet below them.

Stretching out across the river lay a huge fallen pine that looked as though passersby had used it as a bridge for some time. All of its branches were broken or cut away, leaving an unobstructed, yet perilous crossing. Kyrin sucked her breath as Geric stepped onto it, balancing her on his shoulder as he walked across.

Kyrin stared down at the churning dark river. Would she stand a better chance braving the rushing water than staying with these ryriks? All she had to do was throw her weight to one side and both she and Geric would go over. However, in a swift river like this, it would probably be suicide. She never had been a strong swimmer, and she had the disadvantage of having her hands tied.

When they reached the safety of the opposite bank, Kyrin prayed she hadn't just wasted her only opportunity to escape. Once again, they plunged into the thick pines of the forest on the other side. Kyrin didn't expect them to stop for a while, but a couple of miles from the river, she caught the scent of smoke on the breeze. After another half a mile or so, voices echoed in the trees, and they stepped into a clearing. Kyrin caught sight of a large fire burning and several ryriks sitting around it. Would they all keep away from her if Geric told them to?

Elôm.

At the fire's edge, the man finally put her down. Her ankle protested, but she shifted her weight to her other foot. She peered around the fire, her throat closing as she met the other ryriks' too-interested stares.

"You only caught one of 'em?" an especially burly ryrik asked.

"We had the half-ryrik too but had to leave him to the wolves," Geric answered, and Kyrin's heart reacted painfully.

Another of the ryriks spoke up. "Well, if you had to bring just one of them, you made the right choice in bringing the girl."

He traded cruel laughter with his companions, and Kyrin took a step back from the fire feeling as though she were surrounded by wolves herself. She glanced up at Geric, praying he would protect her despite being one of them.

"She goes to Daican as is." Geric gave them a stern look.

The first ryrik scowled. "What does he care? He can still behead her. We just want to have a little fun first."

"I won't risk his wrath or the gold. She's the most valuable thing we have. With her, we can draw in her brothers, if not more from their group. The king may not give himself up, but just imagine if we hand over four Altairs to the emperor. You can take your gold and go buy yourself a whole string of women if you want."

The ryrik grumbled, but he didn't argue.

Kyrin swallowed with dread. How did they even know her brothers were here in Dorland or that Balen was with them?

Movement on the other side of the fire drew her attention. A man stood there who clearly wasn't a ryrik—he was a crete. Her eyes widened as his gaze met hers. Something sparked familiarity, and she searched her memories until one came to her. She'd seen him the night of the celebration in Arvael. He hadn't spoken, but he'd been amongst Cray's group. It all made sense now. He must have followed them when they left the city and alerted the ryriks when they'd arrived at the ford.

Kyrin glared at the traitor, but he just stared at her, his expression hard and unchanging.

Geric motioned to one of the nearest ryriks at the fire. "I'm putting her in our tent. You can stand watch. The rest of us need to eat."

The ryrik looked her up and down with a half grin and a chilling gleam in his eye as he stood. Kyrin fought not to show any intimidation, but she feared she did a poor job of it. He looked all too pleased to be her guard.

Geric led her toward one of the canvas tents at the tree line. Kyrin limped along with him, her ankle smarting. It swelled against the inside of her boot. They ducked into the tent supported by a single thick pole propped up in the center. She glanced at the two bedrolls on either side and couldn't suppress a shudder. Would she have to share the tent with these men?

Geric turned her to face him and tugged at the knots in the rope around her wrists. When her hands came free, she rubbed the bruised and chafed skin with a wince.

"Sit down." Geric gestured to the ground at the base of the tent pole.

Kyrin hesitated, reluctant to give up her momentary freedom but didn't wait for him to force her. Careful of her ankle, she sat down against the pole, and Geric tied her arms back around it. Without a word, he left her alone. His footsteps took him away from the tent, but her guard stood just outside, his bulky figure silhouetted against the canvas by the glow of firelight. She gulped, praying he wouldn't sneak inside while no one was looking.

Kyrin scanned the tent again, though it was difficult to see in the darkness if anything could be used to her benefit. She tested her bindings, but they were too tight to work loose. She felt around the base of the pole. Maybe she could try to work the ropes under it. However, even if she managed to raise the poll up enough, the entire tent might collapse on her and give her away. She let out a long, shaky breath. Unless Elôm provided a miraculous way of escape, she was trapped.

THE MILES CRAWLED by while the hours did the opposite. They flew past, leaving Kyrin in harm's way for longer and longer. Though the ryriks' trail had become easier to read, Jace still felt as though they would never catch up.

A couple of hours after nightfall, Saul called the group to a halt near a small stream. "We'll stop here for a short time." He glanced at Jace. "The horses need a rest, especially if we have to leave quickly once we have your girl."

Every instinct and desire inside Jace fought against stopping, but Saul was right. The horses did need to rest if they were to be of any use later. He slid down and led the mare they'd let him ride to the stream to drink. Suddenly aware of how dry his throat had become again, he cupped his hands and scooped up some water for himself. When he finished, he turned to where Saul was digging through his pack.

"Now that we've stopped, we'll tend your wound properly."

He motioned to a mossy log, and Jace took a seat, pulling off his shirt. Though not saturated, some blood had seeped through the bandages—another reason to stitch the wound. He didn't want to provide any more scent for the wolves to follow.

Saul drew a leather pouch from his pack and then unwrapped the bandages. After cleaning away the fresh blood, he pulled a vial from the pouch that looked like the one Leetra always carried with her. Jace drew a deep breath, knowing how it would sting. Saul said nothing but cast him a look as if asking if he was ready. Jace nodded, and the man poured the clear liquid carefully along the wound. It seeped in and set the nerves on fire. He sucked in his breath through his teeth and swallowed down a groan. As the pain subsided, Saul threaded a thin needle and went to work closing the wound.

"So, what's her name?" he asked, distracting Jace from the unpleasant sensation of the needle.

Jace sat quietly for a moment. They'd talked some during the afternoon, but even though Saul and the others professed belief in Elôm, a part of him still hesitated at sharing such personal information with them. They were ryriks. He told himself it shouldn't matter, but it did. Still, he'd seen the looks of evil men so many times, and Saul had been nothing but helpful and genuine.

"Kyrin." Just saying her name stabbed his chest with the longing to reach her. "Kyrin Altair." Though he watched for a reaction, Saul gave none. The name didn't seem to mean anything to him. Maybe the infamy of it hadn't reached out here in the wilderness. "We're wanted by Emperor Daican. That's why they took us. So they could hand us over to him."

Saul frowned. "They're working for the emperor?"

"Apparently. I think he's offering them gold to attack the giants. I guess they figured they could get more by delivering anyone he considers a traitor."

Saul just grunted in agreement and finished stitching the wound. Once the bandages were back in place, Jace pulled on his shirt and accepted more berries and some jerky from Saul. Though not hungry, he felt the way his body craved energy. If rescuing Kyrin came down to a fight, he needed to be prepared.

"What were you doing out here when you found me?" he asked as they ate.

"Tracking the wolves," Saul answered. "They've been hanging around our village and getting after our livestock. We thought we'd thin out the pack and bring back some pelts."

Jace thanked Elôm for placing them nearby. His desire to reach Kyrin had eclipsed the miracle of it, but now it sank in. Not only had they saved his life but, without them, would he have even had a chance of saving Kyrin on his own?

"Thank you for rescuing me. I must confess I didn't know if I should trust you and questioned your motives. I've never heard of any ryriks who believed in Elôm." Jace hesitated. "And I wasn't completely sure it was possible given what most people believe about ryriks' souls."

A moment of quiet followed his confession, but instead of looking offended, Saul nodded slowly. "Who could blame you, considering the reputation ryriks have? There haven't been enough of us to change it."

"How many of you do follow Elôm?"

"More than most would think, but we tend to keep hidden here on this side of the Trayse River and away from Arcacia. There are many villages south of here set up for ryriks who don't wish to follow in the violence that is so prevalent among our race. At least half of us follow the King."

"So you do have souls," Jace said, more as a statement than a question.

"Yes," Saul replied with certainty. "Not all of us rebelled against Elôm. There has always been a faithful remnant of us who have followed Him. What most people don't know is that Elôm created ryriks, with all of our fire and passion, to fight for justice and righteousness. Such a thing has been long since forgotten by Ilyon, but we're diligent in passing the knowledge down through our faithful generations."

Amazement swelled inside Jace. He'd accepted his ryrik blood and its origins as a fact that didn't define who he was, but Saul's words changed everything. It meant his blood didn't just belong to a race most of Ilyon viewed as monsters but a race created by Elôm for a noble purpose. *Is it true, Lord?* A quiet affirmation settled in his heart. He had let go of his former insecurities and doubts, but some of them must have remained because they released now.

He shook his head, his voice a little rough. "I never would have known that."

Saul smiled in understanding. "Perhaps someday, Elôm willing, more people will know."

They fell silent for a few minutes as Jace contemplated how such knowledge could change things. Yet, even if others never found out, he knew, and it had the potential to affect his entire life. He couldn't wait to share it with Kyrin. She would be overjoyed. He smiled faintly as he imagined the way her eyes would light up and how pleased she would be.

Then his chest constricted, and he prayed hard. Hanging his head, he stared down at his hands, and his gaze rested on the thin scar below his right thumb. He rubbed it, and his throat clogged up. He'd gotten it the day he had finally admitted to himself how deeply he loved Kyrin. He cleared his throat and pressed his fingers against his eyes.

"When was the last time you slept?" Saul asked.

Jace shook his head, having to take a moment to think about it. Everything seemed like one long blur. "Two days."

"We won't be here long, but you should try to rest."

Jace released a heavy sigh. "I can't. Not when I know she's still out there."

He grimaced. All day, his one goal had been to reach her before nightfall—before she found herself completely vulnerable to the ryriks. But he'd failed.

He spoke quietly, hardly able to form the words. "My mother was attacked by a ryrik. That's where I came from. I just can't bear the thought of Kyrin having to face such horror."

It was hard to say, but in a way, sharing his fears—letting them out instead of holding them inside—helped.

Saul gave a sympathetic nod. "I understand. I would feel the same if it were my wife, Jayna, or my daughter, Liese. But Elôm is with her and even more capable of protecting her than you are."

Though every part of him wanted to be with Kyrin and protect her himself, he had to agree. "You're right."

Even if he were with her, he'd be just as helpless to keep her safe as he was right now. That rested entirely in Elôm's hands.

For another twenty minutes, they let the horses rest and graze while Jace explained what had brought his group to Dorland. However, he didn't mention that Balen was head of that group. Though he believed now that he could trust Saul and the others, it wasn't his place to make Balen known to them. He discovered that Saul knew Jorvik and his brothers well and that they often traded crops and livestock. No wonder none of the giant brothers had ever questioned or even seemed to notice the hints of his mixed race.

At last, Saul gathered up his pack and everyone rose. More than ready to get moving again, Jace retrieved the mare, and they set off. For one of the first times in his life, Jace thanked Elôm for his ryrik blood, which enabled him to see in the dark. Though Saul and the others could follow the trail, it helped Jace to see the signs for himself. They were getting fresher.

A few miles from where they'd rested, the ryriks' trail led them right to the edge of the Trayse River and a large log that spanned across it.

"Looks like they crossed here." Saul turned in the saddle to look at the others. "We'll have to leave the horses. Ross, why don't you stay with them?"

The man nodded, and they all dismounted. Jace looked across to the other side and prayed they were close. He turned at a tap on the shoulder, and Ross offered him his sword.

"Take this. You might need it more than I will."

"Thank you." Jace buckled the sword belt on and joined Saul at the log where they crossed over single file. On the opposite bank, they paused where the ground was soft and clearly distinguished several sets of footprints. Jace bent down to study them, looking for one set in particular. A knot twisted in his stomach.

"I don't see her tracks." He looked again in case he missed them, but all he could find were boot tracks made by men.

"These here are deeper." Saul pointed out one set. "Are any of them a lot larger than the others?"

Jace shook his head.

"Then he must be carrying something . . . or someone."

Jace clenched his teeth until his jaw ached. If they were carrying Kyrin, what did it mean? Was she hurt? He squeezed his eyes shut and stopped himself from going too far down that road. He couldn't know the answer and speculating would only torture him. With the prayers that never ceased to flow from his heart, he straightened and pushed on. He just had to find her.

Saul and the others let him lead the way now. His heart rate accelerated at how fresh the signs were. They couldn't be more than an hour old. Then, a couple of miles from the river, Jace stopped. Firelight flickered in the trees ahead. He pointed it out to Saul.

"We'd better be careful from here," the man whispered. "They might have watches at the perimeter."

They crept ahead, keeping to cover as much as possible. With every step, his anxiousness grew, but he had to move with extreme caution. If they alerted the ryriks to their presence, there would be nothing to stop them from using Kyrin against him, just like last time. The only way to rescue her safely was to get to her before they realized what was happening. As he crept along, placing one foot carefully in front of the other, he prayed for Elôm to provide them just the opportunity they needed to get Kyrin away from her captors without any harm coming to her.

When they finally drew near enough to observe the camp, Jace took stock of the situation. Close to twenty ryriks sat around the fire. He scanned the faces and immediately picked out Geric and Ruis. But where was Kyrin? His gaze darted around the camp and landed on a ryrik standing a few yards from the fire in front of a tent. He nodded to it and barely whispered, "She must be in there."

Saul nodded. "If we can work our way around, maybe you can get to the back of the tent without being seen. We can cover your escape from the trees."

Jace gave the camp a final look to be sure there weren't any factors they were missing. Just before he was about to move, a shorter figure approached the fire from the opposite side of camp. A crete. Jace glanced at Saul, who spotted the man too, but then Jace ducked behind some bushes and crept around the edge of camp. Kyrin was his priority right now. Whatever the ryriks and the crete were up to could wait until after she was safe.

Though Jace was desperate to get to her, he forced himself to move slowly and place every step deliberately. One snap of a twig or rustle of leaves would blow their secrecy. After a few minutes, a drop of sweat rolled down the side of his face from the intensity of his concentration. He'd never had to be so careful in the woods before. The couple of hundred feet to reach the area behind the tent felt more like a mile.

When they stopped in the cover of a thick grouping of pines, Jace drew long deep breaths to steady himself and peeked around the trees toward the fire. So far, not one of the ryriks appeared to know that anyone crept around in the forest. He turned to Saul and the others, who silently strung their bows.

Saul pulled a knife from his belt and handed it to Jace. "You might need it to free her."

Jace stuck it in his own belt and tested the sword Ross had loaned him, making sure it drew smoothly and easily.

"Give us a minute to spread out and get into position before you move on the tent. If you're spotted, we'll do what we can to slow them down. You just grab her and get to the river."

Saul motioned to the others, and they moved off with barely a sound. While he waited for them to get in position, Jace leaned back against one of the pines and bowed his head to pray. After the long day, he'd run out of words beyond a simple plea that he would get Kyrin safely away from here and that she wasn't hurt. It didn't seem like enough, yet he knew Elôm could see the aching plea of his heart.

A couple of minutes later, he looked over to where Saul had moved, and the man signaled him. With another steadying breath, he crept out of the pines and toward the tent. If he stayed low, the shrubs and low pine boughs kept him hidden from anyone near the perimeter. Now he only needed not to alert the guard at the front of the tent. More sweat rolled down his face and neck.

He crossed the ten yards to the tent without a sound and paused. Thankfully, the tent had a back flap, and he wouldn't have to try to cut through the canvas. With a quick glance around to be sure no one was nearby, he went to work on the flap's ties. Knowing Kyrin was just inside urged him to move faster, but he loosened the ties slowly. Any abandoning of caution could be disastrous. At least the ryriks at the fire, with all their rowdy talk and raucous laughter, would cover any slight sounds.

At last, the final tie came loose. Holding his breath, Jace pushed aside the flap and looked inside. Kyrin sat against the support pole facing the front flap, her arms tied behind her. She sat still, her head hanging. His heart thumped his ribcage. Was she all right? Was she hurt? Was she even conscious? But then her head lifted, and she tugged against her restraints. He barely held back a sigh.

Now what? He needed to let her know he was there, but he dared not utter a word with the guard right outside, barely ten feet away. However, if he startled her, any noise she made might alert him. Praying this was the best course of action, he slipped inside the tent without a sound. In a swift but silent move, he put his hand over her mouth and his arm around her to keep her from struggling. She went rigid in his grip, and it hurt him to scare her like this, considering what she had been through. Leaning close to her ear, he barely breathed, "It's me."

Almost at once, she went limp in his arms, and he took his hand away from her mouth. Her breaths trembled in and out as if she were about to cry. She looked over her shoulder, meeting his gaze. Tears built in her eyes, though she did not try to speak. Jace wanted nothing more than to hold her and make sure she was all right, but he went carefully to work on freeing her. He pulled out Saul's knife and cut through her bindings, glancing to the front of the tent to make sure the guard hadn't moved. Judging by his silhouette, he still faced the fire, intent on the conversation.

Once Kyrin was free, Jace took her arm to guide her toward the back of the tent. However, she grasped his shirtsleeve and drew him closer to whisper in his ear.

"I hurt my ankle."

Heat burst through his chest to discover she was hurt, but he forced it aside for now. He slipped one arm around her shoulders and the other under her knees to lift her up. She wrapped her arms securely around his neck, and he stepped cautiously to the back of the tent and through the flap. It was more difficult to stay low with her in his arms, but he took it one careful step at a time.

When they reached the grouping of pines, he looked at Saul, who motioned in the direction of the river. Jace moved deeper into the woods, giving the camp a wide berth. He didn't relax until a mile later. Finally, he breathed out a long breath and increased his pace. He wanted to ask Kyrin if she was all right, but it still felt dangerous to utter a word out loud.

Just before reaching the river, Saul and the others caught up. Holding Kyrin tightly, Jace crossed over the log first. When they reached the other side where Ross and the horses waited, he set her down gently, keeping his hands on her arms to support her until he was sure she could stand on her own.

"Are you all right?"

She nodded, but her cheeks were wet with tears.

The heat ignited in Jace's chest again, quickly overtaking his entire body. However, a chill chased after it as he cupped his hands around her face and searched her watery eyes. He struggled to form the words. "Did they hurt you?"

"No."

Jace stared deep into her eyes, not sure he should fully believe it, and she said, "They didn't hurt me."

"Your ankle?"

"I stepped in a hole and twisted it. I'll be all right."

The chill lifted, allowing Jace to breathe a little easier and thank Elôm. Gently, he wiped the tears from her face.

She sniffed. "What about you? Are you all right?"

"I'm fine."

Fresh tears welled in her eyes. "I was so afraid for you."

Jace couldn't help the breathless laugh that escaped. She'd been afraid for him? He'd nearly gone out of his mind with worry for her. He leaned closer and spoke quietly. "We're both all right."

He would have kissed her right there if Saul hadn't spoken.

"We shouldn't linger here. They could discover her missing any time."

Jace agreed and took Kyrin's hand securely in his. Whatever it came down to, he would not let her fall into the ryriks' hands again.

Saul turned to instruct his men, "A couple of us should stay behind. I want to find out what they're up to here."

Two of the men volunteered.

"They have a crete traitor from Arvael with them," Kyrin said. "He must have a dragon nearby. I also heard them mention something about 'Daican's force' showing up."

"See if they say anything more about that," Saul told the men. He then focused on Jace. "If you'd like, we can take you to our village where you can rest and recover. It's closer than Jorvik's farm, and your captors won't expect you to head that way. Even if they follow, we have enough fighting men to protect you."

Jace considered it a moment. Right now, his number one priority was to get Kyrin to a safe place. Then they could decide what to do next. He agreed, but said, "Our friends will be looking for us. If they were able to pick up our trail, it could lead them straight into the ryriks."

Saul gestured to Ross. "Backtrack and see if you can find them. If you do, lead them to the village."

"They'll be suspicious," Jace warned. "Tell them Jace Ilvaran sent you." Not many besides their closest friends knew his family name.

He returned Ross's sword to him, and the man rode off in the direction they'd come. Everyone else, save the two men remaining behind, mounted up. Jace swung up onto the mare and then reached down for Kyrin.

Saul stepped forward and said, "Let me help you."

Kyrin glanced at him, uncertainty crossing her expression. Could she tell in the dark that they were ryriks? Yet, she nodded, and Saul gave her a careful boost up onto the horse. She settled in behind Jace and wrapped her arms around him. Taking the reins in one hand, he laid his arm across hers. He needed to hold onto her, just to assure himself that she was truly safe and right there with him.

303

Saul took the lead and they rode away from the river, angling more to the north than their previous path. After a few minutes of silence, Kyrin spoke softly near Jace's ear.

"Are they ryriks?"

He squeezed her arm reassuringly. "Yes, but they're friends. They saved my life."

THE SUN ROSE, filling the forest with light and waking the birds. It transported Jace's thoughts back to the days he and Kyrin had gone out hunting every morning just after they first met. A smile grew on his lips at the warm feel of Kyrin's head against his back, her arms draped loosely around his waist. He wasn't sure if she had fully slept during the ride, but she did doze, and he was glad she was able to rest. One of her hands rested in his, and he rubbed his thumb gently over her soft skin, thanking Elôm for the millionth time for keeping her safe. Though he wouldn't let his guard down until they were safely within Saul's village, after the quiet night of travel, he didn't expect to see their ryrik captors again.

The horror of what they'd been through still hung in his mind, and he clutched Kyrin's hand a little more tightly. In response, her own grip tightened. Twice, he'd almost lost her to ryriks. If only he could take her somewhere far away from the struggle that surrounded them and live the quiet sort of life he'd known on the farm. He sighed lightly. Of course, he'd need to marry her first.

Just ahead, Saul turned in his saddle. "The village is only another mile from here."

Kyrin straightened, lifting her head from his back. He felt her draw a deep breath and reclaim one of her hands.

He looked over his shoulder to find her rubbing her eyes. "How do you feel?"

"All right."

"Does your ankle still hurt?"

"Just a little."

That was one of the first things Jace would make sure was properly tended once they stopped. Surely, she would have told him if she thought it was broken, but he wanted to make sure.

Very soon, the trees ahead of them thinned out, and a tall wooden palisade came into view. As they neared, Saul dropped back to ride beside them.

"You'll probably draw a lot of interest. You're the first non-ryriks we've had in years besides Jorvik and his brothers. But we have good people in our village, and they will welcome you."

Jace anxiously looked forward to seeing the village. After all, they were just as much his people as humans were, and his ryrik side always seemed dominant. He couldn't have imagined feeling this way a few days ago before meeting Saul. However, now that he'd learned ryriks weren't all brutal monsters, curiosity to discover more about this side of his heritage had taken over.

"Most of us live within the palisade," Saul explained, "though we have pastureland outside for some of our animals. As you can imagine, we don't have many newcomers out here, but the wall keeps out the wolves and bears as well as any ryriks who don't agree with our way of life."

"How long has the village been here?" Jace asked.

"Over a hundred years. I came here as a boy with my family from farther south when our area was too overrun by hostile ryriks."

"It seems like a peaceful way to live." Tucked away in the forest with little intrusion from the outside world was just the life Jace had always wanted.

"It is, and we strive to keep it that way."

A few moments later, they arrived at an open gate, where a tall ryrik man appeared. His gaze, bright with intensity, landed immediately on Jace and Kyrin before shifting to Saul.

"What's this? I thought you were hunting wolves."

"That's what we set out to do, but Elôm had other plans. I'll tell you about it after I get these two home to Jayna and looked after."

The guard nodded and stepped aside to let them pass. On the way through, Saul paused to say, "Just don't let any strange ryriks inside. We may have a few following us. However, if a group of humans shows up, send word to me. They're likely friends."

"I'll keep a lookout," the guard responded.

They rode into the village, and Jace took in the sight of simple yet sturdy log homes. Many had their own small barn and fenced in areas holding chickens, milk cows, and goats. From deeper in the village came the sound of a hammer against metal. Men and women milled about or worked near their homes, while children played and dashed around in groups—all of them with piercing blue eyes and black hair. Jace had never seen so many ryriks at once, and he would never have expected it to be such an incredible experience.

What struck him next was the number of animals other than livestock. Nearly every house had at least one wolf lounging or sniffing around outside—normal wolves the size of Tyra, not the giant wolves that had nearly killed him yesterday. Most were gray, but a few had either black or white fur. There were a couple of red foxes as well, and Jace noticed children with a variety of birds perched on their shoulders. He'd always suspected his bond with animals came from his ryrik blood, and this confirmed it.

As Saul had said, their presence did cause a bit of a stir as many of the villagers they passed turned to stare at them curiously.

Until yesterday, Jace could never have imagined ryriks looking at anyone in a non-hostile way.

Halfway through the village, they parted from the other ryriks in their group, and Saul led them down a pathway to one of the village farms. Chickens strutted around in front of the cabin, and a couple of goats and cows stood in the corral. Two impressive-looking gray wolves jumped up from where they lay on the porch of the cabin and trotted over to them as they halted at the barn. Saul dismounted and gave each of the creatures a pat on the back. They sniffed at Jace and Kyrin but were very calm.

"Don't mind them," Saul said.

Jace slid off the mare first and turned to Kyrin. Taking her by the waist, he lifted her off the horse and set her down gently. A moment later, a female voice called from near the cabin.

"Saul?"

They all turned as a tall ryrik woman approached them. Her long hair rested in a thick, black braid over her shoulder, and her well-rounded belly filled out the front of her linen dress. She was a lovely woman who reminded Jace of his mother, Rachel, though her clearly ryrik features set her apart. It occurred to him that, before today, he'd never seen a ryrik woman. Though very feminine, she seemed strong and certainly not delicate.

With a warm smile, Saul reached for her hand and drew her closer to meet Jace and Kyrin. He introduced her as his wife, Jayna, and briefly explained how he'd met them.

"Oh my," Jayna murmured with true concern. "Do please come in. You must be exhausted." She motioned them toward the cabin.

Jace looked at Kyrin, nodding to her ankle.

"I think I can make it, if I'm careful," she said.

He offered her his arm for support and guided her slowly up to the cabin. The inside offered cool relief from the sun, which already shone very warmly. Jace glanced around, finding the cabin serviceable and homey, much like Kalli and Aldor's cabin had been. It wasn't nearly the size of the giants' cabins, but close quarters were much more familiar to him.

"Please, sit down." Jayna pulled a chair from the dining table to their right, and Jace helped Kyrin to it. The woman looked at her. "Is it a sprain?"

Kyrin nodded. "I stepped in a hole."

"Let me get you something to soak it in." Jayna walked around the table and put a kettle over the small fire in the fireplace. Looking over her shoulder, she asked, "Are you hungry? I still have some breakfast leftover."

"That would be wonderful," Kyrin answered.

While waiting for the water to heat, Jayna served Kyrin, Jace, and Saul each a plate of fried potatoes, ham, and slices of fresh bread. Between bites, they told her everything that had happened with the ryriks. When they finished, her hand rested over her stomach as if protecting the baby she carried. Her eyes shone a brilliant, bright blue.

"That is terrible. Thank Elôm you were not seriously hurt," she said, looking specifically at Kyrin. She turned to her husband. "We must find out what's going on. These attacks can't be allowed to continue like this."

Saul agreed. "Hopefully the others will be able to gather enough information for us to figure out how to put a stop to it."

Just then, two children dashed in from outside—a girl about ten and a boy about eight. A chickadee flitted in right after them and landed in the rafters, chattering. The moment they spotted Saul, their faces lit up.

"Papa!" they cried in unison.

Saul rose from his seat and lifted them both up in a big hug.

"Did you get any wolves?" the boy asked.

"Only a couple, but I did bring back some friends." Saul turned to the table, setting the two children in front of him. "Jace, Kyrin, this is my daughter, Liese, and my son, Kal."

Jace smiled at them, and they shared hellos. They were beautiful children with their striking ryrik features. Kal brushed his slightly long hair out of his eyes and behind his pointed ears as he studied them. Is that what Jace had looked like as a child?

The little boy focused on Kyrin, tipping his head as he stared at her. "You look different."

"That's because she's a human," Saul told his son.

Kal's eyes grew huge. "Really? I've never seen a human before."

Saul chuckled and tousled his hair. "Yes, and we'll treat her and Jace very well while they're our guests, won't we?"

The children nodded enthusiastically and scrambled into chairs at the table, their faces curious. They both had questions for Jace and Kyrin, though Jayna kept them from asking everything all at once. Jace smiled at the way Kyrin laughed and answered the sometimes slightly outrageous questions they had about humans. She always was good with children.

As they were talking, Jayna brought a pan for Kyrin to soak her ankle in. Once it had been soaking for a while, Jayna wrapped it for her. Though still swollen and a bit bruised, at least it was not broken. It would just take a few days to heal. Jayna also cleaned and applied a salve to the cut on Kyrin's jaw. She then said, "You look like you could use some good rest. If you'd like, I can show you to our room to sleep."

Kyrin glanced at Jace and nodded. Her face was heavy with weariness. He couldn't imagine how the trauma of the last two days had worn on her. It was amazing she had held up so well for this long.

"I would appreciate that," Kyrin told Jayna.

Jace stood and helped her up. Supporting her arm, he guided her along with Jayna to a door off the main living area that led into a bedroom. Though not large, it contained a bed, wardrobe, washstand, and a cradle waiting for use in the corner. Jayna stepped to the wardrobe and pulled out an off-white nightgown and then a dress.

"You can wear these. There's water in the pitcher for you to clean up, and I can wash your dress for you."

Kyrin offered her a grateful smile. "Thank you."

When Jayna left the room, Jace remained at the doorway and looked down at Kyrin, who stared up at him.

"Do you feel safe here?" He didn't want to leave her alone if she had any doubts.

"Yes, I do."

"Good." For a long moment, he just stared, thinking of how close he'd come to losing her. He didn't ever want to leave her, but finally he backed away. "I'll let you rest."

She smiled softly and then closed the door. Jace stood by it for a moment more before returning to the kitchen, where Saul was waiting for him.

"You should get some rest as well. Come, I'll show you upstairs to the children's room. It's the only other room we have. Later, we'll figure out better arrangements."

Jace followed him up the stairs to the room in the peak of the cabin, which was divided in half by a canvas curtain. Saul motioned to the side that obviously belonged to Kal with all his toys and boyish trinkets.

"Kal was eager to offer you his bed," Saul said.

Jace smiled. "Let him know I appreciate it."

Once he was alone, Jace pulled off his boots and ducked under the slanted ceiling to lie down in Kal's bed. Though a bit small for him, he sighed as his whole body relaxed into the mattress. His arms and back were sore, and the wound to his shoulder throbbed dully, but none of it mattered. He closed his tired eyes. At first, sleep wouldn't come as he kept thinking about

Kyrin. He couldn't help feeling that he wanted to keep a watchful eye on her at all times, but after a time of prayer, he succumbed to his weariness.

"Over here!"

Kaden spun around to the sound of Halvar's voice. Scanning the thick forest, he could just make out the giant's head above a wall of ferns. He sprinted forward and joined up with the others as they pushed through the ferns and found a large hollow.

"Looks like this is where they stopped the first night," Halvar told them.

Kaden looked around. They had spent the entire day yesterday from sunup searching for the ryriks' trail. And now what signs Halvar had managed to find had only led them as far as the ryriks' first camp? He shoved his hand through his hair. It meant the monsters who had Kyrin and Jace were still more than a full day ahead of them.

"There's a lot of blood here," Rayad said from near a tree at the other side of the hollow.

Kaden walked over to him with Marcus, and his stomach twisted. Dried blood spattered the ground at the base of the tree as well as the ropes lying there.

"Whose blood do you think it is?" Kaden asked.

Before anyone could form an answer, Halvar reached up and pulled a bloodstained piece of cloth from the branches above their heads—a shirtsleeve. "Recognize this?"

Rayad took it, his expression grim. "It's Jace's."

And no doubt Jace's blood.

Kaden scanned the clearing again. "Is there any sign of Kyrin?"

Halvar studied the ground. "A couple faint footprints. There are wolf tracks too."

The knot in Kaden's stomach yanked tighter. Blood, ropes, and wolf tracks? What had happened here?

Halvar crossed the clearing again and pointed. "Looks like they continued on in this direction and didn't take as much time to cover their tracks."

Finally, some good news. Maybe now they could gain ground . . . before it was too late, though judging by the blood, it could be already. Kaden shook these thoughts off and hurried after Halvar with the others.

With a clear trail to follow, they moved more quickly than they had since the beginning of this search. Halvar pointed out the obvious tracks to them, including those left behind by wolves. The prints were three times the size of Tyra tracks—as wide as Kaden's hand with his fingers spread apart. He cast wary glances into the forest for the beast that made them. The others seemed on edge as well, and Kaden kept thinking back to the blood and ropes. Surely there would have been more blood and evidence if the wolves had been the cause . . .

A couple of hours later, the entire group halted when a man stepped out of the trees just ahead of them. At the sight of his black hair and blue eyes, Kaden yanked out his sword, as did everyone else except for Halvar.

The ryrik lifted his hands. "I'm a friend."

Halvar stepped forward. "Ross."

Kaden frowned at his friendly tone. His confusion deepened when the giant reached out to shake the ryrik's hand. Kaden exchanged a glance with Marcus, who looked just as bewildered.

Halvar turned to them. "You can put your weapons away. Ross is a longtime friend."

No one moved. Kaden just stared at them, the words ryrik and friend not registering together in his mind. How was that even possible?

"I know you are suspicious," Ross said. For a ryrik, he

313

managed to appear remarkably unthreatening. "I was told to tell you that Jace Ilvaran sent me."

"Jace," Rayad's voice echoed Kaden's own surprise.

They all looked at each other. Hardly anyone knew Jace's family name.

Rayad slid his sword back into its scabbard first and stepped forward. "He's alive."

Ross nodded.

Kaden sheathed his weapon next. "What about Kyrin?"

He held his breath, his gut clenching before Ross nodded. "Yes."

Kaden blew out his breath. "Are they injured?"

"Only minor injuries that I'm aware of."

Kaden hung his head, breathing out heavily again. Next to him, Marcus did the same. In that moment, Kaden felt like he could sink straight to the ground as the desperation that had kept him going all morning dissolved. He hadn't slept in two nights, terrified for Kyrin's life.

"Saul took them to the village," Ross told Halvar, and Kaden raised his head again. "He thought they would be safest there."

Halvar turned to the group and motioned to them. "The village is not far. We'll take you there."

He and Ross took the lead, turning east. Kaden and the others followed. How it had come to be that a ryrik was now leading them to Kyrin and Jace he couldn't even begin to process, but right now his only concern was getting to his sister.

Jace came to slowly at first but then jerked to full awareness when he heard his name. Blinking the sleep from his eyes, he looked up. Saul stood near the bed.

"Your friends have arrived."

The last remnants of sleep left Jace as he got up. He pulled on his boots and followed Saul downstairs.

"They're at the gate. Halvar is with them," Saul said as they walked outside.

Jace followed Saul through the village with growing anticipation. The danger of the last couple of days had a way of making it feel as though he and Kyrin had been separated from their friends for even longer. When they neared the gate, Jace spotted the group and smiled. He hurried the last few yards. Kaden caught sight of him first and called his name. He and Marcus stood at the head of the group, their expressions anxious yet marked with weariness.

"Where is Kyrin?" Kaden asked the moment Jace reached them.

"She's all right. She's asleep."

Kaden blew out a long breath, and Marcus's shoulders sagged noticeably, as if releasing a great weight.

"She's not hurt?" Marcus winced. "The ryriks didn't . . ."

"No." Jace shook his head firmly to assure them. "She has a sprained ankle and a small cut, but she's fine."

All the tension of the last two days slowly drained from her brothers' faces.

Now Rayad stepped forward, his eyes reflecting his own deep relief. "What about you? Are you all right?" He nodded to the bandage visible beneath the collar of Jace's shirt before his gaze dropped to Jace's bandaged wrists and raw hands.

"Nothing that won't heal," Jace said.

Rayad gripped his shoulder gently. His voice came out a little hoarse. "You and Kyrin had us real worried."

"Thanks to Elôm, we both made it out alive and relatively unharmed." Jace turned then to Saul, who waited behind him, and motioned him forward. "This is Saul. If not for him and his friends, I would be dead and Kyrin would still be a captive."

Rayad greeted him first, and then Kaden and Marcus before the others stepped up. Though Jace caught some looks of confusion and curiosity over the fact that Saul and the other men at the gate were ryriks, they seemed too thankful to let any suspicions show through. Holden was the most uneasy. He greeted Saul respectfully, but Jace sensed his hesitation. His eyes held an underlying discomfort in sharp contrast to his calm actions. Jace couldn't blame him after what had happened to his parents.

"Welcome to our village," Saul told the group. "You can bring your dragons inside, if you wish."

Jace now noticed the creatures waiting just outside the gate. Once they were given the command to enter, Gem nearly bumped Kaden out of the way to reach Jace. With an exuberant chirp, she eyed him as if checking him over and then nuzzled his chest. He patted her neck and glanced at Saul.

"That's quite an animal you've got."

Jace smiled. "She is indeed."

As they followed Saul back toward his cabin, Jace fell into step beside Holden. His friend's gaze darted around the village to all the people watching them. He finally looked at Jace and whispered, "Are they all ryriks?"

"Yes. And I know this can't be easy, but they are good people. Most, if not all, are believers. They've done nothing but help me and Kyrin."

Holden drew a deep breath and nodded. "If you trust them, I'll trust them."

"I do."

By now, they neared Saul's cabin. When it came within sight, Jace spotted Kyrin standing on the porch, waiting. A grin lit up her face. Kaden rushed ahead with Marcus right behind him, and Kyrin hobbled down the steps to meet them. Kaden reached her first, and they hugged tightly.

"You had us worried sick," he said.

"I know. I'm sorry," Kyrin replied, her voice wobbling a bit.

They pulled apart, and Kaden gave her a look-over before letting Marcus in to embrace their sister. Kyrin then greeted the others before Saul ushered everyone inside, where they had a lot of catching up to do.

THE CONSTANT UP and down emotions left Anne in a continuous state of exhaustion. Sometimes her grief led to cold, hard resolve that strengthened her against it. However, most of the time, it left her so fragile she felt sure she would crumble. It was hard to find an in-between. Especially tonight. An invitation had arrived the day before to a gathering in Landale to celebrate Goler's rise to baron. When her father first received it, Anne immediately refused to attend, but with Baron Grey gone and Goler in such a powerful position, it left them no choice.

So, she prepared for the celebration and fought to shore up her waning resolve as Sara helped her slip into a dark blue gown. Anne initially wanted to wear black, but such an open display of mourning might not be the wisest course. The darkest blue she had would have to suffice.

Once she was dressed, Sara styled her hair before Anne dismissed her. After that, she sat for a while at her dressing table and stared at her reflection in the mirror. Her face was pale and a bit gaunt looking. She hadn't slept well in days. Her heart ached too much, and more than ever, she wanted to be with Trask. So many times she'd had to fight off the urge to give up and go out to the forest, never to return to this life again. She didn't want to be part of this act anymore. But she couldn't escape it; at least, not this very night. There were too many other lives to consider between her parents, Elanor, and the servants.

With a deep sigh, she pushed up from her chair and crossed the room. At the door, she paused and closed her eyes.

"I don't know how to face this, Elôm. How do I face Goler after what he did and not let my true feelings show? Please give me strength."

She pressed her hand to the nauseous ache in the pit of her stomach and walked out into the hall. Downstairs, her parents and Elanor waited. She shared a beleaguered look with Elanor. Anne hadn't seen a hint of her sunny disposition in days. She then locked eyes with her father, and sorrow passed between them. Tonight would be just as difficult for him. He'd lost one of his closest friends. Tears bit Anne's eyes, but she blinked them back, determination hardening inside her. Her father seemed to gather his resolve as well.

"Let's get this over with," he said, his voice husky.

He opened the door and ushered the women out into the soggy twilight, where Elian and their carriage waited.

The ride to Landale passed in silence, but Anne's dread mounted with each mile. She hadn't visited the village since that fateful day last week. Her stomach threatened to heave, and she didn't think she could eat anything without becoming violently ill. When they rolled into the courtyard of Landale Castle, her heart beat erratically. Her father exited the carriage first and helped her mother and then Elanor out. He turned back for Anne last, but she couldn't move. How could she go inside where so many memories resided without Baron Grey there? The pain of it choked her.

"I can't do it." She shook her head, her eyes burning mercilessly. "I can't go in."

Her father reached for her hand and squeezed it. "Annie, we must be strong tonight."

Anne drew in a tremulous breath, battling the emotions that had such a tight grip on her. Finally, she nodded and let her father lead her out. Before he released her, he said, "Let's just get through tonight."

Reaching out to Elôm again for strength, Anne remained close to Elanor and followed her parents inside. It was every bit as hard to enter the castle as she'd anticipated. Everything looked familiar—Goler hadn't had time to change much—but without Baron Grey, the castle felt cold and empty despite the gathering guests. The butler greeted them, and Anne's heart squeezed. Though maintaining a proper manner, the older gentleman's eyes revealed his true sorrow. Everyone on staff here had served Baron Grey for many years. How awful to have to serve the man partially responsible for his execution.

The butler admitted them into the sitting room with the rest of the guests. Just as Anne expected, Goler was watching the door, and his gaze latched onto her the moment they entered. Her stomach recoiled. Would becoming sick be a good enough excuse to escape his presence tonight? She pushed the thought aside for now but didn't discard it as a last resort.

Goler made a beeline for them—for her. He carried himself proudly, yet his pride faded a little when he locked eyes with her. She couldn't call it concern or contrition in his expression— she wouldn't allow him any such redeeming qualities—but he wasn't entirely comfortable. He greeted each of them with a surprising amount of politeness.

"My lord." Anne's father inclined his head respectfully. "Sorry we are a bit late."

Anne dropped her gaze and tipped her chin down in what would look like a respectful gesture, but it was only to gain a moment to collect herself. She'd forgotten Goler was now their superior and had to be addressed and treated as such. It was almost too much to bear. Trask should be baron right now.

"Not at all," Goler replied, trying his best to sound refined. "Supper is just about to be served."

She lifted her eyes again, taking in Goler's tailored jerkin and deep red shirt. She'd never seen him clothed in such finery. He'd probably taken the outfit from Baron Grey's wardrobe. She had to fight the urge to glare at him.

A moment later, he offered her his arm. "Let me escort you to the dining room."

Anne stared at his arm for a moment, working herself up to taking it. Then, reluctantly, she wrapped her hand around it, swallowing down her distaste. With a smile, he led her toward the dining room. When they entered, he guided her down the length of the table. Anne's feet dragged the entire time. He only stopped when they reached the chair just to the right of what was now his place at the head of the table.

"Sit here, next to me," he invited, his voice too low and silky.

Anne glanced at her father, but it hit her right then that he could do nothing. Goler now outranked him. Even if he did try to intervene, it would only lead to trouble. A shudder ran through Anne, but she slid into the seat. It rattled her even further when Dagren took the chair directly across from her. The glance he sent was probing, as if he would be measuring every move she made tonight.

The rest of the guests sat down along both sides of the table with quiet murmurings. Aside from a few who didn't seem affected, an air of unrest hung over everyone. They seemed to know, as Anne did, that death was only one small mistake away. The servants silently served their meal, and the conversation livened up, but it all became a blur to Anne as she picked at her food. She considered taking a bite here and there for appearances, but even the smell made her ill.

After a while, Goler leaned toward her. "Are you unwell?"

Anne clenched her jaw and couldn't meet his eyes. "Yes, I am."

A moment of silence followed before he responded. "You're still upset about the execution."

She glanced across the table at Dagren, but he was too intent on a conversation with the baron seated next to him to pay this exchange any attention. "Of course, I'm still upset."

Goler's eyes narrowed. "He was guilty of treason."

"So you keep saying," Anne ground through her teeth, "but he was also a friend. Just give me time to mourn and stop gloating. A man died. It's barbaric to be so pleased about it no matter why it happened."

Goler sat back in his chair, brooding.

Eventually, Anne gave up on her pretense of interest in her food and fiddled with the necklace Trask had given her. She'd debated over wearing it, but felt the need to have a piece of him with her. Goler must have noticed. Once again, he leaned toward her.

"I've never seen you wear that piece before."

"It was a gift," she said in a short tone that discouraged further questions. She reached for her goblet and took a small sip of wine. She would do what she must to appease him, but she didn't have to fawn over him or cater to his every wish.

He didn't speak to her again for the rest of the meal.

Near the end, Dagren rose and all eyes lifted to him. He raised his goblet. "To the new Baron of Landale. May he bring honor to the gods and put a permanent end to the rebellion that has poisoned this community."

Murmurs of assent trickled along the table as everyone raised their goblets, but Anne had to choke down her swallow of wine and pray for the strength to hide her true feelings. How much sniveling must Goler have done to gain this position? She couldn't think of anyone less deserving or more ill-suited.

Once everyone had finished, they rose from the table, and Anne hoped to find a quiet corner somewhere to spend the rest of the evening. Yet, once again, Goler offered his arm. She had no choice but to let him escort her out of the dining room and into the ballroom, where everyone mingled.

Goler led her along with him from group to group as if he were showing off a prize. Anne's anger simmered. She wasn't his to claim. She sent several looks to her father, who watched closely from nearby. Anne searched for a good excuse to extricate herself from Goler's presence, but without Charles there to help, she came up empty.

Then the music started. Goler leaned close enough that his hot breath warmed Anne's ear and neck and made her want to squirm away. "Let's dance."

A refusal sprang to her tongue, but she kept her lips tightly sealed. He took her silence as acceptance and led her to the dance floor. When he wrapped his arm around her and pulled her close, she almost gagged on his scent—too much fragrant oils mixed with sweat. She could barely focus past his presence and the exhaustion dragging at her feet.

After the fourth dance, Anne numbed to it all. However, adrenaline surged through her when Goler swept her past a couple of the onlookers at the far side of the room and through a doorway into one of the darkened halls. Her heart leapt into her throat, and she jerked against his hold on her arm.

"What are you doing?" she gasped.

"I just wanted to talk privately."

Every instinct screamed for Anne to break away from him and call for her father, but if he did confront Goler, how would it end? Goler held all the power now. She'd seen the way he had looked at her father in the past for coming between them. She wouldn't put it past the former captain to have her father arrested and executed just to get him out of the way. Fear for him outweighed the fear for herself.

"I wanted to discuss the future . . . and us," Goler said softly.

Anne stiffened her back. She did not buy his attempt at tenderness. She'd witnessed too much of his cruelty to believe it didn't lurk just under the surface, waiting to be provoked.

"What about us?"

Goler straightened a little, inflated by pride. "I have a place of standing and power now. I know you need time to accept the circumstances, but . . . I want you as my wife. You know I've long admired you, and you're more than suited for such a position. Marry me and help me rule and bring peace to Landale."

Anne just stared at him for a moment before a solid answer formed in her mouth. "No."

His hopeful expression fell, and hardness crept in. "Why not?"

Her voice cold, Anne answered, "For one, you don't have my father's blessing. And I will not accept any offers while I am still mourning the death of a friend and am in no frame of mind to give it any consideration."

Goler's brows sunk in a dark frown. "It isn't as if you haven't had time to consider this. I've made my intentions clear in the past."

"And I have in no way invited those intentions."

Anne turned away from him and tugged against his grasp, but then he grabbed her with both hands and pulled her into him, subjecting her to a ravaging kiss. Panic and fury burst through Anne. She struggled mightily and ripped from his hold, slapping him as she backed away.

"How dare you!" She fisted her shaking hands at her side. "I will not be pressured into marriage. Not by you or any man. I don't care how much power he commands."

Goler stared at her, his eyes wide with surprise from either his own actions, her slap, or both. He almost looked sorry as he took a step toward her and murmured her name.

"Stop!" Anne put her hand up and backed another couple of steps toward the door. She wouldn't let him get near her this time.

Even so, the fear of how helpless she was to fend him off from this point forward seized her. She grasped at the only thing that might buy her time. "Unless you want Viscount Ilvaran to go to the emperor and remove you from this position, you will not touch me again."

With these words, she spun around and fled back into the ballroom. However, his unwelcome presence clung to her in the phantom feel of his possessive hold and his damp lips pressed to hers. Trask had been the only man she'd ever kissed before tonight. Goler had robbed her of that. Tears seared her eyes. She fought them at first but then gave in. Let the other guests see her cry and know what a beast the new baron was. He'd stolen something precious from her, and she hated him for it.

Her father broke through the guests in front of her and grabbed her shoulders. "Annie! What happened?"

By now, the room had gone quiet and everyone stared at them. Anne bit her lip and shook her head, unable to voice what she'd just experienced. "Please, can we go home?"

Her father nodded and put his arm around her. Her mother and Elanor met them, and they all left the ballroom. The butler brought them their cloaks at the front door, his face solemn, and they stepped out into the drizzle to wait for Elian and the carriage. Here, Anne's father took her by the shoulders again and looked her in the eyes.

"Did he hurt you?"

"He kissed me." She shuddered. She knew she should thank Elôm that Goler had done no worse, but she couldn't stop her tears or her shaking.

A moment later, Elian rushed up to them, his hand grasped around the scabbard of his sword. "What happened?"

"Goler," Anne's father ground out.

They both looked toward the door of the castle. A spark of anger had kindled in her father's eyes that Anne didn't witness often. She grabbed his arms, finally working her tears under control. "Don't go back in. Please. We just need to go."

He hesitated but then nodded with grim acceptance. There wasn't anything they could do about this.

Over the remainder of the afternoon and during a hearty meal that evening, Jace and Kyrin recounted their tale of captivity. They also learned from the others how Halvar had tracked them to the spot where the ryriks had first camped for the night and then got a good start on Jace's trail before Ross found them. It was a lot to take in, and they had much to discuss as to what the ryriks were doing here and what other force Daican was sending. They wouldn't know more until Saul's men returned with information and they had a chance to talk to Balen. Leetra and Halvar had left shortly after arriving in the village to take the news back to Jorvik's farm.

Though crowded in the cabin, Jace welcomed the companyionship of their group and Saul's family. Everyone was curious about the ryriks' way of life. Jace's satisfaction grew deeper the more he learned and experienced the true kindness of Saul and those in this village. Though it had come about through a terrible trial, he thanked Elôm for the opportunity to witness this half of his blood in a completely different light. It somehow made him feel more complete than he had his entire life.

Sometime after dark, Saul rose to answer a knock at the door. A ryrik man stood on the other side.

"The lights are out if anyone wants to see them."

Jace glanced around the cabin, but like him, most didn't seem to understand.

"The northern lights," Talas told them, pushing up from the floor. "You'll want to see this."

Curiously, they all got up to follow Saul and Talas outside. Jace took Kyrin's hand and helped her up, guiding her to the door. Outside, they stepped carefully down the steps. Several yards from the cabin, Saul motioned to the sky and everyone tipped their heads back. Overhead, ribbons of green, pink, and pale blue light weaved through the starry sky. Jace heard Kyrin's breath catch. It was indeed a breathtaking sight. The soft shafts of light slowly bent and flowed, almost like sheer curtains of light in a breeze. Jace had heard stories of people who had seen them in the more northern parts of Arcacia and in Samara, but he had never witnessed them himself.

"It's so beautiful," Kyrin murmured in awe.

Jace glanced down at her wonderstruck face and smiled. He squeezed her hand. She leaned closer into his side, and he breathed out contentedly. He never wanted her to leave that place at his side. Ever. His heart did an odd flip and then pounded as he looked down at her again. What better time or place would come along to make that a reality? He could do it, right here, under these lights. He only had to ask.

His intent staring caught her attention, and she looked up at him. She studied his face for a moment, a smile on her soft lips. "What are you thinking?"

Jace drew a shallow breath. "I . . . wanted to ask you something." He swallowed, his throat suddenly drying out. She watched him expectantly. *Don't back out now.* He tried, but the words just wouldn't come. Defeat set in, and he hung his head. "Never mind. Just forget I said anything."

He couldn't bring himself to look at her until a bit of the sting wore off. He'd failed her. What a coward he was. When his gaze did stray back, she was still watching him.

"I know what you wanted to ask."

His heart socked his ribs. "You do?"

She nodded, and though he couldn't fight off his first instinct to fear the worst, her face held understanding. Her voice soft and caring, she said quietly, "You've wanted to ask before. What always stops you?"

Jace sighed and rubbed his neck. He should have had an honest conversation with her long before this. He glanced at the others, but they were all spread out and paying too much attention to the sky and their own conversations to notice him and Kyrin.

He refocused on her and winced. "Fear. I thought after what happened with Elon I could leave my old fears and insecurities behind. Some I have, but others I still have to fight." He paused before admitting, "I'm afraid I can't be the husband you deserve."

"Jace," she said, her smile returning full-force, "you don't have to be afraid of that. I believe in you completely."

If only that were all and his fears would leave him. "Thank you . . . but that is not my only fear. I think, maybe, a bigger one is . . . my fear of being a father. Growing up the way I did, I don't have any experience in what parents even do."

Kyrin tipped her head thoughtfully. "I don't have much experience either. I'm not even sure I'd be a good mother but, if it came to that, I think we could figure it out together . . . just like everything else we've been through."

Jace couldn't imagine Kyrin being anything but a wonderful mother, considering her relationship with Meredith and her interaction with Saul's children. He let her words sink in before another thought took over.

"They would be part ryrik . . . our children." He swallowed hard. "I couldn't bear for them to face the same hatred I did."

Kyrin drew Jace around so they stood facing each other. "You were alone, but they would have loving parents, and uncles, and grandparents, and friends who would all show them how much they are loved. We would raise them to see their mixed blood as a blessing, not a curse. Especially now with what we've learned here in this village."

Slowly, her words soothed the fears he'd been carrying. Though he would still have to conquer them completely, she'd helped him gain ground.

"I don't want you to make this decision right here or any time just because you think you should," Kyrin told him. "I will wait. You don't *ever* have to worry about me leaving."

All the tension drained from Jace's body. "Thank you."

She smiled and turned to look at the lights again, but Jace stopped her. Drawing her a little closer, he bent his head close to hers and looked her in the eyes. "I *do* want to marry you, Kyrin."

Her smile widened. "I want to marry you too."

They shared a grin, and Jace had to work mightily to resist kissing her. No doubt it would bring everyone's attention straight to them. So he pressed his lips to her forehead instead, and then lifted his gaze to the sky, though she consumed his mind for the rest of the time they stood there.

DESPITE HAVING TO sleep in the loft in the barn—the only place Saul had room for all the men—Jace awoke refreshed and well-rested. Once sleep cleared completely, the first thought on his mind was Kyrin and their conversation last night. Talking it out together left him significantly lighter. Now that she knew he wasn't just balking at the idea of marriage, a burden had lifted. He just wasn't quite ready for that step yet, but he was confident it would come. Thank Elôm that Kyrin was so patient with him.

The barn door squeaked open below, and Saul and Kal's quiet voices drifted up to Jace. He listened as they went about their morning chores. Kal giggled when Saul teased him, and Jace smiled wistfully. What would it have been like to grow up with a father like that? Elian would have made a good father. Jace hoped someday he would be too, if that was the future Elôm had planned for him.

Pushing aside his blanket, he sat up and glanced at the others. They appeared fast asleep still, though Talas's hammock in the rafters was empty. Jace left his bedroll in the hay and climbed down from the loft. Saul and Kal had left the barn, so Jace wandered out to the corral where the two of them were milking the cows. Jace walked up to Saul and laid a gentle hand on the cow's hip so as not to startle it. "Good morning."

Saul glanced up with a smile. "Morning."

"Is there anything I can do to help?"

"You're a guest here. There's no need for that."

"Actually, I'd enjoy helping out."

Saul cast him another glance, this one in interest. "Are you a farmer back home?"

Jace shook his head. "I'm not sure if only three years of experience before joining the Resistance makes me a farmer, but I would like to go back to it if I could."

"Well then, Tula over there still needs milking." Saul gestured to the third cow. "There's another bucket just inside, and you should find another stool in the corner."

Jace headed back to the barn and gathered the items. Though he hadn't milked a cow in some time, the motions still felt familiar and satisfying. Being around farms and farm animals the last few days stirred his deep yearning for this life. In fact, it was surprisingly easy to picture—the little valley, a new cabin, sitting down to supper with Kyrin every night. He prayed it would work out someday despite the struggles they faced now with the emperor.

"What kind of animals did you have on your farm?" Kal asked from over at his cow.

"Actually, the farm belonged to a couple that Rayad and I lived with," Jace told him, "but we had a few milk cows, some horses, chickens, and sheep." He could still clearly see Kalli spinning wool during winter months. "Once in a while we had some pigs, but there were enough pickerins in the area that it wasn't always necessary."

"Papa hunts pickerins sometimes. He brought back a real big one last fall."

"There are some big ones in Arcacia too."

Jace's mind flashed back to the last pickerin he had ever hunted—the biggest one he'd ever come across. It was the day just before Kalli and Aldor had died and everything in his life had changed again. He fell silent for a moment at the pain that rose up and then slowly faded.

When the three of them finished milking, Saul carried the pails to the cabin and Jace helped Kal feed the rest of the animals. Saul returned a couple of minutes later to say that breakfast would soon be ready and sent Kal to the cabin to wash up. While the man closed the gate to the corral, Jace stood at the fence. He watched the animals and then glanced around to the small neighboring farms where other families finished their morning chores.

"You have an amazing community here." If Jace had grown up in a place like this, he never would have developed such a cynical view of people.

Saul joined him at the fence. "We work hard to keep it that way. It's not always easy. People are bound to butt heads, but we always come together when the need arises." He looked at Jace. "If you were ever looking for a change of scenery, you'd be more than welcome here."

Jace took a long moment to consider the offer. It was an appealing invitation. After all, no community of humans had ever accepted him so readily. The seclusion of this place and the acceptance did tug at him, but he shook his head. "It's tempting, but I could never live so far away from everyone I love." And, as surprising as it would have been to him a couple of years ago, he did have a good number of people he loved.

Saul smiled. "It never really matters where you are as long as you have your family and friends with you."

Jace agreed.

After breakfast, Saul showed most of them around the village. Jace offered to stay with Kyrin, since she couldn't join them, but she insisted he go. She did seem perfectly content to sit and visit with Jayna.

Just before noon, Leetra returned to the village with Michael, Balen, and the others from their group. Jace smiled at the reunion between Kyrin and Michael. After the flurry of greetings, Saul led everyone inside where it was almost twice as crowded now, though no one seemed to mind. Jace and Kyrin gave them a brief retelling of their capture and rescues, and then Darq asked, "What can you tell us about this traitor crete?"

He had that intensity in his eyes like he was ready to fight someone.

"I don't know who he is, but I know I saw him in the group backing Cray in Arvael," Kyrin said. "He's the only one who could have informed the ryriks where we were and who we are."

"I wonder if he's still with them." Darq glanced at Talas. "Maybe after dark we can fly over the area."

Knowing him, he was thinking about grabbing the crete.

"Leetra mentioned you heard something about Daican having a force on the way," Balen said.

Kyrin nodded. "I didn't catch much, but I distinctly heard one of the ryriks say, 'when Daican's force shows up.' I can only assume they meant here, and if they're calling it a force, it must be large."

"Two of us stayed behind to see what more they could find out," Saul said. "Elôm willing, they haven't been captured and will soon return with information."

Soon turned out to be shortly before suppertime. They were just about ready to eat when the two ryrik men arrived, dragging the bound crete traitor along between them. The man tugged against his captors, his hair hanging in a tangled mess, and a deep scowl on his face. His eyes flashed coldly as he glared at the group.

"You," Darq said in disgust.

"Do you know him?" Kaden asked Talas.

"Chand," Talas answered. "His father is leader of the Owl Clan."

One of the ryrik men said, "We grabbed him when he was leaving. He had this on him." He handed over a folded parchment.

"This is addressed to Lord Vallan," Saul said after inspecting it. He gave it to Darq.

"And it's sealed with Daican's seal." Darq broke it open and began reading. His expression grew harder until it bordered on a scowl.

"What is it?" Balen asked.

"Basically, a declaration of war on the Dorlanders. It's warning Lord Vallan and the cretes not to interfere. According to the emperor, if we turn our backs, we'll be left in peace." He shook his head, crunching the parchment as he refolded it, and sent another glare at Chand.

"That's not all of it," the other ryrik said. "Just before we left, that force they talked about showed up."

"How many?" Balen asked.

"More than fifty foot soldiers and twenty of these great black dragons with their riders. As far as we could tell, they are a preliminary force and plan to march straight on to Bel-gard and either weaken it or take control. Reinforcements will arrive in a couple of weeks. They'll reach the ford the day after tomorrow and the city in about four days. The ground force won't be much threat to the giants. They'd never make it beyond Bel-gard's walls. But those dragons . . . The giants wouldn't have anything to combat them if the cretes don't help. All they need to do is weaken Bel-gard's defenses and whatever force is coming after them can just walk in and take control."

Captain Darq grabbed Chand by the jerkin and yanked him close. "How large is the force still coming?"

Chand just glared at him and clamped his mouth shut.

"No doubt large enough to ensure Daican's control of the

area," Rayad said. "He probably intends to set up his rule here same as he did in Samara."

"Not if the cretes have anything to say about it," Darq replied.

At this, Chand broke his silence. "You'd do well to heed Daican's offer and stay out of this fight."

Darq pinned him with a steely gaze again. "Just stand by and watch while he destroys every one of our allies? What then? What's to prevent him from turning on us once our allies have fallen?"

Chand lifted his chin. "Daican's power to conquer comes from the firedrake force, and Falcor commands them. If Daican wants them on his side and not against him then he'll agree to our terms to leave the cretes out of his conquest and return the land we lost."

"So you're willing to not only allow, but *help* him destroy innocent lives and take over Ilyon just so long as we can occupy our former territory—a territory we left by our own choice?"

"What happens between the other races is none of our concern. There will be only two ruling forces in Ilyon after this—Daican and the cretes. It's a lot better than we have now where we're merely an afterthought shut away in the wilderness with no say in what goes on around us."

Darq looked angry enough to hit him. "You worthless scum. I knew you came from a family of fools, I just didn't realize how foolish. You've deceived yourself into believing a warped view of history. You act as though cretes were victims in some crime. We left Arcacia by our own choice. We *abandoned* Arcacia. Maybe if we had stayed and fought harder in our opposition to what was happening instead of turning our backs and walking away, things wouldn't be as they are now."

"It's cretes like you who won't live long enough to see our people returned to our former glory," Chand sneered.

"Yeah, well, I will see Lord Vallan deal with you." Darq shoved the crete toward Talas and Kaden. "Keep an eye on him."

Talas gripped Chand's arm. "Gladly."

Now Darq turned to face Balen. "We need to warn Jorvik and the other giants who will be in the path of Daican's men. They need to leave now."

Balen nodded, but Saul said, "If I know Jorvik, he won't go anywhere. He takes guarding the ford seriously. There are many defenseless villages right in Daican's path if his men get past the river."

"Then we must at least warn him so he can prepare," Balen replied. He turned to the group. "Gather your things. We need to go."

All the men turned and hurried to the barn. In the loft, Jace hastily rolled his bedroll and stuffed his belongings into his pack. As soon as he finished, he climbed down the ladder where they all met Saul at the door to the barn.

"Jorvik and his brothers won't stand a chance against Daican's men," Saul said grimly.

Balen gave a slow nod, looking as though a weight of the situation rested on him. "We'll see if there is anything we can do to help once we get there."

Saul grimaced. "I'll talk the men here and try to get word to the other nearby villages. If I can, I'll gather a force to aid you, though it will take some time."

"I know Jorvik would be grateful, as would we," Balen said.

As he and the others headed toward the dragons with their packs, Jace hung back with Saul. If things did not go well in the next few days, this might be the last they saw of each other.

"I don't know how to thank you for everything you did for me and for Kyrin." Jace had planned to find a more fitting way to show his gratitude, but now time didn't allow for that. "Also for giving me a new view of ryriks I never would have gained anywhere else. I've enjoyed it here more than most places I've been in my life, and I wish I had more time to spend here."

Saul smiled. "I'm glad Elôm caused our paths to cross. I don't know what the future will hold, but I do hope someday you will visit again . . ." He glanced toward the cabin with a smile. "Perhaps with a pretty wife at your side."

Jace ducked his head with a smile of his own. "I hope so."

Saul then offered his hand, and Jace gripped it firmly.

"You're always welcome here," Saul told him.

Darkness had long since fallen and Aertus and Vilai hung high overhead when they arrived back at Jorvik's farm. Amid the chorus of crickets from the surrounding fields, they landed in front of the cabin. Slowly, they all dismounted, wearied by the late hour, but Jace sensed the tension running through all of them. He'd spent most of the last several hours wondering how they would stop Daican from gaining ground in Dorland. Because they would try. He had no doubt of that. They wouldn't leave Dorland to fight or fall on her own.

Captain Darq pulled Chand down from his dragon and motioned to Talas and Kaden. "Help me get him tied up where he can't cause any trouble."

They led him up onto the porch, sat him down against one of the support beams, and wound a rope around him.

The commotion of their arrival must have alerted those in the cabin. The door opened, spilling candlelight out into the dark farmyard. Jorvik walked out onto the porch, followed by his brothers.

"What's going on?" He eyed Chand before he turned to Balen.

"Nothing good, I'm afraid," Balen answered.

Leaving Naeth to guard their prisoner, they all filed inside where Halvar and Levi lit more candles. Gathered in a circle in the living room, Balen relayed the information about the coming attack.

"The firedrakes will no doubt destroy any farm or village they come across on their way to Bel-gard. Anyone in the area must be warned to leave."

Jorvik shook his head. "There are too many. They'd never get out in time." His gaze settled on Halvar and Levi. "We will have to try to stop them at the ford, or at least slow them down to give the people time to flee. If not, it will be a slaughter."

"But what about the firedrakes?" Halvar asked. "All we can hope to do is slow down the men on the ground. We won't even be able to do that if those firedrakes take us out first."

Jorvik shook his head. "I don't know, but we have to do something. Hundreds, if not thousands, will be killed if we don't."

Off to the side, Jace caught Darq murmuring to Talas, who nodded. The captain then stepped forward. "Talas and I will do what we can to stop the firedrakes. I'm sure Naeth will join us."

Kaden stepped up as well. "So will I."

Beside Jace, Kyrin tensed, wrapping her arms around herself. Jace rested his hand against her back.

"We can't ask you to do that," Jorvik replied.

Darq shook his head. "You aren't. This is our choice."

"You'll also have help against their ground force." All eyes turned to Balen, and he said, "I will fight with you."

More than one person appeared ready to protest, but Darq beat them to it. "My lord, at risk of overstepping, you're the king of Samara and cannot put yourself in this sort of danger. This is likely a suicide mission, and I, for one, can't let you make that sacrifice."

"But what will it mean that I'm king if Daican succeeds in his conquest? If Dorland falls to him, any hope to free Samara falls with it, and I will never be her king again. Daican will have won. I would rather fight and die here than stand on the sidelines watching Ilyon fall to him. I understand your concern, but my life is no more important than anyone else's in this room, and if I'm not willing to fight and make sacrifices, then I'm not worthy of being king anyway."

Darq hesitated but then gave in with a slow nod.

All around the room, the men traded looks of a silent agreement that they would remain here to fight. After all, if Saul couldn't gather men from amongst the ryriks, then those in this room were the only form of help Jorvik would receive. Jace drew a hard breath. Somehow, he had known from the moment they learned of Daican's plan that it would come to this. That it would be them standing against Daican's force in a desperate attempt to hold them back.

Kyrin's arm slipped around him, and he looked down at her. Her eyes held both resignation and fear. As Darq had said, this would no doubt be a suicide mission. Daican's force outnumbered them at least five to one, probably more. It was hard to see any of them coming out alive . . . except Kyrin. He would make sure she survived.

Before he could act on this, Darq spoke again. "King Orlan will need to be warned of the attack." His attention rested on Kyrin. "We'll send you back to Bel-gard to inform him of what has happened." He then switched his gaze. "Leetra, you'll fly straight to Arvael and gather together as many riders you can. If, by Elôm's grace, we can hold out here, perhaps you will make it back in time to aid us. If not, then at least you can stop them from burning a path to Bel-gard."

As much as Jace knew Leetra hated to leave the fight, she nodded. Someone had to go, and it was only logical to get the women out of harm's way. And if anyone could gather an army from the reluctant cretes, it was her.

"Give your dragons a few hours to rest and leave at first light," Darq said. "Other than that, we just need to pray that Elôm provides us with the ability to hold back Daican until help arrives."

JACE SHOULD SLEEP. He needed his strength for this battle they had never expected to fight when they'd left Landale. However, too many thoughts and people crowded into his mind—Kyrin, Elanor, his mother. The anticipation of battle wasn't new to him. After all, only a year ago he and the others had faced it in Samara. Yet, there they'd had every expectation to win. Here . . . this wasn't to win. This was a desperate stand—an effort to save lives and slow Daican long enough for Dorland to prepare for the attack and for the cretes to come to their aid . . . if any of them came. Surely Lord Vallan would aid the giants and wouldn't accept Daican's offer, but what of the clan leaders? If they remained split, would they let Dorland fall?

Whatever happened, Jace had a terrible feeling he and the others wouldn't be here to see it. The thought of losing the entire group of people he'd become so close to through so many trials tore at his heart. It would be so senseless. His eyes stung at the same time heat burned through his chest.

Unable to stand the pressure of it building inside him, he sat up and pushed aside his blankets. Grabbing his boots, he stepped to the door and let himself out of the bedroom as quietly as he could so he wouldn't disturb anyone who might have been able to sleep the last few hours.

He needed fresh air, so he walked out to the porch. Chand still sat tied up near the stairs, while Naeth guarded him from a bench near the door. Darq stood and stared out toward the river as if Daican's men would show up any minute, and Talas and Leetra sat on the porch railing. They all looked at him.

"Couldn't sleep?" Naeth asked.

Jace shook his head. "No." He glanced down at Chand. The man looked very uncomfortable all trussed up, and yet he still managed to retain his fierce crete pride, judging by the sharp angle of his chin as he glared at Jace.

Jace scanned the others again, but their grim expressions only added to his unease. He stepped to the edge of the porch, where he peered up at the sky. Dawn was only about an hour away. Daican's force would soon be on the move.

Leaning against the support post at the stairs, he stared out at the open meadow in the direction of the ford. He imagined Daican's force marching across it, cutting them all down while the firedrakes destroyed the dragons and their riders. They would have no such protection as a fortress or walls to shield them. They'd make easy targets right out in the open . . .

Jace straightened and turned to Darq. "We should ambush them."

Darq looked at him, his brows lifting. "What?"

"Daican's men have no reason to assume we know they're coming. That means they won't expect or be prepared for an ambush. If we fight them out there—" he gestured to the meadow, "—we'll have no cover. If the firedrakes don't pick us off first, Daican's men will march on us full force and cut us down. But if we set up an ambush on the other side of the ford, we can use the forest to our advantage. It will force them to spread out instead of stay in a strong formation, and it will go against their training. Plus, the trees will provide us cover, not only from Daican's men, but also from the firedrakes. It won't help against the ryriks if they are with them, but I still think it might be better than exposing ourselves in open battle. We'd never last."

Darq considered it and nodded firmly. "You're right. It might not give us a significant advantage, but it would rob some of theirs."

"It could help us riders too," Talas said. "We can maneuver through the trees. The firedrakes can't, at least not well."

Darq nodded again. "The ambush will be on Arcacian soil, but it's not like Daican hasn't declared war. We'll let everyone know once they're up and spend the day scouting for the best location."

The first light of dawn brought everyone down from the bedrooms. Jace waited at the stairs for Kyrin as she gingerly took each step. He met her gaze and knew by the shadows around her eyes and her pale skin that she probably hadn't slept any more than he had. He took her by the hand and helped her down the remaining steps. She had her brave face on, but everything about it spoke of fragility.

Jorvik looked at her and Leetra. "I'll make breakfast for you so you can be on your way."

Kyrin shook her head. "Nothing for me, please. I'll eat along the way when I'm hungry, but not right now."

"Me neither," Leetra said, unusually subdued. "It's best if we just get ready and go."

Kyrin lifted her gaze to Jace. "My pack is still in my room by the door. Will you get it for me?"

He nodded and went up to the bedroom. The pack was where she said it would be. He picked it up, and a stabbing sensation filled his chest at the thought of her leaving. But she had to go. She had to be safe. He turned to the stairs again. Halfway down, he heard Marcus say, "Michael, go get your things. You're going with Kyrin."

Michael's eyes flew to his brother. "What? No way. I'm staying with you."

Marcus shook his head. "I will not argue over this. I let you come because I didn't think there would be any danger, and I promised Mother I'd keep you safe. I intend to keep that promise."

Michael straightened. "I think I'm man enough to decide whether to face the risk or not."

"Michael . . ."

"I won't go." He folded his arms stubbornly and reminded Jace very much of Kaden standing there. "You need every fighting man you can get, and you know I can fight. I'm not ten years old, Marcus. I can decide this for myself."

Marcus hesitated, sharing a look with both Kyrin and Kaden as if to gain their opinion. Neither one said anything.

After a long moment, Marcus released a heavy sigh. "All right, but that doesn't mean I have to be happy about it."

Michael drew his shoulders back and puffed out his chest. He would finally get his chance to fight. However, Kyrin's face crumpled just slightly, despite remaining silent.

Everyone left the cabin then and gathered by the dragons. Jace saddled Ivoris and secured Kyrin's belongings before turning to her. That brave mask of hers looked right on the verge of shattering. She reached for his hand, gripping it tightly as she led him around Ivoris and away from the others. Here, he watched the mask break, piece by piece.

"Please, just talk to me," she said, her voice hoarse and trembling. "I don't know if I can do this. I prayed so hard I'd never have to sit again and wonder if I'd lose all of you, but it's happening. I was able to hope in Samara, but I don't know if I can here. I'll probably lose three of my brothers and most of my closest friends." She paused, choking on her next words. "I'll probably lose you, and I don't know if I can bear that."

Her tears finally won out, spilling down her cheeks. Jace pulled her close and wrapped his arms tightly around her as she curled against his chest. He struggled for a way to comfort her that would be truthful and more than simply telling her everything would be all right. Would it be? It was difficult to see in these circumstances.

"I don't want to go," Kyrin's voice muffled against his shirt. "Whatever happens, I just want to stay here with you."

Jace pried her away just enough to look down into her face. "We need you to go to King Orlan and warn him. And *I* need to know you're safe. If you were here, I'd worry sick over you, but as long as I know you're safe, I can focus on what needs to be done. So please, whatever you do, stay safe, all right?"

Her breath trembled in and out, and she nodded, her voice barely a whisper. "All right."

Jace wiped the tear tracks from her face, careful of the cut along her jaw. That was when reality seized him as well. In all likelihood, these would be their final moments together. The loss of a future they could share sucked the breath out of his lungs, and each heavy, sluggish beat of his heart shot a stab of pain through him. He slipped his arm around her and drew her close again. Bending his head, he kissed her longer and deeper than he had in the past, drinking in everything about her. When he broke the kiss, he pressed his forehead against hers, never wanting to be parted from her. He spoke, though his words came rough through his clogged throat.

"I love you more than anyone else in this world. Bringing you into my life is the greatest thing Elôm has done for me aside from saving me. And despite my fears, it's been my dream for a long time to spend the rest of my life with you."

Kyrin choked on a quiet sob. "Me too. I love you so much."

Jace looked her in the eyes. "I will not give up on that dream. Yes, this situation looks bad. Yes, we are outnumbered, and by all accounts, have no chance at surviving. But Daican's men, no matter how many there are or how strong they are, do not have the power to kill us unless Elôm grants it. *He* is in control of who lives and who dies in the next few days. None of us are going anywhere unless it's His will. I won't lose hope that He brought us together for more than saying goodbye now."

Kyrin reached up to wipe her face. "I won't either."

"Take this to Lord Vallan so he knows the situation."

Leetra accepted Daican's letter from Darq and tucked it safely inside her vest as the captain continued.

"As soon as you've spoken with him, find Glynn and Novan. They'll know who will fight regardless of Daican's offer and will help you gather a force together."

It ate at her to leave this fight, but she understood how dire it was for her to get reinforcements. "I'll bring them back here as fast as I can."

Darq nodded and then turned away as Talas approached. He had a smile on his face.

"Don't let any of those clan leaders get in your way."

Leetra scoffed. "Not a chance."

"If only they had half of your fighting spirit." A moment of silence stretched between them before he spoke again. "So listen, if this all ends horribly . . ." at first he tried to sound unconcerned, but his voice lowered, "will you just let my family know how much I love them?"

Leetra had forced herself not to dwell on the outcome of the battle—to focus solely on her mission and what needed to be done—but hearing her cousin speak such words made it all too real.

"Of course." She winced at how thick her voice was. If she lost control of her emotions now, how much more painful would it be later when there would be true reason for sorrow? She wrestled the feelings back into their cage, but the sight of moisture in Talas's eyes almost destroyed her resolve.

"Well, this has been one crazy adventure for the two of us," he said. "Never would have expected it when we signed on to try to find Josan and the Scrolls, huh?"

"Nope. And there will be plenty more craziness for us to come, I'm sure." She refused to let this be goodbye. She just wouldn't.

Talas's smile resurfaced. "I'm sure." He cast a glance at the others before facing her again. His expression grew more serious. "I think you should talk to Timothy before you go."

Leetra frowned, and her heart gave an uncomfortable and irregular beat. "Why? I really shouldn't take the time."

But Talas's face had grown too solemn to ignore, and his voice echoed grimly. "Because this might be your only chance."

Leetra shook her head stubbornly, but he didn't give up.

"At least let him say what he has to say. You should give him that."

Every muscle in Leetra's body tensed up. She did not want to do this right now, and her sense of self-preservation screamed to flee, but . . . what if this was the only chance? Did she care enough not to rob him of that?

Talas turned away but paused to look back. "Maybe it's too late, but I really think the two of you . . ." He left that hanging there and smiled.

Before she could retaliate, Talas joined the others, and when Timothy turned to look at her, her heart beat like a celebration hand drum, only without the excitement. Her panic escalated when he walked toward her, but with a jolt of defiance, she stiffened her spine. She was a fighter—she would let him say his piece, but she would not change her mind.

However, it was not as easy as that when they came face to face.

"I would like to talk before you leave," he said. "Would you mind?"

Leetra nodded stiffly. She followed him just around the corner of the porch where they could talk privately. Crossing her arms tightly across her chest, she avoided his eyes. If there was one thing she'd learned, Timothy had a way of looking at her that melted the frozen pieces she kept on ice.

"All right. What did you want to say?"

He waited until she looked at him. "We haven't talked about the night we danced. If we don't do it now, we may never."

"What about it?" Leetra grimaced at her own harshness, but if she let her walls down now, it would rip her heart to shreds. The aggravating thing was scarred enough already.

Yet, despite her caustic tone, he was sweet and kind.

"It showed me something I suspected but was never completely sure of . . . I think you care for me, but you fight it."

Leetra tilted her chin defiantly. "Of course, I care. You're an important member of our group."

He shook his head. "You know that's not what I mean."

She looked away, refusing to acknowledge any other meaning.

"See, you're fighting it right now."

Her gaze snapped back to him, to those eyes looking at her so gently. But there was more. He couldn't hide a trace of disappointment, and she nearly screamed when her eyes started to sting. No, she would *not* do this. She would not let herself feel. Feeling hurt. Feeling led to loss. To betrayal . . .

"I've been down this road once before, and we both know how that turned out," she said bitterly.

"Lee," he spoke her nickname tenderly.

No one but Talas and her family ever used it, but it was the tenderness in his voice that undid her. All at once, her walls crumbled around her, leaving her already bruised heart completely exposed. Timothy's face blurred as her tears welled, but his voice came to her softly. "Do you really believe I would ever betray you?"

He stepped closer, taking her arms in his hands. She flinched, but he didn't pull away. The warmth of them seeped through her thin sleeves and spread all the way to her fingertips. Before she could stop it, her mind drifted back to the night in Stonehelm when he'd touched her hand and how her heart had reacted in a way it never had with Falcor, even when he'd kissed her. She clenched her fists, willing the tears not to fall, waiting until she could trust her voice, but even then it came out broken and thick. "No, you would never betray anyone."

Voice still tender, he said, "Then what is it? Why do you fight me?"

She blinked his face into focus, found him earnestly searching her eyes, and the raw wound that had festered and never fully healed in almost two years finally burst to the surface in a choked cry.

"How could you ever want me? I'm a stupid, foolish girl. I let Falcor into my heart. I should've been the first one to see through his lies, yet I was the most blind of everyone. I looked right past his flaws and any signals that things were not right, and people died." A sob tore at her throat as she remembered what she had been like then. "Josan *died* because I was too blinded and prideful to see that my betrothed was a traitor."

The seconds after her outburst were unbearable as she waited for him to finally understand he should hate her for not suspecting the man who had taken his uncle's life. He had every right to. Still, if he did, it would strike the deepest wound to her heart of all.

But his eyes did not grow hard—they softened, filling with compassion. He shook his head. "Leetra, you're not the only one he fooled. What about Darq and Talas and Glynn? Do you think they would have allowed him on such a critical mission had they any sense he would betray us? Falcor is the guilty one. Regardless of how you feel about me, you can't let him rob you of future happiness. You would only be punishing yourself for no reason. Elôm doesn't want that for you. *I* don't want that for you."

Like the ointment she always carried with her, his words seeped into her wounded heart, painful at first, but healing. The tears she'd held back for so long trickled down her face one after the other. At first, it stung her pride, but she couldn't stop even when she tried, and the effort left her trembling.

With a quiet murmur, he drew her against him and soothed her back. Her first instinct was to stiffen, but the strong shelter of his arms cocooned her and calmed the trembling. She sagged in surrender, her hands caught between them, curling in his shirt. After a long moment, he pressed a kiss to her forehead. To her temple. To the crest of her cheek, which was wet with her tears.

He reached up with one hand to thumb them away, his eyes running over her face as he spoke words she would never forget.

"I don't know how much of this you will want to accept, but I have to say it now while I still have the chance. In the last two years . . . I have come to love you. I hope, if Elôm allows me the time, you will let me prove it to you. But I also love you enough to let you go, if that's what you want. I just don't want you to keep on living as if, by punishing yourself, you'll somehow make up for Falcor's betrayal."

Still held by him, Leetra stood speechless in the wake of his quiet declaration. He loved her. Falcor had never spoken such words. She'd always accepted they were simply understood, but she'd been wrong. This man was one she could trust, and when he took his arm from her back and stepped away, the loss and longing surprised her.

"You need to go now," he said, as reality settled in all its painful truth. "Elôm willing, we will talk about this again."

She nodded feeling bereft of her usual fearlessness. If only he would just hold her again. She swiped her hands across her cheeks and drew a resolute breath, her crete strength flowing back. They had a mission to accomplish, a duty toward those they loved. She had to go. And he had to stay. There was no way around it.

Still, she couldn't leave him wondering. If she never saw him again, she wanted him to know. With a step, she flung her arm around his neck and hugged him desperately. His arms pulled her tight, and she whispered against his neck. "You don't need to prove anything to me."

And then she spun around, hurrying toward her dragon.

DANIEL AWOKE WITH a nauseating ache in his gut. He squinted toward the slightly parted drapes and groaned at the morning light. His father's birthday had dawned. And it just happened to be sunny too. He pressed his fingers against his eyes and then let his hand flop back down on the bed. He could happily sleep the morning away. A couple of years ago, he would have. But then, a couple of years ago, he wasn't *trying* to appease his father. Still, what he would have to face this morning soured his stomach to the point of truly feeling ill. He doubted that excuse would work though. Even if he went so far as to refuse to attend the grand opening of the Draicon Arena and the first day of celebratory games, he had a hunch his father would have him forcefully escorted. If only it were pouring rain. That would cut the games short.

"Elôm, give me strength. And a downpour."

The door in the sitting room opened, and he raised his head as his manservant, Walter, walked in. Thin as a twig, he looked like he hadn't eaten a full meal in his life. Despite this and his wrinkled features, he stood stiff and proper.

"Your outfit for today, my lord." He lifted the hanger of perfectly pressed black and gold attire.

Daniel eyed the clothing but resisted a scowl. After all, it wasn't Walter's fault he was in a bad mood. "Thank you. Just hang them up."

The man dipped his pointed chin and hung them neatly from a hook on the inside of the wardrobe door, meticulously smoothing out any wrinkles. He then turned to Daniel. "Is there anything else you require, my lord?"

Daniel shook his head. "No, I've got it from here."

"Very well, my lord." Walter started for the door but paused. "I was instructed to remind you that breakfast will be served in half an hour."

"I remember."

Walter cast him a look as though he wasn't so sure. Not that Daniel could blame him after years of disobedience and rebelliousness.

"I will be down on time."

With another quick nod, Walter left the room. Daniel sighed and threw back his covers. Sitting on the edge of the bed, he prayed for a few minutes. Today would require patience and fortitude he wasn't sure he possessed in adequate supply. And, as he had innumerable times in the last weeks, he prayed for an opening of his father's eyes and heart. Though his father always cut him short the moment he spoke of anything even hinting of his faith, Daniel prayed that perhaps, one day, his father might finally listen.

Determined to make good on his promise to both his mother and Walter, to attend breakfast on time, Daniel pushed up from the bed and walked over to the washstand to scrub his face. He then turned to the wardrobe for his outfit. Now alone, he did scowl. The heavy gold-embroidered brocade doublet would be insanely uncomfortable in the summer heat, especially with its high collar. He glanced longingly at his usual linen shirts and leather jerkins but resigned himself to the fact that today would be full of discomfort—from his attire to his father's company to the games. Come tomorrow, he'd distance himself from it as much as he could.

He tugged on the pants and shirt and then the boots Walter had polished to a high shine last night. Reluctantly, he slipped on the doublet and worked the gold buckles before stepping in front of the mirror to inspect his appearance. He straightened his collar and smoothed his hair. Time to face the day.

He walked out of his bedroom and through the sitting room to his door. When he opened it and stepped out, he found two guards stationed in the hall—just like every morning. His father apparently didn't believe the gate behind the temple had been his only means of escape.

Ignoring them, he hurried downstairs and strode toward the dining room. He arrived just ahead of his parents. When they walked in, his mother smiled, clearly pleased by his punctuality.

"Daniel," she said happily.

"Good morning, Mother." He offered a smile in return, though it died when his focus shifted. "Father." He nodded in acknowledgement but couldn't bring himself to wish his father a happy birthday. That would require a far closer relationship than they shared currently.

Davira arrived a moment later. She shot Daniel a poisonous glare before her expression changed entirely upon facing their father. A bright smile lit her face.

"Happy birthday, Father." She gave him a tight embrace and kissed him on the cheek.

He responded with a smile of his own and used the nickname he'd had for her since she was a baby. "Thank you, Virie."

Something pinched in Daniel's chest. It wasn't as if he didn't desire a close relationship with his father—a close father and son bond. They could have done so much good together if only they were united to help people. As much as his father valued power, Arcacia would be much stronger if they would build their people up instead of destroying many of them. Daniel had no doubt of that.

They took their seats at the table, and the servants served some of his father's favorite breakfast foods—poached quail eggs, cinnamon glazed ham, and apple tarts. Daniel took a couple of bites of the rich feast, but his stomach didn't accept it well. He'd rather eat a bland piece of toast this morning. Silently, he stared at his plate as his father and sister talked animatedly about the day's "festivities." He wanted to ask Davira how death could possibly be festive, but she had a disturbingly warped view of things, and he held his tongue.

Halfway through the meal, his mother spoke.

"Come, Daniel, have some more of your breakfast. You haven't eaten enough lately."

He looked up, careful not to sound too accusing and rile his father. "I'm sorry, Mother, but considering what I'll have to watch today, I'm afraid I can't stomach it right now." And being a prisoner in one's own home didn't exactly boost a man's appetite.

Her lips thinned, but she said nothing more.

Davira, however, sneered at him. "Weakling."

Daniel fought to check his temper. "I don't see how valuing life is weak."

"You're valuing the lives of traitors," she hissed. "But, of course, you are one and should be in the arena with them."

"Davira," their mother said firmly. "We will not have such arguments today." She turned her attention back to Daniel and changed the subject. "Will you join us in the coach on the way to the arena, or would you prefer to ride?"

"I'll ride," Daniel replied without even thinking about it.

He caught a suspicious glance from his father. No doubt he expected him to try to bolt as soon as he was outside the gate.

Daniel knew better than to try, but if this were his only opportunity to ride his horse, he'd take it.

His mother nodded and instructed one of the footmen to send word to the stablehands to have his horse saddled.

Daniel kept silent for the remainder of the meal for his mother's sake. The situation weighed on her enough already. After all, how could she take one side or the other? She had to walk a fine line between him and his father. He didn't envy her position.

When all plates were empty, save for Daniel's, they left their seats.

"Time to go to the arena," his father said, a hum of excitement in his voice.

If it were for any other purpose, Daniel might have been excited too. But he couldn't summon even a drop of anticipation. He was more likely to retch his breakfast all over the floor.

His father offered his mother his arm and guided her out of the dining room. Daniel glanced at Davira as she came alongside him to follow. Under normal circumstances, he should offer his arm to her, but she gave him a 'don't even think about it' look that contained more violent connotations. He wouldn't put it past her to stab or try to maim him in some way.

Outside, the gilded royal carriage awaited, along with Daniel's gray gelding whose coat shone from a thorough grooming. His mane was even braided with black and gold ribbons that Daniel would have skipped, but he wasn't about to complain considering this bit of freedom.

"Hey, boy." He patted the horse's neck and offered him the sugar cube he'd pilfered from the table.

The horse crunched it eagerly, and Daniel pulled himself up into the saddle, careful not to dishevel his clothing, though the doublet was so stiff, he doubted he could have if he tried. He took up the reins, and the gelding pranced, ready for a good run.

"Sorry, not today," Daniel murmured, as antsy as his mount. He could use a run as badly as his horse to work out his nerves.

The carriage pulled away from the palace with three mounted guards, including Aric, leading the way. Daniel followed. Ten more guards took up positions around and behind him. Were they for his protection, or to keep him from escaping? Most likely the latter. He couldn't deny the urge to let his horse have his head and bolt the moment they passed through the gate. However, the guards did an excellent job of boxing him in.

They turned along the road that led toward the new arena. The sight was impressive—a mountainous monument to his grandfather, its freshly cut stone fitted together with expert precision. Gold and black banners rippled from their poles along the very top of the arena, while thinner streamers fluttered from the outside balcony of the highest level six stories up. So disgustingly festive.

A buzz of voices and commotion drew Daniel's attention away from the arena. Just ahead, people lined the streets to watch them pass. Both children and adults alike waved small flags, while young girls tossed handfuls of golden colored flower petals into the air above the street. Daniel caught a glimpse of his father waving from the window of the carriage as people called out birthday greetings.

Daniel let loose a huge sigh when, as the carriage passed, attention turned to him. Women and girls shrilly shouted his name, the rising pitch making him squirm. He ignored them and refused to wave. Instead, he scanned the crowd for anyone he knew. Of course, in a gathering this size, recognizing anyone would be nearly impossible. However, halfway to the arena, a face caught his eye. Snapping his gaze to the man, he spotted Ben and Mira. His heart reacted, though he didn't let it manifest outwardly. He longed to stop and speak with them but did not slow his pace. Just before he lost sight of them, Ben gave him an encouraging nod that bolstered Daniel's resolve.

"Thank You, Elôm," he whispered. He'd needed that more than he could put into words.

When they arrived at the arena, Daniel stared at the number of people filing through the multiple entrances. They swarmed like ants surrounding an anthill, though not nearly so industrious. Of course, gladiator fights were popular among the people. His father had taken him to several in the old arena during his youth and teen years, but he'd refused to go once he'd reached young adulthood—another reason his father considered him weak. It wasn't the gore that bothered him as much as the barbarity of it all. No one should have the power to force men to fight and kill each other for sport. Today would be even worse. At least gladiators had training, and some even chose the life. Today people would be slaughtered without any hope of defending themselves. Did the spectators realize this was what they had paid to see?

Ahead of the carriage, Aric called for people to make way, and the carriage slowly rolled through as the crowd parted. Daniel's guards stayed particularly close, making his gelding skittish.

"Easy," he murmured as the horse tossed its head and tugged at the reins. But if they bolted, it wouldn't be his fault. The only problem would be the people. He didn't want to trample anyone.

A moment later, they arrived at the private entrance partitioned off for his family. One of the attendants there took his horse's reins as he slid down and walked to the carriage. While he waited for his parents and sister to climb out, he craned his neck back to look up at the arena. The muted echo of thousands of voices drifted from the arched openings of each level's balcony. The arena must be more than half-full already.

When they walked inside, the shadows of the thick stone halls offered immediate shelter from the hot sun. It didn't dispel the dampness in the air, but at least the sun wasn't beating down on his black doublet anymore.

Aric led them all through one of the perimeter halls and up a flight of steps. An ornate barred gate opened up to their right. Taking another short hall, Daniel found it opened up to a section of viewing boxes set aside for nobility. Those who had already arrived greeted his father, wishing him a happy birthday and congratulating him on the completion of the arena.

Daniel exchanged brief greetings with the men and their wives before following his father to the royal viewing box. He had only visited the arena a couple of times during construction. To see it in its completion was admittedly incredible.

Thirty feet below, the elongated, sand-covered floor waited to receive its victims. All around, rising up at an angle, were the six levels of the viewing stands. Just as he'd expected, they were nearly full of people. Like a giant, oval-shaped bowl, it gave everyone a perfect view of the carnage that would take place in just a short time. His gaze traveled around the perimeter of the arena before snagging at one end. Towering figures of Aertus and Vilai flanked the main gate as if presiding over the proceedings. Daniel scowled and swallowed down his disgust.

His parents took their seats on their padded chairs with Davira to their mother's left. An attendant gestured for Daniel to take the chair to his father's right, and he slowly sank into the cushions. He winced at the agitated gurgle in his stomach, especially when he noticed the table off to the side laden with decanters of wine and platters of delicacies. A young woman stood at either side waiting to serve them.

For the next several minutes, spectators continued to fill the stands—both men and women. It looked as though more than half the city attended. Once the arena was full, his father motioned to one of the attendants, who stepped forward and blew a gold trumpet. As the echo of it died, so did the voices, and the arena grew silent. His father rose from his chair and stepped to the edge of the viewing box. Daniel's mother and Davira did as well. Daniel didn't move until his mother motioned to him. With a sigh, he joined them just behind his father, who addressed the crowd.

"Citizens of Arcacia, welcome to the grand opening of the Draicon Arena. May it forever stand in memory of my father, the great King Draicon." He paused and thunderous applause surrounded them, reverberating and bouncing off the curved walls before finally finding escape through the open roof. Once it died, he continued. "May it also stand in honor of the might of our gods and the prosperity they have granted us."

In a sweeping motion, he drew all eyes to the idols at the end of the arena. As if controlled by some unseen puppeteer, every person bowed toward the idols, the motion sweeping through the crowd like a wave. It made Daniel sick. His parents and Davira also bowed, but Daniel just stood straighter and looked up at the blue sky instead, sucking in a calming breath as he prayed. *Give me strength and show me how to serve You amidst this madness, Lord.*

Everyone straightened again in the same sweeping motion.

"Thank you all for attending," his father said. "Now, let the games begin."

Another roar of applause hit Daniel's ears and vibrated in his chest.

As they turned back to their seats, his father's fingers closed around his arm in a vice-like grip. "You'd better hope anyone who might have noticed you standing there will consider your refusal to bow as an act of youthful defiance and not an act of treason."

Daniel resisted the urge to yank away and cause a scene. "I still don't see how refusing to worship your gods makes me a traitor when I'm perfectly loyal to my country and my people."

"It's the gods who have bestowed on us this power and prospered this country. To dishonor them is to betray their favor and provoke their wrath."

Daniel barely stopped himself from rolling his eyes. Now was not the time or place to hash this out or test his father's patience. His father gave him one final glare before switching his attention to the main gate.

Another trumpet blew, and the barred gate opened. Led by two heavily armored men, who must have been champion gladiators riding a pair of white horses, a long procession circled the perimeter of the arena—first the mounted fighters and then a troupe of gladiators on foot arrayed in a variety of armor and weapons. They were a group of hard-faced, brawny men ready to prove their strength and skill against each other. The men in the stands hooted and cheered as if they were heroes, while the women all but swooned.

At the very end of this parade of combatants came an uneven line of chained up men and women. Daniel stiffened. They shuffled past the royal viewing box, giving him a perfect view of the fifty or so individuals, all of whom would likely die here today. And it showed on their faces. Many of the women had tears staining their cheeks, while some of the men looked up at the stands with terror flashing in their eyes. Others seemed to have grimly accepted this fate.

Daniel curled his fists. How could he sit here while his brethren met death for the amusement of a crowd? He had to restrain himself from calling down to them and commending them for their faith. His father would probably toss him over the edge to join them. That is, if Davira didn't beat him to it.

Daniel leaned to his left, his voice low but sharp. "Father, look at them. They are your citizens. Do they really look like traitors to you?"

His father ignored him.

After a full circle of the arena, the procession disappeared back through the gate. Once the arena had emptied, a buzz of curious conversation came from the crowd as they waited for the first show. A few moments later, a side gate opened and four wild horses bolted out into the arena. They trotted and galloped around, snorting loudly as they searched for an escape. A second gate opened. This time, two muscular wild cats with sandy-colored coats, faint stripes, and long fangs that jutted past their bottom jaw slunk out of their dark tunnel.

Daniel grimaced. As if the day wasn't unpleasant enough, first he'd have to watch wild animals tear each other apart. Where was the sport in that? His father drew great pride in how civilized Valcré had become during his family's reign, yet people flocked in droves just to see these spectacles of violence. And they thought the ryriks' thirst for blood was barbaric!

Amidst yowls and hisses from the wild cats and the horses' terrified shrieks, this first show came to a gory end. Next was a match between a large pickerin boar and a bear. One match after another pitted the wild animals against each other, ranging from more bears and wild cats to wolves and bulls.

When animal carcasses littered the arena, slaves entered and carted them away, though the bloodstained sand remained. To up the excitement, the next bouts featured fighters against animals, the first being a burly man with a spear versus a huge male bear. Each match whet the people's appetites for the main attraction of gladiators later in the afternoon and evening. Daniel did all he could to block out both the fights and the uproar of the crowd. These contests lasted most of the morning before moving on to a couple of horse races in which it was perfectly acceptable to unseat your opponent or ram them and their horse into the wall.

At noon, servants brought generous portions of food to the viewing box. While his family ate eagerly, Daniel declined any for himself. The rising stench of sweat and blood bothered him more than it would have under different circumstances.

The nauseous rolling of his stomach only increased when the main gate opened and a group of soldiers prodded three unarmed men and two women into the arena. Daniel recognized them as a few of the prisoners from the procession. Left alone in the middle of the arena, they looked around. Though he couldn't make out their faces, he could almost feel their fear and uncertainty. His heart thudded in his chest, dreading what would come next. All around the stands, people quieted in anticipation.

Then, after a long, suspenseful minute, a chilling roar echoed through the arena and one of the largest side gates rose. Out slunk a bulky, black reptilian creature the size of a large horse. It had a long neck, angular head, and large maw full of sharp teeth. Its claws dug into the sand as it slowly stalked toward the prisoners, who gripped each other in fear. Daniel had never seen such a creature before, though it resembled his father's firedrakes. Two long scars on its shoulders and along its sides told him it had once had wings someone had cut off. It must have been a cave drake.

Daniel gripped the arms of his chair so tightly his nails dug into the wood as the drake drew closer to the prisoners, hissing and growling. Foamy saliva dripped from its scaly lips. The group backed away, but they would only have so far to go before the arena walls blocked their escape. They backed closer and closer to the viewing box, and Daniel could feel the drake's menacing growl in his chest. If he had a sword, he didn't think anything could have prevented him from jumping down there and killing the beast. But he was powerless. *Elôm, please do something.*

The beast lunged, and Daniel closed his eyes and turned his face away. Screams pierced his ears. His eyes burned behind his eyelids. The cries of terror and pain seemed to go on and on, but then everything fell silent. Daniel struggled not to heave up what little might be left in his stomach from breakfast.

"Open your eyes," his father hissed. "I'll not have you display such weakness in front of an audience."

Daniel did open them but kept them away from the arena and the slaughter he couldn't bear to witness. He ground his words through his teeth. "You can force me to sit here, but you can't force me to watch."

IF DANIEL DIDN'T get away from his father soon, he didn't know if he could keep himself from striking him, or strangling him, or *something* to knock some sense into him. *Lord, give me strength!* It was all he could do not to run from the arena the moment it was time to return to the palace for his father's dinner celebration. Not that his legs would have supported such a flight. They shook as they took his weight, and his head pounded so hard he could barely see straight. He wasn't sure if it was just the headache or the anger that pulsed through every nerve in his body. His throat was bone dry, but the first sip of liquid he took he would heave all over the stones. He just had to get out of here. If his father wanted him to attend any more games, they would have to drag him here and chain him to his chair.

He clenched his jaw and fists as he followed his family back through the halls of the arena. Just outside, his mother took hold of his arm and drew him to a stop.

"Daniel, are you all right?" She touched his cheek. "You're pale. Maybe you should ride with us in the carriage."

"No." He pulled away from her. He'd been in close proximity to his father for long enough. Any longer and he'd probably do something that would have him in the arena during the next games. After today, that sent a wave of chills through his body. "I'll ride."

He strode away before she could protest and mounted his waiting gelding. The motion made him slightly dizzy, but he shook it away. The sooner they left here the better.

The ride back was brief, since there were no crowds waiting for them this time. As soon as they reached the palace, Daniel dismounted and went straight up to his chambers. Inside his sitting room, he sank into one of his chairs. He rubbed his eyes, but he couldn't erase the disturbing images of carnage burned into them any more than he could stop the echoes of screams from ringing in his ears. How would he even sleep tonight? He rested his head back to let his taut muscles relax. It wasn't easy, though, with the way the back of his skull throbbed.

He flinched at the sudden knock at his door, soft as it was. "Come in," he called, reluctant to leave his chair.

The door swung open slowly, and his mother stepped in with a small tray against her hip. When was the last time he had seen her carry anything? She closed the door and walked over to him, setting the tray on the low table. A small teapot, a cup, and a plate of scones rested on it. Immediately, she poured a cup of tea and offered it to him. "Drink this."

Daniel held up his hand. "I don't think I'd keep it down."

"You haven't had anything to eat or drink since this morning. You have to get something in you. Just take it slowly."

Sighing, Daniel took the teacup and brought it to his lips. It wasn't as sweet as he liked it, but that was probably a good thing right now. He took a tiny sip and let it settle in his stomach before braving another. At first, it made him queasy, but his stomach seemed to recognize the need for sustenance. After he'd downed a few more swallows without it coming back up, his mother offered him a scone. By now, he felt ravenous. He finished one and grabbed another before giving his mother a grateful look.

Swallowing, he said, "I don't think I can go back down tonight."

"You must. Everyone will be expecting you."

"Just tell them I'm too ill." That wasn't stretching the truth too far. Though the tea and food helped, an underlying nausea still occupied his stomach.

His mother shook her head. "I think you're overreacting. You've been to these sorts of games before."

"And I've always hated them," he snapped. He cringed and softened his voice. "But it's not the games that did this. I had to sit there and listen to the dying screams of people mauled to death by wild animals or used as unarmed targets just for believing in the same God I do. How am I supposed to handle that? I mean, you can't enjoy watching such barbarity."

His mother straightened. "I don't, but I will support your father, and tonight, you need to as well."

Daniel groaned, wanting to fight this with everything inside of him. He couldn't support his father.

"I'll go for you," he said finally.

A smile ghosted across her face. "Thank you." She stood. "I'll let you change. Please be down as soon as you can. You may not wish to eat it, but dinner will begin shortly."

She left him alone again. After swallowing down another scone, Daniel pushed to his feet and entered his bedroom. Walter had another pressed outfit hanging on the door of the wardrobe. He changed into it, thankful to find it slightly more comfortable than the attire he'd worn all day. He stepped to the mirror and saw for himself how pasty his skin was.

With no power to do anything about it, he left his room and headed slowly back downstairs. The buzz of conversation hummed down the hall as he neared the gathering room. When he entered, he found the most guests Auréa had hosted in quite some time. He paused just inside the doorway to collect himself.

371

He had to be careful tonight, especially if anyone noticed his lack of enthusiasm. His father had warned him that if anyone at the party found out about his faith, there would be consequences—deadly consequences. Perhaps not for him but certainly for whoever learned his secret.

He'd barely taken two steps into the room when a shrill female voice sent a zing straight through his still throbbing head. His attention snapped to the source—a slender young woman with jewel-like green eyes and luscious blonde hair cascading past her hips. He suppressed a wince at an uncomfortable barrage of memories. She was one he'd spent far too much time with a few years ago.

She latched onto his arm. "It's been absolutely ages."

She stared up at him expectantly, and he stared back, racking his brains. Her father was an earl, but for the life of him, he couldn't remember her name. Especially not with this headache.

"Angela," she supplied finally, quirking her brow.

"Angela, yes, I'm sorry." He tried to formulate a better apology, but she just laughed giddily.

"Had a bit much to drink at the games, did we?"

Daniel opened his mouth but then snapped it shut again. Letting everyone believe he'd overindulged would probably be safer for them than knowing he condemned everything about today.

Finding his manners, he asked, "How are you? I hope your family is in good health."

"Oh yes, Father has been much improved."

"Good," Daniel replied, though he hadn't the slightest idea what ailed the earl.

"This rain, however, is quite vexing. How fortunate it held today, thank the gods."

Daniel nearly snorted. While he didn't know why Elôm had allowed a break in the rain today of all days, it certainly had nothing to do with fake idols whose only real use was firewood.

A playful smile lifted Angela's full lips, and she leaned inappropriately close, batting her eyelashes. "Perhaps we can take another moonlit walk around the garden."

Daniel cleared his prickly throat. There would be no sneaking off with her tonight, or any girl in this room for that matter. He struggled to form a suitable reply. Thankfully, his father invited everyone to the dining room, providing the perfect escape. He gently extricated himself from Angela's possessive clutches.

"Excuse me. I must join my family."

He strode away before she had a chance to speak again and crossed the room. However, he didn't fail to notice the adoring eyes of several other young women, all of whom he'd spent time with at one point or another. All his idiotic and immature choices were coming back to bite him. He knew full well these women were only after him because he was royalty. It hadn't really mattered to him when he was young as long as he was having a good time, but it mattered now. *Lord, help me deal with the consequences of my life before I knew You, and help me make much better decisions in the future.*

He met his parents at the door of the dining room and fought to retain his composure and a cool head as they took their places at the main table. Two more tables had been prepared to accommodate everyone. When the servants set a heaping plate of braised lamb, roasted garlic mushrooms, and stewed onions before Daniel, he was glad to find he still had a bit of an appetite. It was hard to pass up such a feast. Though he didn't come close to cleaning his plate, he did manage to enjoy much of it in spite of all the talk of the games that surrounded him. Thank Elôm he wasn't required to participate in these conversations.

After the meal, everyone filled the ballroom. Daniel positioned himself to the far side in hopes of remaining inconspicuous for the final couple of hours of the evening. He caught sight of Aric stationed at the perimeter of the room and contemplated joining him, but his father wasn't stupid. If he caught Daniel spending too much time with the head of security it might just cast suspicion on Aric's beliefs and loyalties. So he remained where he was.

A few of the young lords eventually found him. The games were a popular topic until they must have sensed he had no desire to speak of them. They moved on to hunting and other sports Daniel had no notion of when he'd ever get to partake in again. Then the women sidled up to him, sometimes two or three at a time. His old self would have eagerly engaged in their flirtation, but he remained distantly polite until they gave up. Though a tedious cycle, he was willing to endure it if it meant staying out of trouble until he could go to his bed for the night.

When the dancing started, it only grew worse. Even more women hovered around with expectant gazes, but he offered no invitations. He would honor his parents with his presence, but it did not mean he had to participate in all the activities. He was in no mood to dance.

An hour later, Daniel caught sight of a familiar face among the crowd. Excusing himself from his latest gathering of flirting females, he worked his way around the dancers.

"Alex?"

A man with short black hair turned to him. Something unhappy flashed in his eyes, but a smile quickly hid it. "Daniel."

Daniel offered his hand to his friend, and they clasped each other's arm. He hadn't seen him since before the fatal "accident" that had befallen Alex's father two years ago. Of course, Daniel knew better. He'd suspected his own father had something to do with Baron Arther's demise, and now he had no doubt.

"I didn't know you were here. It's good to see you."

Alex gave a brief nod. "I couldn't really pass up the invitation, now could I?"

"You should have let me know you were coming."

"Well, it was a rather last minute decision."

"So how are things in Keaton?" Daniel asked, realizing how much they had to catch up on.

Alex's smile disappeared entirely and that cool look returned to his eyes. "My *esteemed* uncle has deemed me unfit for the task of ruling Keaton due to the indiscretions of my wayward youth. Everything is under his power now."

"But that was years ago. We may have been a bit wild, but we didn't do any true harm."

"Yes, well, try telling him that."

Daniel shook his head. "I'll talk to my father about it."

Alex cast him a doubtful look. "You do that."

He then walked away without another word. Daniel called to him and stood stunned when he did not turn back. The two of them had been such good friends growing up—Daniel's only true friend, really. How had that changed so much in just a couple of years? And yet, how could it not have if Alex suspected how his father truly died? If Daniel knew it, chances were Alex did too.

Daniel let his shoulders slump as the heaviness of the whole day descended once more. He backed away to the perimeter of the room again, contemplating what seemed to be the loss of a longtime friend. He sighed. Maybe he could talk to Alex again before he left and assure him that he did not condone his father's actions. Maybe it would even lead to deeper topics . . . if he was very careful about it.

Sometime later, a servant offered him a glass of wine, but he declined. He was in the middle of a benign conversation with two older barons when Alex's voice came from across the room. The musicians were resting between dances so it carried easily and drew everyone's attention to where Alex stood.

"A toast to our illustrious emperor. May he enjoy many more such birthdays as he so rightly deserves." He lifted his wine glass toward Daniel's father and then drank. Everyone else with drinks followed suit while the others applauded.

Daniel frowned deeply. Why would Alex honor his father with a toast if he were so upset? He set off across the room. As he neared, he found Alex talking to his parents.

"Thank you for that," Daniel's father said.

Alex smiled. "I wanted to make sure there would be no mistaking my loyalties." He glanced at Daniel and then said, "Excuse me. I have a young lady awaiting a dance."

He walked away before Daniel could get a word in. Daniel stared after him, and his mother touched his arm consolingly at Alex's painfully obvious avoidance of him. It just made no sense. What had Daniel done to deserve such treatment? Alex couldn't possibly think he had anything to do with his father's death, could he? That would be ridiculous.

He reluctantly turned his attention to his father, who was just finishing a sip of his wine. At least he could try to fix things between him and Alex.

"I need to talk to you about a situation in Keaton."

His father raised a brow. "And what situation is that?"

"Alex should rightfully be baron, but his uncle has taken over the province." Daniel drew a breath to ease the discomfort of speaking with his father and to make sure his tone remained respectful. "I would appreciate it if you would restore power back to Alex. I know the two of us pulled some crazy stunts in our youth, but he has every right to govern Keaton. I have no doubt he can manage it."

His father stared at him for a long moment before he finally nodded. "I'll look into it."

A pleasant thankfulness settled inside Daniel, and he actually smiled. "Thank you."

The moment the current dance finished, Daniel looked around for Alex. He couldn't rest until he made things right between them. Peering through the mingling guests, he spotted Alex at the far door. His friend glanced around the room and then slipped out. No doubt a young woman had exited just ahead of him. Maybe his friend hadn't matured as much as he thought.

Daniel worked his way to the door and stepped out. Looking up and down the hall, he found it empty. Of course, Alex knew every secret corridor and private nook inside this palace. Unless Daniel wanted to spend the rest of the evening searching him out, he would have to wait for him to return or catch him at breakfast in the morning.

Resigned to waiting, Daniel reentered the ballroom, though he remained near the door in case Alex did return before the evening was over. He chatted with an elderly noble couple and firmly resisted an obnoxious mother's attempts to nudge him toward her daughter, who happened to be ten years his senior. Avoiding that catastrophe, he turned to the nearest server, ready for something to wet his throat.

Shattering glass echoed across the room. Someone must have had their wine glass refilled too many times. He turned, but it was not a tipsy party guest amongst the glittering shards of glass. Daniel's father stood there, his hand splayed across his stomach. His face clenched in a tight grimace, and his pale skin was more than a match for Daniel's earlier. Then, before any solid thought could form, Daniel watched his father collapse.

GASPS AND MURMURS filled the room. Daniel blinked, but his father was still on the floor, his mother kneeling over him. Breaking from the shock, Daniel rushed through the guests and reached his parents the same time as Davira did.

"Father!" his sister cried.

Daniel knelt next to his mother, who grasped his father's hand and touched his cheek.

"Daican, what is it? What's wrong?"

He only groaned, his eyes squeezed shut as his grimace deepened. Something was very wrong. Daniel touched his mother's shoulder. "We have to get him up."

She nodded, and Daniel looked around. Aric stood at his side.

"Help me get him upstairs," Daniel said.

They each took one of his father's arms. Draping them over their shoulders, they lifted him up and held him securely between them. To one of the other security guards, Daniel instructed, "Bring a physician to my parents' quarters immediately."

The man hurried away, and Daniel and Aric carried Daniel's father upstairs. Daniel's mother rushed ahead of them to open the door. Daniel and Aric eased Daniel's father down on the bed, and Aric took a step back as Daniel's mother and Davira crowded around.

"What happened?" Daniel asked his mother.

She shook her head, her eyes wide. "I don't know. Everything was fine until I noticed him pressing his stomach. He said it was nothing, but then he dropped his wine and collapsed." She leaned over his father and rested her hand against his cheek again. "Daican, can you hear me?"

He moved fitfully and his eyes fluttered, but he didn't appear to be conscious.

Davira leaned closer. "Come on, Father, wake up." Daniel had never seen her so worried. She shook her head and cast a desperate look at their mother. "What could be wrong with him?"

"I don't know," their mother murmured.

A minute later, the physician arrived. Daniel moved aside to let the wiry, balding man have room.

"What happened?"

Daniel repeated what his mother told him so she wouldn't have to.

The physician's lips pursed. "His pulse is elevated. What did he eat?"

Daniel's mother named off some of the main courses served at dinner and shook her head in bewilderment. "Nothing out of the ordinary, and nothing we didn't all have."

"How quickly did he fall ill?"

"I don't know . . . from when I first noticed his discomfort to when he collapsed was about five minutes."

The physician's expression turned grim.

"What is it?" Daniel's mother asked. "What's wrong with him?"

"Considering the speed of the onset . . . I believe it may be poison."

"Poison!" Davira shrieked. "How could he be poisoned?"

Out of nowhere, realization struck Daniel like a violent blow. He gasped.

All eyes swiveled to him.

"What?" Davira demanded.

He swallowed convulsively. Surely it couldn't be, yet it was too coincidental. He shook his head. If he was wrong . . .

"Tell me!" Davira screamed at him.

Daniel winced. He couldn't withhold information that could be useful. "I don't know anything for certain, but Alex seemed upset about the situation in Keaton. He wouldn't talk to me, and I thought his toast to Father was strange. Then I saw him leave the room shortly before Father took ill."

Davira's eyes flared and flashed to Aric. "Find him and arrest him!"

Aric glanced at Daniel before he left the room.

Once he was gone, Davira turned her attention back to the physician, all the fury melting into worry. "What can you do for him? Can you stop the poison?"

"Without knowing the poison used, I can only guess what might neutralize it." The physician hesitated. "I can make no promises."

"You have to save him!"

"I will try, my lady." He opened his medical kit and rummaged through the many vials stored there before choosing.

Daniel stood at the foot of the bed, his eyes hardly leaving his father's unconscious but taut face. His father had always been such a strong man. He didn't remember ever seeing him ill. To see him so stricken like this turned everything upside down. What really gripped him was his mother's distress. Though she remained calm, talking soothingly to his father and stroking his face and hair, every worry line in her face deepened. Even Davira lost all her cold, hard edges. The fear widening her emerald eyes gave her a much younger, almost childlike appearance. Though they'd never gotten along, he was still her big brother and his instinct was to protect her.

Overcome with these emotions, Daniel did something he would never have imagined needing to do. He bowed his head, closed his eyes, and prayed that Elôm would spare his father's life—that He would guide the physician and would halt the poison's effect. *I know what he's done and what he plans to do, but maybe he will change. Maybe this will give me the opportunity to help him understand.*

The physician continued to administer different remedies and then wait to see if they had any effect. Daniel watched hopefully for an improvement. At least his father didn't appear to be getting worse. Maybe he would fight through it. He was an incredibly—*infuriatingly*—stubborn and determined man. Yet, it was ultimately in Elôm's hands, so Daniel did not cease his prayers.

When Aric returned to the room, Daniel turned with an ache in the pit of his stomach. He didn't condone what Alex had done, but the punishment would be a death sentence for his friend.

However, Aric shook his head. "I'm afraid he's gone. He told the guards he was going to one of the taverns, but I'm sure it was just a story to avoid suspicion. All his things are gone from his room."

Davira rose, her eyes like fire. "Have them thrown into the dungeon."

Aric spoke carefully. "My lady, they had no way of knowing what he'd done."

"I don't care," Davira snapped. "They let him escape. I don't care what it takes, I want him found. Close off the city if you have to. I want every available man out there looking for him, now!"

Aric nodded slowly. "Yes, my lady."

He turned, and Daniel followed him to the door where Davira wouldn't overhear them.

"Do what she says. Finding Alex may be our only chance at discovering what poison he used. Just make sure the guards at the gate are well treated. I'll sort this out as soon as things calm down. I'm sure Father will understand." At least he prayed his father would find it in his heart to understand. None of this was on the guards.

Aric accepted these orders with another nod. Just before he left, he said, "I'm sorry. I know you and Lord Alex were friends."

Daniel sighed heavily. "Thank you."

He then returned to his position at the foot of the bed. His mother squeezed his father's hand, not moving for several minutes until she rose from her seat on the edge of the mattress.

"I should go see to the guests." Fear strained her expression, her eyes never leaving her husband's face.

"I'll do it," Daniel offered. She shouldn't have to leave his father's side.

Her eyes pooled with moisture and gratitude, and he walked out of the room. He felt heavy and slightly lost as he walked the dim halls. He wasn't used to taking charge of things like this, but he would do it for his mother. He'd never cared for Sir Richard, but he did wish the man was here right now instead of in Samara. As his father's closest advisor, he would have handled everything smoothly. But it was now up to Daniel.

When he entered the ballroom, the guests stood around in groups, talking in muted, concerned tones. Servants had cleaned up the shattered glass and spilled wine. Daniel cleared his throat to gain everyone's attention, and the room went instantly silent.

"I apologize for having kept you here waiting for news. I'm afraid it appears that my father has been poisoned."

Women gasped and men murmured, some looking fearfully into their wine goblets.

"Don't be alarmed for your safety," Daniel assured them. "I have no reason to believe anyone but my father was targeted."

Surely someone else would have fallen ill by now if that were Alex's intent.

"Who would do such a thing?" an elderly baroness asked, her hand to her throat.

Daniel hung his head but then raised it. "We believe the culprit was Alex Avery."

Murmurs started again, many raising questions, but Daniel didn't elaborate. How could he possibly tell them it was because his father had murdered Baron Arther? At least, that was what Daniel assumed had triggered Alex's assassination attempt.

Finally, one of the earls stepped forward. "How bad is it?"

Daniel shook his head. "Since we don't know what poison Alex used, our physician can only guess, but my father didn't appear to be getting any worse when I left. It is my hope he will fight through this." The guests exchanged looks and murmurs again, but Daniel quieted them. "You may spend the rest of your evening here if you wish. Or you can retire to your rooms. Please make yourselves comfortable. I will see that you are informed of any major changes in my father's condition. Hopefully, by morning, he will be conscious and well on his way to recovery."

However, a rock formed in Daniel's gut. If Alex had gone so far as to poison the emperor of Arcacia, he wouldn't have done so with an impotent poison. He shook the thought away, clinging to the hope his father would recover.

His attention snapped back to the guests when the earl said, "I, and anyone who wishes to join me, will go to the temple and pray for him."

All around, the others nodded. Daniel looked at them, struck with sadness. How powerful would the prayers of so many be if offered to Elôm instead of to idols?

"Thank you." He didn't know what else to say, though he knew it would do no good. "If you need anything, just have word sent to me and I will take care of it."

Leaving them to their own devices, he turned and trudged back to his parents' room. His feet dragged as he climbed the stairs, his heart still heavy over the guests' offers to pray. As far as he knew, only he, and perhaps Aric, prayed for his father's healing to a God who could actually hear them. If only he could get word to Ben and Mira. It would be strange to ask people to pray for a man who would have them killed for their faith, but he didn't have a single doubt that they would do it.

When Daniel arrived upstairs, he found that his mother and Davira hadn't moved from their places beside his father. Daniel took a seat at the end of the bed near his mother.

"Any change?"

She shook her head, and Daniel chose to see that as a good thing.

"Has everyone been settled?" she asked without looking at him.

"Yes. Most of them are going out to the temple to pray for Father's healing." Daniel rested his hand on her shoulder. "I'm praying too."

Davira made a scoffing noise in her throat, but his mother offered him a grateful look.

Silence settled around them, broken only by his father's ragged breaths and the rustle of the physician sorting through his remedies. Living in the palace had meant always having people around—from servants to security—but in the quietness of the room, Daniel almost felt as though it were just his family and the physician. What would it have been like if they'd not been royalty—if they were just a normal, working family? Would he and his father have been close? Would they have worked together, sweated together, hunted together? Maybe they could have done some of that even here, but he'd never wanted to compromise enough to try. Why now, when his father could be dying, did the desire grip him so strongly? *I'd like another chance, Elôm.*

Time slipped by unnoticed. Sometime after midnight, Daniel rubbed his gritty eyes and considered going to his room to change into something more comfortable, but then his father groaned. They all focused on him.

"Daican," Daniel's mother called.

Grimacing, his eyes fluttered open. They didn't focus at first, but he turned his head, and his gaze locked on his wife. He didn't speak, just stared at her.

"You're going to be all right, Father," Davira said from the other side of the bed. "You're going to fight this and be all right."

Slowly, he turned his head to look at her next. She smiled at him, though tears wet her eyes. "You'll be all right," she whispered again.

Then his gaze shifted to Daniel, who leaned a little closer. In that moment, he felt as though his father truly looked at him with love for the first time. It was both painful and comforting. Then his father's eyes slid closed again. His chest lowered as he released a wheezing breath but failed to rise again. Daniel held his own breath, his heart pounding in his ears as he waited . . . and waited.

"Father?" Davira said shakily. Nothing happened. Her voice shrilled in panic. "Father?" Still nothing. She grabbed the physician's arm. "He's not breathing! Do something!"

The physician sprang into action, diving into his medical kit and trying remedy after remedy. Daniel sat paralyzed as if watching through someone else's eyes. This couldn't really be happening. His father couldn't just die so suddenly.

After a few minutes, the physician stopped and shook his head. "I'm sorry," he barely whispered, and cold flushed through Daniel.

"No!" Davira screamed. She shook their father's arm as tears poured down her cheeks. "No, Father, please! Come back!"

Sobs broke from their mother's chest, and before Daniel knew it, tears ran hot down his own cheeks. He stared at his father's still face and could hardly make himself believe it. He wasn't finished talking to him yet—wasn't finished trying to tell him about Elôm. Pain exploded in his chest. His father had lost his only chance to save his soul. Daniel would *never* see him again. *Why did you do it, Father? Why didn't you listen?* His tears fell harder, but he finally broke himself from shock and reached for his mother, holding her against his chest as they both cried quietly. Davira's louder sobs filled the room as the three of them huddled on the bed.

Morning light filtered into the room in the midst of an overcast sky. Daniel still cradled his mother in his arms, and Davira sat across from him staring blankly, her pale face streaked with tear tracks and smeared cosmetics. Aric had checked on them sometime during the night, but other than that, they were left alone.

Daniel stared down at his father's motionless body. He shuddered at the way death hung so heavily in the room. Preparations had to be made for a funeral and burial. And, of course, there were guests to see to. Aric must have given them the news, but someone from the royal family should address them. Someone like him. But his body was so heavy. He didn't have the energy. Yet, if he didn't, his mother would have to.

Slowly, he pulled away from her. "I am going to go change." His voice came out hoarse. "Then I will see to things downstairs."

His mother didn't respond.

He rose stiffly. "I will see that your maids are sent up to assist you." He glanced at Davira, but neither one even seemed to hear him. His sister had fresh tears trailing down her cheeks though her face was set as stone. Daniel almost walked around the bed to hug her, but he thought it best just to leave her alone.

He stepped out of the room and walked numbly to his own. After lighting a few candles, he went to the wardrobe and reached for a plain green shirt, but paused. Black. They were in mourning now. He pulled out a black shirt instead, and a plain black jerkin.

All his fatigued muscles protested as he changed into the fresh outfit, but he was almost too numb to notice. When he finished, he sank down on the edge of his bed and stared at the wall.

His father was dead.

The thought hung suspended in his mind. In one evening, everything had changed. His father's commanding presence and ideals had been the heartbeat of this palace. How empty it suddenly felt. What would happen now?

That's when it crashed down on Daniel, the enormity of what his father's death meant. His breath snagged his chest, and his heart almost failed to beat.

He was now the king of Arcacia.

KYRIN PRAYED FOR daylight. Huddled next to Ivoris for warmth on the breezy grassland, she hadn't felt so uncertain or lonely since awaiting her own execution in Auréa's dungeon. She'd flown almost nonstop the day before. She would have flown throughout the night to reach Bel-gard, but she was too afraid she would veer off course in the dark. She needed to see the landmarks they'd passed on the way to the ford. And as much as she desired to push on, Ivy did need the rest.

Kyrin, however, sat awake for most of the night. When she did doze off, she would jolt awake only a short time later with a sick ache gnawing inside of her. Twice she'd succumbed to tears, crying mournfully in the darkness. She prayed for a miracle— that Elôm would protect Jace, her brothers, and their friends long enough for help to arrive.

The moment light appeared in the east, and she could see a good distance across the grassy terrain, Kyrin pushed to her feet and stretched her legs. "Time to go, Ivy."

She tightened the saddle straps and climbed onto the dragon's back. Before taking off, she reached into her pack for enough food to satisfy the empty pinching in her stomach. With a command, Ivy spread her wings and took to the air. The wide-open grassland stretched out farther and farther as they climbed toward the sky, seeming to symbolize how alone she was. Yet, she wasn't alone. The same God who had created these grasslands was with her as surely as if Jace were flying beside her. And He was at the ford too, with power far greater than Daican's force.

The sun climbed steadily as Kyrin scanned the terrain and compared it with her memories. A little over an hour after sunup, she caught her first glimpse of mountain peaks straight ahead. Bel-gard appeared a short time later, and her heart rate accelerated. Her main concern had been to reach the city, but now she had to confront King Orlan and convince him to send help to the ford. Considering his refusal to aid them last time, would he simply send her away? Still, this time they had proof of Daican's intentions. The king would have to take action to defend his people . . . unless he chose to surrender. Kyrin grimaced. That would destroy everything they had fought for all this time and make any sacrifice of life at the ford meaningless.

She shook her head. No sense in dwelling on that before she'd even spoken to him.

Coming up over the walls of the city, she flew straight to the castle and landed in the courtyard. Hopefully the giants would receive her as well as they had the entire group. She wasn't a crete like Captain Darq, but at least as a woman, she didn't appear threatening.

Ivy crouched down for her, and Kyrin dismounted. Two castle guards already strode toward her. Now that she was here alone, the men did seem rather intimidating with their size and those giant swords, but she strengthened her resolve and thought of Leetra. Small as she was, the crete girl would never back down from anyone.

Ignoring the twinges in her ankle that made her limp, Kyrin walked toward the giants. When she met them, she said, "I am Kyrin Altair. I was here with King Balen of Samara several days ago. I must speak with King Orlan immediately. Dorland will soon be under attack."

The two giants looked at each other, and then one motioned for her to follow. "Come with me."

She hurried to keep up with his stride. Jace would fret over the strain she was putting on her ankle, but that didn't matter right now. At the stairs, however, his absence made the climb much more difficult. She gritted her teeth when the pain increased after the first three steps.

"Let me help you." The guard offered his large hand.

She gave him a grateful smile and wrapped her hand over his top two fingers. With his support, she climbed the remaining stairs more easily. Inside, he took her to the throne room and guided her to a chair along the edge of hall.

"Stay here. I'll get the king."

With echoing footsteps, he left the room. After hoisting herself up in the chair, Kyrin lifted her leg and massaged her ankle through her boot. It would probably start swelling up again after this. Her gaze strayed around the silent hall, but then she bowed her head and prayed about her meeting with the king.

A couple of minutes later, footsteps approached. King Orlan entered the throne room, followed by the guard and another giant with dark blond hair. Kyrin slid off the chair and met them near the throne. The third giant had to be just shy of ten feet tall as he towered over her. A keen glint in his eyes showed his interest in what she had to say. When she glanced between him and King Orlan, they looked so similar that she knew he must be Prince Haedrin. This heartened her, considering what Captain Darq had said about him.

"Miss Altair," the king said. "You were with King Balen."

"Yes, and I'm afraid I bring grave news. Daican has declared war on Dorland. There will be Arcacian troops at the Andros Ford in a matter of hours if they haven't reached it already."

She paused, her mind too quick to imagine everyone at the ford already fighting . . . maybe dying. She gulped. "They intend to march on Bel-gard. A second force will arrive in a couple of weeks."

Orlan's bushy white brows lifted. "How do you know this?"

"Because we intercepted a message from Emperor Daican to Lord Vallan telling the cretes that if they stay out of the fight when he attacks your people, they will be left in peace. Those ryriks attacking at the ford were hired by Daican to weaken your border. King Balen and the rest of our group are at the ford now to try to slow Daican's men down, but they are greatly outnumbered. Daican's men will reach the ford today. Please, you must send reinforcements." Kyrin had to swallow again with the way her throat tightened up. "I don't know how long they can hold them off . . . if they can at all."

King Orlan's eyes narrowed. "You're sure of this?"

"Yes," Kyrin replied a bit sharply. She drew a deep breath to calm herself. "I saw the message for Lord Vallan myself. I could quote it to you word for word, but there isn't time. Everyone at that ford—including Jorvik, Halvar, and Levi—is likely to die if they don't get help quickly. Every minute of delay dooms them further."

Before Orlan could say a word, Prince Haedrin stepped forward. "How large is Daican's force?"

"More than fifty foot soldiers and twenty firedrakes and their riders, plus over a dozen hostile ryriks if they choose to fight. We sent a messenger to Arvael to gather crete dragon riders to aid us, but I don't know if they'll arrive in time."

Haedrin didn't wait for her to say more. He turned to the guard. "Gather fifty men armed and ready to ride out with me within the hour. I want the rest of them at the walls preparing for an attack should the enemy get this far."

The guard nodded and rushed off.

King Orlan took his son's arm. "Perhaps you should remain and oversee the men here."

"King Balen and his people are putting their lives at risk to defend our country. I aim to see it isn't in vain. If we had dealt with this sooner, then none of this would be happening."

He turned his intense gaze to Kyrin, and his expression softened. "I will send servants to show you to a room and fetch anything you require to make your stay here comfortable."

Kyrin shook her head. "No, I will fly along with you and your men."

"You're sure?"

"Yes."

Jace wanted her to stay safe, and she would. If there was any sign of danger, she would hang back and return to Bel-gard or Arvael if she had to. But she couldn't just sit here and wait for news. As much as she dreaded what would await her, she had to return to the ford.

It seemed some of the rain they'd left behind in Arcacia had finally made its way to Dorland. Thunder rumbled in the distance, and sheets of rain drifted across the meadows. Jace watched it from the cabin porch as he sipped a large cup of coffee. The liquid settled warmly in his stomach with the light breakfast he'd eaten, but it didn't soothe the ache. The day had come. Soon, Dorland would be at war with Arcacia. They'd spent all of the previous day scouting the terrain and creating whatever obstacles they could to hinder Daican's men. The rest was in Elôm's hands.

He looked toward the forest to the south. Every time he glanced that way he hoped to see an army of ryriks led by Saul, but the open plain remained empty. Even if Saul had gathered men, it would have taken time to prepare and make the journey from the village. Jace prayed they would still arrive before it was too late.

He wrapped his left hand around the sword at his side, trying to get used to the unfamiliar grip. It was one of the Arcacian swords taken from the dead ryriks. Though a finely constructed weapon, it was not his sword. That one still resided with the ryriks. He frowned. Rayad had given him that sword a year after they'd come to the farm. He'd purchased it from a traveling merchant in Kinnim and given it to Jace on his birthday, or at least the day they'd chosen to celebrate his birthday. He'd rarely parted from it in the last four years. Not that it would really matter now, but if he had to go out fighting, he would have preferred to have a familiar weapon and not one that had so recently belonged to their enemy.

He glanced at the others, who stood on the porch with him. Some drank coffee while others inspected their weapons. It reminded him of the hours leading up to the battle at Stonehelm. Like Kyrin, he'd hoped not to face such an experience again. He could only pray that everyone would come out of this alive the same as they had then. He had to be realistic, though, at the improbability of them holding off Daican's men. It would take a miracle.

At last, Captain Darq spoke. "I'm going to make sure Chand hasn't worked himself loose and then saddle up."

He left the porch and headed toward the barn where they'd left the crete for the night, looking like a giant spider had bound him to one of the support beams. Kaden, Talas, Naeth, and Aaron stepped out into the rain as well and walked toward the dragons. It would be up to the four of them and Darq to take on the twenty firedrakes and their riders.

Jace returned his coffee cup to the cabin and walked out after the riders to the dragons. Gem didn't seem to mind the wet weather at all. She looked at him and purred when he stroked her rain-slicked scales.

"You're a good girl," he murmured.

She chirped and nosed his cloak before resting her chin on his shoulder. He wrapped one arm around her neck and continued stroking her with the other.

"I'll keep an eye on her."

Jace looked over at Kaden, who stood next to Exsis. Everyone had agreed without question that Kaden and the others should take all the dragons with them. Even without riders, they could still fight. The extra dragons could mean the difference between life and death for them, and stopping the firedrakes had to take priority. They would do the most damage if they reached Bel-gard or any of the villages along the way.

"Just don't risk your life to do it." No dragon was worth a person's life, even one as beloved as Gem.

A few minutes later, the rest of their group left the shelter of the porch. Marcus and Michael approached—Michael with a sword hanging from his belt. He walked with a confident stride, almost as tall as Marcus, yet uncertainty flickered in his eyes. Jace had been only a couple of months older than Michael when Jasper had thrust him into the arena for the first time. He remembered the fear leading up to it. It was easy to fake bravery outwardly, but not so much in the privacy of your own head. And this was the first time Michael would have to kill anyone. Jace had already known the horror of it before the arenas. He winced but shoved the past behind him where it belonged.

The two brothers stopped near Kaden, who turned from his dragon and faced Marcus.

"Well, you two take care of yourselves. Try not to take any more spears to the side."

Marcus nodded. "And you try to avoid any more burns and dislocated limbs."

They grinned at each other, and then Marcus shook his head, glancing at Michael. "You know, if we survive and make it back to Landale, Mother is going to kill us for this."

Kaden raised his brows in agreement.

"You couldn't make me leave," Michael said.

"Don't be so sure," Marcus responded. "With Kaden's help, I could have tied you to Kyrin's dragon . . . I probably should have."

Michael folded his arms. "Come on, I have as much right to stay here and fight as Kaden does."

Marcus didn't respond this time. As calm as he was, Jace still sensed his misgivings over allowing his little brother to get involved in this. Yet, the truth remained that they were at war. They needed every available swordsman, even if they were young.

Kaden then focused on Michael. "Just keep in mind everything Marcus has taught you. He knows what he's talking about."

"I will."

Kaden hauled first him and then Marcus into a crushing embrace. "All right, let's go get this taken care of so we can all sit down to a good supper tonight."

Marcus smiled grimly. "Sounds good."

He and Michael turned to join the others, who gathered nearby. Jace gave Gem a final pat and turned as well but paused to face Kaden. "Be careful."

He nodded slowly, glancing toward the river. "I don't know what it'll be like out there for you, but keep yourself alive for Kyrin. She might lose us, but the two of you could have a good life together. I don't want her to lose that too."

Jace dragged a deep breath into his lungs, which had begun to tighten up. "I'll do my best. But that good life would be even better for her with all of her brothers around too."

"Elôm willing, we will be."

Jace clasped Kaden's arm. "See you at supper."

Kaden echoed him, and they parted.

Jace joined the others in their ground force—twelve men in total, including Jorvik and his brothers—and they stood back as the dragon riders mounted. In a moment, they took to the air and called the riderless dragons after them. Most obeyed, though Gem hesitated, her brilliant eyes staring at Jace. He told her to follow and watched her spread her wings to obey him.

As she flew away, his eyes stung, and he cleared his throat. He drew another deep breath, but the ache in his chest only intensified as he looked around at his companions. Twelve against more than fifty. Jace had faced bad odds before but nothing like this. And yet, how many impossible situations had Elôm rescued him from? He reached out to Him, craving the reassurance of His presence, and prayed for deliverance.

"We should go," Balen said, his voice deeper than usual.

Jorvik and his brothers took the lead, each carrying a pole with a long banner the same color as those on the walls of Belgard. They left the farmyard and trekked across the meadow as a light rain fell around them. A breeze caught the banners, sending them curling and flapping deep crimson against the slate colored sky.

They marched in silence. Rainwater dripped from Jace's hair. When they arrived at the ford, they found the river had risen with the rain. They looked across to the other side, but so far, it lay empty. At the water's edge, Jorvik stuck his banner forcefully into the sand and pebbles. Halvar and Levi did the same.

"I will die before I let an enemy of Dorland set foot beyond these banners." Jorvik hung his head. "Elôm willing, it won't come to that . . . for any of us." He turned to face them. "Last chance to change your mind. We brought this on ourselves with our complacency. You need not risk your lives."

Balen shook his head. "Whatever happens here affects the entire future of Ilyon. All of us—Arcacia, Samara, Dorland—

we've all failed in some way and are all in part responsible for what has happened. It's as much our fight as yours."

Together, they crossed the ford, sloshing through the cool water to the opposite bank, and entered the forest. They proceeded cautiously, avoiding the trip ropes they had set and the hollows they had concealed. Jace peered ahead to pick out any movement or sound of approaching soldiers. About a mile from the ford, they stopped in a thickly wooded area of pines and tall ferns—the perfect ambush point. Here, they strung their bows and found cover. Nearby, Jace heard Marcus tell Michael, "Just stay close to me."

Jace looked over to see Michael nod. Now that they were in position and there was no going back, his fear was more evident in his taut expression.

Jace scanned the trees ahead of them again before looking at Rayad, who waited at his side. "Have I ever told you how glad I am that you talked me into going to Landale? I can't say it has been easy, but I would never trade everyone we've come to know for the solitude I thought I wanted."

Rayad smiled faintly. "As nice as retirement and peace would be, I wouldn't trade it either."

"I can't see you sitting with your feet propped up and lazing around anyway." Even at the farm, he'd worked hard with Aldor.

Rayad chuckled. "You're probably right. My father never slowed down either."

"I look forward to meeting him one day." Perhaps even soon, depending on how today went.

"He'd be right here with us, that's for sure."

Jace smiled at the thought of it. He imagined Rayad was very much like his father.

A distant sound snapped his attention back to the forest. He strained his ears to pick up a faint rustling. Jace waited a moment until the sound of marching feet grew more distinct.

"They're coming."

He signaled to the others and reached back for an arrow. After fitting it to the bowstring, he took a position next to a large tree where he'd be mostly hidden but still have a clear view to aim. Rayad and Holden took their positions to his left, while the others spread out to the right. Everyone with a bow stood ready.

Jace's heart pumped hot blood through his body as the marching drew closer, though muffled by the wet conditions. After a couple of minutes, flashes of gold and black interrupted the green of the trees. The distance between them and Daican's men decreased another several yards. Jace drew back his bowstring and peered down the arrow shaft, focusing on one of the soldiers.

His mouth went dry. He'd never killed anyone in a surprise attack before. This ambush was his idea. Had he been wrong to suggest it? *Elôm?*

For a brief moment, he wavered with the morality of it, but then he steeled himself. This was war. Their enemies had come to destroy, and it was up to the few here to defend Dorland to the best of their ability.

Two heartbeats later, he let his arrow fly. With a grunt, the soldier went down. A slight twinge of regret passed through Jace just before several of the other soldiers fell. But he reached for another arrow from his full quiver as chaos ensued among the enemy ranks.

Perched in the branches of the giant pines for camouflage, Kaden waited and watched the sky with Exsis. His heart beat a steady rhythm. His experiences while leading his men in Samara eliminated the fear of the unknown. He knew what he was facing and what he would have to do. Still, grim anticipation had his muscles wound taut. He rolled his shoulders to loosen them.

Exsis must have sensed it and released a low grumble, his leg muscles rippling as he gripped the branches. Kaden patted his dragon's neck and then swiped at the raindrops dripping down his face. This moisture would make his saddle and weapons slick. On the bright side, his clothing would be less likely to catch fire.

He glanced downward but couldn't see the forest floor through the dense foliage. They were close to the ambush site, and he listened, but all was silent . . . so far. If their calculations were correct, Daican's men should show up any time now.

Black shapes materialized through the mist in the distance. Kaden sat up straighter, his pulse elevating. This was it.

The firedrakes rapidly grew in size as they drew closer. Exsis growled, lowering his head as he peered at the oncoming drakes. He exhaled loudly, and two streams of smoke curled around his nostrils.

"Easy," Kaden murmured.

By now, the firedrakes had nearly reached them, but they maintained their position. They needed to give their ground force the opportunity to attack first before engaging the firedrakes and alerting Daican's men of the danger. They waited until the firedrakes were just about to fly over before commotion erupted below them. Men cried out somewhere in the forest. With one look from Captain Darq, Kaden knew it was time.

He gripped the saddle bar. At the captain's signal, all five of them burst from the forest canopy, straight toward the firedrakes. The riderless dragons followed. Kaden remained close to Talas. Working together gave them the best chance of survival. Two could take out a firedrake much more easily than one.

Exsis released a thundering roar as they shot up through the firedrake force. The air around them filled with the ear-piercing shrieks and surprised roars from the beasts. Kaden evened out the moment he cleared them and flew straight for the nearest firedrake, flaming its left wing and its rider before they had a chance to react. Talas flew directly behind him. The heat of Storm's fire warmed his back. The firedrake released a panicked screech, unable to stay aloft with both its wings severely burned. It plummeted toward the forest in a trail of dark smoke. Two others joined it.

But the element of surprise died after this first attack, and the firedrakes fought back. Kaden dove sharply, barely missing a head-on collision with a drake, whose maw gaped open to spill out fire. He looked over his shoulder for Talas. His friend had managed to soar over the top of the firedrake and hit it with a good burst of fire in the process. This only incited the beast, and it pursued them.

Kaden glanced around for Gem. She and the other riderless dragons swooped among the firedrakes, blasting them with fire whenever they could. Satisfied she was all right for now, he focused again on the firedrake that still chased him. He pushed Exsis into a dive again, straight toward the trees. Their greatest advantage against the beasts was their mobility within the forest canopy. When he drew closer, he looked to his right to make sure Talas was with him. His friend gave him a nod and slowed a little, gaining the firedrake's attention. Kaden split off from them, and the firedrake pursued Talas. Just as the beast came close enough to blast the crete with fire, Talas banked sharply around a pine. The firedrake struggled with the sharp turn and took it wide.

Kaden curved around in the opposite direction and cut across over the top of the firedrake, searing its wings, though not enough to immobilize it. A blasting roar from just behind him warned of approaching danger. He swung Exsis around one of the trees right before a ball of fire crashed into the pine just ahead. Now it all came down to a dangerous game of out-maneuvering and outwitting each other.

Jace reached for another arrow. His quiver was almost empty. Though their arrows had kept Daican's men at bay, the enemy steadily gained ground. The soldiers still proceeded with caution, using the trees for cover as best they could. However, once they realized they were only up against twelve men, Jace had no doubt they would push forward for a full-scale attack.

Overhead, roars and screeching echoed across the sky like thunder. Every so often, tree limbs crackled and splintered, followed by the solid thud of something large hitting the ground. Every time, Jace prayed it was a firedrake and not a dragon.

After firing a shot at a soldier who tried to change positions, Jace motioned to Rayad and Holden. Staying low, they sprinted to a thick patch of undergrowth a couple of yards away. Every few arrows, they changed positions so the soldiers wouldn't have one area to focus on.

Still gripping his bow, Jace looked over his shoulder. Four arrows left. Once they ran out, it would be close quarter combat. He couldn't tell how many men they had taken out but certainly not enough to even the odds.

Just as he reached for a final arrow, soldiers burst from the brush to their left. Jace dropped his bow and yanked out his sword. Metal rang through the forest as his blade collided with that of the first soldier. Though he'd hardly wielded a sword in a year, instinct took over, and his blood pulsed hot. After trading several back and forth blows, Jace left the man wounded on the ground and turned his attention to the next.

Swords clashed around him as the others engaged in battle. Jace took down another foe before looking ahead. Soldiers surged forward. Heat raced through his body and down into his hands with his desire to protect everyone. But even the advantage his blood might give him was not enough to make up for their lack of numbers.

Several more soldiers rushed at him, Rayad, and Holden. Jace barely blocked one before another lunged. He dodged the blade and used the man's momentum against him, but others moved in.

Then, behind him, Marcus yelled, "Fall back!"

Making sure Rayad and Holden were with him, Jace snatched up his bow, and they regrouped with the others to retreat to a new area of cover. Jace scanned the group. So far, they had not lost anyone, but they only had a couple dozen more arrows between them. They might be able to slow the advance of the soldiers again, briefly, but after that . . .

Forcing it from his mind, his attention jerked back to their pursuing foes, and he nocked an arrow from the handful Holden shared with him. Careful to make one of his precious few shots count, he released, and a soldier went down. The others fired. The soldiers did dive for cover but didn't hide for long. They approached more boldly now. In only a couple of minutes, Jace and the others were out of arrows. Dropping his bow again, Jace gripped his sword. It would all be close combat from here.

They stood together as the first soldiers rushed in. Though they took down many, they continually had to give ground to avoid being overwhelmed by the numbers. Out of the corner of his eye, Jace saw Rayad fall. His heart plummeted, knocking the breath out of his lungs just before a fresh explosion of fire burst through his chest. He brought down his opponent with one powerful swing and turned on the man who stood over Rayad. With a shout, he engaged the soldier in a brief confrontation. He then turned his full attention to Rayad. His breath returned to find Rayad already pushing back to his feet. Jace grabbed his arm to help him up. Blood stained a rip in his pants just above his knee.

Rayad grunted, but said, "I'm all right."

Jace didn't have time to make sure. More soldiers were on them in a moment, and they both had to redirect their attention to the fight. Still, a part of Jace's mind couldn't release the sight of Rayad falling. Some, if not all of them, would die here. They couldn't escape that reality. Next time one of them went down, they probably wouldn't get back up. Everything inside Jace cried out against it, driving him to fight harder, faster, fiercer—anything to keep them alive.

A flash of gold snapped his attention to his left. Soldiers worked their way around the group.

"They're flanking us!"

Marcus gave another command to fall back. Once they were able to disengage, he shouted, "Just run!"

Jace agreed. They couldn't stand up to this. They needed time to strategize—to catch their breaths. To keep fighting would lead to slaughter. If it took that to save the villages, so be it, but it hadn't come to that yet.

So they ran. Jace came alongside Rayad, who limped slightly, but enough adrenaline coursed through each of them to keep them going in spite of any wounds. His gaze darted over the group, and he thanked Elôm they were all present. His mind then hurried to work on a plan. Perhaps, if they lost the soldiers, they could circle around to the ambush site and gather more arrows. He'd had to drop his, but a few of them still had their bows. It was a long shot, but maybe they could pick off more soldiers that way. Whatever it took to slow them down without having to engage them again.

All thoughts vanished when men burst out of the trees just ahead of them. The group skidded to a halt. Geric, Ruis, and the other ryriks spread out in front of them, cutting off their escape. Jace looked back. The soldiers closed in. He scanned the forest frantically for an opening, but they advanced too quickly in a ring of black and gold.

Like a noose, the deadly ring drew tighter around them. The group stood, their backs together, waiting. Would the soldiers offer them a chance to surrender? A chance to live long enough for rescue to arrive? However, Ruis's cruel voice stomped out the hope.

"Kill them all."

The ryriks rushed toward them. Jace squeezed the hilt of his sword, setting his gaze on Ruis, whose expression promised death. His pulse thundered in his ears, and an ache spread through his chest. This was it. They'd failed. They'd barely had a chance to defend Dorland and already it was all over. He reached for Elôm's presence, already devastated by what was coming.

He raised his sword just before the ryriks reached them, ready to fight to the very last breath as a loud shout rang out.

The ryriks slowed, and everyone turned. From off to Jace's right, more dark figures rushed from the trees, straight up behind the soldiers. Jace's heart gave a jubilant leap. At least thirty ryrik men charged into the fray led by Saul. For the first time in the last two days, Jace found a tangible hope for survival.

KADEN DOVE EXSIS sharply, almost lifting out of the saddle, and soared under an outstretched tree limb. A smaller branch slapped him with a sting across the shoulder, but all he cared was that the firedrake right behind him barreled right into the tree. A tremendous crash and crackling of wood echoed out, followed by the beast's roar. He looked back. The firedrake floundered, coming dangerously close to being lost among the trees before shaking off its daze and righting itself. Even its rider managed to stay in the saddle by some twisted miracle. Kaden almost swore.

They had managed to thin the firedrake ranks to fourteen with minimal difficulty, but now they'd lost their momentum. He went through every tactical maneuver he'd ever practiced with no success. Not even Captain Darq seemed to know how to handle so many foes without being killed in the process.

Kaden looked around for Talas but didn't spot him in the immediate vicinity. He probably had his own firedrake right on his tail. Kaden could practically feel the one behind him breathing down his neck. *That's it.* He'd had enough. At a high-reaching pine, he swung Exsis around in a tight curve so fast he managed to come up behind the firedrake. Streaking right over the top, he scorched the rider and turned in the opposite direction.

Once again, he scanned the area for Talas. This time, he found him flying nearby in pursuit of a riderless firedrake. Kaden turned to help finish the beast off when he spotted a second firedrake barreling straight for Talas and Storm at an angle.

"Talas!"

But it was too late. The beast smashed into them as if it were a flying battering ram, and sent Storm spinning limply through the air. Kaden's eyes latched on her falling rider. His gut lurched. *Talas!* He dove Exsis toward him, but he was too far away. He'd never reach him before he hit the canopy. Storm recovered and dove straight down after him. A moment later, both of them disappeared into the trees. Kaden held his breath, his heart thudding off the seconds. First two, then five, then ten. Cold seeped through his veins. They did not reappear. *No!*

Tears scalded Kaden's eyes, and for a brief moment, he couldn't move. Anger and grief struck him in the same brutal blow. He choked on the cry of agony rising in his throat, and he locked his gaze on the firedrake and rider who had knocked his friend out of the sky.

Exsis reacted as if he knew what had just happened. Before the rider even realized what was coming, Kaden and Exsis were on top of him. Exsis reached out with his sharp claws and swiped the man right off the beast's back. Apparently, firedrakes weren't trained to rescue their riders because the beast didn't even react as his rider plummeted toward the trees.

Instead, it focused on Kaden as he flew past and pursued him. Straight ahead, another riderless firedrake trailed after one of the dragons. Gem. Clenching his jaw, Kaden pointed Exsis toward them. He urged his dragon for more speed, aiming directly for the other firedrake's side. He cast a glance back. His trailing firedrake flew only a few yards behind. He dug his feet in the stirrups and held on tightly, not pulling up until the very last second. They skimmed just over the top of the firedrake in pursuit of Gem, narrowly avoiding its wings. Less than a second later came a solid impact and two enraged roars.

Kaden looked back again in grim satisfaction. The two firedrakes had turned on each other. They clawed and bit at one another, their wings entangled as they fell toward the trees. He prayed for them both to fall to their deaths, but they detached just before they reached the canopy. One, however, disappeared into the forest, too injured to right itself in time.

Heat scorched the back of Kaden's neck and across his left shoulder with a roar of flames. Ducking, he swung Exsis to the right, and slapped at his smoldering shirtsleeve. The drake's flames seared through the material even wet. So much for avoiding burns. He caught sight of the firedrake that had flamed him. The rider glared, apparently not pleased with him setting their drakes against each other.

Kaden groaned in both pain and frustration. How would he defeat his latest foe? He wasn't sure how long they'd been fighting, but he was already exhausted. After executing a few unsuccessful evasive maneuvers, his anger and frustration rose. He was about to try something more daring when a dragon came screeching overhead, blasting the firedrake with a perfectly aimed fountain of fire. The beast veered away, and Kaden swooped around to get behind it.

He gasped the moment he spotted the dragon that had come to his rescue. Storm! And she wasn't alone. Talas sat in the saddle. Kaden nearly sagged as relief flooded in. How in Ilyon had he survived? The way Talas clutched his arm to his middle told Kaden he was hurt, but hurt was significantly better than dead.

Jace batted away an attack aimed for his neck and pressed forward, careful to keep from tripping on the littered forest ground. These weren't young, inexperienced soldiers. Whoever had put together this force had chosen men of skill and experience—men who fought with confidence and wouldn't have hesitated when faced with destroying Dorland villages.

Thoughts of why they fought kept Jace energized. This was what his ryrik blood was meant for: protecting and fighting for others. Though he had already put away the guilt he'd struggled with for years, now he embraced the advantages of his blood completely.

After a hard fought battle, his current opponent fell. Before he had a chance for a breather, two soldiers charged him. They weren't the first group to try to take him out together. He would always despise Jasper, but if the man hadn't trained Jace to face multiple opponents, he wouldn't still be alive today.

They came at him from different angles, but he dodged one attack and parried another. Constantly in motion, he didn't give them a chance to find him open. He blocked their attacks and waited for an opening for his own until they grew frustrated. When it came, he clipped one of the men across the ribs. Though it didn't put him out of the fight, it did slow him down. This left Jace the opportunity to put more pressure on the second soldier.

To avenge his injured friend, the man drove into Jace hard, bordering on reckless. Jace met three successive attacks, angling sideways so he could still keep an eye on the wounded soldier. The moment he let up, Jace pushed forward. The man back-pedaled. His foot snagged on a root, and he fought for balance, leaving himself undefended. Jace took him down. He then turned his gaze on the second soldier, who held his hand to his injured side.

Jace looked him in the eyes. "Surrender." He prayed he would.

Yet, the man raised his sword and advanced. Jace winced. This wouldn't be a long fight. Though the man fought well, his injury hindered him, and he fell after a poorly-timed defense.

He raised his eyes to find his next opponent. The rushing of water caught his attention. They must be near the river. Glancing that direction, his gaze snagged on two mismatched combatants, and his hot blood turned to ice. Michael stumbled, driven back by one shattering attack after another delivered by Ruis. Blood stained Michael's jerkin, and though he blocked the ryrik's blade, the only reason he wasn't dead yet was that Ruis wasn't done toying with him. Jace read the cruel amusement on the man's face.

Michael tripped, landing hard on his back. Heat flushed through Jace's system again and galvanized him to action. He sprinted forward. Ruis raised his sword to finish Michael off but then spun to face Jace. Their swords collided, sending a jolt through Jace's hands. Ruis growled in his face, his eyes flashing, before shoving him away to take another swing. Jace blocked and thrust his blade toward Ruis's middle. The ryrik reacted lightning fast and avoided the attack.

His sword arced toward Jace's head. Jace barely ducked in time, and it whirred right over him. Before Ruis could regain his defense, Jace lashed out with his blade and caught flesh just above the man's hip. Ruis bellowed and stumbled but was on Jace in a moment. Each progressively vicious strike forced Jace back a step. The wound had only added fuel to the heat driving the man on. He probably didn't even feel the pain. Not in such a blind rage.

Jace blocked, waiting for the man to slow. When he did, he swore as if cursing Jace for not dying already. Jace recalled the man's advances toward Kyrin, and his energy redoubled. Blood surging, he mounted his own attack. Though Ruis was bigger, Jace drove him back one step at a time.

He backed the ryrik toward a tree, hoping the man wouldn't notice the obstacle behind him. However, at the last second, Ruis sidestepped. Releasing an enraged yell, he swung hard and batted Jace's sword against the tree. Before Jace could pull it free, Ruis's hand closed around his wrist. Using all his weight, he shoved Jace into the tree.

Jace's forearm took the impact. With a crack, gut-wrenching pain lanced up his arm like a streak of lightning and numbed his hand. A cry tore from his throat. He tried to maintain his grip on his sword, but Ruis knocked it away. The man's own blade rose and then descended toward Jace's chest.

Jace twisted away. The blade caught his injured arm instead, sending another white-hot streak of pain to punch the air from his lungs. He stumbled, only then seeing how close he'd come to the riverbank. His foot slipped, and he tumbled over the edge. He reached out to catch himself with his good arm, but the impact with the rocky slope jarred another yell out of him right as he splashed into the cold river. Water flooded his nose and mouth. Floundering, he got his feet under him and pushed up, coughing.

He barely blinked water out of his eyes in time to catch Ruis looming over him. The man's knee smashed into his face. Jace fell, plunging back under water, the river rushing in his ears. He scrambled to get upright, but hands gripped his shoulders, pressing him down against the rocky riverbed. Panic ignited a burst of adrenaline.

He clawed at Ruis's arm with his right hand and fought to shove the man off him. His pulse thundered in his head, matching the roar of the river. He kicked at Ruis, but the water absorbed his power. His lungs burned. He needed air.

His knife! He reached for his right leg, but Ruis was kneeling on it. Pulling as hard as he could, he worked his leg free. He couldn't hold his breath any longer. Water seeped into his nose, and the panic almost overtook him. He reached down and wrapped his fingers around the hilt of his knife. Yanking it out of his boot, he stabbed upward, too panicked to aim.

The blade pierced flesh up to the hilt. The pressure against his shoulders released, and he pushed himself upward. Breaking the surface, he gasped in a huge gulp of air and choked water out of his burning lungs. Deep throbbing encased his skull, and his limbs lacked strength. He looked around for Ruis, still gripping his knife. The man stood a few feet away, his hand pressed to his side. A lethal amount of blood already stained his shirt.

Ruis turned on Jace as if about to lunge but stumbled against the current. He took one more step before he fell. He struggled in the water, staining it red, but eventually it carried him away.

Shaking, Jace stumbled out of the river and collapsed on the mud-slicked bank before the water could sweep him away too. Every movement weighed on him, and air filled his head. He examined his injured arm, but the unnatural angle of the broken bone wasn't what sent waves of fear through him. Blood flowed free and fast from a gash along the underside of his arm, turning his soaked sleeve scarlet. He covered the wound with his hand, but hot blood seeped through his fingers. His heart rate climbed even as he begged it to stop pumping so much blood. He squeezed the wound more tightly but couldn't stop the flow.

No. He shook his head. *Please, Elôm.* He didn't want to die here. He didn't want to leave Kyrin. Gray fog swirled around him, and he swayed. He breathed out heavily. *All right. If it's my time.*

"Jace!"

He blinked enough to see Rayad slide down the bank near him, followed by Michael. Before he could speak, he tipped sideways into the mud unable to keep his eyes open.

Only three left.

Kaden didn't know how he was still breathing right now, let alone on the brink of achieving victory over the firedrakes. He glanced to his left. Talas still flew with him. He'd just spotted Captain Darq as well. He didn't know about anyone else. Right now, he just had to focus on the remaining threat.

With Talas right behind him, he pursued the only firedrake that still bore a rider. The beast's wings were already tattered and singed, so it didn't take long for the two of them to debilitate the beast. Working together on the next, they quickly overpowered the drake, and everything grew incredibly quiet. Kaden looked around. The gray sky was clear of everything but their few dragons.

A breath gusted from Kaden's lungs. They'd done it.

Just ahead, Captain Darq motioned to them. Not far from the river, they landed in the meadow at the forest's edge, and Kaden finally took stock of who was left. Talas landed beside him. A moment later, Aaron and Naeth followed, sporting both blood and burns. Talas had a long cut across his disturbingly pale face and still clutched his arm to his stomach. In a flurry of wings, two more dragons landed near them—Gem and Timothy's dragon. Both were burned and looked a little rough but alive.

Kaden looked up at the sky. The gray clouds offered no signs of the other five dragons. He winced but then a ringing echo of metal drifted from the river.

"We need to get to the others." A knot tied in Kaden's stomach. Who would be left when they arrived? He looked over at Talas. "Can you make it?"

His friend looked ready to keel over. He wasn't going to have Talas survive the attack only to pass out and fall from Storm.

Talas straightened a little but grimaced at the motion. "Yeah. Just a broken collarbone. I'll be fine."

Kaden nodded. They didn't have time for discussion. Without another word, he prompted Exsis back into the sky. Now his concern shifted to his brothers. How would he face their mother if they were dead? He grew ill just thinking of it. *Please Flôm, let them be safe. All of them.*

The minute it took them to reach the ford was torture. When they arrived, he found the sight both stomach-turning and encouraging. Several ryriks fought against Daican's soldiers just within the trees. Kaden signaled Exsis, who let out a blasting roar. Captain Darq's and Aaron's dragons echoed him. Even before they set down on the edge of the forest, the soldiers had already turned to run. Within seconds, their flashy uniforms disappeared into the undergrowth. Just as in the sky, everything grew quiet.

Kaden jumped off Exsis and scanned the faces of those who turned to meet them. He spotted Saul along with Jorvik and his brothers but not a single person from Landale. Had they all been killed before Saul and the others joined them?

"Marcus! Michael!" He held his breath.

"Kaden!"

His eyes snapped to the voice and found Marcus stumbling out of the trees. Timothy and Trev were just behind him supporting a more seriously wounded Mick. Kaden rushed to his older brother.

"Where's Michael?"

Marcus shook his head. "I don't know." His eyes and voice held more fear than Kaden had seen in past situations, and it doubled his concern. Marcus almost never let his emotions show.

Kaden turned, scanning the entire area. "Michael!" He looked everywhere for a glimpse of their brother, at the same time wondering what had befallen the rest of their group. What about King Balen? And Jace?

The king appeared, helping one of the injured ryriks. Kaden breathed out a sigh, but fear took over again in an instant. Marcus called their brother's name.

A moment later, a voice came from near the river. "Over here!"

Kaden and Marcus both spun toward the river as Michael appeared up over the bank. Blood spattered his sleeve and smeared his jerkin just below his ribs, but he was alive. Kaden's shoulders sagged, and he thanked Elôm. Yet once again, elation died when Rayad and Holden appeared along with him, carrying a limp form between them. Jace.

Kaden sprinted forward as they set Jace down on the flat ground. He focused on Jace's arm, which was clearly broken and already swelling. Right above it, a deep gash left a steady blood trail down his bare arm. Rayad and Holden had torn off his sleeve and used it for a tourniquet. Kaden's gaze lingered on the blood before shifting to Jace's face. His skin was gray. Was he even breathing?

"Is he alive?"

"Yes, but he's close to bleeding out," Rayad said, his voice urgent.

Footsteps rushed up behind Kaden. He glanced over his shoulder. Saul. He took one look at Jace and turned to call out, "Toris!" He then looked back down at Jace. "Toris is our physician."

Kaden knelt beside Jace. He'd seen him in horrible condition but never so disturbingly close to death. He swallowed with difficulty. "Hang on, Jace." He clenched his teeth. He couldn't bear to face Kyrin if Jace died. It would be even worse than facing their mother.

A moment later, one of the ryriks rushed over to them. Grim-faced, he inspected Jace's arm and said, "We need to get him somewhere I can work on him."

"Kaden, take Jace back to the cabin," Darq's strong voice broke in. "I'll take Toris."

Kaden nodded. After making sure the tourniquet was secure, Rayad, Holden, and Saul lifted Jace up again. Kaden rushed ahead and helped them get him into the saddle. Sitting behind him, he wrapped his arm securely around Jace's chest. Now he could feel the slight rise and fall of each weak breath.

"Keep breathing, Jace. Just keep breathing."

PEOPLE WERE RIGHT when they said time healed. Even a week helped Anne recover from the horror of Baron Grey's execution. Tears still came, though not as often or regularly. Life moved on, somberly most times, but surely. And she refused to let the night of Goler's party drag her down. Instead, she let her anger with Goler fuel her determination, not paralyze her. She and her father had already begun weighing their options. They couldn't openly oppose Goler without risking everything.

In the end, they both agreed that, perhaps, they had held out long enough. Perhaps it was finally time to let go of this life and move out to camp. Just the thought of it lifted Anne's spirits. Such a move, however, required careful planning and preparation. She and her family weren't the only ones who called this estate home.

While her father and Elian saw to these preparations, Anne kept herself from getting impatient by occupying herself with her spinning. She was starting to get the hang of it, and she enjoyed sharing the activity with her mother. She was also grateful for the quiet afternoon. Her nerves had been wound so tightly for days. She recognized the need to let herself rest from all the turmoil—to give herself moments to recover.

Without warning, the door burst open, and Anne jumped, tangling her yarn. In rushed Sara, who had ridden into Landale with one of the stablehands to visit her family. Tear streaks wet her flushed face. Anne pushed up from her chair to meet her, dread turning her cold.

"Sara, what's wrong?"

"I'm sorry!" she choked out, gasping for breath and sobbing at the same time. "I didn't want to tell him, but he hurt me and threatened my family."

Anne stiffened, and her mother rushed to the stairs to call her father. He hurried down as Anne asked her maid, "Who hurt you?"

"Captain Dagren." Her face contorted. "He knows."

"Knows what?" Anne's father asked gently, but urgently.

"He knows you believe in Elôm." Sara sobbed hard. "I told him. I'm sorry! I ran back as fast as I could."

Ice formed in Anne's body, freezing her to the spot. Doom pressed down on her as if an invisible sword already rested against her neck. *He knows.* Their secret was out.

Sara blubbered another apology, snapping Anne from the grip of dread. She looked to her father, who rushed to the door and shouted for Elian. He then turned back to them. Though his face was taut, he spoke calmly as he instructed Sara. "Go to the kitchen and tell everyone to leave immediately. Do not take time to gather anything."

Sara nodded and ran to the kitchen.

A second later, Elian burst through the door. Anne's father spun to face him.

"We need to leave. Get the horses, but do not take time to saddle them. Tell everyone to leave now. They can use whatever horses they need."

Understanding registered in Elian's expression. Without a word in question, he left the house. Anne's father then turned to face them. "Wait for me outside."

He rushed upstairs. His words prompted Anne to act. She grabbed her mother, who looked about the house as if unable to believe what was happening, and guided her outside. Elanor followed. They stopped in the yard and looked back. They were leaving everything. Anything that carried any sentimental value. Yet Anne didn't even care. She was ready to run.

Her father joined them, sword in hand. He ushered them toward the stables, where the servants gathered. Elian led out the family horses. They hadn't made it ten feet before the sound of hooves pounded the soft ground. Soldiers burst from the forest into the yard. Anne gasped, and her mother released a fearful cry.

"Run!" Her father pushed them toward the forest behind the house.

Soldiers appeared there too, cutting off their escape. They closed in and surrounded them. Anne clung to her mother and Elanor as her father and Elian faced the men with their swords drawn. Doom thumped inside Anne's chest. They would never be a match for the soldiers.

The ring of mounted men parted and Goler rode up. "Drop your swords, unless you want to die in front of the women, in which case I'll happily oblige you."

A moment of thick, pressing silence passed before Anne's father let his sword fall into the mud. Elian's joined it. Goler dismounted and marched up to them, sneering in her father's face.

"John Wyland, you and your household are under arrest for treason against the emperor and the gods." He offered a challenging look. "Unless you can prove otherwise."

Anne's father didn't say a word. He only drew himself up taller and faced Goler straight on. Anne followed his example. If Baron Grey and so many others could die so courageously for their faith, so could she.

Goler motioned to the soldiers. "Bind the men."

The soldiers promptly obeyed. Then they gathered everyone in front of the house, and Goler ordered them all to kneel. Anne sank slowly to her knees in the soggy grass beside her parents. Would it all end here, or did he have some other cruel torture in mind first? Despite kneeling, Anne held herself stiffly. She would not cower before the fiend for one second.

To one of his men, Goler ordered, "Go inside and bring me a comfortable chair. This could take a while."

The younger soldier hesitated. "I thought Captain Dagren said to bring them straight back to the village."

Goler glared at him. "Are you questioning my orders? *I* am baron of Landale."

The soldier ducked his head and rushed to obey.

To a few of the others, Goler said, "Sweep the house and bring out anything of value."

As they strode past, Anne looked to the forest and then to the sky, praying Trask had scouts or dragons nearby. Her attention snapped back to Goler as he stood over them, glaring down at her father.

"I should have known you were with the rebels."

Anne bit back the urge to insult his intelligence.

Her father stared up at him. "Do what you will with me, but surely you can show leniency to the women. Lady Elanor is merely our guest. I'd beware of her father if you do not treat her with respect."

Goler focused on Elanor. "Get up."

She exchanged a quick glance with Anne, but everything about her hardened as she rose to her feet and tipped her chin. Anne wished to cheer her on for not backing down either. Goler leered over her, yet she didn't waver in her stance.

"You will go to wherever it is you rebels like to hide and get Trask. I want him here in one hour. If he fails to show up in time, I'll kill Sir John. And for every ten minutes he keeps me waiting

after that, I'll kill one of the servants, starting with your bodyguard."
He leaned closer, his face menacing. "And you let him know he
is to come alone. If I even suspect he's brought extra men or
dragons, I will kill *everyone*, including Anne. Do you understand?"

Elanor swallowed and looked down at them. A little of the
fire had gone out of her eyes, and Anne didn't know how to react.
Everything inside her screamed not to draw Trask into danger.

Finally, Elanor looked back up at Goler. "All right, but I will
need a horse otherwise I'll never reach him in time."

Goler gestured to the horses milling near the stable. "You'd
better get riding. Time's wasting."

Gathering up her skirt, Elanor dashed across the yard to
the horses. She grabbed her mare's bridle and led her to the
porch where she could hoist herself up onto the horse's back.
With a fearful glance at Anne, Elanor pointed the horse toward
the forest road and took off at a canter.

Just as she left the yard, Goler ordered two of his men,
"Follow her. Find where their camp is."

Anne barely bit back a cry as the men mounted and rode
off. *Elôm, no! Don't let them find it.* Her attention jerked back
to Goler. He reached down, locking his hand around her wrist,
and hauled her up. She pulled against him, and her father pushed
to his feet. One of Goler's men intercepted him and punched
him hard in the gut. He stumbled, and the man hit him again,
this time across the face, which sent him back to his knees.

"No!" Anne fought to get to him, but Goler yanked her arm
hard.

"Then quit squirming," he snapped.

Anne stilled, locking eyes with her father. He was breathing
heavily and blood welled from his lip, but he didn't appear to
be in significant pain.

With another tug, Goler turned her around to face him.
"Now, right here, you will accept my offer to become my wife."

Anne gritted her teeth. "You think I would ever marry you after this? I would never marry a beast like you."

Goler leaned close, his hot, unpleasant breath striking her face. "I think you'll reconsider after a bit of persuasion."

Anne refused to shrink away. "I will die before I marry you. And if you force me to, I will make every day of your life miserable."

Goler reached for her arm again and squeezed it viciously. "Not if you want your mother to be treated well."

The glare disappeared from Anne's face.

"Make no mistake about it, your father will die for his treason, but I'm inclined to show your mother mercy *if* you cooperate."

A heavy weight settled inside Anne. How could she not do anything she could to save her mother's life?

"Don't agree to this, Anne," her mother cut in.

In response, Goler motioned to one of the soldiers, who backhanded her mother across the cheek.

Anne cried out and fought to pull away from Goler. "Monstrous pig!"

She struggled until he squeezed her wrist so tightly that pain shot up her arm. A whimper escaped her throat, and she stopped fighting.

"That is no way to address your lord and fiancé," he growled near her ear. "Now, will you marry me willingly and spare your mother?"

Tears burned Anne's eyes, wavering her vision. She ground her teeth, every fiber of her being fighting against the idea. Finally, she nodded. "Yes."

She could hardly stomach the horror of living as his wife, but she couldn't condemn her mother. She had to save at least one member of her family.

Goler's grip loosened a little. "Good."

He dragged her to the padded chair one of the soldiers had brought out and sat down before pulling her down to sit on his lap. He hooked his arm around her, and Anne had to fight every impulse to escape his hold.

"Now we wait for Trask to show up so we can settle this permanently."

ELANOR HAD NEVER pushed a horse so hard. Her mare panted loudly, but she would not let up. She *couldn't* let up—not when everyone's life depended on it. She had to reach Trask in time, even if it meant sacrificing her beloved mare. Tears blurred her eyes, but she fought to keep them at bay. She could not lose her head now.

Her horse slipped in the mud. Elanor lurched sideways and almost lost her seat but clung to her horse's mane and managed to right herself. Now at a standstill, the mare's gasping breaths echoed through the forest.

"I'm sorry," Elanor cried, "but we must keep going."

She urged the horse on. At first, the mare wouldn't move, but after a little more prodding, she worked her back into a steady canter. *Please Elôm, let us make it.*

Ten minutes later, they rode up to a towering oak tree where a thick red rope hung from one of the outstretched branches over the road. She looked over her shoulder. The road appeared empty, but she did not go any farther. Instead, she raised her voice and called out as loud as she could.

"Help! Please help!"

Over and over again, she called until her voice grew hoarse. Just when she thought she would have to go on, two men appeared from the trees.

"Lady Elanor?" one said in surprise, and she recognized him from camp.

She slid down and rushed up to him. "I have to get to Trask right away, but I think I was followed."

The man turned to his companion. "I'll take her to camp. You make sure no one follows us." He then faced Elanor. "Come on."

He guided her deeper into the woods where he had his horse hidden. He swung up into the saddle and then reached down to pull her up behind him.

"Please, hurry," she urged him.

He turned his horse in the direction of camp. Elanor's heart beat to the steady cadence of the horse's hooves. Tears assaulted her again, and now that she didn't need to see where she was going, they spilled over and ran down her cheeks. What if Trask didn't reach Marlton in time? And what if he did? Goler would surely kill him. *Oh, Elôm, please do something!* Would she be the only one to come out of this nightmare alive?

At last, they rode into camp. Elanor shouted Trask's name before they even stopped. The door to his cabin ripped open just as they reached it, and he rushed out, his eyes wide.

"What happened?"

"Goler is at Marlton." Elanor slid down from the horse. "He knows we're all believers. He is going to kill Sir John and all the servants if you don't come. He only gave you an hour starting from when I left."

Before she could finish, he turned back to the cabin and grabbed his sword from just inside the door. Immediately, he set off for where the dragons rested, but Elanor grabbed his arm.

"Wait! He said you had to come alone. If he suspects you have dragons or men with you, he will kill everyone, including Anne."

This stopped him in his tracks. Indecision warred on his face, but then he changed course and set off for the stable. Warin and Elanor followed.

"What do you want us to do?" Warin asked.

Trask shook his head. "I don't know." He rushed into the corral and grabbed his horse, not bothering to do more than tie the lead rope to the halter as a pair of reins. He swung up onto the horse's back. The only thing that stopped him from taking off was Warin standing in his way.

"If you go alone Goler will kill you and you won't be any help to anyone."

"I know," Trask said, the struggle clear in his voice, "but if I don't get there right now, Sir John and everyone else will be dead too. I won't let that happen." He gave Warin a dire look. "Whatever you do, don't bring the dragons."

With those final words, he took off. Elanor stood beside Warin and watched him disappear, an awful churning in the pit of her stomach.

Anne didn't know what was worse—watching the soldiers loot her home or the stickiness of Goler's hot breath on her neck. She leaned away from him, but he only pulled her more firmly against his chest. Every muscle in her body drew tense in protest, and she could think of so many ways to hurt him if only she could.

"You know," he said, his bearded chin tugging at her hair, "it wouldn't have had to be this way. I asked you nicely and you refused. You chose the hard way."

"I refused because I knew exactly what kind of man you are," Anne replied through her teeth. "The kind who would force a woman to comply with his wishes instead of respecting and cherishing her."

Goler simply shrugged. "I'm an ambitious man, and if I can't get what I want one way, I'll get it another."

"By destroying anyone who gets in your way?"

One of the soldiers walked up to him. "We've cleared the house of valuables, my lord."

"Good. Now torch it."

"What?" Anne gasped.

Her gaze followed the soldier back to the house, where he and the others lit torches and carried them inside. Anne strained against Goler, her mouth open in horror. After a couple of minutes, the men hurried out and smoke soon poured from the door and windows. It wasn't long before the crackling of wood echoed inside and flames licked at the roof. Hot, angry tears dripped down Anne's face as the flames consumed her home. Her mother's quiet sobs only fueled her grief.

Amidst the roar and the heat of the fire, Goler glanced toward the road.

"Trask should have been here by now. His hour is up." He rose abruptly, dumping Anne into the vacant chair, and motioned to his men. "Bring him forward."

Two of the soldiers grabbed Anne's father and dragged him closer to Goler.

"No!" Anne jumped up and latched onto Goler's arm. "You can't do this. You can't just kill him."

Goler brushed her off and shoved her at his men to restrain her. "I can and I will."

Anne fought against them, her tears flowing faster. "No, please!"

Taking a stand beside her father, Goler pulled out his sword. "John Wyland, you have been found guilty of treason, and as baron of Landale, I sentence you to death."

Anne screamed for him to stop, but he raised his sword.

"Goler!" a voice echoed.

Trask pulled his horse to a sliding halt, sickened by the sight of Goler about to behead Sir John. Goler looked up, a twisted satisfaction growing in his expression. Trask jumped down from his horse and glared at him. The entire way here, he'd tried to formulate a plan, but he had nothing. All he knew was that he had to buy his men time to figure something out. Though he fought to banish feelings of vengeance, he wanted nothing more than to take Goler down for what he had done to his father and to Anne.

He whipped out his sword. "Are you going to hide behind a bunch of captives like a coward, or will you face me like a man?"

He didn't care what happened to him next; he just wanted the beast away from Anne and her family.

Goler took a step toward him. "I could just kill them if you don't drop your sword and surrender."

Trask glanced at Anne. He would surrender if that's what it came to, but he needed more time. "And that would prove to every man here that you're too afraid to fight me one on one. Proof you're a coward and don't have the backbone to rule Landale. It doesn't take much to order the killing of unarmed people while you strut around pretending to be something you're not. You're just afraid to fight me because, deep down, you know you could never defeat me in a fair fight. You're afraid because you know I'm the true leader of Landale, and you're nothing but a pretender."

With every word, Goler's face turned a deeper shade of red until he snapped and stalked toward Trask, his sword raised.

"I'll show you who the true leader is."

With an enraged roar, Goler swung and brought his sword crashing down against Trask's. All the years of animosity between them would be settled here. As Trask had always predicted, it would surely end with one or both of them dead.

Their swords clashed with ear-shattering blows that sent shockwaves all the way up Trask's arms and into his shoulders. The emotion drove each of them forward relentlessly. For every strike, Trask saw all of the moments he and Goler had faced each other before. All of the misery the man had caused those closest to him—to Anne, her family, his father, and the people of Landale. He fought for them.

Trask used all the moves he'd learned and practiced with his father, but Goler met each of them with maddening precision. He'd always considered the former captain a fool, but that didn't diminish his skill with a blade. They were an even match, but eventually, one of them would fall.

Their swords came together, and Trask leaned into his to shove Goler off balance. Slightly larger, Goler didn't move. Instead, he lashed out and kicked at Trask's shin. Jumping back, Trask almost fell. He caught his balance but released his sword with one hand. Goler stepped forward and swung hard, driving the sword from his other hand. Before he could catch him unarmed, Trask grabbed Goler's arm and slammed it down across his knee. Goler cursed as his own sword dropped into the mud. Trask then threw a hard punch across Goler's chin.

Swords abandoned, they traded punches. Goler's attacks caught Trask in the jaw and the ribs, but he gave back as good as he received. Though panting for breath, he would not let up or back down. To do so would be to die, and every pounding heartbeat rebelled at this man taking him down.

A hammer-like blow to the cheek brought an explosion of stars and sent Trask staggering. Goler rammed him, and he landed hard in the mud. He scrambled to regain his feet, but his battered body reacted clumsily, and he slipped in the mud. Goler jumped on top of him, a manic light in his eyes. A dagger glinted in his hands. Trask gasped and grabbed his wrists just before the weapon would have plunged into his chest.

He held it just inches above his ribs, but his arms shook. Goler put his entire bulk behind the weapon, and it inched closer. Trask couldn't hold it. With the very last of his strength, he struggled to push it aside. His arms gave out, and the blade sank into his shoulder. He yelled in pain, but adrenaline surged with it. He raised his elbow and smashed it into Goler's head. Goler grabbed at his face and rolled away. Trask reached for the hilt of the dagger and pulled it from his shoulder, fighting away the shadows that narrowed his vision.

He raised the dagger just as Goler lunged at him again. The momentum brought him chest first into his own weapon. He froze, staring down at Trask as if unable to process what had just happened. Defeat flashed in his expression followed by a burst of fury. He stumbled away from Trask, the dagger still in his chest, and looked toward his men.

"Kill them!"

"No!" Trask fought to rise as Goler fell beside him.

The soldiers drew their swords. Agony ripped through Trask's heart greater than any physical wound. *Elôm, no!* He would never reach them in time. "Anne!"

Just before the soldiers reached her, one of them cried out and stumbled forward. Four others did the same. A roar shattered the air, and several dragons burst from the trees. Cretes rushed from behind the stable, their bows fitted with fresh arrows matching those already embedded in the fallen soldiers. The other soldiers dropped their swords immediately and backed away with their hands upraised. One of the dragons landed between them and the captives with Warin in the saddle.

In that moment, all of Trask's strength drained out as relief flooded in. As much as he wanted to get up, he let himself fall back, not even caring about the mud or his wounded shoulder. All he could do was draw deep breaths amidst the pain of his throbbing ribs.

"Thank You, Elôm," he gasped skyward.

"Trask!"

Groaning at the effort, he slowly maneuvered himself back into a sitting position as Anne rushed over to him, falling to her knees at his side. He cupped her tear-streaked face with his hand. "Are you all right?"

Anne looked at him as if he were crazy. "Am I all right? You're the one who's bleeding and beaten half to death."

Despite the concern in her voice, a small laugh escaped him. He couldn't help it, though smiling didn't help his swollen jaw. "I'll be fine."

He glanced to his right. Goler lay a few feet away, unmoving. Trask looked at him in disgust, but he wouldn't hurt anyone ever again.

Footsteps drew Trask's attention away from the body, and he looked up at Warin. He attempted a frown, but it stung his face. "I thought I told you no dragons."

Warin shrugged. "Occasionally, a man has to disobey orders if convicted."

Trask's smile broke out again. "Well, I'm glad you did."

Warin reached down for his good arm and helped him to his feet. Trask hissed out a breath, but he managed to stay upright under his own power even though Warin hovered close, ready to reach out and help him.

"We need to get you back to Josef. That shoulder needs to be looked after."

Trask nodded slowly, glancing around the yard before his gaze settled on Anne. "Just as long as she comes with me."

She wrapped her hand around his arm. "I'm coming . . . and this time I'm not leaving."

PAIN SEARED THROUGH Jace's arm, shocking him into a hazy semi-consciousness. He had no strength to hold back the cry that followed. He pulled away from whatever caused it, but something pinned him down. He couldn't move at all. Not even his eyelids would work. The pain shot through his arm again, more intense this time, dragging a groan from his aching throat.

"Easy, Jace. Hang in there."

The quiet voice floated around him. *Rayad?* He couldn't make his lips form the name or his voice to follow. A sinking sensation descended on him, tugging him with it. He wasn't sure if he wanted to or could fight it, so he let himself sink, and the lingering pain faded.

Whether time passed or stood still, he couldn't say. Yet, when awareness returned, clarity slowly joined it. The awareness grew instead of leaving him in a confusing numbness. Pain returned, though not the sharp, intense pain of before. More of a deep throb in his arm letting him know something was not quite right. Yet, he felt comfortable—warm, dry. He struggled to open his eyes again. It took great effort, but they opened this time, heavily. His surroundings were only a blur that faded as his eyelids slid closed again.

"Jace."

The quiet voice helped anchor his focus. This time he knew with certainty it was Rayad. He desired to respond, but everything from his eyelids to his tongue felt incredibly heavy. He forced his eyes open again, blinking to clear away the fog. Slowly, Rayad's face came into focus. The man smiled and released a sigh. "Praise Elôm."

At last, the fog clinging to Jace's mind lifted and images of the battle came back to him. He tried to move and look around, but that jolting pain speared through his left arm. He sucked in a breath.

"Careful," Rayad said gently. "Your arm is broken."

Jace winced. "How is everyone? Michael?"

"Michael's all right, thanks to you."

This new voice came from Jace's left, and he shifted his gaze to Kaden.

"He's learning all about healing from battle wounds," Kaden said. "But it's nothing too serious. Some sliced ribs and a shoulder wound."

Jace let his breath seep out slowly and turned back to Rayad. "What about everyone else?"

Rayad's expression sobered. "We lost some men from Saul's village. A few others are in rough shape. We also lost five of the dragons. You gave us quite a scare. If not for the resilience of your ryrik blood, you probably wouldn't still be here."

As weak as he felt right now, Jace believed it. Not even in Auréa's dungeon had he felt so frail. He doubted he could even raise his head.

"How long has it been?"

"The battle ended yesterday afternoon."

Jace's eyelids grew heavy once more. Just talking drained what little energy he had. Weakly, he looked over at Kaden. "Gem?"

Kaden smiled. "She's tough, like you. She's got a few scrapes, but she'll be all right."

Jace let himself smile too but could no longer hold his eyes open.

"You just rest," Rayad said as he drifted away again.

Trask eased into a rocking chair near the cold fireplace and bit down on a groan. He'd managed to dress himself without Warin's help, though the man had come over early and hovered nearby. The action did set fire to his shoulder and pulsated in every bruise across his upper body. However, inside, he hadn't felt so settled in a long time. All he had to do was simply walk across camp to see Anne, and that soothed any aches and pains. A contented smile grew on his face. Before yesterday, he hadn't smiled in a week. He still ached keenly for his father, but knowing Anne and her family were safe eased his pain. Now that they were here, he wouldn't have to worry about the same fate befalling them.

Moments later, a light knock sounded at the door. Warin answered it and let Anne step inside. Trask's smile widened as she approached and pulled up a chair beside him.

"How are you feeling?" she asked.

Trask traced her lovely face with his eyes. "Very well, especially now that you're here. I was just about to come over and see you."

Anne frowned lightly. "Don't you dare get up. You need rest."

"There's nothing wrong with my legs."

Her expression turned scolding, and he chuckled, holding his ribs with his good arm.

"Trust me, I'll be fine. There's no way I'm leaving this world without first making you my wife unless Elôm tells me otherwise."

This seemed to please her, and he asked, "How are your parents?"

"Father is a little sore, and I'll feel better once the bruise on Mother's face goes away."

"Are you settling in all right?"

Anne nodded. "It will take some getting used to, but I, for one, am glad to be out here . . . finally."

"Well, you know how I feel about you being here."

She smiled, and he motioned to the opposite wall. "See that trunk over there? Since you've forbidden me from getting up, why don't you go over and open it?"

Anne rose and walked over to the trunk to lift the lid.

"Find the bundle wrapped in blue silk and bring it here."

She picked through the trunk and brought back the bundle. "Open it."

Taking her seat again, she laid the bundle in her lap and untied the ribbons. When she folded the silk aside, it revealed shimmering white fabric. She took it in her hands and held up a beautiful satin gown—a wedding dress. Her wide eyes darted to him.

"It was my mother's," Trask told her. "I know under normal circumstances, you might have worn your mother's . . . but, if you'd like, my mother would have loved for you to wear hers. You can take it as is or make it your own. It's your choice."

Anne's eyes shimmered, and she smiled. "I'd love to wear it."

Trask let his own smile grow. She would look beyond lovely in the dress. Then he reached for her hand. "Let's get married tomorrow."

"Tomorrow? Don't you think we should wait until the others return from Dorland?"

Trask forced out an exaggerated sigh. "All right, but as soon as they get back, let's get married. I don't even care if it's a big deal or not. I just want to marry you."

"Yes, as soon as they get back, we'll get married." But she frowned as she eyed the bruises on his face. "At least this way you'll have a little time to recover."

"I don't have to recover as long as I have you to take care of me." He gave her a little grin and chuckled at the blush that crept into her cheeks.

She sent him a reproving look and glanced at Warin, who was clearly pretending not to pay any attention. But he was a married man now. He understood.

Then Anne rose. "I have to go. Lenae is cooking breakfast for us, and I don't want to be late or keep Warin here. I just wanted to make sure you were all right. Clearly, you're just fine."

Trask grinned as he watched her leave the cabin. He wished she would have breakfast with him, but soon enough she would, every day. And not just breakfast but all meals and every other moment they wanted to spend together.

When Jace woke again, he could tell by the light in the cabin that it was much later in the day. He still barely had strength to move, but his head didn't take as long to clear. He wasn't used to being so weak. The last time he was right on the brink of death, Elon had healed him, and he hadn't needed to go through a recovery process. He wished for that healing now.

Movement drew his attention, and Rayad limped to his side.

"I have to say it's good to see you awake again."

Jace offered a bit of a smile, and his gaze shifted down to Rayad's leg. "Are you all right?"

Rayad nodded, touching where a bandage bulged under his pant leg. "It'll hurt for a while, but it'll heal." He paused. "Can I get you anything?"

"Water." Speaking scraped his dried out throat.

Rayad stepped away and then returned a moment later with a cup of water. Carefully, he helped Jace lift his head and put the cup to his lips. Jace drank deeply, and then lay back with a sigh.

"We should get some food in you," Rayad said.

Jace nodded. His stomach felt shrunken, though the thought of eating made him tired. Rayad left again, and Jace rested his eyes. He drifted off a little, but not completely, before Rayad returned. When Jace opened his eyes, he found Holden had joined them. His friend smiled widely.

"Now I get to see you awake for myself."

"Barely," Jace responded.

Holden helped Rayad prop Jace up with folded blankets. Now that he could look around better, Jace found himself on a cot in the living room of the cabin. A few others lay around him, recovering.

Rayad sat down on a chair next to Jace with a bowl in hand. "I've got a little soup here for you."

Jace pulled his right arm out from under the covers, bothered by how heavy it was, and reached for the spoon as Rayad held the bowl closer. He gripped it but couldn't lift the spoon out of the bowl without shaking it so much he lost the whole spoonful.

"Here, let me," Rayad said.

Jace grimaced at the idea of being spoon-fed, but he'd never recover without nourishment. Swallowing down his pride, he accepted a spoonful of savory chicken broth. The liquid trailed down his throat and warmed his stomach. Members of the group came to visit while he ate. It overjoyed him to see all of them alive. Talas seemed to be one of the most seriously injured with his arm in a sling.

Just after Jace finished the small bowl of soup, Saul came to see him.

"You don't look so near to death now."

"Rayad said that's because of your physician."

"Thank Elôm that Toris was with us and wasn't one of the wounded."

"Thank Elôm you were all here," Jace replied, "otherwise none of us would be."

Saul smiled. "I'm glad we could help. We want to keep Daican out of Dorland as much as the rest of you. I only wish we could have arrived sooner. We prepared and traveled as quickly as we could."

"You showed up just in time," Jace told him.

They talked for a bit before it was only Jace and Rayad once more. Jace hated how little it took to make him want to sleep again, but at least he'd lasted longer this time. Before letting himself drift off, he asked, "No one has come from Arvael or Bel-gard yet, have they?"

Rayad shook his head. "Not yet. Tomorrow, I would expect."

Now that it was all over, Jace longed to see Kyrin. Maybe no one was coming from Bel-gard, and she was waiting there for news. If he'd had even the strength to get to his feet, he would've been sorely tempted to go after her. However, the grip of sleep grew too strong for him to resist.

THE MORNING SUN shone warmly on Kyrin's back, but it didn't dispel the cold dread mounting inside of her. As fast as Prince Haedrin's force moved, it was agony not to fly on ahead when she could reach the ford in half the time. But she honored Jace's desire that she stay safe and stuck with the company. That is, until last evening when a large dragon force, led by Lord Vallan himself, had intercepted them. Kyrin had joined the cretes, and they'd pushed on through the night.

Sixty dragon riders in all had come from Arvael, including Leetra, Glynn, Novan, and Captain Darq's brothers—more than enough to crush Daican's army and any that came behind it. But would they be in time? Fearfully, she scanned the horizon for any firedrakes that might appear. If they did, it meant everyone at the ford had failed.

Yet, as midday approached, the sky remained empty, and the villages they passed along the way sat peacefully untouched. By noon, she spotted Jorvik's cabin in the distance. Her fingers grew sweaty and slick on the guide bar of the saddle, and little tremors of anxiety passed up and down her arms. She pressed her free hand to her stomach in a vain attempt to rub away the tight knot there. As desperately as she needed to know everyone was all right, the terror of what she would find was stronger. *Oh, please, Elôm, let them be all right.* She sucked in a deep breath, but her throat squeezed together. The likelihood of survival had been so slim. She had to prepare herself for the worst.

As they drew nearer, Kyrin spotted men in the yard—many men, yet no firedrakes. Instead, there were dragons—familiar dragons like Exsis, Gem, and Storm. The first blooming of hope sprang up inside her. They must have held Daican's men back . . . but who had survived? Her hope grew further when she recognized the men in the yard as ryriks from Saul's village. Had they come in time to save everyone?

When Lord Vallan and the rest of the company landed at the edge of the yard, Kyrin didn't even wait for Ivoris to fold her wings before she scrambled down and rushed toward the cabin, heedless of her ankle.

"Jace! Kaden!" Despite the signs of hope, fear burned every nerve in her body, almost paralyzing her. "Marcus! Michael!"

Why were none of her loved ones in the yard? But then a tall figure exited the cabin.

"Kaden," she cried, tears welling.

He hurried down the stairs to meet her, and Marcus and Michael followed just behind him. Kyrin rushed into Kaden's arms. Tears streamed down her face as she hugged her brother with all her might.

"You're alive," she gasped. Deep down in the recesses of her heart that she had fought to ignore, she truly hadn't expected this reunion.

She hugged Marcus next. Before she could grab Michael, her older brother said, "Better take it easy with him. He's got a few cuts and bruises."

"It's nothing," Michael replied, though his face was a bit pale.

Kyrin looked around the yard again. By now, most of the others had left the cabin, though one person was alarmingly absent. Kyrin's heart missed a beat and her stomach wrenched. She looked up at Kaden, her voice wavering. "Where's Jace?"

His solemn expression almost sent her to her knees.

"He was injured pretty badly, but he should be all right. He's inside, resting."

Kyrin's breath poured out in a gust, her legs still wobbling. The moment they solidified again, she rushed up the stairs and into the cabin. Just inside the door, she paused to look around. Several cots sat in the living room bearing wounded men, but her gaze went straight to the one where Rayad sat. His face lit up to see her, and she hurried forward.

Her gaze then locked on Jace. She'd expected to find him conscious, but his eyes were closed. Her throat swelled up again, and she drew a gasping breath. His face, particularly around his right eye, bore bruises, and a cut split his bottom lip. His left arm lay at his side, bandaged and splinted. But most disturbing was his ghostly pale skin. She'd seen him injured before but not like this. Her tears welled again.

"What happened?"

"His arm is broken," Rayad answered quietly.

Kyrin winced and waited for the rest. A broken arm hadn't put Jace in this state. Not when he was so strong.

"He was cut too. He came close to bleeding out." Rayad shook his head. "Very close."

Kyrin brushed the stray tears from her cheeks and thanked Elôm for sparing Jace's life. Carefully, she reached for Jace's right hand, glad to feel the warmth of it in hers. A moment later, he stirred, and his eyes fluttered open. He blinked a couple of times and then his gaze fixed on her face.

"Kyrin."

She smiled widely even as a couple more tears worked themselves free. "Jace."

His fingers squeezed around hers. "When did you get here?"

"Just now. I followed Prince Haedrin and his men. Then we met up with Lord Vallan and the other riders, and I flew with them the rest of the way. I made sure I was safe."

Jace gave her a warm smile. "Good."

Leetra stood stiffly near the dragons, her feet refusing to move. She'd watched Kyrin rush up to the cabin calling for Jace and her brothers. Leetra should have followed, except for one startling fact—she wasn't that brave. Despite how strong she always presented herself to be, fear held her in place. Fear to discover if *her* loved ones lived or were dead. It encased her in ice that didn't begin to thaw until she spotted Captain Darq. He'd been her mentor for a long time. At least if the worst had happened, she could count on his strength to help her face it. Then she spotted Talas. Finally, her feet moved forward, and she hurried to meet her cousin.

"Talas." Her voice came out breathless in spite of how she fought to project a brave front. She eyed his arm and sling. "What did you do to yourself?"

"Collarbone."

She winced, knowing firsthand how that felt, but his injury quickly flew from her mind as she glanced around the yard, searching. Looking back at Talas, she swallowed hard, but couldn't work any words loose. She was still too afraid.

What if he was gone?

The question almost paralyzed her again. All the way to Arvael and back, Timothy had barely left her mind. She had relived his words so many times she could have recited them perfectly. And every time she did, regret tore her apart. She'd had so many chances to let Timothy into her heart but had pushed him away. Her stubbornness would be her ruin. She didn't fool herself about that.

Blinking hard against the moisture making her vision waver, she forced her mouth open to speak. However, right then, her gaze drifted past Talas. On the porch looking at her stood Timothy. A slight, welcoming smile lifted his lips, and Leetra's heart tripped over itself before leaping in her chest. He was alive!

Talas stepped aside, and Leetra raced to the porch, where Timothy met her at the bottom of the stairs. By now, her eyes watered so heavily she could barely make out his face. "You're all right."

She didn't know whether she actually meant it as a question or a jubilant declaration, but he nodded.

"Yes, I'm all right."

She breathed hard, fighting the flood on the brink of overwhelming her. Failing, but trying her best to speak calmly, she asked, "Are you hurt at all?"

"Not badly."

Leetra nodded in relief, the pressure in her throat and eyes giving way. Before she could say anything more, Timothy stepped closer and reached out for her. She readily stepped into his arms and laid her head against his chest just as the dam to her tears broke. *It's true, Elôm, I am a foolish girl sometimes, but thank You for giving me another chance to try to change that.*

Kyrin remained at Jace's side for most of the day and helped him with his supper. By late evening, the long, trying days had caught up with her. Though reluctant to leave Jace, as soon as he had fallen asleep, she took Rayad's suggestion to go upstairs to rest.

When she reached the top of the steps, she glanced back and found that Leetra had followed. Though cretes didn't sleep as much, a need for rest weighed on Leetra's expression. From what Kyrin had heard, she'd hardly rested the whole way to Arvael. Either Timothy or Talas must have convinced her to get some sleep.

In the bedroom, Kyrin closed the door, and they both quietly changed into their nightclothes. Kyrin crawled up onto one side of the bed, while Leetra used the bedpost to hoist herself up on the other since she hadn't discovered a way to hang her hammock. She then sat brushing out her long, black hair. Kyrin crawled under the covers and laid back against the pillows, too tired to care about her own messy braid. She'd brush it in the morning. Silently, she thought back over the day, thanking Elôm that the battle had not been the massacre they so feared.

"How did you know you loved Jace?"

Kyrin blinked, snapping out of her prayers, and looked over at Leetra. The girl was still brushing her hair but sent her a curious look.

Kyrin shrugged against the pillow. "I've always loved Jace, probably from the very first week I got to know him. Of course, it was just friendship for a while. It really hasn't changed all that much, it's just . . . deeper. Now, instead of loving him just as my closest friend, I also want to spend the rest of my life with him."

Leetra's forehead creased deeply. "I thought I loved Falcor."

"Did you love him or just the idea of being his wife?"

Leetra contemplated this a moment before hanging her head. "I guess I don't really know what true love is."

"Sure you do," Kyrin said gently. "You love your family. You stick with them, put up with them on their bad days, you fight for them and sacrifice for them. *That* is true love."

Leetra looked up again, understanding in her eyes. "You don't give up when they're being stubborn and foolish and try to push you away."

A smile grew on Kyrin's face. "Exactly."

Leetra then set her brush aside and blew out the candle next to the bed, darkening the room. The blankets rustled as she settled in and then all fell silent.

"Thanks." Her voice broke the silence a moment later.

Kyrin smiled in the darkness. "You're welcome."

FOUR DAYS OF rest and Jace was ready to leave the cot for good. Mentally, at least. He needed to get out and get some fresh air. The walls might start to close in on him otherwise. Kyrin fussed about him getting up, but he assured her that he would be fine.

With Rayad's help, he shuffled into a separate room to change. His broken arm made it nearly impossible to do much for himself. And despite being on his feet, his entire body trembled with weakness. If he had to fight right now, he couldn't have even lifted a sword. It frustrated him, but he reminded himself to be thankful that he even had any life in his body. He didn't doubt how close he had come to death. He'd fully expected it that day on the riverbank.

Once he was fully clothed, he made his way out to the porch, barely. The moment he reached it, he sank down on one of the benches, lightheaded. When the dizziness cleared, he looked out over the yard. Tall cream and crimson tents stood in the meadow. Prince Haedrin's men moved among them. Off to the right, the dragons basked in the sun. Most of Saul's men had returned to their village, though Saul had remained. Jace spotted him standing with Balen, Lord Vallan, and Prince Haedrin, who seemed to be holding a small conference. A moment later, Talas approached from that direction, matching Jace with his arm in a sling. He climbed the stairs slowly, without his usual vigor, careful not to jar his arm.

"What's going on over there?" Jace asked.

"They want to hold a meeting and discuss what's next for Dorland," Talas said. "This should be interesting."

Several minutes later, everyone gathered inside the cabin, where their leaders assembled around the table. Most people stood around to listen, but Holden offered Jace a chair. He didn't want to admit how much he needed it. It was as if his body only had a small reserve of energy that he'd already spent just on getting dressed.

When all were present, Lord Vallan handed Prince Haedrin the same parchment Jace had seen in the ryrik village. "These are the terms Emperor Daican has offered to the cretes."

He gave the prince a moment to read it over before saying, "Regardless of whether or not Daican truly intends to honor this agreement, I will not accept it. The Dorlanders have been our closest allies for a long time. Dorland is our home, and the emperor has declared war on it by bringing this attack against your people. You won't have to stand against him alone. You can count on our full support."

Prince Haedrin nodded gratefully. "Thank you."

"I will leave riders here to stop Daican's second force when it arrives," Vallan continued. "We'll make it clear that to try to cross the Trayse will not be tolerated." Now his attention shifted to Balen. "Once we've established that and Dorland is secure, then we will turn our attention to liberating Samara. Whichever way the council leans is irrelevant now. Daican has made his true intentions clear."

Despite the tired expression on his face, Balen smiled. "Your aid is greatly appreciated."

"You will have our aid as well," Prince Haedrin announced. "Whatever you need, we will help you reclaim Samara. After all, you saved many lives here at great risk to your own."

Saul spoke up as well. "I'll get word around to our other villages. I'm sure there are many of us who would be willing to help you fight and defend both Samara and Dorland."

Balen and Haedrin both thanked him.

"That means if all has gone well for Sam in Arda," Rayad said, "then Ilyon truly will be united against Daican."

Balen nodded. "And once Samara is free again, all believers from Arcacia are welcome to make their home there. We may not be able to change the way Daican rules, but we can create a safe haven for those endangered by it."

Anticipation thrummed inside Jace. Perhaps the quiet life he longed for lately wasn't so unobtainable after all. His mind already rushed ahead, picturing a farm on the edge of the forest in Westing. But it wasn't so much the farm that tugged at his desire; it was the return of a normal, peaceful life. He looked over at Kyrin. She met his eyes, and he read the same dreams in her expression. What a glorious future it would be if they could just attain it. *Please, Elôm, let it be.*

Once they had spoken of these future plans, they focused on the immediate. They received invitations from Jorvik, Prince Haedrin, and Lord Vallan to stay with them for however long they chose to remain in Dorland. Balen thanked each of them for their hospitality, but said, "I think once we're all fit for travel, we should return to Landale. We left a difficult situation there, and I am anxious for any news that has come from Samara."

Besides Talas, Jace was the only one who would find travel difficult. Still, he said, "I'm ready to return." For right now, camp was home, and he was ready to get back.

Balen looked at him. "You're sure you're up to it?"

Jace nodded. After all, he only had to ride his dragon. Even with this lack of strength, he should be able to manage that.

"All right then, we'll take another day to prepare and then start back."

The morning of their departure dawned with a clear sunrise and a sense of newness and hope that Jace hadn't experienced quite like this before. The future excited him with all its possibilities. Of course, it wouldn't be as easy as it sounded. There would be fighting. More people would probably die. But he wouldn't let go of the hope. It was worth fighting for.

They ate a filling breakfast with everyone who could fit inside the cabin and then gathered their things to take out to the dragons. Jace tried to carry his belongings, but Holden stepped in immediately to take them from him. Good thing too. He probably would have collapsed halfway out of the cabin, though he wouldn't admit it to anyone. According to Leetra, it would take weeks before he fully recovered from the blood loss.

Outside, Holden also took over saddling Gem for him. Jace felt terrible that his friend had lost his dragon, Brayle, but he took it well. Without the aid of those extra dragons, Kaden and the others probably wouldn't have succeeded in defeating the firedrakes.

Gem cautiously sniffed his splinted arm but seemed to know to be gentle. She released a sad warble, and Jace patted her neck. "It'll be all right."

He looked her over. She had patches of burns and scrapes, but they were already healing.

Rayad approached and held a sword out to Jace. After one look at it, Jace's brows rose in recognition. He took the familiar blade in his hand.

"My sword," he said in surprise. "Where did you get it?"

"We found it near the river where you fought Ruis. Seems he was using it."

Jace shook his head at the irony. "I was almost killed by my own blade."

He turned and handed it to Holden, who attached it to the saddle with the rest of his belongings.

"You're sure you feel all right to make this trip?" Rayad asked as he turned back. His eyes narrowed slightly. After all, Jace didn't exactly have a reputation for being honest about his health.

"A few more days wouldn't make much difference." He shrugged. "All I have to do is sit anyway."

"And I'll be there to make sure it isn't too much for him."

They both turned. Kyrin walked up to them with one of her supply packs and looked at Jace. "I'll ride with you. That way Marcus and Michael can ride Ivoris."

Jace smiled. He certainly didn't object to sharing her company for the next several days. It seemed to please Rayad as well. Apparently, they thought he might overtax himself. Not that he could blame them.

Once they'd all packed their replenished supplies and figured out who would pair up now that they were short on dragons, it was time for goodbyes. Though anxious to return to camp, Jace would miss certain people, particularly Saul. He was glad the man stuck around a couple of extra days.

"It must be nice to know you're heading home," Saul said as Jace walked up to him.

"Yes. This trip wasn't what any of us expected."

Saul smiled in agreement. "Well, I wish you the best. I hope, now that we're all working together, we can change things and you can get back to a more normal life. We'll be praying for that."

"Thank you. And I'm very thankful for the opportunity to have met you and your family. I think I can finally embrace who I am. I had learned to accept my ryrik blood, but I still tried to ignore it and pretend it wasn't really part of me. Not anymore."

"Perhaps, someday, others will come to see the truth and ryriks can return to being protectors and fighters for justice as Elôm intended."

"I hope so."

They shook hands, and Saul said, "Remember, you're always welcome to visit. Come any time and stay for as long as you want."

Jace smiled. "I will."

With their goodbyes concluding, everyone gathered around the dragons to mount up. It was a little difficult for Jace, but Gem crouched down low enough to make it easier. Once he'd settled in, Kyrin climbed up behind him. Just being so near to her after how things could have ended restored some of his strength.

Before flying off, Lord Vallan approached Balen. "We'll keep in touch, and I'll have dragons sent to replace those you lost."

"We appreciate that," Balen said, "and we are very grateful for your help."

Lord Vallan nodded. "Daican has been allowed to go un-challenged long enough. It's time for that to change."

DANIEL RUBBED HIS sore eyes and craned his neck from side to side. The past two weeks had passed in a blur. He hadn't slept a full night in all that time. First, he'd focused on his mother and being there in her grief. Though he'd wanted to do the same for his sister, she refused his sympathy. Then he'd had to arrange his father's funeral. Looking back on it still felt too strange to be real.

Yet, now that it was over came the most surreal part of all—the preparation for his coronation and ascension to the throne. For the last three days, he'd spent almost every waking moment in his father's study with the secretary—Henry Foss—trying to catch up on all his father's affairs that would now be his responsibility.

One of the first things he would do once he was officially crowned was pardon everyone arrested in the last two years for believing in Elôm. If only he could find a way to make amends to all those who had suffered so terribly. Maybe Ben and Mira would have an idea, but he hadn't had time yet to visit them.

"I just found this letter from one of the generals, my lord." Mister Foss held out a parchment. "It appears your father had two forces sent to invade Dorland."

"What?" Daniel snatched the letter and skimmed it, groaning when he reached the end. His father had seemed bent on systematically making enemies of everyone who had once been an ally of Arcacia. "Send someone immediately to put a stop to this. And I want all of our troops pulled out of Samara and King Balen restored to the throne."

He prayed both King Balen and King Orlan would understand that he wasn't his father and that he sought to restore peaceful relationships.

"It will be done, my lord, but it must wait until after you are crowned."

Daniel groaned again. "People could be dying in Dorland by then." For all he knew, they were already. He sighed. Three more days and then he could make things right.

A knock sounded at the office door, and Foss answered it. One of the footman stepped in and addressed Daniel.

"Excuse me, my lord, Sir Richard Blaine has arrived."

Daniel knew his sister had sent for him. "Where is he now?"

"With the princess, my lord."

Though Daniel had never particularly liked him, Richard was like an uncle to Davira. Maybe his presence would help her through her grief. Daniel had barely seen her since the funeral. When he did, her gaunt appearance disturbed him. She almost seemed to have given up on life.

"Thank you," Daniel said, dismissing the footman. He'd let Davira have her time with Richard before he sought him out. He didn't look forward to explaining the changes he planned to make anyway. In fact, the dread of it had weighed on him for days. Richard had been the staunchest supporter of his father's plans. Not to mention what he'd gained from it—rule over all Samara. He would probably have a good deal to say in opposition to the changes. Daniel would have to learn good diplomacy skills and fast.

He turned his attention back to Mister Foss. "Any other hostile operations I should be aware of?"

The secretary shook his head. "I will keep looking, my lord."

It surprised Daniel how willing the man was to see things changed. He was another one Daniel would have expected to remain fiercely loyal to his father, but that didn't seem to be the case.

He glanced at the letter concerning Dorland again and set to work writing his orders to pull out of Samara and Dorland and restore rule to their rightful parties. They may not be official documents yet, but at least he'd have them here waiting to go out the moment he was crowned.

For the next hour, he sifted through document after document, recruiting Mister Foss to explain most of them. This made it painfully clear how his refusal to work with his father had left him ignorant as to what it took to rule Arcacia. He just prayed he would learn quickly without any catastrophic mistakes.

Just when he thought about taking a break for lunch, the office door burst open. His head shot up, and he frowned as Richard marched in followed by four guards. Pushing to his feet, Daniel glared at Richard. The man might have shared a close friendship with his father, but Daniel wouldn't stand for him barging in whenever he pleased. If he didn't demand respect now from the start, he might not be able to enforce it later.

Before he could get a word out of his mouth, two of the guards strode around the desk and grabbed him by the arms.

"What are you doing?" Daniel jerked against the men. "Unhand me immediately."

The guards dragged him around the desk to Richard. Daniel's mind spun. He hadn't expected a power play for the throne—not when Richard had been so loyal to the family—but then Davira stepped into the room. Her eyes seemed to pierce right through him.

"You are under arrest for treason."

Daniel's mouth dropped open. "What? You can't do that."

Davira tipped her chin up and motioned to the guards. "Take him down to an interrogation room."

Any protest died on Daniel's lips, shocked that she would actually do this and that Richard was in it with her. Quick to follow her orders, the guards hauled him out of the office. In the halls, he looked around for Aric. He would put a stop to this. Then he spotted his mother. Her eyes went wide, and she rushed up to them.

"What's this?"

"I'm preserving Father's legacy," Davira said, her voice like ice.

Their mother stared, dumbfounded, and then shook her head. "You can't do this." She looked at the guards. "Release him."

Daniel tugged against them, ready to have Richard escorted to the dungeon instead. He'd be sorely tempted to have Davira thrown down there for a while too. However, the guards didn't relinquish their hold. His mother drew herself up, her eyes flashing.

"I am still the queen, and I command you to release him immediately."

Still, the guards refused to obey. Glaring at their mother, Davira ordered, "Carry on."

The guards shoved Daniel forward again, simply brushing his mother off to the side. He looked back at her, meeting her wide eyes. That was the moment reality crashed in. Davira and Richard had the guards entirely under their control, and not even the queen could stop them. That left Daniel at Davira's mercy. He swallowed convulsively. All the murderous looks she had sent him over the years floated into his mind. How much hatred had she stored up ready to release on him now?

They led him down one of the dark staircases into the dungeon. Daniel gritted his teeth. He'd always avoided this place.

The cool, damp air seeped into his skin, and he shivered. Down a long hall, they shoved him into an interrogation room and clamped a heavy pair of shackles to his wrists.

Forcing aside his apprehension, Daniel sent his sister a hard look. "You won't get away with this."

She merely smirked. "I already have." She walked up to him, her eyes like cold emeralds. "Now, why don't you tell me who and where your traitorous friends are? I bet you know exactly where Alex is hiding."

Daniel shook his head. "Of course I don't know where he is."

Davira turned and motioned to the guards. "Looks like he needs his tongue loosened."

Before he had a chance to prepare for it, one of the guard's fists smashed squarely into the side of his jaw. He stumbled and caught himself, but another fist drove into his ribs. He raised his arms to try to shield himself from the attacks. The blows came one after the other, some to the head and some to the body, until he fell to his knees, gasping. Pain ricocheted inside his skull and pulsated through his chest. He shook his head to clear his senses.

"Now chain him up."

The guards grabbed Daniel's wrists and attached a long chain to the shackles. They yanked on the opposite end threaded through a ring in the ceiling and hauled him to his feet, leaving him standing with his arms suspended over his head. The metal dug into his wrists.

"Davira, what are you doing? I'm Father's heir."

Davira placed her hands on her hips. "I will produce a new heir. Once I have a son, I will raise him up in your place, and he will continue Father's legacy. Three days from now, the people will gather to see your coronation. What they will witness instead is your execution, and I will be crowned queen

463

of Arcacia. No one, not even the prince, gets away with treason."

Daniel breathed out hard. He'd always suspected his sister was capable of murder, but to actually go through with it? "Do you really think killing me is what Father would have wanted?"

Her face flushed as she stepped closer. "What Father wanted was to create a strong and powerful Arcacia, and all you plan to do is destroy everything he worked for his entire life."

"Power is not what makes a country great. It's—"

"Silence! You don't know anything! You were never involved in any of Father's affairs. You didn't sit with him and learn what it takes to run a country. You didn't want anything to do with him!" Her chest heaved, and her eyes flashed. "I *did*."

Daniel released a long sigh, guilt weighing on him. "I know. And I know how you loved him. I didn't learn the things you did, but I do care about the people of Arcacia—"

Davira snorted. "The people of Arcacia. The traitors, you mean. I'll deal with your precious people. Now tell me the location of every Elôm-worshipper you know."

Despite how his ribs protested, Daniel stood up straighter and refused to speak. She wouldn't get a single name out of him.

A solid blow to the gut robbed him of breath. With another, a cracking in his ribs forced a groan up his throat. The guard backed off, and Daniel struggled to catch his breath, but it set fire to his side.

Gritting his teeth, he locked eyes with his sister. "You must know you're wasting your time."

"Oh, really? Because we're just getting started. If you think this is the worst we can do, you're sadly mistaken. After all, you don't need your eyes, or your fingers, to talk. If that's how you want to be seen at your execution, that's perfectly fine with me."

A chill slithered through Daniel's body. "Davira, I'm your brother. We're not enemies."

She released a short, hard laugh. "You are not my brother. Not since you joined up with those Elôm-worshipping rebels who wanted my father dead."

"Alex acted on his own personal vendetta against Father. He had nothing to do with the believers in Elôm."

"You expect me to believe they didn't want him dead too?"

"Not anyone I know."

Davira scoffed. "I don't believe you. You're my enemy, they're my enemies, and so is everyone who ever opposed Father. And let me tell you, *brother*, you will *all* pay for it."

Daniel let a breath hiss out through his teeth. The struggle to breathe grew worse the longer he stood here with his arms secured over his head. Davira and Richard had left him alone hours ago. Unless he stood up straight, which pained his ribs, he hung from his wrists. By now, his legs and arms ached almost as badly as his chest. He winced and blinked, though his left eye was almost swollen shut. Not that it mattered since it was too dark to see anything.

The darkness weighed on him like a physical manifestation of the despair that sank into his heart. *I had a chance to make things right. I could've changed everything. Why would You allow this? You said You could use me. I don't understand. Did I miss something I should've done to prevent this?* If only Elon would appear to him here as He had on the cliffs.

Daniel straightened up to draw another deep breath and groaned. How long would Davira keep him in this position? Until his execution? He grimaced and considered how many others had endured torture here for their beliefs. Kyrin Altair, her brother, the half ryrik Elon had sacrificed Himself to save. Though he'd been well aware of the danger, Daniel never actually believed it would come to this. He was the prince. He choked out a dry, painful laugh. What a stupid, arrogant fool. Maybe it was that stupidity and arrogance that had put him down here. He should have been more wary of Davira. *I thought I was doing the right things, Lord. I'm sorry if I failed.* He hung his head.

The bolt on the door slid open, and Daniel looked up, bracing himself for more questions or torture—whatever Davira felt in the mood for. A torch bobbed in first, followed immediately by one man.

"Aric," Daniel gasped. A friendly face immediately lifted his heavy heart.

The man closed the door and stuck the torch in a holder before crossing the room to remove the shackles. When Daniel's arms lowered, he gritted his teeth, hunching over as pain tore through his shoulders and chest. His legs wobbled, but he managed to stay upright. Flexing his fists, he worked some feeling back into his fingers.

"We need to get out of here now," Aric said. "We may need to run. Can you do that?"

Daniel straightened, wincing. He hurt worse than he ever had in his comfortable, pampered life, but he wouldn't let that stop him from escaping this place. He nodded firmly.

Aric handed him the extra sword he had stuck in his belt. "In case you need it."

Daniel took it, and Aric turned for the door. He grabbed the torch and peered into the hall before motioning for Daniel to follow. Walking briskly, Aric asked, "You don't know of any more secret exits, do you?"

"Unfortunately, no."

"We'll have to use the main gate then."

They hurried through the dungeon and up a long staircase, where Aric put out the torch. Easing the door open, he peered outside before the two of them crept out into the courtyard.

Daniel looked around. The sky and moons were cloud-covered, thankfully. At least they had that to their advantage.

"We'll sneak to the wall and follow it to the gate," Aric whispered. "It'll be safer than trying to cross in front of the palace undetected."

They made their way to the wall, using anything they could for cover. When they reached the dark shadows at the base of the wall, they paused, and Daniel braced himself to catch his breath. Though his adrenaline dulled some of the pain, he still could hardly breathe without groaning.

"Once we're out, we'll need someplace to hide so you can rest," Aric said. "Do you know a place?"

"Yes."

"Then once we're out, you lead the way."

Daniel nodded, and they moved on again, keeping close to the cover of the wall. When they drew near the gate, Aric stopped again. "Whatever happens, you need to go. Don't stop. I will get the gate open. Wait here until you have an opening and then go."

A protest jumped to Daniel's mouth, but Aric moved away before he could voice it. Silently, he crouched in the shadows as the man strode toward the gate. In a moment, the two gate guards spotted him. Their hands jumped to their swords, but they relaxed when they realized who it was.

"I was just working my way around the perimeter and thought I'd have a look around outside," Aric said.

One of the guards frowned. "Alone?"

Aric shrugged. "I don't anticipate trouble. Besides, I think I'll head down into the city for a while."

The guards hesitated at first, but then one turned to the gate and swung it open. When the man turned back to Aric, Daniel's heart skipped a beat. Now was his chance. Gasping a prayer for success, he sprinted toward the opening and slipped through.

"Hey!" one of the guards shouted.

Daniel glanced over his shoulder. The guards sprinted after him, but Aric yanked out his sword and cut them off. Despite what Aric told him, he paused to hear him say, "He is heir to the throne and rightfully our king."

However, the guards drew their own swords, and one said, "The princess is our ruler now."

With this declaration, one of the guards attacked while the other shouted toward the palace, "Help! Prince Daniel is escaping!"

Daniel gripped his sword as both guards engaged Aric. He looked to the street, considering Aric's instructions to go no matter what, but then the man grunted in pain. With more guards on the way, he wouldn't last long on his own. Daniel stood, torn for just a moment, before rushing back through the gate. He wouldn't leave a loyal friend. Catching one of the guards by surprise, he slashed down across the man's arm. This gave Aric a chance to debilitate his own foe.

"Go!" Aric shouted, grabbing his shoulder and urging him toward the gate.

They both rushed through as the pounding of footsteps grew behind them. Taking the lead, Daniel ran down the street. Every one of his footfalls sent a fresh stab of pain to his ribs, cutting off his breath, but he kept moving. Swerving left, he led Aric into a dark alley. They had to lose the guards before he could get them to safety.

Weaving in and out of alleyways, eventually, all sound and sign of their pursuers died away. Daniel changed his course, taking the long way around to Ben and Mira's street. When they arrived, he stopped at the corner to wait and make sure they'd lost the palace guards. Braced against the side of the building, he panted, but the agonizing pain made him dizzy. He swayed a little, but Aric grabbed his arm to steady him. Gripping his ribs, Daniel pushed away from the wall and moved toward Ben and Mira's house. At the door, he knocked twice and then three times.

A few moments later, Ben opened it. The eagerness in his expression grew serious upon seeing Daniel's face. He immediately reached for him, helping him inside.

"Daniel!" Mira gasped, rushing to him.

"I'll be all right," he tried to assure her, though he wasn't all that convinced of it himself at the moment.

They led him and Aric into the living room, where several other believers were gathered. Daniel hadn't even considered that tonight was their weekly meeting. They all looked at him, murmuring in concern.

After helping him ease down into a chair, Ben asked, "What happened?"

"Davira has taken the throne. Now, she wants me dead." Daniel winced at the persistent throbbing in his chest as well as the circumstances. "I need a place to hide."

THE FAMILIAR FORESTED hills of Landale had never looked so welcoming—so much like home. When they landed at the edge of camp, Jace took in the site of the cabins and released a deep sigh. Though he'd managed the journey, it would be good to rest and not spend the days traveling. Even after almost two weeks since his injury, he still hadn't recovered his full strength.

Kyrin climbed off Gem first and then turned to make sure he dismounted all right. His splinted arm was cumbersome, but he'd learned how to work with it. By the time they all dismounted, everyone from camp started to gather around. Tyra bounded up first, her tail wagging frantically. Jace smiled and knelt down to pet her. She nuzzled his face, then sniffed at this injured arm.

He patted her head. "Don't worry. It'll be all right."

He spotted Trask and Warin as he rose back to his feet. Trask's smile said how glad he was to see them, though his face bore the remnants of bruises and healing cuts. The last time Trask sported such injuries, Goler had nearly executed him. What had happened this time? More questions arose in Jace's mind when he saw Anne and her parents just behind him.

"Jace!"

His gaze jumped to the sound of his sister's voice. She ran up to him, Elian only a short distance behind.

Her eyes grew wide and serious. "What happened to your arm?"

Jace glanced at Elian, and then at Anne and her parents again. They never all came out to camp except on special occasions.

"It's broken," he answered, distracted as his attention swung back to his sister. He frowned. "What are you doing here?"

Elanor raised her brows and looked over at Trask, who said, "It looks like we all have stories to tell."

But they waited until after everyone had a chance to greet each other. The sheepish looks Marcus, Kaden, and Michael traded with their mother amused Jace. They had a lot of explaining to do.

"We're all perfectly fine," Marcus assured her, though she didn't appear convinced.

Once everyone had helped them unload and unsaddle the dragons, they gathered in the meeting hall to catch up on all that had taken place in Dorland and here in Landale. It deeply saddened Jace to learn about Baron Grey, but he thanked Elôm that Elanor and the others had escaped Goler relatively unharmed. It could have ended in disaster. The sadness that hung around them over Baron Grey's death was comforted by the fact that they now had support from Dorland and the prospect of new lives in Samara.

When they had shared all the details of the last few weeks, they left the meeting hall, dispersing to different cabins for lunch. Jace gave Kyrin a smile as she went off with her mother and brothers while he followed Elanor and Elian.

Walking beside his sister, Jace asked, "How are you settling in here?"

"Quite well." She shrugged. "Obviously, the smaller quarters take some getting used to, but everyone is so accommodating."

Jace nodded, recalling when he'd first come to camp and how he'd missed having a private bedroom. At least his sister had a cabin to sleep in. Still, he wished for a way to offer her better. She was used to a much more comfortable life.

"I am glad to be out here," she continued. "Now I can see you whenever I want." She grinned at him.

"But you don't get to go home now that you're a known traitor."

"I couldn't go home before, either. Not unless I wanted to end up in an arranged marriage. And I was always in danger of discovery. Even at home. I'd rather be here, in the midst of things, than waiting around at Ashwood to see how everything plays out."

She did have a point.

"My only concern now is Mother, but I know Uncle Charles will take care of her." A bright smile bloomed on her face for such a serious discussion. "He visited while you were away."

Disappointment took hold of Jace over having missed his uncle.

"He brought incredible news," Elanor said, taking a little of the sting away, "James is a believer now."

Jace stopped in his tracks and turned to face her. "Really?"

She nodded, still grinning. "Really."

Jace stood in stunned silence. That was the last bit of news he ever would have guessed.

"Apparently, ever since the night you spoke to him, Elôm was working on his heart and gave Charles an opening to present him with the truth."

Jace shook his head, still unable to speak. He'd carried a lingering regret over what he'd done to James that night, but the fact that it might have led to his change of heart filled Jace with joy. His throat clogged up a bit. Even if he never saw them here again, he, his mother, and both his siblings would be together one day. It was more than he ever could have hoped.

In the cool darkness just before dawn, Daniel pulled on a pair of rough workman's clothing. Even when he used to disguise himself, he'd never worn anything this plain, but he prayed it would keep anyone from suspecting his identity. He gritted his teeth as he maneuvered his arms through the worn leather jerkin. Though he'd spent two full days in Ben and Mira's care, his ribs still ached fiercely. Only time would heal that.

He left the bedroom and met Ben, Mira, and Aric in the foyer. Thank Elôm that Aric's fight with the guards the night of their escape had only resulted in a minor wound.

"Ready?" Ben asked.

Daniel nodded, though reluctance weighed on his heart. He hated to leave this house—to leave two of the best friends he'd ever had. Would he ever see them again? The future was a mystery to him beyond today. All he knew was that it was too great a risk to stay here, and he had to reach the Resistance camp in Landale. He prayed Elôm would direct him after that.

However, before that could happen, he had to say goodbye. He faced Mira. The woman's kind eyes welled with moisture.

"Thank you, for everything," Daniel told her. "I'm not sure where I'd be without you and Ben." Dead, probably, or about to be, considering his execution was scheduled for this morning.

Mira smiled. "It has been a blessing to watch your faith grow and witness the miracle of it. I don't know why Elon chose to send you to us, but I'm so thankful He did."

Daniel put his hands on her shoulders. "So am I, and I do know the reason. It's because you two are amazing at displaying His love. It's your faith and encouragement that has helped me grow."

Two large tears fell from her eyes, and she wiped her cheeks. "Goodness. You give us far too much credit."

"Not at all." Daniel hugged her as tightly as he was able with his aching ribs, his own eyes watering.

When they parted, Mira wiped her eyes again, though a few more tears leaked out. "You take good care of yourself. Elôm's not done with you yet—of that, I'm certain. We'll be praying for you every day. You can count on it."

Daniel gave her a bittersweet smile. "Thank you. Please, pray for my mother as well."

He thought of the letter his mother had given him through Aric—a letter that urged him to run far away and start a good life somewhere. The sort of life she knew he'd always wanted. Tempting as it was, that wasn't the life Elôm had called him to pursue.

"I think, given time, she could turn to Elôm. But I worry for her. My sister has proven that, beyond our father, family doesn't matter to her."

"Of course we'll pray," Mira promised.

"We better get going," Ben urged.

Daniel nodded, though he'd do almost anything to put off this moment. "Goodbye, Mira."

"Goodbye, Daniel."

They hugged again, and her tears flowed more heavily. Daniel had to blink hard to keep his own from spilling. He then forced himself to turn and follow Ben and Aric out of the house. The emotions weighed heavily on him, but the cool air helped relieve some of it. A fine mist fell from the dark sky, but that made it less suspicious to pull up his hood and hide his face.

Ben led the way out of the courtyard and into the street. Daniel looked around, his heart beginning to pound. This was one of the most dangerous parts of their escape plan. They made their way through the city toward the docks, and Daniel's muscles remained taut until they reached one of Ben's warehouses. Here, one of his employees, who also attended the weekly meetings, waited with a loaded supply wagon. He greeted them quietly, and then Ben turned to Daniel. Now it was time for the final goodbye.

"This should get you past the city gates," Ben said. "Elôm willing."

Daniel drew a deep breath. Every moment they stood here brought risk of discovery, so he offered his hand to Ben, and they clasped arms. "You are one of the most honorable men I've ever met. Thank you for the risks you've taken for me."

"I would do it again and more."

They embraced each other, and before Ben released his arm, he said, "Keep seeking Elôm. He will direct you."

Daniel nodded firmly. "I will."

Trading their goodbyes, Daniel climbed up into the wagon and stepped into one of two empty barrels. He crouched down and tried to get comfortable, but his ribs protested no matter how he sat.

"Will you be all right in there?" Ben asked.

"I'll have to be."

With that, Ben lowered a round board into the barrel that Daniel braced up just above his head. Then came a thudding sound as Ben covered it over with potatoes. Any bit of light disappeared, and Daniel sat in the darkness. A couple of minutes later, he heard Ben jump down from the wagon. It then rolled forward, and Daniel drew the best breath he could manage. He was leaving Valcré.

As the wagon rolled through the city streets, he struggled to brace himself against the bumps and jars. Even the slightest jolt set fire to his ribs. He squeezed his eyes shut to block it out. After all, what was worse? This temporary discomfort, or hanging in the dungeon waiting for his sister to come torture him?

Without being able to monitor their progress, the journey to one of the city gates seemed to stretch on forever. Claustrophobia was just setting in when the wagon jerked to a halt. Daniel's eyes popped open, and his heart hammered at the sound of muffled voices. He couldn't make out any words, but then someone stepped up into the wagon bed, their footsteps clumping against the wood.

"Open the barrels," a stern voice commanded.

Daniel's heart pounded so loud, he was sure it echoed in the barrel. He held his breath as the cover was pried off above him. Seconds passed. Finally, the guard moved on to the next and Daniel let out a painful breath. Sweat rolled along the sides of his face, down his neck, and into his shirt, but he didn't dare move.

After an eternity, the wagon rolled forward again.

"Thank You," Daniel gasped.

He knew they had passed through the gate when the cobblestone gave way to rutted dirt road. He had to bite down on a groan as they rolled along. Another long while elapsed, and his muscles cramped to the point he wondered if he'd be able to straighten out once they did stop.

But, finally, they came to a halt, and the cover lifted off his barrel. The driver scooped out the potatoes, and in a moment, he had the board out and helped Daniel stand up. Daniel braced himself against the rim of the barrel to let the blood flow through his limbs while the driver freed Aric. He breathed deeply of the clean air. He hadn't even realized how stale and close it had gotten in the barrel.

Once Aric was out, they climbed down from the wagon and shrugged on the supply packs Mira had put together for them.

Looking down from the wagon, the driver said, "Elôm protect you on your way."

Daniel thanked him, and then stood back as he drove off. He watched him for a moment before his gaze turned in the direction they had come. Though he couldn't see Valcré through the trees, he knew it was there, along with his sister and all the guards who would search for him for days yet. He shook his head at the way life had been turned upside down in the span of just a couple of weeks—his father had died, his sister had usurped his throne, and now here he was, an exile escaping his own city.

ANNE SMOOTHED HER hands down the front of the wedding dress that had once belonged to Trask's mother. With a few alterations, it fit her perfectly. Her motions were as much to smooth any wrinkles as to calm the butterflies tickling her stomach. She wasn't so much nervous as giddy with anticipation. Four days had passed since everyone had returned from Dorland. It had given them a chance to settle in and rest from their journey home. For Anne, the days had been incredibly full and busy with preparations, and yet they'd seemed to drag. But, it was here at last—the day she would become Trask's wife.

She turned to her mother, Elanor, and Kyrin, who were helping her get ready. Her mother smiled even as tears wet her eyes.

"You look breathtaking," she said.

Anne grinned. She couldn't wait for Trask to see her, especially in this dress. She knew how much it meant to him.

A moment later, her father entered the cabin. He paused a moment, looking her over. His smile and watery eyes matched her mother's. He shook his head. "Look at you. You look beautiful."

Anne gave him a warm smile, thankful the signs of his confrontation with Goler's men had faded. "Thank you."

"Everyone is ready if you are."

Anne nodded and took his arm. She was more than ready.

Together, they left the cabin and walked to the meeting hall. Though the clouds hung heavily, the rain held for now. Surrounding the meeting hall, canvas and lanterns hung in the trees so they could still enjoy their celebration outdoors and avoid the rain. Yet, at this point, nothing could dampen Anne's mood, not even a full-blown thunderstorm. As long as she was Trask's wife at the end of the day, that was all that mattered.

At the door to the meeting hall, her mother, Kyrin, and Elanor entered first. Before following them, her father looked down at her.

"You will always be my little girl, but I'm so happy you and Trask will finally be together."

Anne rose up to kiss his cheek. "Trask might be the most important man in my life now, but that will never change how much I love you."

Her father squeezed her hand and then led her inside. Anne noticed immediately how packed it was. There was hardly any space at all except for the cleared path to the end. Anne's gaze followed it to where King Balen waited to preside over the ceremony. After all, Trask had teased that soon they might all be citizens of Samara anyway. Her gaze shifted from the king, straight to Trask. He stood at the end of the aisle, his eyes glued to her. The smile on her face grew to the point she didn't think anything could wipe it away.

As they drew nearer, she saw how Trask's eyes shone and moisture sprang to hers as well. She had to blink to keep her vision clear. How adorable he looked being so close to tears. They'd both waited so terribly long for this. She almost couldn't believe it was really happening.

Yet, when they reached the end and her father handed her off to Trask, the reality set in, and her heart pattered. Together, the two of them stood before Balen. Anne gazed up at Trask, delighted by his adoring smile. Never in a million years could she have doubted his love for her, and she counted herself incredibly blessed. Parts of their relationship had been rocky and uncertain at times. There were even moments she doubted this day would come or if they would both survive to see it. But they were here. It was happening.

When Balen asked Anne if she took Trask as her husband, she responded with an eager "I do" that she spoke as a lifetime promise. Then, after all the years of longing and waiting, he pronounced them husband and wife. Joy raced through Anne as Trask pulled her into his arms and kissed her like he never had before. All around them, cheers and applause erupted so exuberantly that it set Anne to giggling before they even parted from their kiss.

Jace smiled as he watched Trask and Anne. While everyone else talked and enjoyed the celebration meal under the canvases outside, those two had eyes only for each other. Jace didn't blame them after how long they'd waited. They deserved such a moment of uninterrupted bliss. Trask had sacrificed so much for the people in this camp, and Anne was such a good friend to Elanor.

Happily, he looked over at Kyrin, who sat close to his side. Unlike the last wedding, none of his nerves took over. One of these days, it would be the two of them. Soon. He was determined of that. They'd even talked of a wedding the previous day and how they would want only a small celebration. He smiled as he studied her, anticipation taking hold of him. She caught his look and smiled back, so lovely and pure. It stole his breath away.

He gazed at her until Tyra give a little woof behind him. He looked up and spotted four men striding across camp. Two were the men who stood watch at the road. Though the other two looked strange at first, recognition hit him the same moment Kyrin exclaimed, "It's Prince Daniel and Sir Aric."

Questions poured into Jace's mind as murmuring swept through everyone gathered at the tables. Aric was an ally, but Prince Daniel? What was he doing here?

As they drew nearer, Jace noticed the bruises and cuts on Daniel's face that spoke of a recent beating. The prince also had his arm wrapped around his ribs. No one seemed to know how to react. Trask broke away from the shock first and rose from the table, though his voice still echoed surprise when he invited them inside the meeting hall out of the rain drumming on the canvas stretched above the tables. Everyone from the core group hurried to follow. Inside, Trask offered Daniel a chair, and the prince sank down with a quiet groan.

At first, no one said a word. Only Daniel's heavy breathing filled the room until finally Trask asked, "What brings you here, my lord?"

The prince grimaced. "My sister wants me dead. Her men spotted us on the road yesterday. We barely eluded them and made it here."

Trask traded confused looks with everyone. "Why would she want you dead?"

Daniel shifted in his chair, still gripping his ribs. "Because I'm a believer in Elôm."

Everyone reacted at once, looking at each other and then to Aric, who nodded confirmation. Shocking as it was, it was true.

"Is your father in on this?" Trask asked.

Daniel frowned as if this were a strange question. "You don't know?"

"Know what?"

"My father is dead."

The news sent a shockwave straight through to Jace's core.

Trask shook his head. "How?"

"He was poisoned at his birthday celebration. He died that night."

Daniel looked around the meeting hall, taking in all of their reactions, until his eyes caught on something that seemed to distract him. Jace looked to see what it was. Not something, *someone*. Elanor. She looked down shyly, and Daniel's attention slowly returned to Trask.

"I was supposed to be crowned three days ago, but Davira knew I would reverse everything my father has done. She had me arrested and planned to have me executed as she was crowned queen. She intends to rule until she can raise a new heir for my father."

Long seconds passed as they all let this sink in. For years, Daican had been the enemy. All of their plans revolved around stopping him. In one moment, everything had changed.

Finally, Trask said, "Lenae, Josef, take them to one of the cabins and see that they have everything they need. I'll be there in a moment."

The two of them nodded and led Daniel and Aric out of the meeting hall. As soon as they were gone, Trask turned to face the group, his expression one of astonishment. He shook his head, just standing there a moment before speaking.

"Do you realize what this means? The opportunity Elôm has given us? We now harbor two exiled kings in our camp. If we can stop Davira and restore Daniel and Balen to their thrones, Ilyon will be a different place. All of this could be over. We could be free to live our lives again. Free to worship Elôm without fear."

Hope built in Jace's chest, releasing in a long breath. He looked down at Kyrin, and she met his eyes, sharing in the anticipation beating inside him. He reached for her hand. Perhaps his dream to return with her to the little valley near Kinnim might come true after all.

EPILOGUE

DAVIRA PACED IN front of the throne. One of the servants offered her a goblet of wine, but she slapped him away. She would not sit and relax until the riders brought her their news.

Finally, the company of travel-weary men strode in, and Davira spun to face them.

"Well?" she demanded, when they slowed a few feet away.

The leader flinched, and Davira curled her fists. If they brought bad news, so help her . . .

"We spotted the prince and Aric on the road traveling east. They fled into the woods. We pursued them, but . . . we lost their trail. We picked it up near Landale, but then it disappeared again." The man swallowed. "We believe they've joined up with the rebels."

Fury boiled inside Davira, exploding with an enraged scream. She snatched the goblet out of the servant's hand and flung it at one of the pillars. Glass and red wine sprayed across the marble floor and dripped down the pillar. Shaking, she glared at the men.

"Find my brother and find that camp! Bring me their blood!" She spun around to face Richard. "As for whoever helped them escape the city, gather the people tomorrow. I wish to make a decree. As of tonight, it is permissible to kill anyone suspected of Elôm worship and sacrifice their blood to Aertus and Vilai. And to anyone who brings these traitors to me alive, five hundred gold pieces. Triple if they're from the Landale group. I want them all dead."

CHARACTERS
AND
INFORMATION

RETURNING CHARACTERS

Aaron—A half-crete and former miner from Dunlow. Timothy's older brother.

Aertus (AYR - tuhs)—Arcacia's male moon god.

Altair (AL - tayr)—Kyrin's family name.

Anne—The daughter of Sir John Wyland.

Aric (AHR - ick)—Emperor Daican's head of security.

Charles Ilvaran—The Viscount Ilvaran and Jace's uncle.

Daican (DYE - can)—The emperor of Arcacia.

Davira (Duh - VEER - uh)—Daican's daughter, the princess of Arcacia.

Elanor—Jace's sister.

Elian (EL - ee - an)—Elanor's bodyguard.

Elôm (EE - lohm)—The one true God of Ilyon.

Falcor Tarn—A crete traitor and Leetra's former fiancé.

Glynn (GLIN)—A crete from Dorland. Captain Darq's lieutenant.

Goler—An Arcacian army captain and bitter rival of Trask.

Grey—The baron of Landale.

Holden (HOHL - den)—A former informant for Daican but now part of the resistance.

Jace—A half-ryrik former slave and gladiator.

Jeremy—Lenae's son.

John Wyland—A retired knight.

Kaden (KAY - den)—Kyrin's twin brother.

King Balen (BAY - len)—Exiled king of Samara.

Kyrin (KYE - rin)—A young Arcacian woman with the ability to remember everything.

Leetra Almere (LEE - truh AL - meer)—A female crete from Dorland. Talas's cousin.

Lenae (LEH - nay)—A widowed Landale woman.

Liam—Kyrin's older brother.

Lydia—Kyrin's mother.

Maera (MAYR - uh)—Kyrin's dappled buckskin horse.

Marcus—Kyrin's eldest brother and captain of the Landale militia.

Meredith—Lenae's adoptive daughter.

Mick—A Resistance member from a wealthy mining family.

Michael—Kyrin's younger brother.

Niton (NYE - tuhn)—Jace's black horse.

Rayad (RAY - ad)—One of Jace's close friends and mentor.

Richard Blaine—A knight and old family friend of Daican.

Ronan "Ronny"—Kyrin's youngest brother.

Sam "Endathlorsam"—A talcrin man and Tarvin Hall's wisest scholar.

Talas Folkan (TAL - as FAHL - kan)—A friendly crete from Dorland. Leetra's cousin.

Timothy—A half-crete young man from Dunlow, and the Resistance's spiritual leader. Aaron's younger brother.

Trask—Resistance leader and son of Baron Grey.

Trev—A former member of Daican's security force. Now part of the Resistance.

Tyra—Jace's black wolf.

Verus Darq (VAYR - uhs DARK)—A crete captain from Dorland.

Vilai (VI - lye)—Arcacia's female moon god.

Warin (WOHR - in)—An Arcacian man active in the Resistance against the emperor. Lifelong friend of Rayad.

New Characters

Ben—Wealthy merchant and leader of the believers in Valcré.
Cray—Hostile crete.
Dagren (DAY - gren)—Arcacian captain with a vendetta against Rayad and Warin.
Gerric (GAYR - ick)—Half-ryrik captain.
Haedrin (HAY - drin) —Prince of Dorland.
Halvar (HAL - vahr)—Jorvik's younger brother.
Jayna (JAY - nuh)—Saul's wife.
Jorvik (JOHR - vick)—A giant whose family has always guarded the ford at Dorland's border.
Kal—Saul's son.
Katia (KAY - tee - uh)—Naeth's love interest whose father is leader of the Eagle Clan.
King Orlan—King of Dorland.
Levi—Jorvik's youngest brother.
Liese (LEESE)—Saul's daughter.
Lord Vallan (VA - lan)—The crete lord.
Mira (MEER - uh)—Ben's wife.
Naeth Tarn (NAYTH)—Falcor's older brother.
Novan Tarn (NOH - van)—Falcor's father.
Raias Almere - (RYE -as AL - meer)—Leetra's father.
Ruis (ROOS)—Cruel ryrik man.
Saul—Friendly ryrik in Dorland.
Sonah Tarn (SOH - nuh)—Falcor's mother.
Trenna Folkan—Talas's younger sister.
Tress Folkan—Talas's mother.

Thel Folkan—Talas's father.

Tolan Silvar (TOH - lan)—Timothy and Aaron's grandfather.

Varn Folkan—Talas's grandfather.

DRAGONS

Exsis (EX - sis)—Kaden's dragon.
Gem—Jace's dragon.
Ivoris "Ivy" (EYE - vohr - is)—Kyrin's dragon.
Storm—Talas's dragon.

LOCATIONS

Andros Ford (AN - drohs)—The only safe crossing into Dorland by foot along the Trayse River.

Arcacia (Ahr - CAY - shee - uh)—The largest country of the Ilyon mainland.

Arvael (Ahr - VALE)—The crete's capital city.

Auréa (Awr - RAY - uh)—Daican's palace in Valcré.

Bel-gard—Capital of Dorland.

Dorland—Ilyon's easternmost country. Inhabited by cretes and giants.

Ilyon (IL - yahn)—The known world.

Landale—A prosperous province in Arcacia ruled over by Baron Grey.

Marlton Hall—Home of Sir John Wyland.

Trayse River (TRACE)—A swiftly flowing river along Dorland's border.

Valcré (VAL - cray)—Arcacia's capital city.

RACE PROFILES

RYRIKS

HOMELAND: Wildmor

PHYSICAL APPEARANCE: Ryriks tend to be large-bodied, muscular, and very athletic. They average between six, to six and a half feet tall. They have thick black hair that is usually worn long. All have aqua-blue colored eyes that appear almost luminescent, especially during intense or emotional situations. Their ears are pointed, which makes them very distinct from the other races. They have strong, striking features, though they can pass as humans by letting their hair hide their ears and avoiding eye contact. Ryriks typically dress in rough, sturdy clothing—whatever they find by stealing.

PHYSICAL CHARACTERISTICS: Ryriks are a very hardy race and incredibly resistant to physical abuse and sickness; however, they have one great weakness. Their lungs are highly sensitive to harsh air conditions, pollutants, and respiratory illness. Under these conditions, their lungs bleed. Short exposure causes great discomfort, but is not life-threatening. More severe, prolonged exposure, however, could cause their lungs to fill with blood and suffocate them. It is said to be a curse from choosing to follow the path of evil. Ryriks' eyes are very sensitive, able to pick out the slightest movement, and they can see well in the dark. Both their sense of hearing and smell are very keen—much higher than that of humans. In times of great distress or anger, ryriks can react with devastating bursts of speed and strength.

RACE CHARACTERISTICS: Ryriks are the center of fireside tales all across Ilyon. They are seen as a savage people, very fierce and cunning. To other races, they seem to have almost animal-like instincts; therefore, it is commonly believed they don't have souls. They are a hot-blooded people and quick to action, especially when roused. They have quick tempers and are easily driven to blind rage. They prefer decisive action over conversation. Most have a barbaric thirst for bloodshed and inflicting pain. They view fear and pain as weaknesses and like to see them in others. They are typically forest dwellers and feel most comfortable in cover they can use to their advantage.

SKILLS: Ryriks are highly skilled in the woods and living off the land. They are excellent hunters and especially proficient in setting ambushes. They're experts in taming and raising almost any type of animal. They make the fiercest of any warriors. A ryrik's favorite weapons are a heavy broadsword and a large dagger. Ryriks aren't masters of any type of craft or art. Most of their possessions come from stealing. What they can't gain by thieving, they make for themselves, but not anything of quality. They think art, music, or any such thing to be frivolous. Most ryriks can't read or write and have no desire to.

SOCIAL: Ryriks are not a very social race. Settlements are scattered and usually small. They have no major cities. Families often live on small farms in the forest and consist of no more than four to six people. Children are typically on their own by the time they are sixteen or seventeen—even younger for some males. Ryriks have a poor view of women. They see them as a necessity and more of a possession than a partner. Once claimed, a ryrik woman almost never leaves her home. She is required to care for the farm while the men are away. Most ryrik men group together in raiding parties, pillaging and destroying unprotected villages and preying on unsuspecting travelers. Ryriks have an intense hatred of other races, particularly humans.

GOVERNMENT: Ryriks have no acting government. Raiding parties and settlements are dictated by the strongest or fiercest ryrik, so the position can be challenged by anyone and changes often.

PREFERRED OCCUPATIONS: The vast majority of ryriks are thieves. A few hold positions as blacksmiths and other necessary professions.

FAITH: Ryriks disdain religion of any kind. They were the first to rebel against King Elôm and led others to do so as well.

TALCRINS

HOMELAND: Arda

PHYSICAL APPEARANCE: Talcrins are a tall, powerful people. Talcrin men are seldom less than six feet tall. They have rich, dark skin and black hair of various lengths and styles. Their most unique feature besides their dark skin is their metallic-looking eyes. They have a very regal, graceful appearance. Men often dress in long, expertly crafted jerkins, while women wear simple but elegant flowing gowns of rich colors, particularly deep purple.

RACE CHARACTERISTICS: Talcrins are considered the wisest of all Ilyon's peoples. Some of their greatest pleasures are learning and teaching. Reading is one of their favorite pastimes. They have excellent memories and intellects. Talcrins are a calm people, adept at hiding and controlling strong emotion. They are peace-loving and prefer to solve problems with diplomacy, but if all else fails, they can fight fiercely. They have a deep sense of morality, justice, loyalty, and above all, honesty. They are an astute people and don't miss much, particularly when it comes to others. Besides learning, they are also fond of art and music. Most talcrins are city dwellers, preferring large cities where libraries and universities can be found. Of all the races, they live the longest and reach ages of one hundred fifty, though many live even longer. Because of this, they age slower than the other races. Talcrin names are known to be very long, though they use shortened versions outside of Arda.

SKILLS: Talcrins excel in everything pertaining to books, languages, legal matters, and history, and are excellent at passing on their wisdom. They are often sought as advisors for their ability to easily think through situations and assess different outcomes. They are master storytellers and delight in entertaining people in this way. Though they strive for peace, most talcrin men train as warriors when they are young. They make incredible fighters who are highly skilled with long swords, high-power longbows, and spears. When not reading, many talcrin women enjoy painting and weaving. Their tapestries are among the most sought after. Both men and women enjoy music and dancing. They are expert harpists. Beautiful two-person dances are very popular in talcrin culture and are considered an art form. Metal-working is another skill in which talcrins are considered experts. Their gold and silver jewelry and armor are some of the finest in Ilyon.

SOCIAL: Talcrins are a family-oriented people and fiercely loyal to both family and friends alike. Families are average in size, with between three to seven children. Men are very protective of their families and believe their well-being is of utmost importance. Their island country of Arda is almost exclusively populated with talcrins. Scholars from the Ilyon mainland often come to visit their famous libraries, but other races rarely settle there. Many talcrins inhabit the mainland as well, but are widely scattered. The highest population is found in Valcré, the capital of Arcacia. They get along well with all races, except for ryriks. Though generally kindhearted, they can hold themselves at a distance and consider others ignorant.

GOVERNMENT: The governing lord in Arda is voted into authority by the talcrin people and serves for a period of two years at a time, but may be elected an unlimited number of times. His word is seen as final, but he is surrounded by a large number of advisors, who are also chosen by the people, and is expected to include them in all decisions. Those living on the mainland are under the authority of the king or lord of whichever country they inhabit.

PREFERRED OCCUPATIONS: Scholars, lawyers, and positions in government are the talcrins' choice occupations, as well as positions in artistry.

FAITH: Talcrins are the most faithful of all races in following King Elôm. The majority of those living in Arda are firm believers, but this has become less so among those living on the mainland.

CRETES

HOMELAND: Arcacia and Dorland

PHYSICAL APPEARANCE: Cretes are a slim people, yet very agile and strong. They are the shortest of Ilyon's races, and stand between five foot and five foot ten inches tall. It is rare for one to reach six feet. They are brown-skinned and have straight, dark hair. Black is most common. It is never lighter than dark brown unless they are of mixed blood. Both men and women let it grow long. They like to decorate their hair with braids, beads, leather, and feathers. Crete men do not grow facial hair. A crete's eyes are a bit larger than a human's, and very bright and colorful. A full-blood crete will never have brown eyes. They dress in earthy colors and lots of leather. All cretes have intricate brown tattoos depicting family symbols and genealogy.

PHYSICAL CHARACTERISTICS: The crete's body is far more resilient to the elements and sickness than other races. They are very tolerant of the cold and other harsh conditions. Their larger eyes give them excellent vision and enable them to see well in the dark. They don't need as much sleep as other races and sleep only for a couple of hours before dawn. Their bodies heal and recuperate quickly.

RACE CHARACTERISTICS: Cretes are tree dwellers and never build on the ground except when absolutely necessary. They love heights and flying and have a superb sense of balance. They are very daring and enjoy a thrilling adventure. They mature a bit more quickly than other races. A crete is considered nearly an adult by fifteen or sixteen and a mature adult by eighteen. They are a high-energy race and prone to taking quick action. Cretes are straightforward and blunt, coming across as rather abrupt at times. They are not the most patient, nor understanding, and they have high expectations for themselves and others. They are a stubborn, proud, and independent people, and don't like to conform to the laws and standards of other races.

SKILLS: Cretes are excellent climbers, even from a very young age, able to race up trees effortlessly and scale the most impassible cliffs and obstacles. Because of this fearlessness and love for heights, they are renowned dragon trainers. They are masters at blending in with their surroundings and moving silently, which makes them excellent hunters. All crete males, as well as many females, are trained as skilled warriors. Their choice weapons are bows and throwing knives, though they can be equally skilled with lightweight swords. Cretes are also a musical race, their favorite instruments being small flutes and hand drums.

SOCIAL: Cretes live in close communities and often have very large families, maintaining close connections with extended family. They are very proud of their family line and make sure each generation is well-educated in their particular traditions and histories. They consider it a tragedy when a family line is broken. Still, all children are cherished, both sons and daughters. Every crete is part of one of twelve clans named after various animals. Men are always part of whichever clan they are born into. When a woman marries, she becomes part of her husband's clan. Though cretes are proud of their clans, they show no discrimination, and their cities always have a mixed-clan population. Cretes are hospitable to their own people and well-known acquaintances, but suspicious and aloof when it comes to strangers. It takes time to earn one's trust, and even longer to earn their respect.

GOVERNMENT: The highest governing official is the crete lord. He is essentially a king, but directly below him are twelve men who serve as representatives of each of the twelve clans. The lord is unable to make any drastic decisions without the cooperation of the majority of the twelve clan leaders. Each crete city has a governing official who answers to the twelve representatives. Directly below him is a council of men consisting of the elders of each major family in the city. In the past, the cretes ultimately fell under the authority of the king of Arcacia, but with the deterioration of the Arcacian government, they've pulled away from its rule.

PREFERRED OCCUPATIONS: Hunters, dragon trainers, and warriors are the favored occupations of the cretes. But leather-working is another desirable occupation. This is typically done by the women of a household.

FAITH: Most cretes have remained faithful to King Elôm, or at least are aware of Him.

GIANTS
(Also known as **Dorlanders**)

HOMELAND: Dorland

PHYSICAL APPEARANCE: Giants are the largest race in Ilyon. Standing between seven to nine feet tall, they tower above most other peoples. They are heavily built and powerful, but can be surprisingly quick and agile when the occasion calls for it. They are fair-skinned, and their hair and eye color varies greatly like humans. They dress simply and practically in sturdy, homespun clothing.

RACE CHARACTERISTICS: Despite their great size and power, giants are a very quiet and gentle people. They dislike confrontation and will avoid it at all cost. They are naturally good-natured and honest, and enjoy simple lives and hard work. To those who don't take the time to get to know them, they can seem slow and ignorant, but they are very methodical thinkers, thinking things over carefully and thoroughly. While not quick-witted, they are very knowledgeable in their fields of interest. They are generally a humble race and easy to get along with. They tend to see the best in everyone. Their biggest failing is that, in their methodical manner, it often takes too long for them to decide to take action when it is needed.

SKILLS: Giants are very skilled in anything to do with the land. Much of the gold, silver, and jewels in Ilyon come from the giants' mines in the mountains of northern Dorland. They are also excellent builders. While lacking in style or decoration, the architecture of their structures is strong and durable, built to last for centuries. They have often been hired to build fortifications and strongholds. Unlike other races, it is not common for giants to train as warriors. Only the king's men are required to be able to fight. While not a musical or artistic race, giants do love a good story, and they've been said to have, beautiful, powerful singing voices.

SOCIAL: Giants typically live in tight farming or mining communities. Family and friends are important. Families usually consist of two to three children who remain in the household for as long as they wish. Many children remain on their parents' farm after they are married, and the farm expands. Giants are known throughout Ilyon for their hospitality. They'll invite almost anyone into their homes. Some people even find them too hospitable and generous. They are very averse to cruelty, dishonesty, and seeing their own hurt. Despite moving slowly in most other areas, justice is swift and decisive.

GOVERNMENT: Giants are ruled over by a king who comes to power through succession. However, most communities more or less govern themselves. The only time the king's rule is evident is when large numbers of giants are required to gather for a certain purpose.

PREFERRED OCCUPATIONS: The majority of giants are farmers, miners, or builders.

FAITH: Almost all giants agree King Elôm is real, but in their simplistic and practical mindset, fewer giants have actually come to a true trusting faith.

BITTER WINTER

ILYON CHRONICLES – BOOK FIVE

When a catastrophic event leaves the Landale camps reeling and stricken by a deadly illness, Jace must face the dangers of Valcré and an impossible choice to gain the cure.

COMING SOON

For more "behind the scenes" information on Ilyon Chronicles,
visit: **www.ilyonchronicles.blogspot.com**

To see Jaye's inspiration boards and character "casting" visit:
www.pinterest.com/jayelknight

ABOUT THE AUTHOR

JAYE L. KNIGHT is an award-winning author, homeschool graduate, and shameless tea addict with a passion for Christian fantasy. Armed with an active imagination and love for adventure, Jaye weaves stories of truth, faith, and courage with the message that even in the deepest darkness, God's love shines as a light to offer hope. She has been penning stories since the age of eight and resides in the Northwoods of Wisconsin.

To learn more about Jaye and her work, visit:
www.jayelknight.com

Made in the USA
Columbia, SC
22 January 2018